A SEASON FOR THE DEAD

David Hewson is a weekly columnist for the *Sunday Times*. *A Season for the Dead* is the first novel in an Italian crime series set in Rome and featuring Detective Nic Costa. The fourth in the series, *The Lizard's Bite*, is his most recent novel. The author lives in Kent.

www.davidhewson.com

DAVID HEWSON

A SEASON FOR THE DEAD

PAN BOOKS

First published 2003 by Macmillan

First published in paperback 2004 by Pan Books
This edition published 2007 by Pan Books
an imprint of Pan Macmillan Ltd
Pan Macmillan, 20 New Wharf Road, London N1 9RR
Basingstoke and Oxford
Associated companies throughout the world
www.panmacmillan.com

ISBN 978-0-330-45486-5

2 4 6 8 10 9 7 5 3

A CIP catalogue record for this book is available from
the British Library.

Typeset by Intypelibra, London
Printed and bound in Great Britain by
Mackays of Chatham plc, Chatham, Kent

Visit **www.panmacmillan.com** to read more about all our books and to buy
them. You will also find features, author interviews and news of any author
events, and you can sign up for e-newsletters so that you're always first to hear
about our new releases.

A SEASON FOR THE DEAD

One

The heat was palpable, alive. Sara Farnese sat at her desk in the Reading Room of the Vatican Library and stared out of the window, out into the small rectangular courtyard, struggling to concentrate. The fierce August afternoon placed a rippling, distorting mirage across her view. In the unreal haze, the grass was a yellow, arid mirror of the relentless sun. It was now two o'clock. Within an hour the temperature beyond the glass would hit forty degrees. She should have left like everyone else. Rome in August was an empty furnace echoing to the whispers of desiccated ghosts. The university corridors on the other side of the city rang to her lone footsteps that morning. It was one reason she decided to flee elsewhere. Half the shops and the restaurants were closed. The only life was in the parks and the museums, where stray groups of sweating tourists tried to find some meagre shade.

This was the worst of the summer. Yet she had decided to stay. She knew why and she wondered whether she was a fool. Hugh Fairchild was visiting from London. Handsome Hugh, clever Hugh, a man who could rattle off from memory the names of every early Christian codex lodged in the museums of Europe, and had probably read them too. If the plane was on time he would have arrived at Fiumicino at ten that morning and, by now, have checked into his suite at the Inghilterra. It was too early for him to stay with her, she knew that, and pushed from her head the idea that there could be other names in his address book, other candidates for his bed. He was an intensely busy man. He would be in Rome for five days, of which two nights alone were hers, then move on to a lawyers' conference in Istanbul.

It was, she thought, possible that he had other lovers. No, probable. He lived in London, after all. He had abandoned academia to become a successful career civil servant with the EU. Now he seemed to spend one week out of every four on the road, to Rome, to New York, to Tokyo. They met, at most, once a month. He was thirty-five, handsome in a way that was almost too perfect. He had a long, muscular, tanned body, a warm, aristocratic English face, always ready to break into a smile, and a wayward head of blond hair. It was unthinkable that he did not sleep with other women, perhaps at first meeting. That was, she recalled, with a slight sensation of guilt, what had happened to her at the convention on the preservation of historical artefacts in Amsterdam four months before.

Nor did it concern her. They were both single adults. He was meticulously safe in his lovemaking. Hugh Fairchild was a most organized man, one who entered her life and left it at irregular intervals which were to their mutual satisfaction. That night they would eat in her apartment close to the Vatican. They would cross the bridge by the Castel Sant'Angelo, walk the streets of the centro storico and take coffee somewhere. Then they would return to her home around midnight where he would stay until the morning, when meetings would occupy him for the next two days. This was, she thought, an ample provision of intellectual activity, pleasant company and physical fulfilment. Enough to keep her happy. Enough, a stray thought said, to quell the doubts.

She tried to focus on the priceless manuscript sitting on the mahogany desk by the window. This was a yellow volume quite unlike those Sara Farnese normally examined in the Vatican Reading Room: a tenth-century copy of *De Re Coquinaria*, the famed imperial Roman cookery book by Apicius from the first century AD. She would make him a true Roman meal: *isicia omentata*, small beef fritters with pine kernels, *pullus fiusilis*, chicken stuffed with herbed dough, and *tiropatinam*, a soufflé with honey. She would explain that they were eating in because it was August. All the best restaurants were shut. This was not an attempt to change the status of their relationship. It was purely practical and, furthermore, she enjoyed cooking. He would understand or, at the very least, not object.

'Apicius?' asked a voice from behind, so unexpected it made her shudder.

She turned to see Guido Fratelli smiling at her with his customary doggedness. She tried to return the gesture though she was not pleased to see him. The Swiss Guard always made for her whenever she visited. He knew – or had learned – enough of her work in the library to be able to strike up a conversation. He was about her own age, running to fat a little, and liked the blue, semi-medieval uniform and the black leather gun holster a little too much. As a quasi-cop he had no power beyond the Vatican, and only the quieter parts of that. The Rome police retained charge of St Peter's Square which was, in truth, the only place the law was usually needed. And they were a different breed, nothing like this quiet, somewhat timorous individual. Guido Fratelli would not last a day trying to hustle the drunks and addicts around the Termini Station.

'I didn't hear you come in,' Sara said, hoping he took this as a faint reproach. The Reading Room was empty apart from her. She appreciated the quiet; she did not want it broken by conversation.

'Sorry.' He patted the gun on his belt, an unconscious and annoying gesture. 'We're trained to be silent as a mouse. You never know.'

'Of course,' she replied. If Sara recalled correctly, there had been three murders in the Vatican in the course of almost two hundred years: in 1988, when the incoming commander of the Swiss Guard and his wife were shot dead by a guard corporal harbouring a grudge, and in 1848, when the Pope's prime minister was assassinated by a political opponent. With the city force taking care of the crowds in the square, the most Guido Fratelli had to worry about was an ambitious burglar.

'Not your usual stuff?' he asked.

'I've wide-ranging interests.'

'Me too.' He glanced at the page. The volume had come in its customary box, with the name in big, black letters on the front, which was how he knew what she was reading. Guido was always hunting for conversational footholds, however tenuous. Perhaps he thought that was a kind of detective work. 'I'm learning Greek, you know.'

'This is Latin. Look at the script.'

His face fell. 'Oh. I thought it was Greek you looked at. Normally.'

'Normally.' She could see the distress on his face and couldn't help being amused. He was thinking: *I have to try to learn both?*

'Maybe you could tell me how I'm doing some time?'

She tapped the notebook computer onto which she had transcribed half the recipes she wanted.

'Some time. But not now, Guido. I'm busy.'

The desk was at right angles to the window. She looked away from him, into the garden again, seeing his tall, dark form in the long window. Guido was not going to give up easily.

'OK,' he said to her reflection in the glass, then walked off, back down to the entrance. She heard laughter through the floor from the long gallery above. The tourists were in, those who had sufficient influence to win a ticket to these private quarters. Did they understand how lucky they were? Over the last few years, both as part of her role as a lecturer in early Christianity at the university and for purely personal pleasure, she had spent more and more time in the library, luxuriating in the astonishing richness of its collection. She had touched drawings and poems executed in Michelangelo's own hand. She had read Henry VIII's love letters to Anne Boleyn and a copy of the same king's *Assertio Septem Sacramentorum*, signed by the monarch, which had won Henry the title 'Defender of the Faith' and still failed to keep him in the Church.

From a professional point of view it was the early works – the priceless codices and incunabula – which were the focus of her constant attention. Even so, she was unable to prevent herself stealing a glance at the personal material from the Middle Ages on. In a sense, she felt she had listened to Petrarch and Thomas Aquinas in person.

Their voices remained, like dead echoes on the dry vellum and the ancient stain of ink they had left on the page. These traces made them human and, for all their wisdom, for all their skill with words, without their humanity they were nothing, though Hugh Fairchild would probably disagree.

There was a noise from the entrance, a half shout, not loud in itself but, given the context, disturbing. No one ever shouted in the Reading Room of the Vatican Library.

Sara raised her head and was surprised to see a familiar figure walking towards her. He moved briskly through the bands of sharp light that fell through the window, with a swift, determined intent that seemed out of place in these surroundings, wrong. The air-conditioning rose in volume. A chill blanket of air fell over her and she shivered. She looked again. Stefano Rinaldi, a fellow professor at the university, carried a large, bulging plastic bag and was crossing the empty Reading Room with a determined stride. There was an expression on his round, bearded face which she failed to recognize: anger or fear or a combination of both. He was wearing his customary black shirt and black trousers but they were dishevelled and there were what looked like wet stains on both. His eyes blazed at her.

For no reason, Sara Farnese felt frightened of this man whom she had known for some time.

'Stefano . . .' she said softly, perhaps so quietly he was unable to hear.

The commotion was growing behind him. She saw figures waving their arms, beginning to race after the figure in black with the strange, full supermarket bag dangling from his right hand. And from his left, she saw now, something even odder: what appeared to be a gun, a small black pistol. Stefano Rinaldi, a man she had never known to show anger, a man for whom she once felt a measure of attraction, was walking purposefully across the room in her direction holding a gun, and nothing she could imagine, no possible sequence of events, could begin to explain this.

She reached over, placed both hands on the far side of the desk and swung it round through ninety degrees. The old wood screeched on the marble floor like an animal in pain. She heaved at the thing until her back was against the glass and the desk was tight against her torso, not questioning the logic: that she must remain seated, that she must face this man, that this ancient desk, with a tenth-century copy of a Roman recipe book and a single notebook computer on it, would provide some protection against the unfathomable threat that was approaching her.

Then, much more quickly than she expected, he was there, gasping for breath above her, that crazy look more obvious than ever in his dark-brown eyes.

He sat down in the chair opposite and peered into her face. She felt her muscles relax, if only a little. At that moment, Sara was unafraid. He was not there to harm her. She understood that with an absolute certainty that defied explanation.

'Stefano . . .' she repeated.

There were shapes gathering behind him. She could see Guido Fratelli there. She wondered how good he was with his gun and whether, by some unfortunate seren-dipity, she might die that day from the stray bullet of an inexperienced Swiss Guard with a shaking hand that pointed the gun at a former lover of hers who had, for some reason, gone mad in the most venerated library in Rome.

Stefano's left arm, the one holding the weapon, swept the table, swept everything on it, the precious volume of Apicius, her expensive notebook computer, down to the hard marble floor with a clatter.

She was quiet, waiting, which was, his eyes seemed to say, what he wanted.

Then Stefano lifted up the bag to the height of the desk, turned it upside down, let the contents fall on to the table and said, in a loud, commanding voice that was half crazy, half dead, 'The blood of the martyrs is the seed of the Church.'

She looked at the thing in front of her. It had the consistency of damp new vellum, as if it had just been rinsed. Apicius would have written on something very like this once it was dry.

Still holding the gun with his left hand, Stefano began to unravel the pliable thing before her, stretching it, extending the strange fabric until it filled the broad mahogany top of the desk then flowed over the edges, taking as it did a shape that was both familiar and, in its present context, foreign.

Sara forced her eyes to remain open, forced herself to think hard about what she was seeing. The object which Stefano Rinaldi was unfolding, smoothing out carefully with the flat palm of his right hand as if it were a table-cloth perhaps, on show for sale, was the skin of a human being, a light skin somewhat tanned, and wet, as if it had been recently washed. It had been cut roughly from the body at the neck, genitals, ankles and wrist, with a final slash down the spine and the back of the legs in order to remove it as a whole piece and Sara had to fight to stop herself reaching out to touch the thing, just to make sure this was not some nightmare, just to *know*.

'What do you want?' she asked, as calmly as she could.

The brown eyes met hers then glanced away. Stefano was afraid of what he was doing, quite terrified, yet there was some determination there too. He was an intelligent man, not stubborn, simply single-minded in his work which was, she now recalled, centred around Tertullian, the early Christian theologian and polemicist whose famous diktat he had quoted.

'Who are the martyrs, Stefano?' she asked. 'What does this mean?'

He was sane at that moment. She could see this very clearly in his eyes, which had become calm. Stefano was thinking this through, looking for a solution.

He leaned forward. 'She's still there, Sara,' he said, in the tobacco-stained growl she recognized, but speaking very softly, as if he wished no one else to hear. 'You must go. Look at this.' He stared at the table and the skin on it. 'I daren't . . .' There was terror in his face though, in the context it seemed ridiculous. 'Think of Bartholomew. You must know.'

Then, in a much louder voice, one that had the craziness back inside it again, he repeated Tertullian, 'The blood of the martyrs is the seed of the Church.'

Stefano Rinaldi, his eyes now black and utterly lost, lifted the gun, raised it until the short, narrow barrel pointed at her face.

'Down!' the guard screamed. '*Down!*'

Guido was an idiot. Sara knew that instinctively, knew he could not be seeing this scene and reading it the way she did.

'No!' She insisted, raising a hand, to both men, and

saw, to her dismay, Stefano's gun move in front of her again, going higher. 'Both of you! Stop this!'

Guido screamed, gibberish that was both fear and anger. He was out of control. And Stefano simply stared at her, stared with those mournful, forsaken eyes, an expression that finally began to make her feel cold since it seemed to contain so much dead fatalism inside it.

He mouthed a single word, 'Hurry.'

'Don't,' she said, to both of them, knowing it was useless.

An explosion rang from Guido's gun. The room was enveloped by a sound that made her ears scream with pain. Stefano Rinaldi's scalp opened up and issued a livid burst of blood and tissue. Then Guido was dancing around the dead man, wishing he dared touch the corpse now slumping to the floor, letting the gun jerk in his hand as if it had some mind of its own.

She closed her eyes and listened to the sound of fire, heard the bullets whistling round the room, the quiet room, the place of many splendours she had grown to love.

When it was done, Sara Farnese opened her eyes. Stefano lay still on the floor. One of the attendants was close by, shrieking, his hands holding his stomach as if he dared not let go for fear of what might tumble out.

She looked at Stefano's head. It lay on the floor, resting on the ancient copy of Apicius, staining the page with thick, black blood.

Two

They stood in the shade of the colonnades in St Peter's Square, Luca Rossi wondering how badly the sun might have burned his bald head already that day. A couple of rocks were rumbling around his stomach from the previous night's beer and pizza feast. Then, to make matters worse, he had that very morning been given the kid as duty partner for the next four weeks. It was a kind of punishment, for both of them he guessed. Neither fitted in well with the Rome state police department at that moment, for very different reasons. His were distinct, directly attributable to an obvious and, for him, understandable, source. The kid just didn't look right, full stop. And never even knew.

He eyed his partner and groaned. 'OK. I know you want me to ask. So do the trick then.'

Nic Costa smiled and Rossi wished he didn't look so young. Sometimes they had to arrest the odd vicious type in the hallowed precincts of the square. He couldn't help but wonder how much use this slim, adolescent-looking character would be in those circumstances.

'It's not a trick.' They had never worked together before. They came from different stations. Rossi guessed

DAVID HEWSON

the kid never even knew why some old, overweight cop had been made his new partner. He'd never asked. He just seemed to accept it, to accept everything. Still, Rossi knew something about him. They all did. Nic Costa was one of those cops the others couldn't quite believe. He didn't drink much. He didn't even eat meat. He kept fit and had quite a reputation as a marathon runner. And he was the son of that damned red the papers used to go on about, a man who had left Nic Costa with one very unusual habit. He was a painting freak, one particular painter too. He knew the whereabouts and the provenance of every last Caravaggio in Rome.

'Sounds like a trick to me.'

'It's knowledge,' Costa said, and for a moment looked more like his real age, which Rossi knew to be twenty-seven. Maybe, the older man thought, there was more to him than met the eye. 'No sleight of hand, big man. This is magic, the real thing.'

'Give me some magic then. Over there . . .' He nodded towards the walls of the Vatican. 'I guess they're full of the things.'

'No. Just the one. *The Deposition from the Cross* and they took that from its original location too. The Vatican never much cared for Caravaggio. They thought he was too revolutionary, too close to the poor. He painted people with dirty feet. He made the apostles look like ordinary mortals you might meet in the street.'

'So that's what you like about him? You get that from your old man, I suppose.'

'It's part of what I like. And I'm me, not someone else.'

'Sure.' Rossi remembered the father. He was a real trouble-maker. He never stood to one side for anything,

12

never took a bribe either, which made him one very odd politician indeed. 'So where?'

The kid nodded towards the river. 'Six-minute walk over there. The Church of Sant'Agostino. You can call it *The Madonna of Loreto* or *The Madonna of the Pilgrims*. Either works.'

'It's good?'

'The feet are really dirty. The Vatican hated it. It's a wonderful piece of work but I know better.'

Rossi thought about this. 'I don't suppose you follow football, do you? It may give us more to talk about.'

Costa said nothing then turned on the radio scanner and plugged in the earpiece. Rossi sniffed the air.

'You smell those drains?' he grunted. 'They spend all this money building the biggest church on the planet. They got the Pope in residence just a little walk away. And still the drains stink like some backstreet in Trastevere. Maybe they just chop up bodies and flush them down the toilet or something. As if we'd get to know.'

Costa kept fiddling with the damned radio scanner. They both knew it was supposed to be banned.

'Hey,' he growled. 'Don't you think I get bored too? If Falcone hears you've been messing with that thing he'll kick your ass.'

Costa shrugged his narrow shoulders and smiled. 'I was trying to find some football for you. What's the problem?'

Rossi stuck up his big hands and laughed. 'OK. You got me there.'

They watched the thin crowds shuffle across the square in the enervating heat. It was too hot for the bag-snatchers, Rossi thought. The weather was doing more to reduce the Rome crime rate than anything a couple of cops could ever achieve. He could hardly blame Costa for playing with the scanner. None of them liked being told there were places in the city where they weren't welcome. Maybe Costa had some anti-clerical thing in his genes, however much he told everyone he was apolitical, the opposite of his father. And the Vatican *was* part of the city, whatever the politicians said. It was crazy to think some thieving little bastard could snatch a bag in front of them then scuttle off into the milling masses inside St Peter's and suddenly become untouchable, the property of the Pope's Swiss Guards in their funny blue uniforms and ankle socks.

Costa was never going to hear anything of import on his little pocket scanner. Too little went on in the Vatican for that. But just listening was a form of protest in itself. It said: *we're here.*

Rossi eyed a long crocodile of black nuns who followed a woman waving a little red pennant on a stick. He looked at his watch and wished the hands would move more quickly.

'Enough,' he announced, then, to his surprise, felt Costa's hand on his arm. The young detective was listening intently to a squealing racket in the earpiece of the radio.

'Someone's been shot,' Costa said, suddenly earnest. 'In the Library Reading Room. You know where that is?'

'Of course,' the older man said, nodding. 'Mongolia as far as we're concerned.'

Costa's sharp brown eyes pleaded with him. 'Somebody's been shot. We're not going to just stand here, are we?'

Rossi sighed. 'Say again after me, "The Vatican is another country." Falcone can put it more clearly for you

if you want.' Falcone could, Rossi thought, put it very
clearly indeed. He didn't even want to imagine what that
conversation would be like. He'd been very glad that the
last five years had been spent outside Falcone's reach. He
only wished it could have been longer.

'Sure,' Costa agreed. 'That doesn't mean we can't
look. I mean they never said we couldn't go in there.
They just said we couldn't arrest people.'

Rossi thought about that. The kid was right, up to a
point.

'That's all you heard? Someone's been shot?'

'Isn't that enough? Do you want to go back and tell
Falcone we didn't even offer to help?'

Rossi patted his jacket, felt his gun there and watched
Costa do the same. They looked down the Via di Porta
Angelica towards the entrance to the private Vatican
quarters. The Swiss Guards who were normally there
checking visitors' papers were gone, doubtless called to
the event. Two Roman cops could walk straight in
without a single question being asked. It seemed like an
invitation.

'I'm not running,' Rossi grunted. 'Not in this
damned heat.'

'Your decision,' Costa answered and was off, out of
the square, through the open gate, legs pumping.

'Kids . . .' Luca Rossi grunted and shook his head.

Three

By the time Rossi arrived at the library, some seven minutes later, Nic Costa had quietly established that the man who now lay on the floor, head ripped apart by at least three bullets, was indeed dead. He had watched the injured attendant being taken away by two scared-looking medics. He had quietly, carefully made a few enquiries. The room was in utter chaos, which suited Costa just fine. The terrified Guido Fratelli had immediately assumed that Costa was some kind of Vatican official, which was good enough for the three other Swiss Guards who had come to the room, established there was no imminent danger and now awaited further orders. Costa had no early desire to disillusion any of them. He had, in four years on the force, seen plenty of dead bodies and even a couple of shootings. But finding a corpse and the epidermis of another, and in the Vatican, was a new experience, one he was unwilling to relinquish.

His mind was working overtime. He let it race. The effort almost pushed the smell of the room from his consciousness, making the stench of blood and the way it mixed with the hot, arid air from the open windows just a little less noticeable.

He let Fratelli babble out his story, unable, all the time, to take his eyes off the woman who sat on a chair, back to the wall, watching everything. She was something short of thirty, modestly dressed in a tight grey business suit. She had shoulder-length dark hair, expensively cut, large green eyes and a serious, classically proportioned face, like that from some medieval painting. Not Caravaggio, she was too beautiful for that. No one had that kind of radiance in his work, not even the Madonnas. It wasn't supposed to exist. She looked, too, as if she were holding everything that had happened inside her, trying not to let it explode.

When the guard was done she stood up and walked over to him. He noticed that her grey suit was spattered with blood. She seemed unworried by it. Delayed shock, he thought. Sometime soon she would realize how close she had come to being murdered, how a man had been shot to death in front of her after displaying this strange and gruesome trophy on the desk. The skin still sat there looking like the cast-off from some bad Halloween party. Nic Costa found it difficult to believe it had once belonged to a human being.

'You're city police?' she asked, in a voice which had some odd tinge of accent to it, as if she were half English or American.

'That's right.'

'I thought so.'

The Swiss Guards looked at each other and groaned but had yet to find the courage to argue. They were still waiting for someone.

Rossi, who had been content to let the kid do the talking, smiled at them. The big man was willing to stand back. It felt a touch weird but Costa had got there first.

He already seemed to be in control. All the same Luca Rossi felt a touch grey around the gills. Which he did more and more recently.

The woman said, trying to recover his attention, 'I think Stefano was trying to tell me something.'

'Stefano?' Costa asked. 'The man who was going to kill you?'

She shook her head and Nic Costa couldn't stop himself watching the way her hair moved from side to side. 'He didn't try to kill me. That idiot . . . ,' she indicated Guido Fratelli who went red at her words, '. . . didn't understand what was going on. Stefano wanted me to go with him somewhere. He didn't get the chance to explain.'

The guard muttered something in his own defence and then was silent.

'What was he trying to tell you?' Costa asked.

'He said . . .' She was trying hard to think. He could understand why it would be difficult. There was so much crammed into such a short period of time. 'He said she's still there. To think of Bartholomew. And that we should hurry.'

He watched her deliberate these points and Nic Costa revised his opinion of her. Perhaps it wasn't delayed shock. Perhaps she really was this cool, this detached from what had gone on.

'Hurry where?' he was about to ask when a thick-set man in a dark suit elbowed his way into the conversation, stabbed him hard in the shoulder with a fat index finger, and demanded, 'Who the hell are you?'

The newcomer was about his own size, well built and middle-aged. He wore a dark suit which stank of cigars.

'Police,' Costa said, deliberately cryptic.

'ID?'

He took out his wallet and showed the man his card.

'Out,' the suit ordered. 'Out now.'

Costa looked at his partner, who felt similarly incensed judging by the small amount of colour that came back into his cheeks.

Rossi bent down to the truculent newcomer and asked, 'And we are?'

He looked, Costa thought, like a boxer who had just found God: a big face with florid, pock-marked cheeks and a broken nose. He had a crucifix in the lapel of his black wool jacket which, as far as Costa was concerned, meant nothing.

'Hanrahan,' he grunted, and Costa tried again to place the accent: maybe there was some gruff Irish touch and a little American in there. 'Security. Now you boys just walk along, eh? Leave this to us.'

Costa tapped him on the shoulder and was amused by the anger in his grey eyes. 'You want to know what we found out? I mean, we were just here to help, Mr Hanrahan. This could have been one nasty thing. Someone shooting in the Vatican. Let's face it, you took a while to get here. We could've been stopping something pretty bad.'

The woman looked at the three men fiercely. Costa knew what she was thinking: *they lock horns at a time like this*. She was right too.

'This is a Vatican matter,' Hanrahan said. 'We'll look into it. If we need your help, we'll call.'

'No it's not,' Costa insisted. 'This is our business too.'

Hanrahan said just one word, 'Jurisdiction'.

'You mean,' Costa asked, 'your dumb guard here killed the man on your turf so that's it?'

Hanrahan glanced at Guido Fratelli. 'If that's what happened.'

Costa walked the couple of metres to the desk and picked up an edge of the skin. This had once covered an arm. It felt damp and cold. More human than he had expected.

'And what about this?' he asked.

Hanrahan stared at him. 'What's your point?'

'My point?' The man was not a cop, Costa realized. He wasn't even a Swiss Guard because they always wore some kind of uniform. Security maybe, but he was about defending things, not interested in the slow, careful process of discovery. 'My point is that somewhere there's got to be a body this fits. And for the life of me I don't think that's going to be here.'

'Detective . . .' the woman interrupted.

'Please. Bear with me. What I'm saying, Mr Hanrahan, is that we've got two murders here and if you're a betting man I'll give you good money one of them took place in *our* jurisdiction because we've got the people for this. And you . . .' he cast a withering glance at the miserable Guido Fratelli, now close to tears, 'you don't. Now we're co-operating, we're being nice. Do you think there's some small chance we might get the same in return?'

Hanrahan shook his head. 'You really do not know what you are dealing with.'

'Hey!' Costa's voice rose. He put a hand on Hanrahan's shoulder. 'Are we after the same thing or what?'

'No,' Hanrahan said instantly with a grimace. 'Not at all. Now . . .'

The woman pushed between them and looked Nic Costa in the face.

'Do you have a car?' she asked.

'Sure.'

'He said to go there quickly. Can we do that, please? Now?'

Costa was puzzled once again by how calm she was. All the time they had been arguing she had been thinking, trying to work out the riddle the dead man had left her.

'You know where?'

'I think so. It was stupid of me not to realize earlier. Now. Please?'

Nic Costa patted Hanrahan on the shoulder as they left and said, 'See? You just have to know how to ask.'

Four

Costa thought about the abbreviated story Sara Farnese told them in the car. It raised a host of questions. He wondered too about her reasoning. Maybe the woman was already in shock, only inwardly, and this was just some crazy wild-goose chase.

'Why Tiber Island?' he asked.

'I told you. We have to go to the church.'

Rossi, who was driving, cast him a chilly glance. Costa wondered if he was starting to get bad feelings about this whole thing. It was an odd decision. They should have waited for instructions maybe. But he had no evidence a crime had been committed on city territory. Besides, the woman was adamant: she wanted to get there quickly. Costa thought he could make out a good case in front of Falcone. He normally did.

'Do you mind if I ask why?'

She sighed, as if she were talking to a school child. 'Bartholomew. The saint was flayed alive. Skinned. Stefano worked in that field. He would have known. The church on Tiber Island is Bartholomew's. I can't think of anything else.'

'That's it?' Costa wondered, fast revising his hopes of keeping Falcone sweet.

'That's it,' she agreed testily. 'Unless you have a better idea.'

The two men looked at each other. The August traffic was light. They made their way along the Trastevere waterfront at speed then took a left turn onto the tiny island that sat in the middle of the river.

'This Stefano,' Rossi asked as they pulled into the piazza in front of the church. 'He was a friend of yours?'

She said nothing, and was stepping out of the door before they had come to a halt.

'One scary woman,' Rossi grunted just out of earshot, and shook his head. The two men followed her and looked at the church. It was hard to believe there could be anything wrong here. It was an old, unspoilt corner of the city, with a cobbled piazza where you could sit in the shade away from the murmur of traffic that ran along both banks of the river.

'You think we should call in?' Rossi asked.

Costa shrugged. 'What's the point? Let them hang us in their time, not ours.'

'Yeah,' the older man agreed. 'Let me see if I can find a warden. Get some keys.'

The woman was already at the door of the church.

'Hey,' Costa yelled. 'Wait.'

But she was gone. Costa swore and raced after her, shouting for Rossi to follow.

The place was empty. Costa stood in the nave, framed by the polished columns on either side, feeling the way he always did in churches: uncomfortable. It was a matter of upbringing, he guessed. The places just spooked him out sometimes.

They looked in the dimly lit side chapels. They tried a couple of doors that opened onto tiny storage rooms full of dust.

'There's nothing here,' she said.

They stood in the nave, Costa trying to think of other options. She was disappointed, anxious, as if this were some intellectual puzzle demanding a solution.

'It was worth a try,' he said. 'Don't blame yourself.'

'I blame myself already,' she said softly. 'There has to be more to it than this. We did some work here once. There was a temple, to Aesculapius, before the church. Maybe something underground.'

'Aescoo— who?'

'Aesculapius. He was the god of medicine.' She looked at him. 'That makes it appropriate too, don't you think?'

'Maybe.' He was out of his depth and knew it. There was more going on in the woman's head than he understood. He wondered how much she acknowledged herself.

Rossi returned waving a set of large, old keys. Costa felt awkward. Somehow he seemed to have taken the initiative which was surely Rossi's prerogative. He was older, more senior. He knew more.

'We've been everywhere,' Costa said. 'It's all open anyway. Nothing.'

'Best we call in then,' Rossi said, and seemed relieved at the idea someone else might have to pick up the pieces.

She was staring intently at a small door on the left, before the altar. 'Over there.'

'We tried it,' Costa said.

'No. There's a campanile here too. We didn't find the way into the tower.'

Costa led the way and threw open the door. The room was small and dark. He pulled out the little torch from his pocket and saw instantly why they had missed the exit earlier. The stairs were hidden in the dark far corner, behind an iron screen that was secured with a huge padlock. Rossi grunted then went to it, fumbled with the keys, found the right one and pushed through into the darkness, scrabbling up the stairs.

'Jesus! What was that?'

The big man's screech echoed up the stone staircase.

Costa's hand finally found a light switch. It illuminated the ground floor of the tower and the stone spiral leading upwards through a first floor of old, dry planking.

Rossi staggered down the stairs, still squealing. His bald head was now stained with blood. It ran down his temple, into his eyes. He squirmed trying to clean it, scrubbing at his head with a handkerchief, yelling all the time. For the first time in his police career Nic Costa felt bile rising in his throat. Now they were at the staircase there was a smell inside the hot enclosed oven that was the tower's interior. It stank of fresh meat starting to go sour. He flashed the torch upwards. From the wooden ceiling above the stairs there was a slow, steady drip of coagulating blood that Rossi had walked beneath the moment he put a foot on the first step.

'We need help,' Costa said grimly, pulling the radio from his pocket.

He looked at her, not believing his eyes. Sara Farnese was already on the stairs, squeezing past Rossi. 'Hey!' he yelled, seeing her slim form disappear completely out of view. 'Don't do that. Don't touch anything. Jesus . . .'

His partner was losing it. He was scratching at his face as if the blood there were poison, acid, ready to eat into his skin. Costa took the radio and made a short, urgent call. Then he told Rossi to stay downstairs and wait for him. He didn't like the look on the older man's face. There was something crazy there, something that said this was all travelling a little too far from home. Nic Costa felt the same way but she was gone, she was upstairs with whatever else lived there, and he couldn't accept the idea she might be there alone.

He heard the sound of a switch overhead. A dim, yellow light cast shadows down the stairs. Then Sara Farnese made a noise, something halfway between a gasp and a scream, the first real sign of emotion she had uttered since the carnage in the Vatican Library half an hour before.

'Shit,' Costa cursed and took the stairs two at a time.

She was slumped with her back to the wall. Her hands were over her mouth, her green eyes were wide open in shock and amazement. Costa followed the direction of her gaze. He saw the corpses in the full beam of the single bulb and fought to keep the contents of his stomach down.

There were two bodies in the room. The woman's was fully dressed in a dark skirt and red blouse. It was suspended from a beam by a makeshift noose. Close to the dangling legs was an old wooden chair which might have been kicked from beneath her – or, perhaps, had fallen away as she tried to keep herself upright. Costa did not look too closely at her face but she appeared to be in her mid-thirties, with streaky fair hair and thin, leathery skin.

Two metres away was a second figure, strapped upright to a supporting timber beam: a man with a striking shock of golden hair and a face contorted by the agonies of a terrible death, with a gag tied tightly across his mouth, raising the bloodless lips and perfect white teeth into an ironic smile. He hung by his arms which were tethered above his head to a blackened beam. His legs dangled free to the wooden floor. There was skin on his face, hands, feet and groin alone.

A buzzing cloud of flies hovered over the fleshy torso. Their noise filled the tiny circular room. Around the walls, painted time and time again in the dead man's blood, was the message Sara Farnese had first heard in the Vatican Library, written in rough capital letters: THE BLOOD OF THE MARTYRS IS THE SEED OF THE CHURCH. And, once only, a couplet in English, one Nic Costa could understand enough to realize it was even crazier. It was painted on the wall behind the body so the writing stood behind his head. The words read like the first two lines of a poem . . .

> *As I was going to St Ives*
> *I met a man with seven wives.*

Nic Costa felt his stomach give a single heave then looked at her. Sara Farnese was unable to take her eyes off the bloody, stripped corpse. She looked as if she were going crazy inside her own head.

He crossed the tiny room in two strides and knelt down, between her and the flayed corpse, touching her hands with his.

'You've got to get out of here. Now. Please.'

She tried to avoid the obstacle of his body, tried to see once more. Costa placed his hands on her cheeks and forced her to look into his face.

'This is not your doing. This is not something you should see. Please.'

Then, when she failed to move, he bent down and lifted her into his arms with as much care as he could muster, and walked down the circular stone stairs, feeling her weight in his hands, avoiding as best he could the diminishing drip of blood from the ceiling.

Rossi was outside the door. As they passed he looked back and muttered something about support being on the way. Costa carried her into the nave. At the front he placed her on the bench pew. She was staring at the altar. Her eyes shone with tears.

'I've got things to do,' he said. 'Will you wait here for me?'

She nodded.

Costa beckoned Rossi to stand by the woman's side, then took a deep breath and returned to the tower and the bloody room on the first floor, to sort through what he could. The woman was easily identified from an ID card in her handbag. The skinned man's clothes lay in a tangled pile near his body. In the jacket pocket was a UK passport and the stub of a ticket for a flight from London that morning.

Ten minutes later the teams began to arrive, clambering up the stairs, filling the tiny room: scene of crime, lab people, an army of men and women in white plastic suits who wanted him out of there, wanted to get on with their work. Teresa Lupo, Crazy Teresa, the woman pathologist the police admired in a distant, scared fashion, was leading the way. It made sense; he couldn't see Crazy Teresa passing up on a case like this. She must have known the big man was there too. Station gossip had it that something had been happening between them recently.

Leo Falcone walked in and considered the stripped

corpse as if it were an exhibit in a museum. The inspector was as well dressed as ever: pressed white shirt, red silk tie, light-brown patterned suit, shoes that picked up the full yellow light from the single bulb and still managed to shine like mirrors. He was a striking figure: completely bald, with a perfect walnut tan and a silver beard cut in a sharp, angular fashion, like that of an actor playing the Devil on stage. He stared at Costa and said, with what sounded like venom in his smoker's voice, 'I sent you out to catch bag-snatchers. What in God's name is this?'

Costa thought to himself that one day he would lose it in front of all these people. One day someone would push him just a little too far.

'The woman is Rinaldi's wife,' he said. 'I looked in her handbag. It's with the other one's pile of clothes.'

'And the other one?' Falcone demanded.

Nic Costa felt like screaming at him. He hadn't asked for this. He didn't want to come to this place. Most of all he didn't want to watch Sara Farnese going steadily crazy as she began to accept what had happened in front of her.

'Working on it,' he said and walked down the stairs, leaving them to get on with their business.

Rossi, to his disappointment, had not stayed with Sara Farnese. Costa located him outside trying to find some shade in the hot, cobbled square, sucking on a cigarette as if his life depended on it.

'Did she say anything?' Costa asked.

Rossi was quiet. The horror of the crime was bad enough but Costa knew there was more to his distress than mere shock. There was something about this big, complex man he failed to understand.

'Not a word.' Luca Rossi didn't look Costa in the eye. He frowned. It put a big double chin on his pale, flabby face. 'I was scared in there. I didn't dare go into that room. You could feel it. Bad . . .'

'It's enough to scare anyone.'

'Bullshit!' Rossi hissed. 'You walked in like it was just another day.' He motioned to the scene of crime people outside the church door, smoking just like him. 'They're the same.'

'Trust me. They're shaken. We're all shaken.'

'Shaken?' Rossi mocked him. 'Falcone looks like he could eat breakfast off that corpse.'

'Luca.' It was the first time he'd used the big man's Christian name. 'What's wrong? Why are we working together? Why did they move you here?'

The big man's watery eyes cast him an odd, sad glance. 'They never told you?'

'No.'

'Jesus.' He stubbed out the cigarette with a shaking hand and immediately fumbled for another. 'You want to know? I went to some road accident. Happens all the time, I know. This one wasn't so different. There was the father behind the wheel, dead drunk. And on the road his kid, who'd gone straight through the windscreen and was now in pieces. Dead. Very dead.' Rossi shook his oversized head. 'You know what bothered the father? Trying to wheedle his way out of the accident. Trying to convince me he wasn't drunk.'

'There are jerks in the world. So what's new?'

'What's new?' Rossi repeated. 'This. I picked the jerk up by the scruff of his neck and started throwing him around the place. A lot. If the traffic cop on the scene hadn't been there I would probably have killed the moron.'

Costa looked back inside the church, checking she

was still there. When he turned away Rossi's sad, liquid eyes were burning at him.

'They moved me as part of the deal to stop him suing. To be honest I don't really care, not any more. I'm forty-eight, unmarried, unsociable. I spend my nights watching TV, drinking beer and eating pizza and, right up till that moment, I didn't mind, I didn't care. Then something hits you out of the blue. Sometimes the scales just fall from your eyes for the stupidest of reasons. It happened to me. It'll happen to you one day too. Maybe you get tired, with some bright new kid snapping at your ankles, and then you just see this stuff for the shit it is. Maybe it's something worse. You finally realize this isn't just some game. People die, for no reason whatsoever. And one day it's you.'

'I never thought it was any other way,' Costa replied. There was some personal resentment towards him in Rossi's voice. Costa didn't like to hear it. 'Go home, Luca. Get some sleep. I'll deal with everything.'

'Like hell you will. You think I want Falcone busting my balls tomorrow?'

Costa put a hand inside the older man's jacket and pulled out the packet. It was almost empty. 'Well, in that case just get some serious smoking done. We can talk about this later.'

Rossi nodded at the church. 'You want to know something else too? I'll tell you now. I doubt you're going to listen.'

'What?'

'*She* scares me. That woman in there. A woman who could watch all that stuff and hold it tight inside her. What kind of person can do that? She almost died today. She saw whatever was up in that room – no, don't tell me.

31

I don't want people with no skins on them walking around inside my head at night. It's not healthy. You look at her and you could think she doesn't mind a damn. That might just be where they belong.'

Costa felt his hackles rise on Sara Farnese's behalf. 'You didn't see her there, Luca. You can't judge. You didn't stay long with her at that altar either from what I can work out. You didn't watch her, not knowing where to look, wanting to bawl her eyes out. It takes time with some people. You ought to know that.'

Luca Rossi prodded him in the chest, hard. 'You're right. I didn't see.'

Crazy Teresa came out into the bright sun too, saw them, came over and cajoled Rossi for a smoke. When he reluctantly agreed she climbed out of her white polyester suit and stood there, a heavily built woman in her thirties, with a long black ponytail. She looked like Rossi, a little wasted. She wore the baggiest pair of cheap jeans Costa had ever seen and a creased pink shirt. Crazy Teresa lit the cigarette, blew a cloud of tobacco fumes into the scorching afternoon air and said, with a beatific smile on her face, 'It's days like this that make it all worth while, boys. Don't you agree?'

Costa swore, then went back inside the nave, cursing himself for the way he handled that one.

She was still at the altar, on her knees, hands locked low on her blood-spattered dress, eyes wide open, praying. Costa waited a couple of minutes until she was finished. He knew what she was looking at. Ahead of her, behind a painting of the head of Christ, done in gold, like some Byzantine icon, was a bigger image on the wall. It was Bartholomew, about to die. He had his hands tied above his head, just as the corpse did in the tower. A grim-faced executioner stood next to him, holding the knife, looking into his eyes as if he just couldn't work out where to begin.

Finally, Sara Farnese got off the floor and joined him on the bench.

'We can do this some other time,' he said. 'It doesn't have to be now.'

'Ask what you want. I'd rather get this out of the way.'

'I understand that.'

She was calm again and he wondered about what Rossi had said. Sara Farnese was certainly a woman in control of herself.

'This Stefano Rinaldi,' he asked. 'What was he to you?'

She hesitated then said, 'He was a professor in my department. I had an affair with him. Is that what you wanted to hear? It was brief. It ended months ago.'

'OK. And the woman upstairs in the room. His wife.'

'Mary. She's English.'

'I got that from the papers in her bag. Did she know?'

Sara Farnese peered at him. 'You want all this now?'

Costa said, 'If that's fine with you. If not we can do this some other time. It's your decision.'

Sara Farnese looked at the painting behind the altar again. 'She found out. That was why it ended. I don't know why it began in the first place. It was a friendship that just spilled over into something else. Stefano and Mary's marriage was shaky in any case. I didn't make it that way.'

He pulled out a plastic bag from his jacket pocket. There was a sheet of paper on it, a message from an office notepad covered in handwriting. 'I was trying to work out what's happening here. Not sit in judgement on anyone. I found this in the other one's clothing. It's a note that was left for him at the airport this morning I guess. It says it's from you and asks him to meet you here, at the church, as soon as you can. Says it's really important. Did you send that?'

She shook her head. 'No.'

'How could Rinaldi know he was coming?'

'I've no idea. Perhaps I talked about it at work. I really don't know.'

'The other man was your lover?'

She winced at the word. 'We . . . met from time to time. His name is Hugh . . .'

'Fairchild. I know. He had his passport with him. You want to look?'

'Why?'

'Next of kin. It says he's married.'

'No,' she said coldly. 'I don't want to look.'

'You didn't know?'

'Does it matter?'

Costa wondered. Was he being prurient? And if so, why? 'Maybe not. There was that thing about blood and martyrs written on the wall. You saw that I guess. And that other stuff. Who's this St Ives? Is he another martyr or something?'

'No. It's a place in England.'

'And seven wives?'

'I didn't even know he had one,' she answered with some bitterness.

'So what do you think happened?'

Sara Farnese glowered at him, her green eyes full of resentment. 'You're the policeman. You tell me.'

He hated being rushed but this woman seemed to demand it. 'Anyone who looks at this will say one thing,'

Costa said with a shrug. 'Your old boyfriend found out about your new one and decided it was time to bring things to a close. For all of them, him and his wife included. Maybe you too.'

'I told you. Stefano didn't want to kill me. And they weren't "boyfriends". They were people I slept with from time to time. In Stefano's case months ago.'

Costa didn't get it. Even now, pale and shocked, with grey bags growing under her eyes, Sara Farnese was a beautiful woman. He couldn't understand why someone like her would want to lead such an empty life.

'People go crazy for all sorts of reasons,' he said. 'Not always the obvious ones.' Men walked up a set of stairs and found someone's blood dripping down their face. People you loved walked out in the morning and came home at night with a death sentence hanging around their necks.

'Perhaps.' She didn't look convinced.

'I'm sorry I had to ask these questions. You understand why?'

She didn't say anything. She was transfixed by the painting behind the altar: Bartholomew about to lose his skin.

'It's apocryphal,' she remarked in a matter-of-fact way.

'What?'

'The story of the skinning. He was martyred, certainly. But probably something more mundane. Beheading was the usual method. The early Church embroidered these stories to encourage the waverers. To make sure the movement didn't falter.'

'Hence "the blood of the martyrs is the seed of the Church"?'

She peered at him, surprised, he thought, that he had seen the point.

'Is there some family I can call?' he asked.

'No one, thanks.'

'No one? Parents?'

'My parents died a long time ago.'

'There are people we can get to help in situations like this. Counselling.'

'If I need it I'll let you know.'

He thought again of what Rossi had said. There was much more to this woman than met the eye.

'Don't you ever pray?' she asked unexpectedly.

Costa shrugged. 'Not a family habit. And I never knew what to ask.'

'You just ask the same old questions. Such as, if there's a God, why does he let bad things happen to good people?'

'They were good people? This Englishman? The one who killed him?'

She considered this, Costa noticed. 'They weren't bad people if that's what you mean.'

'Hey,' he added without thinking. 'You should think yourself lucky you're not a cop. We get to wonder that and the other one too: why do good things happen to bad people? Why are the rich so rich and the poor so poor? Why did Stalin die in his bed? My old man's a communist. I used to ask that one a lot when I was a kid and boy did I get whacked around the ear plenty.'

Nic Costa was amazed. There was the slightest flicker of a smile on her face and it made Sara Farnese look like a different person, someone younger, someone with a fragile, interior beauty nothing like the cold, icy elegance that was her normal face for the world. Against his own instincts he suddenly found himself understanding that a man could become obsessed by this woman.

'Families matter,' Costa said. 'They make you a team against the world. I don't envy anyone who has to stand up against all this crap alone.'

'I'd like to go now,' Sara Farnese said. She got up and walked towards the door where the sun was finally starting to lose some of its power and the day was starting to die.

Nic Costa followed her all the way.

Five

The following morning Costa and Rossi found themselves summoned into Falcone's office at eight. The inspector looked grumpier than ever and uncannily alert, his sharp-featured face set in a constant frown. No one liked his temper. No one credited him with any great management skills. But Falcone was a man of talent, and there were insufficient of those in the higher levels of the force. He'd solved some difficult cases, ones that had made big space in the newspapers. He had influence, beyond the police station. There was plenty of respect for him in the Questura, and little in the way of affection.

He had the papers from the Rinaldi case on his desk, complete with a set of grisly photographs.

Falcone waved the reports he had in their faces. 'Skimpy,' was all he said.

'Sir,' Costa answered, 'we're working on something fuller now. You'll have it by ten.'

Rossi shifted uncomfortably on his seat. Falcone was staring at him and both men knew what his look was saying: *so the kid speaks for you now, does he?*

'You have anything on this Farnese woman?' Falcone asked.

Costa shook his head. 'Like what? You mean records or something?'

'That's exactly what I mean.'

'She's clean,' Rossi said. 'I ran a name check last night. There's not so much as a speeding ticket.'

Falcone leaned forward and made sure Costa was looking at him. 'You have to check these things.'

'I know,' Costa agreed. 'I'm sorry.'

'So that's the story?' Falcone asked. 'The old boy-friend killed the new boyfriend and took his own wife along for the ride?'

'Looks like that,' Costa agreed.

Falcone shrugged. 'No arguing there. It does look like that. I talked to forensics this morning. They couldn't find a single trace of anyone else in that tower, ground floor or first. Clean as a whistle except for Rinaldi and the two dead people in there.'

'So what's the problem?' Costa wondered.

'The problem?' Falcone nodded at Rossi. 'Ask him.'

Costa looked at his partner. They still hadn't made up since the near-quarrel the day before. That had to happen, he knew. He respected the big man. He didn't want this coldness between them.

'Luca?' he asked.

Rossi frowned. 'The problem is: why? Rinaldi stopped seeing the Farnese woman, what, three, four months ago? Why now?'

'Maybe he only just found out about the Eng-lishman,' Costa suggested. 'He heard her talking about how much she liked him and just went crazy.'

Falcone stabbed a finger at him. 'Do we know that? It's not in your report.'

Costa thought back to his conversations with her. 'No.'

'We're going to have to go back to that woman,' Falcone ordered. 'Get some detail in all this. Dates. Names. Reasons.'

'Fine,' Costa nodded. Rossi was looking out of the window now, reaching for a cigarette. They had had some conversation beforehand, Costa thought. There could be no other explanation.

'Why did he go to these lengths?' Falcone demanded. 'Why skin a man? Why go through this routine of putting his own wife on a chair as if he wanted the Farnese woman to find her alive? And this stuff he wrote on the wall . . .'

'He was crazy,' Costa said firmly. 'You'd have to be crazy to kill someone like that.'

Falcone snorted. 'Too easy. Besides, even if it's true, do you think there's no rationality behind craziness? It all just spews out for no reason? This man was a university professor. He was intelligent, organized. He was convincing enough for the Englishman to come to him from the airport thinking he was meeting the woman. He managed to get his wife into that tower and string her up. Then he killed the boyfriend, skinned him, went off to the library . . . Or maybe he did her first, in which case how come the Englishman let himself be strung up after seeing her? Can one person handle all those things? I guess so. But how? In what order? You tell me that. And this Fairchild. He was a big man. He didn't just hold up his hands and let Rinaldi tie him. What went on there?'

'I know that,' Rossi said. 'I talked to Crazy Teresa in the path lab just now. They think there's traces of some drug, some sedative maybe.'

'What sedative?' Falcone asked. 'How'd a university professor come to be walking around with medication to hand just when he feels like skinning someone? If it comes to that, how the hell does a man like that *know* how to skin someone? And – this is the biggest one for me, the one I keep coming back to – *why?* Why like this?'

'She's a professor in the same department,' Costa suggested. 'The quotation on the walls is from some early Christian theologian. Maybe it sounded appropriate.'

'*Appropriate?*' Falcone repeated, as if it was the most stupid thing he'd ever heard in his life. 'You mean he's saying to her, "We're all martyrs to you, bitch. And here's the proof"? I don't get it. What was he hoping to achieve? If he was going to kill her it would make more sense. But you claim that's not the case. He just wanted to get her to go, as quickly as possible, to the place he'd left his own wife, still alive. What's the point?'

Costa looked at Rossi for help. His partner was still staring out of the window, working on the cigarette. It was another hot, cloudless day out there. Nic Costa wondered exactly what it was that Falcone expected of him.

'And you're wrong,' Falcone continued. 'I checked. Rinaldi was in the same department but he didn't share the same speciality. His field was Roman law, the Curia, all that ancient stuff the Vatican still thinks we should be listening to today.'

'Is that relevant?' Rossi wondered.

'You tell me. I ran through the records. Four months ago Rinaldi was called as an expert witness for some government tribunal looking at the issue of diplomatic immunity for Vatican officials. They want more. We want less. Rinaldi came up with an expert opinion that said they were right, in law, very old law anyway. Where the hell do martyrs come into that?'

'Are you saying, sir, that you think my conclusion's wrong? That Rinaldi isn't responsible somehow?'

'Hell no,' Falcone answered immediately. 'It's difficult to see how it could have happened any other way.'

'Well, then what? Isn't it enough to know Rinaldi did these things? Sometimes we never know why. We just have to accept that.'

Falcone glowered at him. 'Not yet we don't. I'm an inquisitive bastard. It's what makes me tick. It's what makes every good cop tick. If you're not, you never get to know a thing. I want you to answer some of these questions that keep bugging me. I don't want detectives who think they're elves in Santa's workshop going out there, wrapping things up all nicely with all the right ribbons, all the right answers, dropping them on my desk, getting a pat on the head, then looking for some more toys to play with. This job isn't like that.'

'I know,' Costa replied. 'At least, I never felt the pat on the head.'

Rossi groaned, stabbed out the cigarette and immediately lit another.

Falcone was smiling again. He'd won a response and Costa cursed himself for being so stupid. 'You kids.' The inspector laughed. 'You're so *sensitive*. Listen. I think you've got the right answers. I just don't like the way you got there. Cutting too many corners.'

'Sir.' Costa scowled.

'And one more thing,' Falcone added. 'I'd like you to listen more. I know we're into this youth culture thing that says everyone over the age of thirty is a moron—'

'I'm twenty-seven, sir.'

'Yeah, yeah. I wish you looked it sometimes. The point I want to make to you, Costa, is the only way any of us really learns is by watching our elders and betters. Forget all that crap in the police college. All we do for a living is deal with human beings. Human beings who, for the most part, are trying to lie to us, trying to screw us around. This is a people business. You should talk less and listen more, son.'

Costa grimaced. 'Sir, I—'

'Shut up,' Falcone ordered. 'And here's another thing. That other stuff he wrote on the wall? St Ives?'

'Crazy,' Rossi said, starting to become interested.

'Maybe,' Falcone agreed. 'But I can tell you what it is. I got someone to look it up.'

He stared at a laser printout on the desk and read the words.

> *As I was going to St Ives*
> *I met a man with seven wives.*
> *Every wife had seven sacks,*
> *Every sack had seven cats,*
> *Every cat had seven kits.*
> *Kits, cats, sacks and wives,*
> *How many were going to St Ives?*

The two detectives stared at each other, dumbfounded. Costa grabbed the calculator on the desk and started punching.

Falcone grinned. 'It's a riddle. What's the answer?'

Costa scribbled some figures on his notepad. 'Seven wives. Forty-nine sacks. Three hundred and forty-three cats. Two thousand four hundred and one kittens. That adds up to two thousand eight hundred.' He thought of the tiny enclosed room in the tower and the remembered stink of meat. 'But what the hell does that mean?'

The inspector scowled. 'It means you don't understand riddles. And you just wasted a lot of effort not answering the question you were asked. "I met a man with seven wives . . ." They were all going in the opposite direction. There was just one person going to St Ives. The narrator. You were looking in the wrong place all along. The obvious isn't always the right answer.'

Nic Costa shook his head. 'That's the kind of game a crazy person would play.'

'And not finish the line?' Falcone asked. 'Why would a dead man set an incomplete riddle? Can you tell me that?'

There was no ready answer.

'I want you to go round to Rinaldi's home,' Falcone ordered. 'There's been some people there already but maybe they missed something. Try to work out what kind of man he was, whether there's anything to explain this. And try not to piss off Hanrahan again. He's been on the phone twice to me already. You certainly made an impression there.'

Costa failed to understand the relevance. 'Hanrahan? You know him?'

'Oh, we're just the best of friends.' Falcone was, Costa hoped, being sarcastic. Sometimes it was hard to tell. 'Now . . .'

He was out of his seat, standing in front of the window with his back to them, watching the traffic in the street, thinking, or so he wanted them to believe. Another Falcone ritual. The two detectives knew when their time was through.

Rossi led the way out of the room.

Six

The Rinaldis owned a large restored apartment in a late-nineteenth-century block on the Via Mecenate, a residential street by the park which led from the Via Merulana towards the Colosseum. The neighbourhood was on the cusp of acceptability. It was only a few minutes' walk to the smarter, older quarters of the Caelian Hill. Nero's Golden House lay beneath the parched summer grass a hundred metres from the entrance to the block. The apartment was well decorated in a lean, modern style, generously proportioned and quiet, since it gave out onto the vast internal courtyard of the building, not the street in front. Still, Nic Costa was unable to dispel the idea that the Rinaldis were not exactly rolling in money. The Via Merulana was not a place to wander with pleasure at night. It was only a little distance from the squalor of Termini Station. If he looked closely outside he would see the signs: needles in the gutter, used condoms in doorways. At night the park became a haunt for rent boys. A university professor would prefer to live somewhere else, Costa felt. It was one of those neighbourhoods that was always up and coming but never quite got there.

The apartment had been thoroughly searched already. Costa and Rossi studied the preliminary report: a small amount of cannabis, no messages on the answering machine, no incriminating letters, nothing on the cheap desktop computer that sat in the tiny study next to the bedroom. He wondered how Falcone expected them to come up with something new.

Rossi found the Rinaldis' bank statements tucked into a drawer of the computer desk. Costa's suspicions were correct. They maintained separate accounts and both were in the red, Stefano Rinaldi's to the tune of a quarter of a million euros. There were threatening letters from the bank too. Unless the Rinaldis cleared some of their debt, even the modest apartment in the Via Mecenate was in jeopardy of disappearing from beneath them.

Was this enough to turn someone like Stefano Rinaldi into a multiple killer? Falcone would never accept such a flimsy idea. Where was the evidence? Costa made a note to re-interview the neighbours. The preliminary report came up with so little. All the usual comments they got in domestic incidents, stories that painted the victims as a quiet, solitary couple, with few friends. No one had ever seen Mary Rinaldi with a bruised face. No one had heard her complain about the behaviour of her husband. They were, it seemed, a bland, childless everyday pair struggling to make ends meet. Falcone was right: there had to be more. The bank statements and the threats from the bank were symptoms, surely, of some larger malaise in the Rinaldis' life.

Something else bothered him. Mary Rinaldi didn't work, the report said. Even so, Rinaldi must have earned a decent package at the university. They should have been able to survive. Yet here they were with a sizeable debt outstanding on a mediocre home, fighting to keep their heads above water. Where was the money going? They went back to the bank statements and found the answer: cash. Stefano Rinaldi's salary from the university amounted to almost €6,000 a month after deductions. Even with a tidy mortgage that should have been enough to live on. The statements told a different story. Rinaldi immediately transferred a quarter into his wife's bank account, standing payments accounted for a further half, and the rest disappeared in credit card bills and some huge cash withdrawals, sometimes as much as €1,000 a week.

Nic Costa had been around long enough to understand there were only so many reasons why a man wanted ready money in his hand in this kind of quantity: women, booze and drugs being the main ones. Maybe Sara Farnese had been expensive to maintain, though somehow he doubted that. The woman seemed too independent to rely on someone like Rinaldi for money. Maybe there was someone else now in her place. But if that was the case, why was Rinaldi so furious with Sara that he wanted to kill her current boyfriend?

There was always a simpler answer. While Rossi ran through the answering machine he went into the bathroom which was small, covered in mirrors and had just a toilet, a washbasin with a plain cabinet above it and a shower in the corner. He opened the cabinet door and looked inside: a woman's razor, some headache pills, a packet of laxatives, and two neat rows of white plastic tablet containers from a health store. He read the names: evening primrose oil and ginseng, gingko biloba and selenium. There were eight different preparations in all. One or both of the Rinaldis must have rattled like a pill box when they went out of the apartment in the morning.

Costa picked up the biggest container, the one with evening primrose oil inside, opened it and looked at the round, shiny yellow capsules. There were only about ten left and they sat on a wad of cotton wool. Gelatine health pills nestled on a soft white bed of fluffiness. He hated cotton wool. It stuck to his fingernails. The feel of it gave him the same shivers some people get from running their nails up and down a blackboard. It seemed so pointless. They put cotton wool in pill containers only to stop things rattling around and breaking. A flexible gelatine capsule couldn't break, not easily. Costa turned the container upside down and emptied the visible contents into the sink. Then he righted it and, trying not to screech, gently pulled out the cotton wool from the base.

Beneath it was a small transparent plastic bag containing white powder. Costa swore at the incompetence of the squad who had made the first search. He hated getting people into trouble but, on this occasion, there really was no avoiding it. He took out the bag, unwrapped it, tasted the coke, confirming what it was. The source of the Rinaldis' cash problem was surely apparent. Perhaps dope would explain Stefano's excitable state. Except that the autopsy had so far failed to uncover any trace of drugs.

Costa swore again. It was still significant: it was the only thing he'd found so far that was.

He returned to the living room and showed the dope to Rossi, who commented, 'And these are supposed to be intelligent people? Why do they go around picking up gutter habits like that?'

'No family,' Costa said. It was astonishing how often

that factor cropped up in his line of work. Except every dopehead had a kind of family: the person who fulfilled his or her needs. In the case of the middle classes that was usually fixed, regular, like a visit to the doctor. Those steady withdrawals from the bank each week said as much. Somewhere in the city was the dealer who knew them, a person who, Costa understood, dealt only with professionals, never took risks, and was probably smart too, full of some quick philosophy to justify what he did.

The two of them spent an hour going through the address book in Mary Rinaldi's bag, phoning every number there, talking to hairdressers and doctors, distant friends and a couple of travel agencies. Any of them could be a supplier but it didn't feel right. Then they did the same with the names on Rinaldi's computer, printed off every one, forty in all, mainly academic contacts. The narcotics people could run through the list later and see if any rang a bell.

Rinaldi used the computer a lot. It was full of essays and letters, many to the bank. It was plugged into the phone line too. Costa clicked on the e-mail program expecting it to be protected by some kind of password. To his surprise it popped up and showed an inbox with three messages, each dated from two days before: one was junk mail, the other an invitation to an academic convention in Florida.

He opened the third and stared at it. The message said, simply, 'Money no problem. Be there ten am'. The sender's name and e-mail address were blank. But there was a Rome phone number at the bottom of the screen.

Rossi looked at him, staggered. 'They missed this? Falcone is going to go crazy.'

Costa picked up the phone on the desk and dialled. A woman answered. She said, 'Cardinal Denney's office.'

'Sorry. Wrong number.'

Rossi's long face wouldn't leave him alone. 'Well?'

'It was the office of someone called Cardinal Denney.'

The big man's watery eyes grew wide. 'Someone called Cardinal Denney?'

'The name means something?'

Rossi was making for the door. 'I need a drink. Before one more damn thing. A drink. Now.'

Seven

Costa insisted: if they were going to a bar on duty it would be somewhere he knew. Rossi now glowered at the modest wine glass which was half full of a liquid the colour of straw. He sniffed, tasted it, grimaced, then crammed a piece of cheese on some bread and nibbled artlessly, spilling crumbs everywhere. They sat on tiny stools around a low table in a wine bar Costa sometimes used. It was near his tiny home in the Campo dei Fiori. The place was quite empty apart from the two cops and a woman who had stopped mopping the floor to serve them.

'Why can't we go to a real place and drink beer like normal people?' Rossi moaned. 'Don't you know mathematics? Why do we have to pay twice the price to make our own sandwiches when I can get three times this quantity around the corner for half what it costs in this dump? And they do beer.'

Costa cautiously patted Rossi's colossal stomach. It was an act of some intimacy which the big man tentatively allowed, like a lion allowing its trainer to stroke its head.

'Beer makes you fat,' Costa said. 'Beer makes you fart. Trust me. A partner knows. Diet is important, Uncle

Luca. Particularly for a man of your age, in your . . . condition.'

'I'm happy where I am, thanks. And I'm not your fucking uncle.' Rossi grunted again. 'And what's with this fancy apartment in the Campo? Cops don't live in places like that. That's why I have to drink in a stuck-up *enoteca* . . .'

'It's not fancy. It's just where I like to live.'

'So you can screw the tourist girls when they've had too much to drink on a Saturday night?'

'No. Because I like it. That's all.'

'Inexplicable,' Rossi declared. 'So where's the nearest painting now, huh?'

'Too many to choose from,' Costa answered. The big man looked at him as if to say: *so now I know why you live here.*

'I didn't know about the accident, Luca. What happened there. I'm sorry.'

'I've seen worse,' Rossi grumbled. 'We both have. Yesterday. Sometimes it catches you like that. You just walk along thinking, it's not so bad, I can make it through the day. Then you just stumble round the corner and put your shoe into something that makes you realize the bad stuff was there all along and you just fooled yourself into thinking it could be any other way.'

'There's a painting near here. It's about that. I could show you if you like.'

Rossi almost laughed. 'Me? Look at a painting?'

'Sure. Why not?'

'You won't tell anyone? Some of those bastards take the piss.'

'It's a deal. But I want to hear about Cardinal Denney first.'

Rossi grabbed him by the arm. 'Keep your voice down, for Christ's sake.'

Costa raised an eyebrow. There was still just the woman in the place, mopping away, well out of earshot.

'You never know,' the big man said defensively.

'Know what?'

Rossi shook his head. 'You don't even get to hear the station gossip, do you?'

'Too busy doing a job.'

'Oh my,' the big man grumbled. 'The kid's a saint. Listen. You heard of the Banca Lombardia?'

'Sure.' He nodded. 'I read it was in trouble. Bad investments. Trouble with the authorities. There's supposed to be some mob money in it. Ours. The Americans.'

'Clever boy. Well, let me tell you something. Two partners ago I used to share the Fiat sofa with this grown-up guy who couldn't keep his trap shut. Probably yakked in his sleep, but the funny thing was . . . he was worth listening to. He'd done some secondment work with the spooky people in the Finance Ministry and, my, did he like to talk about all these secret stake-outs he did, and all the good-guy politicians that were really on the take. He knew all the names of the people who pulled the strings without anyone in the outside world seeing. You know what? One of them wore a red cap. Still could if he wanted. Goes by the name of Michael Denney and if it wasn't for the fact he could hide in that place of his we'd be throwing him in the cells right now.'

'The Vatican?'

'Where else?' Rossi waited, hoping for some enlightenment. 'Jesus. The bankers were just the front men. This was a private little operation that Denney spun out of some genuine Vatican venture without telling anyone.' He raised his glass, drained it in one. 'And now it's rapidly going bust. Liquidity problems. No one knows whether it's going to pull through or what. Remember?'

'Yeah,' Costa conceded. 'I think I read about that.'

'You read nothing. Listen to me, Nic. This Denney's been putting his holy hands into stuff no one ought to be messing with, least of all a priest. He had offshore funds in places that don't have offshore funds. Places anyone could put money and no one – not the tax people, not the intelligence agencies – would be any the wiser. There's a queue of people waiting to talk to him about that. Us. The Ministry of Justice. FBI. And probably the Mafia too from what I hear. They don't like it when the man from the Vatican does the laundry wrong. Lucky for him he can hide there trying to get the rest of us to agree that, if we let him walk out, he's covered by diplomatic immunity.' He paused. 'You remember what Falcone said? About Rinaldi?'

Costa did. The dead man had been called to give an expert opinion on the subject only a few months before.

'You think Denney was somehow paying him to come up on the right side?'

Rossi looked around him to make sure no one else came in. 'If he was it didn't work. Maybe that's why Denney got pissed off with him. He quit being a churchman years ago to work on the financial side. Should have filled in the right forms if he wanted to claim he was a diplomat. Too late to start whining when there's money gone missing. A whole lot of money too. I read the file.'

Costa was struggling to make sense of this. 'Why

would he steal it? Why would a man like that want money?'

'Runs in the family. Denney comes from some Irish-American family in Boston. Big in bootlegging in the early days, sidekicks to Joe Kennedy for a while. Moved into politics, finance, all that stuff. But they never could let everything go. It's in their blood, I guess. He was the kid they marked out for the Church while the rest stuck with the family business. Which was all Denney did for a while and pretty well too. Made a name for himself working the Irish ghettos in Boston. Man of the people. Didn't seem to be an act either. Then he hit the up escalator, came to Europe. By the time he's thirty he's in Rome. By the time he's forty-five he's wearing the red cap and suddenly it's no more listening to some local jerk confessing to playing fuck-thy-neighbour. He's gone business, running this bank and he's pumping the Pope's money all ways. Into IBM and General Motors. After a while into funnier places too, companies that are never going anywhere, ever, because that's not why they're there. Suddenly, it's no longer about the Pope's money. It's stuff coming from all over, laundered by God knows who.' Rossi stared at the empty glass. 'Why the hell am I telling you all this?'

'You're keeping me up to date on the gossip.'

'Right,' the big man grumbled. 'So according to this man of mine, along comes the new millennium and Denney's bank's doing like all the rest of them, not good. He's been betting on these dotcom morons. He's been hedging this by betting on the airlines and the telecom people too. In short he's losing his touch. One day in September he turns on the TV and sees a couple of planes fly into a couple of skyscrapers. And what do you know?

Bad turns awful. Bad turns fucking disastrous. Word is that if this bunch was out in the open Denney'd be bust and in the slammer facing some serious incarceration. Which is bad news for him and for all those mob guys who thought they were banking on something that had the Holy Writ on the cover. Now they are people who do not like to lose their money.'

'This man of yours knows a lot,' Costa observed.

'He was a knowledgeable guy. What do I mean "was"? Still is.'

'And he says it in such a memorable way too. Where's he working now?'

'Probably with some dumb smartass kid who doesn't believe a word he says. Do I make myself clear?'

'In a particularly obscure way. Did he get the chance to arrest someone?'

'Like who? Lombardia isn't officially bust yet. Just "suspended". All the money was passing through places like Liechtenstein and Grand Cayman. Try hunting that down. The finance people had one low-grade clerk in their sights, thought he might talk too if they offered him a deal. When they went to collect they found him floating face down in the bath in his apartment in Testaccio. "Heart attack". Very convenient. Who knows? Maybe Denney had him done. Maybe now he's got the taste he's offing a few more people who took the money and didn't come up with the goods.'

'Rinaldi did come up with the goods. He said the Vatican was right.'

'Didn't work though, did it? Remember, Denney has the contacts. To be honest, though, my guess is they're none too keen on him either these days. Which gives him plenty more reasons to stay behind those walls where no one can touch him. Not until the Vatican people themselves wash their hands of the black sheep and kick him out onto the pavement. Yeah. Like that's going to happen.'

Costa was baffled. 'Why not? Why would the Church tolerate any of this?'

It could have been Falcone looking at him. Rossi's expression said just one thing: *don't be so dumb, kid.* 'This isn't about the Church. It's about the Vatican. Another country. Like I said. Mongolia as far as we're concerned. Unless it's in their interests they won't give us anything. Maybe Denney's in some kind of purdah now they know what's been going on. Maybe not. Either way for us it's irrelevant. He daren't set foot outside the place. He knows we'd arrest him on the spot. He knows some of his shady friends might want a word too. They're too picky about their own in there to hang him out to dry. But my guess is he's not a happy little priest. This was a guy who used to hang around with presidents. The way things are going now he's just going to wind up a sad old man stuck in a nice comfy prison for the rest of his life. Unless he gets a fit of conscience, of course, and decides to tell us everything. Which I find somewhat unlikely, to be frank.'

Costa was adamant. 'We have to check it out.'

The big man wagged a finger at him. 'No! Didn't you hear Falcone clearly enough? I shouldn't even have told you any of this. You are not going back to that place. Understand?'

'You said it was gossip. I found out some place else.'

'What about the painting?' Rossi asked, trying to change the subject.

'Still want to see it?'

'My glass is empty. You're starting to scare the shit out of me. You bet I want to see it.'

Costa led him out of the bar, across the busy main road into the warren of streets that stretched between the Pantheon and Piazza Navona. Rossi followed as the kid ducked into a nondescript church in one of the side roads.

'Who'd put a masterpiece in a dump like this?' Rossi demanded in the gloomy interior. 'I've seen better churches in Naples.'

'This is San Luigi dei Francesi, big man. Here you've got two of the greatest works Caravaggio ever painted, exactly where he meant them to be, where he put them on the walls himself.'

'I get to see both?' He didn't sound enthusiastic.

'One at a time,' Costa said and walked forward to deposit some coins in the light meter. A set of bulbs came alive. Rossi blinked at the huge canvas in front of him. Most of it was set in shade: a group of men in medieval dress at a table, counting money. Three of them had turned to look at a pair of figures standing at the right of the scene. From behind came a shaft of revealing light. It burned brightly on the puzzled faces as they sat there, half-cowed, watching the newcomers.

'*The Vocation of Saint Matthew*,' Costa said. 'He's the one in the middle, pointing to himself, as if to say, "Who? Me?"'

'And the couple on the right?'

'Jesus, with his hand outstretched, indicating to Matthew he's been chosen as an apostle. And by his side Peter, who symbolizes the Church which will come to be built on Matthew's gospel.'

'So what's this got to do with me losing it in an accident? That *was* your point, wasn't it?'

Costa nodded. The big man wasn't slow. 'Look at the costumes. The men around the table are in what was, when it was painted, contemporary dress. Jesus and Peter look as if they've walked straight out of a biblical scene. Caravaggio was commissioned to record a specific scene but what he did was make a broader point. This is about a moment of revelation, a moment when, in Matthew's case, he realizes there's more to life than counting money on a table.'

'You sound like a priest,' Rossi grumbled.

'I'm sorry. I didn't mean to.'

'And this,' Rossi nodded at the painting, 'is where you get your kicks?'

'I wouldn't put it that way.' Costa thought about it. 'It's about looking for some meaning, looking for a reason to be alive. Not just working your way through the day and being glad you got to the other end.'

'That's fine as far as I'm concerned.'

'Sure,' Costa replied. 'Until you see something that says otherwise. And then you wind up working with me.'

Rossi sighed. He got the message. There was, Costa knew, no need to labour it.

'So you're a Catholic? In spite of everything they say about your old man?'

'No. Not at all. I just like to look for meanings. It's a hobby if you like.'

A couple of tourists turned on the light for an adjoining painting. It was brightness and shade again, Rossi noticed, but there was more action in this one. Some old guy was lying on the floor, dying, a madman over his body, holding a bloodied sword. There was something deeply disturbing about the work. It was dense, vivid, savage. It seemed poised on the very edge of sanity.

'*Matthew's Martyrdom*,' Costa said quietly. 'Another story. For another time.'

'I never did work out why a religion based around love and peace seemed to involve so much killing.' Rossi grunted. 'You know the answer to that? Or do you need to be a Catholic to understand?'

'It's about martyrdom. Sacrificing yourself for something bigger than one human being. Could be the Church. For my dad it could be the hammer and sickle.'

'Sounds the kind of thing dumb people do,' Rossi mumbled, then wiped his sleeve across his mouth.

Costa knew what it meant. He wanted a beer. He followed the big man outside, watched him working out where to go next.

'Listen.' Rossi's watery eyes hooded over. 'If you want to hear more about this I've an idea.'

'Really?'

'Yeah. We're having dinner with Crazy Teresa tonight. It could be useful.'

'We? *We* have a date with Crazy Teresa?'

Rossi eyed him as if to say: so what?

'We hardly know each other,' Costa objected.

'It's Crazy Teresa. Everybody knows her.'

'I meant *we* hardly know each other.'

Rossi seemed offended by that. 'Look. I know this relationship didn't get off to the greatest of starts. But I'm trying here, kid. I'm doing my best. And there is something in it too. She wants to talk. I know the rumours doing the rounds. There's a touch of truth in them but it's not gone as far as people think. I'm not eating with Crazy Teresa on my own, not tonight.'

Costa couldn't believe his ears. 'Jesus. Why should I be there?'

'She wants you. Don't ask me why. It's only polite. Interdepartmental relations and all that.'

'Wonderful.'

Costa couldn't work up much enthusiasm to complain. He had nothing else to do. Maybe Crazy Teresa off duty would be a different woman.

'Is that a yes?'

'Depends,' Costa said slyly. 'Are we still negotiating?'

Eight

Sara Farnese lived in the Borgo, the residential area that led from the river to the very walls of the Vatican. This was still Rome, still under the jurisdiction of the city. Yet it was impossible to ignore the proximity of the papal state up the hill. Her home was in Vicolo delle Palline, a narrow cobbled lane that ran between the Via dei Corridori and the Borgo Pio. *Il Pasette*, the elevated, fortified corridor which joined the Vatican with the Pope's former fortress, the Castel Sant'Angelo, abutted her medieval, ochre-coloured building. When parties of visiting luminaries were allowed to walk down the passage, treading in the footsteps of long-dead pontiffs sometimes fleeing for their lives, she could hear them through the wall and often listened to their idle chatter. The commercial bustle of St Peter's Square and the hectic tourist trade around it were only minutes away, but in the little street and the close, narrow lanes she favoured, people moved at a different pace. This was still a local quarter, residential, largely untouched by the modernization of the city. Homes were handed down from generation to generation – though not hers, which had been bought at a substantial price.

She had acquired the first-floor apartment four years before when she finally moved to Rome for good at the age of twenty-three, putting on the professional suit of a university lecturer and, shortly after, starting to look older, perhaps more serious, than she felt. College, in London and America, was now a fading memory. Her teenage years, spent in boarding schools throughout Europe and finally in the cold Swiss town of Montreux, seemed remote, as if they had happened to another person. She remembered boarding the steamer and meandering across the great shining expanse of Lake Geneva on her own, trying to escape the prying attention of her classmates, who found her distant, different. She would sit on deck for hours, overlooked by nothing except the towering crown of mountains bordering the eastern end of the glittering inland sea, peering down at her from high, like God from Heaven: some vast, omnipresent watcher over her life, detached from its emotionless daily tedium.

These were Sara Farnese's most vivid memories, ones of physical, geographical objects. The green at Harvard. The college quadrangles of Oxford. A handful of ancient streets behind the Blue Mosque in Istanbul where she could lose herself for hours, following the tangled history of Byzantium, imagining herself into its formative years under Constantine, realizing that the study of early Christianity, the subject she had chosen – or had it chosen her, she was unsure which – was one where she had a certain distinct talent.

There were few people stored in the dark vault hidden within her head. An exception lay in one of the oldest memories of all: Sister Annette, in the convent kindergarten in Paris, taking her to one side on a sunny June morning. This was twenty-two years ago. Yet, seated now in the apartment in the Borgo, she could still recall the nun's gaunt, worried face, framed by a starched white wimple, like a picture waiting to be hung on the wall.

They had gone to a small room she had never visited before. The bright sunlight filtered through a single stained-glass window depicting Jesus with a lamb in his arms. The plangent clatter of the bells of St Eustache drifted into the room, together with the racket of a reggae band busking outside Les Halles shopping complex. The place smelled of dust, as if it were little used, though it was as clean, and as simple, as every other corner of the convent. They sat next to each other on hard wooden chairs, with their hands joined together around an old, battered Bible.

Sister Annette was not as old as she looked, the child Sara thought. Sometimes she imagined the nun's face without the wrinkles, without the tension which seemed to come from some inwardly felt pain. Without the wimple and the habit too, dressed in normal clothes, like the people she saw on the street. When Sara did this, Sister Annette became a different person: full of life, vibrant, restless. Normal somehow. This imaginary person and the real sister who now sat next to her shared only one identical feature. They both had very bright, very intense blue eyes and, on this long-dead Paris day, the real Annette turned them on the infant Sara with a fierce, unbending power which gave the child no room for escape.

Memories were about generalities, not details. Even the child Sara had understood this and never tried to fix each word precisely in her head. It was the meaning which counted and in that, said the nun's eyes, there could be no room for mistakes.

They had spoken about the mysteries of God and how no one, not even the greatest human being who has ever lived, could begin to understand everything in his mind. Not Sister Annette. Not the kindly priest with the foreign accent who came into the convent from time to time, gave them talks she could not understand, then left, touching each child on the head as he walked to the front door and the bright world beyond.

Even the Holy Father himself was outside every last detail of God's great plan she said, which surprised the child Sara greatly since she had been given to understand that the distant white figure who lived in the Vatican was, in some unexplained way, part of Heaven itself.

On occasion God could appear cruel. There would be times when no one would comprehend his meaning. The innocent would suffer, perhaps more than the wicked. There would be pain where it was undeserved, grief which could appear so great it was impossible to believe one would ever escape its morbid clutches. One would ask – and this was quite normal, Sister Annette said, this happened to everyone – whether a loving God could allow such things to happen at all. This was the Devil talking, whispering in our ears at the moment of our greatest weakness. God's grace, though sometimes incomprehensible, was there to make us free. We made our own prisons. We – not him – sent ourselves to Hell. He loved us through our agonies and would, in the end, redeem us with his kindness. Once we had walked the path towards him. Once we had found our own particular path to Paradise.

Life was a mystery, she said, a gift. And like all gifts it

could be taken away. When that moment happened, the faithful didn't complain. They thanked God that the gift was there at all. They acceded to his greater wisdom. They loved him all the more and found, in that love, some solace.

Sara had looked up into the sharp blue eyes, trying to understand. She adored this woman with all her heart. For as long as she had been in the school – and that pre-dated even the haziest of distant memories – Sister Annette had been like a parent. Her own mother and father were infrequent visitors, tall, stern figures, not staying long when they did arrive. They were busy people. She felt fortunate they had the time to come at all. When they did they would kiss her on the cheek, leave endless gifts and promises. Sister Annette had agreed on this point too, and Sara knew she would never lie. This was not an absence of affection on their part. They lived in a different world, one where a quiet, five-year-old child who spoke so little, who spent her time in daydreams she never revealed to another living soul, would never be happy. They did this for her own good and she would one day be grateful.

'God works constantly,' the sister said, 'beyond our understanding.'

She hesitated. There was, the child thought, something wrong with her. A cold. Flu perhaps. Sister Annette was ill and the thought made Sara clasp the nun's hand to the Bible all the more tightly. It was impossible for the child to imagine a world without this woman in it.

'Sara,' the nun said finally. 'God has taken your mother and your father to him. Yesterday. In America. There was an accident.'

She recalled – would always recall – how this made her

mouth go dry, made something hard and painful begin to grow in her throat, like a cancer coming from nowhere.

'They live with God now. They're in his Heaven, where you'll see them one day too, provided you are a good girl, as you are now. God loves you, Sara. We all love you. We will love you every day till he calls us to go to him too and wait for you patiently there until we're reunited. Your parents. All of us.' Sister Annette paused. Her eyes were glassy. 'There's nothing for you to worry about,' she said in a voice that abruptly took on a practical tone. 'We'll look after you, for ever if you like. You can go out into the world too if you choose. You'll have the means to do whatever you want.'

At this point the nun hugged her. Sara could still remember the smell. The stink of death sat upon her, an old, dry stink, like something going off. Within the year, Annette would join God in Heaven. She would become part of the great procession to his door, willingly, smiling perhaps, as she died.

'Be sad,' Sister Annette said. 'But be happy and wise too. And be grateful. You've much to be grateful for.'

'I will,' the child answered, wondering if she had the courage to make good her promise.

The sister smiled. 'I know you will. You're a good girl, my little Sara. You always will be. And one day – on this earth – you'll be rewarded. One day you'll know some great joy in your life.'

Those last words were so fixed in Sara's memory she was convinced they were accurate, the very ones Sister Annette had used. Yet there was another memory too, an inexplicable flaw in the picture: that as the sister spoke there were tears, thick and salty, running down her cheeks, so slowly, so ponderously, she resembled the pale, static figure of Mary in the chapel whose face was stained with drops that were mother of pearl, not human at all.

Sara Farnese looked at her watch and wondered at the power of these memories. Sometimes they stood in the way of the present, she thought, easy crutches on which to lean as a substitute for decision and action. What would Sister Annette make of her present existence? She knew the answer and did not wish to dwell on it.

It was now 2.27 and the press were still making a noise beyond the windows. She was sick of the notes being pushed through the door of the apartment block. She had taken the phone off the hook. Still they waited. Still they haunted her.

She put on a pair of sunglasses and walked to the window. Outside, in the narrow lane, cameras flashed, voices rose, TV crews scrambled to take advantage of this rare appearance by the woman they all wanted to see. A woman the media was already painting as some kind of black temptress, the guilty party to an affair in which one lover – a married one at that – murdered his wife and his ex-mistress's partner in the most bloody of fashions.

People walking down the main road hesitated, stopping to stare at this commotion in the shadow of the Pope's thoroughfare. Would they be any more forgiving? Would they even wish to understand? She doubted it. The best she could hope for from the masses was a lack of interest, which was unrealistic given the curiosity the media was creating in the story.

At 2.29 Sara Farnese walked into her bedroom and unlocked the secure compartment in the small bedside cabinet. The phone still bore the sticker from the mobile operator in Monaco. Calls made using it were, he said, untraceable, unlike those from Italian models. He had one too. If they just used the pair of mobiles, at times they agreed beforehand, everything would be fine. No one need ever know.

She turned on the handset, waited and, sure enough, at half past it rang.

He wasn't angry with her, not this time. Sara Farnese felt grateful to hear his voice which was full of warmth and reassurance, telling her everything would be fine, just to keep calm, keep quiet and never say more than was necessary, particularly to the police.

She cried a little. It was impossible to halt the tears. She told him, too, about the animals on the doorstep and the way the thought of them kept invading her head.

'I'll send you a gift,' he said.

They spoke for no more than four minutes, four minutes in which she felt herself restored to the world, one which Sister Annette would have recognized, even if she found parts of it questionable.

Just after three she walked tentatively to the window, standing far enough back to be able to see without being seen. The street-cleaning vans had arrived in the Borgo Pio, a day before schedule, even though the place was still just dusty, free of litter, thanks to the cruel August weather which was chasing people from the city. Two vans were working their way along the road, spraying water everywhere, big circular brushes turning from beneath their bellies. Then they turned into Vicolo delle Palline, a place no cleaning truck had ever visited before, and made straight for the crowd beneath the window. The media mob scattered, clutching for their cameras, cursing as the vehicles ploughed slowly through their midst.

Sara Farnese watched from behind the curtain and

wished she could laugh. There had been more generous gifts but none so welcome or well timed. Nevertheless, this unwanted attention would return.

The crowd began to reassemble. Through it came two now familiar figures, one large, one smaller and slender. She recognized the policemen from the day before and began, very carefully, to assemble her thoughts.

Nine

Jay Gallo sat on the dry turf of the Esquiline Hill, not far from the Via Mecenate, eating calzone from the pizza rustica shop around the corner: zucchini flowers and salty anchovies wrapped inside mozzarella. The dig was in its fourth day and halted once again. He wondered how long it would be before some anxious producer in New York read the latest accountant's report and pulled the plug on the show, taking his meal ticket with it. Gallo desperately wanted out of this job. There was better money to be made running rich tourists around the city and spinning them rare and occasionally racy stories. He hated TV crews. He hated their dirigible-sized egos. He hated their organizational incompetence. But most of all, Jay Gallo hated their dishonesty. Once, before the drink and the dope took hold and sent his life swerving off in a different direction, Gallo had been a promising scholar at Harvard. He knew his subject: late imperial Rome, though it was now greatly expanded to embrace the needs of a hungry translator and tour guide. Watching this fake archaeology show dig up what may or may not have been an unimportant chunk of the Domus Aurea, Nero's Golden House, and imbue every shard of pottery, every rusting iron nail, with some dubious link to the past was agony. For all his personal deficiencies, Jay Gallo understood intellectual rigour and recognized when it was being tarnished for the sake of pecuniary gain.

Scipio Campion – even the name made his teeth grate – personified this sin completely. A minor Oxford professor with very little chin and an accent that could cut glass, he was born with the fake English academic poise American television adored. If the show were to be believed, Campion had – in one single season – found the camp from which Spartacus's army had surveyed Pompeii; uncovered the remains of a palace in Glastonbury, complete with wall paintings, which he was able to pass off as a possible site of Avalon; and, on the outskirts of modern Alexandria, revealed the tomb – and within it, to much excitement, the decapitated skeleton – of Caesarion, the son of Julius Caesar and Cleopatra. It was all so unseemly. Undeserved too. He had watched Campion go through the motions on camera. There was nothing to it. Jay Gallo knew he could do better if they gave him a chance. The bitch of a producer had laughed in his face when he just happened to mention it.

He finished the calzone and listened in silence to the latest argument between Campion, the producer and the camera crew, which seemed to focus largely on how the star should be lit.

'Morons,' Jay Gallo said miserably to no one, wishing he were not in such an evil mood. Business had been bad of late. He'd been reduced to playing errand boy for people he didn't like, delivering packages that contained God-knew-what to addresses he never wanted to see again. Being stuck on the set of some lousy TV show was better than jail. Just, he mused. Then his mobile phone vibrated in his shirt pocket and with a sweaty, tired hand he pulled it out, got up and walked away from the crew to make sure they didn't start yelling at him for talking on set.

'Mr Gallo? My name is Delgado. I work for a tour company in the Borgo. You won't have heard of us. I have an urgent problem. Are you busy?'

'Very.' It was a stock answer. There was always this ritual with the last-minute customers. You had to make them feel very grateful – and very generous.

'Ah. I'm sorry. Perhaps some other time then.'

'I didn't say I was unavailable,' Gallo snapped. 'Just busy.'

'But we need someone right now. I've been let down badly by one of the agencies. We have a party of very important people due to visit Ostia. I must find a translator for them within the hour.'

'What's the gig?'

'The what?'

'What kind of tour? What am I supposed to talk about?'

'Late imperial finds. The harbour. Nothing too detailed.'

Gallo smiled for the first time that day. 'Hey. I can go into as much detail as you want. I worked on that at Harvard.'

The man hesitated. 'So I heard. Then you're free?'

Gallo knew when a sap was rolling over. 'Let me be honest with you. I've got some personal business. If I'm going to cancel it's got to be double time. Six hundred dollars for the day.'

The voice on the end of the line hesitated. 'That's a lot of money.'

He could only say no, Gallo reasoned. There was just one more day of filming anyway. The crew had paid him in advance. He didn't normally jerk people around but on this occasion it would be a pleasure.

'Take it or leave it.'

'Can I pick you up in thirty minutes? Where will you be?'

'At the bar of the Osteria Capri. In Labicana, the Colosseum end.'

'Drinking coffee?'

'Drinking coffee,' he replied, puzzled. Had people been talking?

'I'll be there,' the man said and cut the call, before Gallo even had time to ask how they'd recognize each other.

He walked over to the crew. They were back to filming now. Campion was holding up a piece of broken pottery and speculating on whether it was an imperial wine goblet which Nero himself had once gripped.

Gallo stepped straight into the scene and prised the shard of unglazed brown ceramic from Campion's fingers.

'Let me interrupt this pile of fancy with a fact,' Gallo said, smiling for the camera. 'Nero lived here two, three years at most before he had his slave kill him to stop the Romans tearing him apart limb from limb. Emperors weren't into Mediterranean peasant chic. They ate off fancy plates. They drank from fancy glasses. This is stuff that never got out of the kitchen. This is stuff a slave would have been ashamed to own. You have excavated imperial Roman Tupperware, my man. Now don't you tell those good people out there otherwise.'

Jay Gallo felt good. Maybe he would fit in a quick beer before the agency man turned up. It could hardly do any harm.

The producer, a small woman with a malevolent dark face, stabbed him in the arm with a podgy finger. 'You're fired, mister,' she hissed.

'Oh calamitous day.' Gallo chuckled and set off down the hill, so happy he began to whistle.

There was time for two beers before the man arrived. Gallo had a pleasant smile on his face. He could do a good job when he felt like this. Everybody loved him.

They went outside and left in a long, black Mercedes. Gallo noticed when he climbed in that it had Vatican number plates, which seemed very odd indeed.

Ten

The mob of damp hacks clustered around the door looking grumpy, determined and somewhat ridiculous.

Luca Rossi scowled in their direction. 'I cannot believe I fell for this.'

'It was a deal. Remember?'

'The deal was I came here. Well, I've done that. Now you go in and talk to the woman on your own. She can't stand the sight of me anyway. You'll likely get more out of her.'

'You're going drinking again?'

'Ha, ha. There's one of these reporters I know. He's been useful in the past. We need to talk. Sometimes they know stuff that's never come anywhere near us. OK?'

Costa shrugged. He wondered if Rossi was being entirely honest with him. There had been times in the Rinaldis' apartment when the big man seemed to be engrossed, puzzled, though he never said a word afterwards. 'If that's what you want.'

'And then I'll make my own way back. Don't worry about me. We can talk again at dinner.'

Costa very much wished to get out of this arrangement. 'She's got the hots for you, Uncle Luca. There can be no other explanation. I'd just cramp your style.'

The big man seemed offended. 'Crazy Teresa's not so bad-looking. A man could do worse.'

'I just don't want to deflect attention away from you, me being young, slim and attractive and all.'

Rossi put out a big hand and patted him on the cheek, not so gently. 'It's a new place in Testaccio. Caligula. Thirteen Alberoni. Eight o'clock. Don't be late. I'm paying.'

'Great.'

Then Rossi was gone into the crowd, pushing his way through, exchanging a glance with one individual Costa thought he recognized. Soon there'd be a beer round the corner, he guessed. Maybe there was something to talk about. It still seemed a slim option. He remembered Falcone and thought: look for a simpler explanation. The big man just didn't want to see Sara Farnese. That was all.

The idea seemed even crazier when she let him into the first-floor apartment. She wore a dark-red cotton shirt and faded-blue designer jeans. Her hair was now tied back behind her neck. Her large and intelligent green eyes had a deep, shining lustre that was new to him. She was about his height and just as slender. She moved with a controlled grace as if she thought everything through first.

The apartment was decorated with a degree of taste Nic Costa associated with the wealthy middle-aged: reproduction wooden furniture, a polished dining table at the centre, and paintings everywhere, landscapes, medieval portraits and some more modern, abstract works that still seemed to fit. The walls were lined with the kind of heavy wallpaper you saw in expensive hotels.

And books, shelf upon shelf of books, all hardbacks, some leather-bound. There was no TV set, only a very pricey-looking stereo system and a pile of classical CDs next to it. None of this made sense to him. The designer jeans and her own magnetic looks apart, it was as if this woman – who could be no more than thirty – was living the life of a rich spinster in her fifties.

He indicated towards the crowd, now out of sight beyond the window.

'There are laws about harassment, you know. If you want me to do something I can call the municipal police.'

She sat down in a stylish high armchair that looked uncomfortable. 'They'll go away, won't they? I still don't understand what they want.'

They wanted a picture of her. He knew that. They wanted to splash her beauty all over the front pages and say: here's the woman some university professor went crazy over, killing himself, his wife and her boyfriend, all for some approximation of love.

He fell into a low sofa feeling awkward and out of place in these surroundings. 'They want your photograph. They want you.'

'Then they'll have a long wait. I'm getting my groceries delivered. The man downstairs brings them to me. I'm not going back to the university until this non-sense is over. They can camp out there for a week if they like. They'll still get nothing.'

That was easy to say, he thought. She didn't understand how soon you wore down under this constant attention, and how that was all part of their game.

'You never told me your name.'

'Costa. Nic Costa.'

'What do you want, Mr Costa?'

He pulled out a notebook. 'Just some simple, basic paperwork. If that's OK. Personal details.'

'Very well.'

In an efficient five minutes Sara Farnese told him all the bare facts. They shared the same age. She was twenty-seven, a little younger than he thought, held both Italian and English passports, thanks to the nationalities of her respective late parents, and was a middle-ranking professor at the university. Her affair with Rinaldi had lasted no more than a few weeks. She had not, as far as she was aware, mentioned Hugh Fairchild's visit in Rinaldi's earshot, though it was possible this had happened. Nor was she aware of Rinaldi's money or drug problems, both of which came as some – genuine, he thought – surprise to her.

She cited from memory the source of the quotation about the blood of the martyrs but was unsure what relevance it had. Just for interest, Costa read her back the full version of the doggerel about St Ives as Falcone had explained it that morning.

'So it's just a riddle?' she asked, bemused.

'You're not reaching for a calculator.'

'Why would I? Isn't the answer obvious? There's one man going to St Ives. The rest are going the other way.'

He began to understand Rossi's discomfiture in the presence of this woman. She was too smart, too cool, too distanced. She made him feel small and stupid, not by any deliberate act on her part but simply from her presence, her way of speaking. This was, he thought, accidental. Some curious air of loneliness hung around her too and it was evident in this antiseptic, overdecorated place she called home.

'Did Professor Rinaldi know many people in the Vatican?'

'He knew the ones we all knew. The academics. The people who controlled access to the library.'

'You need a ticket to get in there, surely? Something that gets you through the private gates without having to queue with the tourists?'

She opened a small blue leather handbag that sat by the chair, one that was, like everything else in the room, too mature for her. Sara Farnese sifted through the contents and pulled out a laminated card. It bore her name and a photograph.

'Of course. The library has more sources on early Christianity than anywhere else in the world. That's why I came to Rome.'

Costa looked closely at the card. 'But this is for access to the Vatican itself. Not the library.'

'Sometimes,' she said a little hesitantly, 'one needs to look at items that are stored elsewhere. This saves time.'

He didn't know anyone outside Vatican staff who owned one of these things. 'And Stefano had a card too?'

'I don't think so. He was waiting for it to come through. Perhaps that's why there was such a fuss when he forced his way in. If he'd had a card there would have been no problem.'

It made no sense. She had been at the university three years and owned one of these precious things. Rinaldi, who had been in the department for more than twenty, had to wait in line with the queues of Japanese.

'Why didn't he have one? If it was essential?'

'I don't know. I'm sorry. We worked in the same department but not on the same courses. Perhaps he felt it wasn't so necessary. You can get a lot of material online these days. I prefer to look at the source. It feels more proper somehow.'

'Why wouldn't he feel the same way?'

'I told you,' she replied a little testily. 'I don't know. I had a brief affair with the man. I wouldn't claim I knew him terribly well.'

Yet Stefano Rinaldi felt he knew her well enough to try to commit suicide in front of her and rely on this woman . . . to do what? To save his wife somehow, in return for the death of her current lover?

A snatch of their conversation from the previous day came back to him. 'Miss Farnese. You said that he spoke in two different voices to you.'

She had forgotten that part. It was obvious in her face, and the return of the memory puzzled her.

'That's correct. When he quoted Tertullian it was as if it were some kind of pronouncement, meant to be heard by everyone. It was loud, purposeful.' She thought carefully before going on. 'It was much quieter when he spoke about Mary. He was just talking to me then.'

Costa racked his head for what that might mean. 'Was there anyone else in the room that you knew? Apart from the guard who shot him?'

'No. They were all strangers.'

'But if he said one thing in a loud voice and the next more softly there had to be a reason. As if someone was watching, someone who needed to hear the first part, and to miss the second. Please. Try to think. Is that possible?'

She considered the idea. 'I'm sorry. The way I remember it, he entered the room in a rush. The first time he said those words from Tertullian he was well past everybody else. Even when he spoke loudly they wouldn't hear. The second time was different. But . . .'

Nic Costa thought about the kind of money the Vatican could spend on security and felt a sudden and urgent need to go back to the place where he had last seen Hugh Fairchild's skin lying on an old mahogany desk.

'I understand. I'm sorry. They must seem very stupid questions.'

'Not at all. They seem very intelligent ones. As intelligent as anyone could ask in the circumstances. I wish I could help more.'

Rossi had been right. It would have been awkward with him in the room. Sara Farnese was an odd mix of strength and timidity. The more she was surrounded by people, the less she would divulge.

He put his notebook in his pocket and got up.

'Would you like a coffee, Mr Costa?'

'Thanks,' he said, smiling. 'But I have another appointment.'

'Will there be another time?'

'I hope we can clear this all up by tomorrow. There shouldn't need to be another interview.'

He nodded towards the window and gave her his card, scribbling his home and mobile numbers on it. 'Remember what I said about harassment. Call any time and I'll get someone to talk to them.'

She looked at the card then placed it in her bag. 'Thanks. I'll bear that in mind.'

'Good. Oh . . .' It was an old trick but sometimes an effective one. 'I almost forgot. Do you know someone in the Vatican? Someone called Cardinal Denney?'

She shook her head and smiled, the fullest smile Costa had seen on her face. 'I'm sorry. I've never heard of anyone of that name.'

'No problem.'

Sara Farnese was looking out of the window again, wistfully.

'Are you sure you don't want to go outside for a little while?' Costa asked. 'A walk. You can't stay here for ever.'

She frowned at the world beyond the window. 'I'm not sure I can face that right now.'

He looked at her and said, 'Maybe . . .'

Eleven

Ten minutes later the door to the apartment block in Vicolo delle Palline opened and the mob outside went wild. In spite of the heat the woman coming out of the building was dressed in a long, full raincoat. Big sunglasses obscured her features and a headscarf covered her hair. She pushed away the forest of TV mikes that were thrust into her face. She said nothing, keeping her head down, trying to look as anonymous as possible in the scrum of reporters clamouring for her attention.

Cameras flashed. Arms and elbows jostled for position. A reporter from one of the tawdrier magazines fell to the floor winded by a sharp stab to the ribs. Another screeched as he was jostled out of position. One of the bigger hacks started to throw punches at a TV cameraman who was trying to push him out of the way. The slender figure at the centre of the mêlée was unable to avoid the photographers but remained silent throughout, pushing forward through the mass, dark glasses fixed firmly on the ground ahead.

Then the centre of gravity shifted. The raincoat forced its way through the final barrier of bodies and was free in the cobbled street. The mob's clamour diminished. This was not what was supposed to happen. Victims gave in eventually. They offered a sight of themselves or a few words in deference to the power of the pack. It was unknown for them to reject the mob's advances so completely, so successfully. One or two of the hacks wondered what to make of it, but then there was no time.

Sara Farnese began to run. The two arms of the raincoat started to pump. Her legs beat on the ground. The figure that eluded them now set up a pace, steady and deliberate, out beneath *Il Pasette* into the broad tourist street beyond, inviting them to follow.

The herd howled and was after her, pausing only briefly to think about how odd this situation was. Close to an ice-cream stand in the Via dei Corridori they almost caught her. Then she picked up speed once more and was away, only just, until the pedestrian lights on the Piazza Pia turned red and a surging sea of cars rolled forward, horns hooting, drivers screaming at each other, a solid sea of metal blocking her way.

The figure turned and saw the mob on her heels, panting, unused to this kind of chase, determined to repay the effort by pinning her down in public, forcing her to remove the disguise, bellowing at her until she said something, anything to explain why three people died in her name, and in such crazy ways too.

The first hack, some way ahead of the rest, pounced, placing a firm hand on her shoulder. This was a mistake. A sharp fist stabbed him in the ribs, the breath went out of his body in an instant, and all he heard for his considerable pain was a low, half-obscene curse.

The traffic was gridlocked in the wide piazza, a mass of overheated vehicles sending out a choking cloud of pollution into the humid forty-degree air. She watched the rest of the pack come close then turned, jumped, mounted the bonnet of a Lexus next to the kerb and raced quickly across the road, leaping from car to car.

The mob watched in anguished amazement. The hacks were out of breath. The photographers scarcely had the energy to lift their cameras. The TV crews were still struggling up the street wondering what was going on. It was just possible for them to see the conclusion once she had navigated the bonnets, roofs and boots that filled the piazza.

Sara Farnese, who was, as far as they knew, a quiet, academic university professor, kicked hard on the pavement, like an athlete setting off for the race. She broke into her pace, a faster pace than she had used down the Via dei Corridori, one which was more natural to her. Then she disappeared past the squat rotund magnificence of the Castel Sant'Angelo sprinting like a pro, arms moving rhythmically, legs pounding the ground, with the raincoat flapping behind in the wind.

Five minutes later a skinny, scared-looking young woman from Kosovo, with a ten-month-old baby in her arms, sat outside the makeshift tent that was her home. It was on the wide footpath by the banks of the Tiber near the Ponte Cavour. She was astonished to see a man walking towards her, a slender man with a woman's raincoat flapping around him. He wore a broad, self-amused smile and was somewhat out of breath.

She held the child more tightly to her and retreated into the shade of the small, tattered tent. He was not a cop, surely, who would move her on again. Cops didn't wear women's raincoats. They didn't smile like this, a nice smile, she realized, one that came from some happiness inside.

He stopped and crouched next to her, looking at the child, breathing heavily. Then he took off the raincoat, bundled it up with a pair of expensive-looking sunglasses and a headscarf and gave them to her.

'Can you use these?' he asked.

She nodded.

The man reached into his pocket and pulled out a €50 note. It was a lot of money. She knew what that meant.

'What do you want?' she said in what she knew was bad Italian. 'I don't . . .' She didn't want to say any more. It was a lot of money.

'Don't worry. It's a family habit. My father told me to give something away twice every day,' he said, in a warm, calm voice. 'Maybe one day I'll be hoping someone does the same to me.'

She couldn't take her eyes off the note in her baby's tiny fingers. It was more cash than she had seen in two weeks. 'A lot of money,' she said again.

'I told you. Twice a day. I was busy this morning, I missed out. You're lucky. You get both.'

She smiled nervously. 'I like being lucky.'

Nic Costa wondered how old she was. Probably no more than seventeen.

'Promise me something,' he said, scribbling on a page ripped from his notebook.

'What?' she said, taking the paper from him.

'You'll go to this address. It's a hostel. They can help.'

'OK,' she replied mutedly, some suspicion in her voice.

'I don't come this way often,' he said. 'Remember that address.'

Then he walked off, back towards the steps that rose

up to road level, back towards the bridge that led on to the Vatican.

He was on the stone staircase when his mobile phone rang.

'I'm in your debt, Mr Costa,' said Sara Farnese, and he could hear the relief in her voice.

'The name's Nic. You're welcome. I lost your coat and things. Sorry.'

She laughed. It was the first time he had heard her make any sound of pleasure and this was, he thought, the real Sara Farnese, not the person she tried to portray to the world. 'It was worth it ten times over. Watching them, chasing you . . . Nic.'

'So you escaped?' he asked.

The line went quiet. It was a direct question, an understandable one in the circumstances. Perhaps she was wondering whether it was personal or professional. He was unsure himself. Nic Costa was curious about where she would go in the circumstances, and cursed his prurience: he wished, automatically, that he had arranged to have her followed.

'Call again, Nic. If you like,' she said, and was gone.

Twelve

The man wore a black suit and dark glasses. He was muscular and probably middle-aged, though he wore such heavy clothing, in spite of the heat, it was difficult to tell from what was on show. For the life of him, Gallo could not work out the accent. Southern? Sicilian maybe? He didn't want to try. There was something serious about him, something that said you just did your job, did it well, got your money, then walked away.

The car struggled through the traffic out to the motorway which led to Fiumicino airport and the coast. He had jazz playing on the music system: Weather Report, with Wayne Shorter's sax wailing like a banshee. Gallo knew Ostia well. He'd taken many parties around the old port area and the ruins of the imperial town.

'Who are they?' he asked.

'Who are who?' the man grunted.

'The people I'm supposed to entertain.'

'Visiting college professors. Not archaeologists themselves, but people with an interest. I hope you know what you're talking about.'

'No problem.'

The car turned off the motorway early. Gallo was puzzled.

'Aren't we going to the town?'

'Not first. There's another area that got cut off from the meander by a flood hundreds of years back. The *Fiume Morto*. The dead river. You know it?'

'No.' Gallo felt his mood starting to wane. No one ever went to the dead river except hardened diggers. It was just mud and mosquitoes. 'You might have told me.'

The black glasses looked at him. 'I heard you were a clever guy. You can make things up if you want. What does it matter? It's all show business. Don't worry. It won't take long. After that we go to the town. Then you run on autopilot, huh?'

'Yeah, right.' He scanned the flat land of the Tiber estuary. The stink of the flat marshes came in with the air-conditioning. It was chemical, lifeless and made the back of his throat turn dry and start to ache. There was nothing ahead, not a coach, not even a single car. Gallo looked at the man again. He was wearing black leather gloves. Odd in the heat.

The driver turned to him again. 'You've heard of Tertullian?'

Gallo laughed dryly. 'Oh wow. What a sweetheart that guy was. Really full of joy and light. What was that wonderful line about women? "Tu es ianua diaboli." You're the doorway of the devil. Boy, do the feminists love that one. What a twisted dude.'

The man at the wheel was watching him and, in spite of the sunglasses, Jay Gallo could tell there was something severe about him, something cold and immovable.

'I was thinking,' he said, 'of another saying.'

'What?'

' "The blood of the martyrs is the seed of the Church." '

Gallo turned to look at the man. Maybe he wasn't as old as he had first thought. He moved with the ease of someone about his own age. The glasses, the clothes seemed to be there to age him.

The travel business, Jay Gallo thought. What a way to earn a living. The mention of Tertullian had put Gallo in full flow. It was rare he got a chance to display his erudition with someone who might begin to appreciate it.

'These early Christians. You know what puzzles me? How did anybody sign up for this thing? What was the point?'

'You mean why did Tertullian call for people to be martyrs?'

'No! Why did the poor suckers take him at his word? Why die just for some . . . idea?'

The dark glasses thought about that. 'You've seen the Caravaggio in Santa Maria deli Popolo? *St Peter's Crucifixion*?'

Gallo knew the church as well as he wished. It was a minor star in the galaxy of Roman sights. A chapel by Raphael, a touch of Borgia history and two famous Caravaggios, all in the perfect Renaissance piazza the tourists loved because it sat at the end of the tawdry shopping street, the Corso.

'Yeah.' He recalled a striking, large canvas of the saint about to be crucified upside down. The cross was being pushed and pulled upright by three largely unseen workers who could have come straight out of any sixteenth-century tavern. Peter stared at the nail running through his left palm with a determination, almost pride, which Gallo never could understand.

'That tells you everything. Peter's executioners believe they're raising the means of his cruel death. In truth, with each inch they build higher the foundations of the Church, as the saint clearly realizes.'

Gallo waved a hand as if to say this was obvious. 'Yes, yes. He's a martyr . . .'

'Furthermore,' the man continued, 'he's bathed in the light of Grace, which even shines on his murderers. He goes to his death out of duty, and happily because he knows there is a better life awaiting him in Paradise. This is a transformation he seeks. He *knows* he goes to Heaven.'

'Crazy . . .' Gallo grunted, shaking his head.

The dark glasses stared at the empty horizon ahead.

Gallo smiled and thought of another Caravaggio, in the Borghese, and the story behind it, one that always went down well with the Americans. 'And anyway, Caravaggio didn't believe that crap himself. Look how he paints himself as the severed head of Goliath. When he did that, my friend, he was under sentence of death himself, for murdering a man during a game of real tennis. He painted his own head there to acknowledge the Pope's hold over him and beg forgiveness. He had good, practical reasons to be afraid. And he was. You don't see him expecting salvation there. Just the grave. And oblivion.'

'You're a cultured man,' the driver said to Gallo's obvious satisfaction. 'And what happened to the painter?'

'He got his pardon. Then died on the way back to Rome. Ironic, huh?'

'Possibly. Or apt. Perhaps that was his punishment.'

But Jay Gallo wasn't listening. There was something he had to say, something important. 'And here's another irony. Tertullian didn't even take his own advice. He was no martyr. He died in his bed at a hundred and two or something. Hypocrite.'

He remembered the Vatican number plate and added quickly, 'Not that I know the first damn thing about religion, of course.'

'Just history?'

'That's right.'

Jay Gallo looked around. They had parked by the low muddy waters of the river. There wasn't a soul in sight. Or anything to look at either. All the usual places to visit were a good kilometre or two away. He wished there was somewhere he could buy a beer or a good coffee with *grappa* in it. He wished the place didn't smell so badly of chemicals and pollution.

'They'll be here soon,' the man said, seeming to read his thoughts. The jazz album came to an end. He hit the button on the hi-fi, removed the CD and carefully put it away in a case he kept on the dashboard. It was an odd action. For some reason it made Gallo think the car wasn't his at all. 'We can still continue our interesting talk while we wait, can't we? You're right about Caravaggio, I think. He did have good, practical reasons to be afraid. But you shouldn't exclude him, or Tertullian, or any of us, you and me, from being agents of God's will. That would be presumptuous, surely, even for one who knows nothing about religion?'

'Really?'

'You don't think God just uses those who believe in him as his instruments? What about Pilate? What about Herod?'

It was only then that Jay Gallo considered his position seriously. He was sitting by a remote stretch of the Tiber with a man he didn't know, waiting for a tour group who wanted to see . . . what exactly? There wasn't a single archaeological artefact in the vicinity as far as he was aware. Maybe they'd turn out to be bird-spotters instead.

Maybe they were reviving that long-lost art-form, the snuff movie.

He looked at the man in the seat next to him. If it came to it, Gallo thought, they were evenly matched. The man was stockier but older, maybe, and he gave him something in height. What was more, Jay Gallo had been in plenty of bar-room brawls over the years. He knew how to look after himself.

'Are you jerking me around?' he asked the man in the dark glasses.

'Mr Gallo?'

'Is this some kind of a joke?'

The man thought about it. ' "The blood of the martyrs . . ." Does that sound like some kind of joke?'

Gallo swore under his breath. The man was starting to annoy him. 'Why do you keep saying that crap? What the fu—'

A black fist, hard as iron, came out at him, flying fast, and caught him full in the eye. Jay Gallo's head went back, his vision narrowed, tunnelling into blackness at the edges. There was little pain; more an absence of sensation altogether. Then, in the limited focus he possessed, something darted at him again. The solid leather shape connected with his nose, there was the sound and the sensation of bone breaking. A warm, salty trickle of blood began to run down his throat.

Thirteen

The official quarters of Cardinal Michael Denney overlooked the Cortile di San Damaso, the sprawling private
courtyard hidden from the outside world by the curving
western wall of St Peter's Square. The Vatican was never
built as a residence. Denney's apartment was one of only
two hundred or so created within the palace walls. On the
far side of the square lay the residency of the Swiss Guard.
In his own block senior Vatican officials jostled for
position to get the best view of the open space. His
neighbours included some of the most powerful figures
in the Holy See. The *camerlengo*, the Pope's chamberlain,
who would briefly oversee the interregnum in the event
of the pontiff's death, was some way down the hall. They
rarely spoke these days. Denney was aware he had
become *persona non grata*, a prisoner in a glittering cell.
Sometimes he spent hours staring at the reflection of the
paintings, the Murano chandeliers and the wall-length
ormolu mirrors, waiting for the most menial of civil servants to return his call. All this must, he knew, change. A
man could go mad in these circumstances.

The agents of that change were now assembled
around the walnut dining table that sat by the long,

eighteenth-century windows looking out onto the court-yard. It had taken him many weeks to persuade these three men to come to Rome and sit down together. Between them they represented a powerful trinity of interests which could, with a little persuasion and the right inducements, resurrect something from the shattered shell of the Banca Lombardia and with it a little of Michael Denney's reputation. Sufficient, he hoped, to allow him to return home and live out the rest of his life in dignified obscurity.

Two of the men present he thought he could handle. Robert Aitcheson, the sour-faced American lawyer who oversaw corporate affairs for the bank out of a base in the Bahamas, had as much reason as Denney to clear this thing up. The Feds were already on Aitcheson's back, chasing up a hot money scam that came to light in the wake of the currency laundering checks introduced after September 11. He needed to get out of the heat. Arturo Crespi was in the same boat. Crespi was a diminutive pen-pushing banker who oversaw the movement of capital in and out of the web of funds that underpinned the bank. The Finance Ministry was asking too many questions of him already. Ostensibly, he was the bank president, though in everything he deferred to Denney, who had assembled the complex network of offshore trusts piece by piece over the years from what had once been a legit-imate, onshore financial enterprise. Crespi was weak and respectable. It had suited Denney at the time. He had been charged with getting an above average return on the money under his care. There had, he believed, been little choice, and, when they began, little in the way of legal obstruction either.

The third man stood by the window, peering down

into the courtyard, sniffing with a summer cold. Emilio Neri was over six feet tall, a giant of a man in his mid-sixties, now beginning to run to flab. He had grey, lifeless eyes, a long, jutting jaw and a head of perfectly groomed silver hair. Today, as always, he wore an expensive suit: thin, pale-coloured silk which now showed damp patches under the arms. He rarely smiled. He spoke only when he had something to say. Neri was, from outward appearances, a successful Roman entrepreneur. He owned a palatial penthouse in the Via Guilia, a pretty young wife, three country houses and an apartment in New York. His name adorned the board of the Fenice Opera House in Venice, where he helped raise funds for its rebuilding, and any number of charitable organizations working with the Catholic poor.

Only once had his image as a man beyond reproach been questioned. It was in the mid-1970s when a radical press untouched by conventional party politics had existed in the city. A scurrilous reporter on a short-lived underground rag had published a portrait of Neri culled from police gossip. It was a story many recognized but few wished to acknowledge. The article told of his upbringing in Sicily as the son of a local Mafia don, his apprenticeship in the racketeering world of black-market tobacco and prostitution and his eventual emergence as a key liaison figure in the continuing dialogue between corrupt government, Church officials and the criminal state that lived then, as now, beneath the mundane façade of Italian society. The piece had accused Neri of nothing criminal. In a way, it was intended as a tribute to the man, who had genuinely come to be something of an art lover, was seen at all the right exhibitions, was always there, in his private box, at the opera and the ballet.

Three weeks after the magazine article, the author was found in a car parked in a lane near Fiumicino airport. His eyes had been put out, probably by a man's thumbs. His tongue had been ripped from his mouth. Every finger and both thumbs had been severed at the first socket with a knife. He survived, blind, dumb and unable, or unwilling, to try to communicate. The street gossip, which Denney later discovered was entirely accurate, claimed that Neri had performed his revenge personally in a warehouse he owned on the perimeter of the airport. He'd then, in front of the tortured hack, changed into evening dress and flown by private plane to Venice to see Pavarotti in a new production of *Turandot*, after which he had attended the first-night party as an honoured guest.

Denney, once he had come to know the man, wondered why he had gone to all that trouble. Emilio Neri could have sucked the life out of another human being just by looking at him. Still, the papers wrote only about Neri's charitable activities after that.

Denney watched Neri's big back at the window, wondering what was going through his head. There was just one thing Neri wanted now: the return of the money he had placed in Denney's hands. If that happened, they would, once again, be on the best of terms.

The door into the room opened. Brendan Hanrahan walked in carrying a tray with coffee on it. Throwing a mint into his mouth, Neri turned to stare at him.

'Don't they provide you with servants any more, Michael?' Neri asked.

'Just helping out,' Hanrahan interjected. 'This is a

private meeting, gentlemen. None of you wants to advertise your presence, I imagine.'

'As if anything's secret in this place these days.' Neri sniffed. He cast a glance out of the window and then at Denney. 'I'm amazed you still have one of the best views in the place. The Church is going soft.'

'Shall we get down to business, gentlemen?' Aitcheson complained. 'I want to be on the ten o'clock plane out of here.'

'Agreed,' Crespi said.

Neri sat down at the table opposite the little banker, grinning at him. 'Have you managed to replace that clerk of yours yet, Crespi? The one who talked himself to death.'

The little banker went white. 'My people are trustworthy. Every one of them. I stake my word on it.'

'You're staking more than that, my friend,' Neri said. 'Enough. You know my position. You know my responsibilities. You people talk. Tell me why we're here.'

'To get ourselves out of a hole,' Hanrahan said and passed around copies of a single printed page.

Neri scanned the document. 'Doesn't say here when I get my money back.'

'Emilio,' Denney replied with as much pleasantry as he could muster. 'I can't work magic. We all want our money back. We can all get it, I think. But it doesn't come out of nowhere. We have to rebuild.'

Aitcheson hadn't been listening. His eyes were fixed on the paper. 'There's this much money still left? Why didn't I hear of this before?'

Crespi threw up his hands. 'We've been liquidating assets for eighteen months. Quietly. Privately. Sometimes . . . we didn't know if we'd get paid. I didn't want to raise anyone's hopes unnecessarily. This is all very complex, gentlemen. We ran away with ourselves. We had so many accounts. In so many places. I couldn't tell you about all of them, my friend. I would have bored you rigid. And for what? You wanted to know what the return was. Not where it was coming from.' He stole a glance at Neri. 'That was all anyone wanted. It's one reason we're in this mess in the first place.'

Neri now seemed interested in the paper. 'Who else knows about this money? Where is it exactly?'

'No one outside this room.' Hanrahan looked Neri in the face. 'No offence but we've been too lax with our secrets already. Where it is, that's my business.'

Some $3 billion had been seized by the US authorities alone, on the basis of tax evasion and money laundering. It infuriated Denney. Had that remained undiscovered he could have weathered the storm. Crespi's feverish bid to liquidate what assets he could find and shift the funds into new, undiscovered accounts had, at least, offered him a lifeline. If only Aitcheson and Neri could be persuaded to grasp this.

'So we're not paupers,' Neri said. 'I walk into this room thinking this was money down the drain. Now you tell me there's, what, sixty, seventy million dollars out there we can lay our hands on. How did this come about?'

'You don't want to know,' Hanrahan said with a scowl.

'We have,' added Denney, 'worked very hard. We've had to persuade people, induce them, get them to see our point of view. It's not been easy.'

Neri sniffed into his hand. 'I heard you'd been spending a lot of money. The price of a Rome whore's gone up ten per cent in the last six months, Michael. Was that your doing?'

'Don't be ridiculous.'

'And none of this for yourself? To get you safe passage out of this place, back to America?'

Denney's hand stole across the table and gripped Neri's arm. The large man stared balefully back.

'Emilio,' Michael Denney said. 'I did this for us. We can be back in business. We can put some new people in place. Let them talk to the banking authorities. Let them run the risks. We just stay behind the scenes and pull the strings, as we should have done all along. This has been a learning experience for all of us. We come out of it stronger. Richer. More powerful. And in the end, yes, I can walk out of here. I can go back to America a free man because we have a whole new field of people in our debt by this stage.'

Neri smiled and looked at Aitcheson. 'You hear this? We're building a new bank. And all it takes is sixty, seventy million dollars.'

'Not enough,' Aitcheson grumbled. 'You know that.'

They hadn't said no. They were interested. Denney could feel it. They had the light of greed in their eyes. 'So we raise more. We still have the contacts. They still have the need. Lombardia wasn't brought down by us. We were the victims of the markets and laws that didn't even exist when we first went into business. We wipe the slate clean, we start again, we stay one step ahead of the pack.'

Denney paused, to give what came next some theatrical effect. 'It requires some investment on our own part. Personally I'll throw every last cent I have into the pot. That's a lot of money. All my money. Whatever you want to come in with, that's your decision. We know this business, gentlemen. We're very good at it. The best. We're needed out there.'

Neri laughed, a big deep sound, and clapped Denney on the shoulder. 'You mean this, Michael? We're back in business. What a salesman. What a guy.'

'We're back in business,' Denney repeated.

Hanrahan's phone rang. He answered it. His face went dark. Then he made an excuse and left the room.

'What do you think?' Denney asked, unable to stop himself stealing a glance out of the window, thinking of the world beyond.

Fourteen

There were two possibilities, Nic Costa decided. Falcone would either love the idea or he would just go plain crazy, unless there were results. Given results, the severe, overdressed man he called inspector would, he thought, forgive almost anything.

The queue to the museums was still fifty metres long though the place would close in an hour. He used his police card to work his way to the front then put it discreetly away and paid for a ticket at the desk. He walked to the library, waved the police card at the dull attendant on the door and entered the Reading Room without waiting to be stopped.

The hard yellow light of the late afternoon streamed in from the courtyard onto a sea of empty desks. The place had a sharp antiseptic smell. Someone had been cleaning up. Costa went first to the old desk where, the day before, Hugh Fairchild's skin had sat like the involuntary cast-off from some giant lizard. He was aware that the attendant was on the phone already. The man's low voice echoed across the spotless, vacant interior. Only one book remained out. It sat on a desk, three along from the one Sara Farnese had occupied. He looked at it:

something incomprehensible in medieval script. This was a place for a certain kind of human being and it was closing now, going to rest for the weekend.

Costa walked through the aisles, examining everything. Sure enough, the library was littered with security cameras: tiny dull eyes glinting back at him from discreet metal housings on the ceiling, in corners, attached to windows. He was no academic but he understood why. The library was priceless. The only way to get access was by obtaining special permission, something even a long-term lecturer like Stefano Rinaldi seemed to find difficult. This was a priceless store of irreplaceable treasures and one that loaned them to a grateful, privileged few to hold in their hands, to touch, admire and then return. The risks required great care. Every entrance into the room, every loan, every moment a work was in the hands of a reader, all these occurrences would be recorded, day in, day out. Whoever kept the tapes would know what Stefano Rinaldi looked like, how he behaved, probably from the moment he entered the library itself on the floor above.

Was this why the man whispered? Or was there someone he feared in the room?

Either way the cameras surely held the key. Still, Falcone's question kept coming back: *why?* Logically, because Rinaldi wanted to set Sara the task of saving his wife, and feared this would be impossible if someone, either in the room or with access to the tape, witnessed what he was attempting. Could he have left his wife standing on the chair in the tower, knowing that if she stumbled she would hang herself? Was it possible that somewhere between Tiber Island and the Vatican he changed his mind and decided to beg Sara to rescue her?

This was extending the craziness theory too far. Nor did it provide a link between Rinaldi's supposed actions and his whispered instructions to Sara. Had he changed his mind Rinaldi could have returned himself and removed his wife from the noose. Costa began to understand Falcone's doubts. The rudimentary logic which reduced these events to some simple act of bloody revenge began to unravel when one thought about the details. There was, now Costa thought of it, only a single possibility that could explain everything, and it was one he found deeply disturbing.

What if Rinaldi was not the lone murderer but an accomplice in concert with another? Or even a victim himself? What if he had come to the Vatican desperate because someone else was in the tower, someone who had entrapped him, his wife and the unfortunate Fairchild? Someone who had used Rinaldi's debts to arrange the initial meeting, murdered the Englishman in front of their eyes, strung up Mary Rinaldi and told her husband that she would be dead unless he sent Sara Farnese back there immediately? Someone who sent the man out on this mission with Hugh Fairchild's skin in a supermarket bag, demanding he spread it out on the desk, say these crazy words, knowing, surely, that the armed guards would think they had some homicidal madman in their midst.

And one more thing too. Someone who, as far as Rinaldi was concerned, would know whether all these conditions had been met. Either because he had an accomplice there, or access somehow to the tapes *even before Rinaldi could return*. Costa rejected this last thought. It could only be practical if someone in the Vatican was in direct contact with the man in the tower.

This was surely a conspiracy too far. No, the conditions that were set – the gun, the bag with Fairchild's skin inside, the repeated and crazy declamations – were invitations to the armed guards of the Vatican to intervene with all possible force because of the nature of the threat they perceived. That must have been the intention – to ensure Rinaldi, and perhaps Sara Farnese too, died in the library.

It was a hypothesis Nic Costa was reluctant to embrace. His years in the police force had taught him that simple solutions were usually the correct ones. The tapes were the key, Costa repeated to himself, then felt a firm hand grip his shoulder. He turned and, as he had expected all along, found himself looking into the cold, rheumy eyes of the man called Hanrahan, still dressed in the same black suit, still with a crucifix in his lapel.

Costa smiled pleasantly. These were different circumstances. He could think more about this curious man who now stood in front of him, blocking his way to the door, not angry, more jaded, even curious perhaps.

'This is tiresome,' Hanrahan said finally. 'Don't you know anything of the protocols that govern how we're supposed to work?'

The voice was thick, rough-edged and familiar somehow. Then Nic Costa remembered. He had briefly played for the force rugby side, before deciding that the more solitary sport of running suited him better. There had been an Irishman who coached the team for a while. He spoke like this. He even had the same kind of coarse features.

'I realized I forgot to give you my details,' Costa said. He took out his wallet and handed Hanrahan the official police card. Then he pointed at his face and the broken nose. 'I know where you got that. You're a player, right? On the field. Rugby.'

Hanrahan read the card then put it in his pocket. 'When I was young. When I thought there was nothing in the world that could harm me.'

'I used to play a little too.'

Hanrahan eyed him, sceptical.

'Fly half,' Costa said. 'Pretty good, even if I say so myself.'

'Falcone told me you ran. He said it was one of your talents.'

Costa nodded.

'In fact,' the Irishman continued, 'I think he said it was your only talent.'

'Sounds like the man.'

'I can imagine you running, Mr Costa. I imagine you excel. But at some stage you have to turn and fight too. How good are you at that?'

Costa laughed. 'Probably not so hot, to be honest. It's a question of size.'

'No, it isn't,' Hanrahan said. 'What do you want?'

Costa nodded at the ceiling. 'A look at the tape. You must have our dead professor covered from the moment he walked into the library. I'd just like to see.'

Hanrahan shook his head, as if amazed. 'Who do you think you are?'

'Just a cop trying to understand why three people are dead. Who do you think you are?'

Hanrahan thought about this and pulled out his own card. 'I'm a consultant here, Mr Costa. I advise on security matters. I have no power to give you your tape . . .'

'Then introduce me to someone who has.'

'Why?'

Costa was starting to feel exasperated. 'Don't you think you're under any obligation to help us crack this thing? Three people dead, Hanrahan. I know none of them are Vatican citizens, but even so.'

The Irishman waved a half angry hand at him. 'Don't give me that crap, son. When you deal with us, you deal with another country. This isn't police work, it's diplomacy.' The sharp, liquid eyes narrowed. 'If I talk to the person who can give you that tape, what do you have to offer in return?'

He knew what Luca Rossi would say if he were here. You never do deals with these people. You never even think you can broker some kind of covenant because there's always a caveat, a get-out you never know about until it's too late.

But Rossi was somewhere else, contemplating dinner with Crazy Teresa. All the relevant information he could think of was here, locked inside this tiny country that just happened to live behind its own high walls in the heart of Rome. If he didn't cut some kind of deal it might never see the light of day.

Besides, some small, quiet voice told him, there was an opportunity here. A moment when you could throw a stone in a pool and wait to see the patterns the ripple would make once the stone hit the surface. Sometimes you had to take chances.

Nic Costa pulled out his notebook and copied the phone number he'd found on Stefano Rinaldi's computer that morning. He gave it to Hanrahan, who stared at the page with a stony expression.

'Someone from here, someone in the office of a

person called Cardinal Denney, was in contact with Rinaldi by phone. On the day he did this.'

Hanrahan seemed genuinely surprised. 'Do you know why?'

'Maybe I should ask Cardinal Denney.'

He was amazed. Hanrahan laughed, a big, hearty laugh, one that, had it lasted, might have brought tears to his eyes.

The Irishman's hand slapped his shoulder, hard.

'You're a funny man, Mr Costa,' he said. 'I just haven't the heart to call Falcone again. Not this time. Now just do me a favour will you?'

'What?'

'Get the fuck out of here. And go sign this thing off whatever way you want. We both know what happened. Some crazy, personal tragedy to do with a rather fine-looking young woman with lax personal morals. Don't turn over stones for the sake of it. Sometimes those little creatures underneath can bite.'

Fifteen

'What do I think? Michael, Michael.'

Neri couldn't stop laughing, couldn't stop slapping Denney on the shoulder.

'You make a good cardinal. Why'd you ever think you could make a good banker too?'

'It was what was asked of me,' Denney replied sharply. 'I know my duty.'

Neri's big face fell suddenly serious. 'And I know mine. You truly believe this money, this hidden crock of gold, is news to me.'

Denney turned to Crespi, astonished. The little man's face flushed. 'I said nothing,' he complained. 'He's making this up.'

'I don't lie,' Neri grunted. 'I'm too rich to have to lie these days. I told you. This place leaks like a sieve. I've known your little secret for weeks, Michael. I've had time to consider it. Carefully. To talk about it with my associates too. What I have to say to you now is painful, but say it I must.'

The door opened. Hanrahan walked in, making his excuses. Denney looked at him in despair. This was all going wrong. Neri had advance knowledge. He couldn't begin to guess how, or what this might mean.

'The choice before me,' Neri continued, 'is simple. Do I lose a friend? Or do I lose a fortune? Do I throw good money after bad for old times' sake? Or do I take what I can and be grateful for that?'

'This is a pittance,' Denney complained. 'It's a fraction of what we could earn if we go back in business. And you need a bank, Emilio. You can't live without that.'

'Banks, banks,' Neri snarled, waving a dismissive hand at Denney. 'You live in the past, Michael. It's the secret, small corporations that attract the interest of those cold-blooded lawyers in the first place. Why waste all our time and money on them when it's simpler just to go to someone more established and pay him for a mutual relationship? It's in the nature of the world we live in now that men like us may hide more easily in the light of day. Scurrying around in dark corners merely calls attention to ourselves. Sadly . . .' Neri seemed genuinely surprised by this insight, 'that's what seems to come naturally to a man like you. Perhaps it's in your background. Perhaps it comes from this place. If the latter, then more fool you, because they've abandoned you, Michael. Even if you don't know that yourself.'

'What?' Denney knew he was out of favour. But a renewal of his business interests, some clearing of debts, these were actions that would surely begin to clear his name.

'I want my cut of this money,' Aitcheson said. 'I want it now and I want it based on what we invested in the first place.'

'You'll walk away with pennies,' Denney repeated.

Aitcheson stabbed an angry finger at him. 'I'll walk

away with something. Listen to me well, Michael. I was on the phone to someone in the Justice Department only yesterday. This present state of limbo isn't going to last. They're closing Lombardia for good soon, not just suspending us. They're preparing the warrants. Your name's on the top. No one else's right now and as far as the rest of us are concerned that's the way it's going to stay.'

Denney glared at them. 'You knew this? All of you? You didn't think to tell me?'

Crespi stared at the table. Neri looked bored.

Aitcheson sighed. 'You've been living in la-la land these last six months, Michael, thinking you can bribe your way out of this mess. It isn't going to happen. Even if it were possible, Emilio's right. Letting you back into the game would just mean we open up a black hole again. You're finished. Face it. We have nothing left to discuss. I wash my hands of you.'

Neri glanced at Hanrahan then nodded at the ceiling. 'They do too. He doesn't know?'

Denney felt hot, confused. He looked into Hanrahan's eyes and saw the future begin to fall apart.

'You don't have a deal?' Hanrahan asked. 'After all this work? All this time?'

Neri shook his head. 'My dear Irish friend. Please don't act so surprised. Do we look like fools?' He paused, enjoying this. 'Well. Tell him . . .'

Hanrahan grimaced then pulled out his phone. Denney heard him calling the janitorial staff, asking them to send a couple of men round. 'If there's no deal,' he said, 'things are very different.'

'What are you doing?' Denney demanded. 'What the hell is going on here?'

Neri smiled at the apartment, appreciating the Murano glass, the mirrors, the paintings. 'Nice place,' he said. 'They'll be scratching each other's eyes out to see who gets it next.'

Sixteen

Teresa Lupo, Crazy Teresa to the Rome police department, sat in front of a varied collection of animal body parts: veal hearts, cartilage, pig thymus glands and a tangle of cow intestines with milk still inside. She was ecstatic and was joined in her joy by Luca Rossi who wore, for the occasion, a Lazio baseball cap, placed backwards on his balding head, and ate with noisy, open-mouthed enthusiasm. This was, it transpired, Rossi's favourite food, *cucina romana*, the traditional working-class fare of the city: the offal which, by tradition, the proletariat had been left after the clergy of the Vatican had picked from the best cuts of meat.

The restaurant was a cheaper clone of the flashy, expensive Checchino dal 1887 around the corner, the city temple to the eating of guts and glands. Its sixteen simple tables were fully booked and heaving with cooked organs which Nic Costa could not begin to identify even if he so wished. This was the big man's joke; to bring a vegetarian to a place where the consumption of arcane flesh was a religion. Or perhaps he didn't even think about it. Costa watched the way he looked at Crazy Teresa as they prodded and poked at some tripe and hoof jelly and wondered if there was the prospect of love in the air.

They made an odd pair. Rossi, with his big, sad face and sprawling body, looked like a man who would stay single all his life and had probably forgotten when he last slept with a woman. Crazy Teresa had run through endless affairs in the department, all of them short, all of them encounters which tended to leave the male party wan and glassy-eyed afterwards. A little taller than Nic Costa, powerfully built, with a handsome face that smiled constantly as it examined every last thing that fell under its gaze, she was an astonishingly skilled pathologist who had worked as a successful hospital surgeon before something – the craving for excitement was her excuse – drove her into the morgue. Costa never really swallowed that line. Her work wasn't exciting. She was so painstaking and exact she found herself working long, tiring hours just to extract every last shred of evidence. The bodies Teresa Lupo called her 'customers' were, in spite of her easy way with them, still the remains of human beings. Her relationship with them went beyond the forensic. At times she was able to offer the kinds of insight that failed the best of cops and that, he thought, was what drove her. She liked playing detective, and often was very good at it.

Rossi and the woman sat together opposite him, picking at the plates, guzzling the cheap house red and sucking at cigarettes when a gap between the delivery of the flesh and the booze allowed. Costa had arrived late, on purpose. He waited until the waitress, a surly looking girl with rings in her nose and ears, came up with a pad then ordered salad and a glass of Cala Viola, a young

Sardinian white which was the only wine he recognized on the list.

'Chicken salad?' the girl demanded.

'Just salad.'

'We don't *do* "just salad",' she snarled. 'You can take the chicken off if you like.'

Costa sighed, digging in his heels. 'Why don't *you* take the chicken off?'

'Hah! And have you moaning when it comes to paying the bill? Do I look that stupid?'

Rossi leaned forward and gave her the serious look. 'Hey. If it comes to it I'll take the chicken off. He's a vegetarian. OK?'

The nose ring twitched. She suddenly looked more sympathetic. 'Sorry,' she said sincerely.

'Me too. Jesus, are we in the wrong place or what?'

When the girl returned with a large plate of rocket and salad leaves and a decent glass of icy wine Crazy Teresa was midway through an explanation of the physical function of the mushy glands sitting in front of them, lightly cooked with garlic and celery.

'Can we not talk food tonight?' Nic Costa asked.

'You're squeamish?' Crazy Teresa enquired, amazed. 'You two, of all people. After what happened yesterday?'

Luca Rossi sided with his partner. 'Maybe it's because of what happened yesterday. I mean, I like eating this stuff. To be absolutely honest with you, I'd really rather not know what it is.'

'OK.' She shrugged. 'But you . . .' she pointed a strong, aggressive finger at Costa's face, 'need to watch this diet thing carefully. Medically, scientifically, vegetarianism is a fad. A dangerous one too. Unless you know how to balance the diet.'

Costa looked at the plate of unidentifiable meats, the pile of spent cigarettes and the near-empty flagon of wine in front of her and wondered who Crazy Teresa was to hand out lectures on eating habits.

'He can run faster than any man in the Questura,' Rossi said defensively. 'They say you should've seen him on the pitch.'

'I did see him on the pitch, before he took up this solitary running thing. He's fast but that doesn't mean he wouldn't be faster if he ate some meat now and again. Look at that guy who plays hooker.'

Teresa was a rugby groupie. That was another well-known fact.

'Lamponi?' Rossi asked, a little jealous perhaps.

'Yeah. Look at the pecs. Look at the thighs on that.' She stabbed a ribbon of tripe. 'That's what meat does for you. Gives a man a body.'

Luca Rossi exchanged a knowing look with his partner. 'He's gay,' he said.

'What?'

'Lamponi. He's gay,' Rossi repeated.

'Hell!'

'Perhaps,' Nic Costa suggested, 'it was something in his diet. Too many female hormones in all those glands he keeps eating.'

'Yeah,' Rossi agreed. 'Things start growing where they shouldn't. Stuff starts shrinking instead of . . .' He shrugged.

Crazy Teresa banged the empty carafe on the table to order a new one, lit a cigarette and glared at them. 'Bullshit merchants. You don't know what you're talking about.'

Nic Costa looked at his watch. It was his turn to go to

the house tonight. He didn't want to be late. 'What are we supposed to be talking about, Teresa? I gathered there was something on your mind.'

She pushed her fork around the remains on the plate. Costa realized he liked this woman. She was smart, fun too, but there was a serious side to her that underpinned everything.

'This skinning trick?' she asked slyly. 'You're happy with the way things have turned out? All nice and obvious like that?'

'It's not closed,' Costa said. 'Not by any means, though I didn't see anything in your report that raised any new issues.'

'To hell with the report. That's just about what I know. Sometimes there are things that grate, and maybe they're nothing at all, but you still ought to hear them.'

Rossi folded his arms and looked at her. 'We're listening.'

'The professor. Did he have any medical experience? Had he worked in an abattoir at some stage?'

Costa shrugged. 'Not that we know of. He was an academic. I can't see how he would have done either of those things. Why?'

Teresa Lupo was unhappy about something. 'I don't know. I may be wrong about this, but it's just a very odd thing to do. To skin someone like that and do it pretty well too at what I assume is his first attempt.'

Rossi's long face grew doubtful. 'Is it that hard? I had an uncle in the country. He used to do this trick when he killed a rabbit. He'd make some little nick in the back of the neck, sort of shake the thing up and down in some way he knew, and the whole skin came right off. Like a glove or something, inside out, clean as anything.'

Crazy Teresa was incredulous. 'You're comparing human beings with furry rodents? Are you serious? What you call "skin" is actually three separate, living organs. The epidermis, which is the outer part, the dermis underneath, the subcutis, the layer of fat below that. You can't make a nick somewhere, throw the corpse up in the air and have it come down stripped. This is complicated.'

She watched some food land on the neighbouring table courtesy of the pierced waitress.

'Wait here. I won't be a moment.'

Crazy Teresa walked into the kitchen. Rossi watched his partner warily from across the table.

'I'm paying,' he said.

'Oh, I know that, Uncle Luca.'

'She said it was important, Nic.'

And maybe it is, Costa thought. More important than Luca Rossi could begin to guess.

Crazy Teresa came back with a side of pork belly, uncooked, and a small kitchen knife. She dropped the meat in front of them and watched the raised eyebrows from the tables around.

'It's OK,' Teresa yelled back at them. 'We're not going to eat it just yet.'

Costa smiled at her. 'That's a relief.'

'Listen. The pig is a pretty close approximation to the human skin system in some ways, which is why it's used for grafts from time to time. You've got to remember, too, that some cannibal cultures call us the "long pig", and there's a reason for that. Physiology *and* taste. So here.'

She gave the short knife to Rossi.

'Try skinning it.'

He grunted then began to slice away at the fat

underneath the thick epidermis. Then he pulled, hoping to lift it away from the carcass. It was impossible, even for a strong man like Rossi.

'There's all that fat,' he complained. 'People aren't like that.'

Teresa eyed him. 'Not all people. You'd be amazed how much fat you can get on a corpse. You're right. It's not an exact match, but it's close. What I'm trying to say to you is there's no easy, quick solution. I looked up some of the classical images of this Bartholomew person on the web. Almost every one shows him about to be martyred and they all have the same idea. The person who wants to do it is staring at him, wondering how to do the job. It's not obvious.'

Costa thought of the painting in the church. This was exactly what it portrayed. Skinning a man required more than just strength and resolution. It surely needed some level of knowledge of the body as a starting point.

'So how'd he do it?' Costa asked.

Teresa took the knife off Rossi, stood up, went behind the big man and made him hold his arms up in the air.

'My guess is he went in behind the neck and circled there, feeling his way, getting an idea for how deep to cut, not trying to remove anything right then.'

Rossi took down his arms, feeling stupid. 'You mean he cut his throat?'

'Not enough to kill him,' Teresa noted. 'That's not the idea. All the reference works on skinning people emphasize how important it is for the victim to remain conscious for as long as possible. In some North American cultures they prided themselves on their ability to remove most of the skin intact and be able to show it to the victim before he died.'

'What happened then?' Costa asked.

'This is all conjecture,' Teresa warned. 'I've tried to come up with a way in which I can estimate the exact sequence of events but it's impossible. I guess he turned him sideways somehow, went down the back, all the way along the spine, lifting a little on each side, then gradually opened it out, up to the shoulder blades, out to the waist until most of the back was off.'

The party at the adjoining table stood up, mumbling, and went to the counter to pay.

'And he'd still be alive?' Rossi wondered.

She shrugged. This was all hypothesis. 'He might have blacked out from the agony, if he was lucky. But then he'd probably come to later. After the back, the knife would work round the groin, the arms, work round to the front. Just very slowly, until he could bring it all to the chest, like a sheath.'

Rossi pushed away the plate in front of him.

'How long?' Costa asked. 'From beginning to end?'

'An hour. Maybe more. And you don't just need a strong stomach for this. You need a lot of physical strength too. This Rinaldi man was in rotten shape. He ate terribly. He drank too much. He had the kind of liver you'd see on a French goose. I don't know . . . This may be all wrong.'

Costa and Rossi waited. Crazy Teresa was about to say what she had wanted to say all along.

She leaned over the table and spoke softly, so that no one beyond would hear. 'My feeling is this. The average surgeon wouldn't have the strength for that. Someone who worked in an abattoir maybe. Someone who had watched a procedure in a hospital could too. But a flabby, out-of-condition university professor? No. I can't give

you any hard scientific fact to put down in a report. But I
don't believe it. Not for one moment. Sorry . . . I know
you thought you had this one fixed.'

The two men looked at each other.

'On the other hand,' she said, 'you're listening to
Crazy Teresa. So maybe you should take that into
account.'

Rossi put a hand on her arm, shocked. 'What do you
mean? "Crazy Teresa"?'

She refilled her glass again. 'I gather that's a nickname
some of them are using now.'

'Who?' Rossi demanded. 'You let me know! You give
me the names!'

Costa said nothing and wished he didn't face the drive
ahead, wished he could order another glass of the good
wine.

'This is a professional organization,' Rossi continued.
'We don't countenance behaviour like that, do we?'

Nic Costa raised an empty glass to his partner.

'Sweet man,' Teresa said, flattered. 'Excuse me now. I
need to go.'

They watched her large, happy frame squeeze through
the restaurant and head for the corridor at the rear.

'I think you've found the perfect partner, Uncle
Luca,' Costa said. 'One who can drink, smoke and eat at
the same time.'

Rossi was offended. 'She's a good woman, Nic. Don't
you say otherwise. And she's not crazy either.'

Nic Costa took the small knife and stabbed at the raw
joint of pork on the table. It was tough. She had a point.
The waitress returned and looked at it too.

'Are you done with this, sir?' she asked Rossi. 'Or

would you like a bag to take it home? I mean, it is going on your bill.'

Rossi sighed as she cleared the table. When she was gone he looked Costa in the eye.

'So what do you think?'

Costa frowned. 'I hope to God she's wrong.'

'Yeah,' Rossi nodded. 'All that work. All that nagging from Falcone.'

'That wasn't what I meant.'

'Well?'

This change in their relationship seemed permanent now. For some reason the big man seemed to look to him for a lead. Perhaps, in spite of his greater experience, he felt lost in these complexities.

'If it was someone else, Luca, we don't have a clue to his motivation. And if we don't know why he did it, we don't know why he shouldn't do it again.'

He hesitated before going further. Rossi's long face was beginning to droop towards the empty plate in front of him.

'All we have,' Nic Costa said carefully, 'is that number to the man in the Vatican.'

Teresa Lupo was coming back from the toilets, smiling, happy, ordering *grappa* from behind the bar. Rossi was right. She was a smart woman, not crazy at all. And she was correct in her analysis. He knew it instinctively.

Seventeen

When Jay Gallo came to it was night. Lying on his back on the hard sand he could see the lights of the planes descending into Fiumicino airport, hear the roar of their engines. It was the only sound around him. He awoke knowing full well where he was: by the banks of the dead river, with its stink of chemicals, and worse, miles from anywhere. It would be a long walk back to the road and, perhaps, a long time before any motorist would pick up a hitchhiker in his present state. Gallo's mouth was full of blood. His head felt as if it had been split open. His nose was shattered and his face ached like hell. But he was alive. His hands moved around his body, feeling for broken bones. He raised himself from the sand on a single arm. He could see only through one eye. He could taste the dead river in his mouth. The water seemed stagnant, poisonous with the scum of algae.

'Bastard,' Jay Gallo spat through broken teeth, wondering who, of the many people he had pissed off over the years, had arranged this particular lesson. It seemed rather pointless without that piece of information.

Gradually his senses began to return. His sight improved, enough to see the lights of the coast at Ostia.

He began to hear the shriek of sea gulls, the far-off sound of a dinghy's weak motor.

And, behind him, breathing.

'Oh, Jesus.' Gallo groaned and began to turn.

The man was still sitting there on the bank, looking as if he had been waiting patiently for hours. He no longer wore the dark glasses. He had removed the jacket to reveal a plain white shirt. There was a reason for this, Gallo thought. The night was desperately close, so hot it was hard to take in sufficient air in a single breath. Then he cursed his own stupidity. The man had shrugged off the jacket because it was part of some disguise, a way of concealing his identity when they had met, in the presence of others. Now that they were alone, and his intent was clear, it was no longer needed.

Gallo fixed his attention on the figure in front of him. He was much younger than he had first thought, possibly about his own age. He was muscular too, in a way that spoke of work-outs and gyms. Oddly, there was sympathy in his face, as if some part of him regretted what was happening.

It was a face that was familiar somehow, which both surprised and irritated him.

'Who the hell are you?' he croaked.

The seated figure looked closely at him. The hint of compassion was there. Gallo did not mistake the expression. 'Just a cog in the wheel,' he said. 'Just a part of the mechanism.'

'We've met.' His head hurt too much to think straight. But the memory was there. He'd done something with this man. Picked up a package maybe. Or delivered one.

'If I ever offended you in some way . . .' Gallo wanted

to plead with this odd, taut figure in the dark, though he knew it was useless. And there was another thought in his head, one that kept getting bigger. If the man intended to kill him – and Jay Gallo could think of no other reason why they had come to the dead river – why had he waited? Why had he sat for hours by his unconscious figure on the sand, risking discovery, just to see him wake? Was there something he wanted? Something Gallo could still provide, maybe barter with?

'You want to trade?' Gallo asked.

The seated man turned. His face came into the harsh moonlight. It was an exaggerated face, one that would turn from beauty to ugliness with a simple change of the light. He had dark, alert eyes glinting in the moonlight, pale skin and full cruel lips. The face of a bit player in a canvas by Caravaggio, Gallo thought randomly.

'What's there to trade?'

'You tell me.'

'Nothing.'

To Gallo's dismay he was rising to his feet.

Jay Gallo tried to struggle to join him but his head hurt too much, his mind was just too woozy.

'Hey,' he said, desperate for anything that could delay what was coming. 'Why did you wait like that? *Why?*'

The strange face was cut in half by the moonlight. It was shocked, offended by the question. 'You think I kill sleeping men?'

Gallo's hands went up in front of him, two out-stretched palms trying to ward off this big, black figure overhead.

'You think,' the man repeated, his voice beginning to rise, beginning to turn into a roar, 'I'd send you to glory without you knowing?'

'Don't,' Jay Gallo whimpered. 'I'll do anything.'

The black figure nodded. 'I know,' he said, calm once more.

The pale disc of the moon disappeared behind blackness. A stone-hard fist came down out of the high dark, punching. The meagre light began to fade, began to be subsumed by blood and shattered bone. He found himself moving, lifted by two strong arms above.

Then there was some final relief: he fell into something cold, something that stank rotten but woke him all the same.

Jay Gallo choked on the stagnant water, wondering whether it made him feel better or worse. Then, under the unrelenting pressure of the hands that gripped his shoulders, his head went below the surface, his eyes stared into black nothingness.

The cold poison began to fill his lungs, no matter how much he struggled against the fists that held him down, how often he tried to vomit out the dank water.

The chill left the dead river and raced into his mouth. Jay Gallo fought it for as long as he could but at some stage the body needs to breathe even if there's nothing out there to pass as oxygen. When he thought his lungs might break he coughed once, felt the coldness win some bitter victory in his chest, and then was still.

Eighteen

Five minutes after Teresa Lupo had returned Costa made his excuses. Rossi had been right. There was a practical reason for the three of them to meet that evening. Nevertheless there was an unspoken one too, one in which he was an unwanted witness. Rossi and the woman were beginning to get too close for him to watch.

He drove through the thick Saturday night traffic, down brightly lit streets into the darkness at the edge of the city. It was a clear, starlit evening with a full moon. Even with the windows down, the interior of the old Fiat was uncomfortably hot. The car swept round the illuminated hulk of the gate of San Sebastiano, out to the old Appian Way, travelled a mile down the narrow road and took the familiar turning to the house, following the rutted drive until he parked beneath the vines of the rough car shelter that leaned drunkenly against the wall. He stepped out of the car and breathed in the smell of the countryside: parched scrub and dust, with the distant fragrance of wild thyme somewhere underneath. Cicadas rattled in the dead grass at his feet. The black, darting outlines of bats, squeaking frantically, broke the perfect night sky.

The house was an old lone farmhouse in the dead land between the old Appian Way and the modern, busy thoroughfare of the Via Appia Nuova. He remembered what he had said to Sara Farnese in front of the altar in the church on Tiber Island. A family was a team against the world, a bulwark against the insanity. He could not imagine what it would be like to be denied its sanctity. He could not begin to understand how anyone could survive the day without some place like this, some safe, holy refuge in which joy and hope, fear and tragedy inter-mingled, became controllable through the mutual regard individuals felt for one another.

The light was still on in the front room. Marco Costa was asleep in an armchair. Pepe, the argumentative little terrier his father loved so much, sat at his feet, curled into a ball. Nic could remember the animal as a puppy, bought after his mother died, as if in compensation. He had been offended at the time, but his father had been right. The dog's ceaseless need for love and attention, and his instant return of the same, made those dark months bear-able. Now the years were taking their vengeance with the same, vicious brutality, for both of them.

Giulia, his sister, had left a note in the kitchen, where the old man could not find it. She had to go to Milan on business for a week. There had been a call from their elder brother in Washington, young Marco. It was hardest for him. The busy lawyer's life and the harsh working regime of America left little time for home visits. The slow process of dying was difficult enough to manage when one lived just a few kilometres from the old man; from the other side of the Atlantic it was impossible. During the coming week, however, some routine could be main-tained. Nic would stay during the evening whenever possible; Bea, Marco's former secretary, from his earliest days in politics, and still a firm friend, would come in for the daylight hours and any other time when work called Nic away. Giulia hated to leave him but she needed the time off too. He read the rest of the note. The old man had taken his pills with his usual bad grace. His mood was up and down. The doctors said . . .

Her writing had faltered as she spelled out the words: *perhaps weeks, not months now.*

He closed his eyes and wanted to scream. His father was sixty-one, half a head taller than him, and once a bull of a man, someone who had, on occasion, stood up to the toughest of Turin union hoods and won his bloody way. Now he was some flimsy human husk, being eaten away each day by this insidious, invisible disease. It was savagely unjust, whatever the doctors said about the old man's habits. To move, in the course of a single year, from such strength to such frailty was a cruel transformation, for Marco Costa and those who loved him. It was also implacable, beyond treatment, something his son still found hard to accept.

There was a sound from the kitchen. Bea came in with two glasses of wine for them. She was still a handsome woman, straight-backed, with short auburn hair, attentive blue eyes and a sharp tongue when it was deserved. As always, she wore bright clothes; on this occasion an orange silk shirt with cream trousers. Gold glittered at her tanned neck and on her slim wrists. She was a little younger than Marco, perhaps fifty-five now, and had been single throughout her life. The relationship puzzled him; there were memories from his childhood, uncertain ones, which suggested Bea had been more than merely a friend to Marco at one time. Seeing him through his illness was now a matter of duty, something she would not shirk. She waved at him to come back into the kitchen, out of earshot of his father.

'Don't believe everything you read,' she said, nodding at the note.

He put down the wine and poured himself some water. 'Bea, the doctors . . .'

'They're all a bunch of quacks and charlatans.'

'But . . .' He waved the piece of paper, feeling stupid.

'But nothing. My own father had the same kind of disease, and the same kind of head on his shoulders. Sure it kills them in the end. But I tell you this, Nic. A man like that dies when he chooses to let go, when he thinks there's no more reason for him to stay around.'

'Of course.'

She gave him a harsh look, with some cause: his answer had been too quick, too easy. 'You think I'm deluding myself? Listen. If Marco finds no reason to live he'll be in a casket tomorrow. If something holds him – and something does right now – he'll be sitting down with us at Christmas.'

Bea owned a tiny apartment in Trastevere which she always said she would sell one day, to return to her native Puglia. He had come to understand over the last few months when that day would be: once Marco was dead.

He took her hands which were still young, the fingers long and supple. 'I can't thank you enough for your kindness, Bea.'

'Then don't. Pay attention to him, Nic. This is a time that will be with you for the rest of your life. There are things that must be said or you'll always regret them. Perhaps things that must be done too. I don't know. A woman never understands the relationship between a man and his father. Still, most of them don't either. There . . .'

She picked up her bag and took out the car keys.

'Lecture's over. I'll be back as usual tomorrow.'

He watched her go, trying to recover those mental images of her when she was young. Bea was beautiful then: a glorious, colourful presence in the family's life. There was a time, perhaps when he was seven or eight, that he felt he was in love with her. The perfume she wore – the same invasive scent she still used – continued to prick his memory. She still had the same exotic air about her, one that his father never seemed to acknowledge. Bea was a mystery. She had never talked of a man, never seemed to need one. Marco Costa, and the cause, had been her life, and now one was dying and the other already dead.

He went back to the room where Marco still slept, undisturbed by the movement around him. It was late. Nic bent down and carefully placed his arms beneath his father, lifting him out of the chair, shocked by how light he had become.

Halfway to the bedroom, Marco's breathing changed. The old man's grey eyelids opened slowly. Nic Costa saw the glint of a welcome recognition in the familiar features which were now creased and wrinkled, like those of an eighty-year-old.

'You should be out chasing women,' his father said in a voice that carried the stain of a lifetime's tobacco.

Nic carried him to the bed and gently laid him on the clean white sheet, newly ironed by Bea. 'I have been.'

'Bullshit,' the old man whispered, then began to smile at some returning memory. 'People have been chasing you. I watch TV you know. I can recognize the way my own son runs even when he's wearing some woman's coat.'

It was the body that was failing him. Marco Costa's mind was as sharp as his son could ever remember.

'Did they know too?' he asked. 'Did the TV people realize it wasn't her?'

'No.' He laughed. 'Do you think I should call? Collect a little tip-off money? I don't understand where you get this theatrical streak. Not from me.'

Nic began to work on his clothes.

His father slapped gently at his hand. 'I can do that. I'm not a cripple. I keep telling Bea that.'

'No,' he agreed. 'You're not a cripple. Bea knows it.'

The old man gave him a curious glance. 'She knows everything, Nic. She's family now. In a way she always was though I was too stupid to tell her.'

'I think she knows. You treat her badly enough.'

'If you pamper me like an invalid I've a duty to be demanding.'

He never gave up, never let go. It was part of his charm and part of his problem too. 'Then you're doing your duty very well.'

Marco Costa's face grew serious. 'She *is* family. When the time comes, when you want to be near, I'd like her around. I say that now. I may not be able to say it when it happens.'

He nodded. 'Bea will be here,' he said, and walked away from the bed, feeling the familiar stinging in his eyes, hiding his reaction by tidying some stray papers on the desk.

The room had once been the family study, until Marco's illness and his inability to climb stairs made it the old man's bedroom. It was still alive with the memories of Nic's childhood, still decorated just as it had always been, with the striking communist posters, the bust of Gramsci, his father's hero, and the piece his mother had insisted upon, a classical head of a handsome man, turning, with an expression of determination on his face, as if to face some unseen enemy. Much of Nic's life was rooted in this room. It was here that all three Costa children had been educated, their parents refusing to tolerate the public schools because, at the time, they insisted Catholicism was the state religion, to be taught to every child. It was here that each in turn learned, and quietly rejected, their parents' own intense brand of politics, here that three studious children read classics and modern stories, Homer and Jack London. And later Marco's most cherished possession, a first edition of Gramsci's own *Letter from Prison* published in 1947, a decade after his death.

It was here too that Anna Costa had died, ten years before, refusing to go to hospital, as Marco would when it was his time. Nic Costa had found her, slumped at the desk as if reading, when he came back from a run. A left-wing magazine was spread out in front of her. Her grey hair, still as long as when she was young, had tumbled across the pages. He could still recall the sharp, painful sense of injustice he had felt. Perhaps it had somehow, illogically, propelled him into the police. It had taken a year before his father had forgiven himself for being absent; he was in Milan, addressing a conference. Nothing had been the same after that. Marco's career entered its decline; winter came into their lives. The bright, vivid joy of childhood – a childhood which Marco Costa had enjoyed alongside his children – was gone. The practical world beckoned and it was a cold place full of solitary people.

Marco Costa reached out with a scrawny arm and touched his son's cheek, smiling.

'So in between the cross-dressing and the athletics have you managed to oppress anyone today?'

'Not as many as I'd hoped. But there's always tomorrow.'

He laughed. 'Of course. There's always tomorrow.'

They had discussed the matter, just once, which was as much as Marco Costa desired. For the old man dying was an inconvenience, like a cab that arrived half an hour before it was due and honked its horn until you came struggling to the door. He was unafraid, more through practicality than courage. People died, he said, usually before they wished it. He hadn't achieved as much as he'd hoped, though he knew it was more than most. He had a good family too: two sons and a daughter whose chosen professions, in the police, in the law and as a professional painter, were so far removed from his own it was impossible for him to feel anything but pride. He did not fear the void that he knew lay ahead. He only regretted that it would disrupt unfinished business, work that would now fall to someone else, someone beyond the Costa clan.

His son felt differently. Even after a year of knowing its imminence, he still could not come to terms with the idea of a world which did not contain his father's considerable presence. This was the only secret he dared not share with the old man, and that made it all the harder to bear.

Nineteen

The phone rang just after he had served the old man breakfast: fresh fruit, orange juice straight from the squeezer, a cocktail of pills. His father watched him as he took the call.

'Don't worry about me,' he said the moment Nic Costa put down the phone. 'Bea will be here soon. I'm not helpless. I'll survive.'

'Thanks.'

'What is it?'

The old man never asked about his work. This was a pact between them. Nic Costa was surprised that was now changing.

'There's been another death.'

'So what? Are you the only cop they've got?'

'It's not that.' He was trying to clarify matters in his own head. 'It's connected somehow by the sound of it.' He had come part of the way to rejecting his earlier ideas already. It should have been no surprise. 'Maybe we've jumped to conclusions about what happened in the Vatican. Maybe . . .' The old man's tired eyes wouldn't leave him. Marco Costa knew when something was badly wrong. '. . . it's all a lot worse than we thought.'

'Tell me about it,' the old man ordered. 'If you want. When you get back. Now . . .' He picked up a bread roll from the table. 'You eat that in the car. No one can live off fruit alone. Not even you.'

Fifteen minutes later Nic Costa was parked outside the old, low church near the Colosseum, by the narrow road that led to the Lateran palace, the first St Peter's. This was a part of the city he never really understood. The Colosseum was two minutes' stroll away. The busy modern thoroughfare of Labicana set up a constant traffic roar to the north. A short walk would take him to the Rinaldis' lonely apartment in the Via Mecenate. There were high, late-nineteenth-century blocks towering over the narrow cobbled streets of the neighbourhood. A few stalls made up the tiny street market that had probably worked here for ten centuries or more. It was a quiet, residential area, one that the tourists rarely visited. And within it lay such odd, unexpected sights: churches and squares that seemed to go back to a different city.

Sara Farnese would, he felt sure, know this area well, would be able to point out a wall here, a crypt there and know its place in the Roman story. He felt lost, all the more so when he walked into the large, elegant courtyard that now bustled with people. The centre was occupied by rows of simple seats, perhaps three hundred of them, pointed towards a low wooden stage. The floor was still littered with cheaply printed programmes: Vivaldi and Corelli performed by a local semi-professional orchestra. An open-air concert had taken place here the night before. That made the morning's discovery even more odd. At 8.15 an Irish Dominican named Bernard Cromarty, a senior member of the order that had administered San Clemente for almost three hundred and fifty years, had opened the doors to the chapel to prepare for the morning service. What he found there led him to run, terrified, from the dark, enclosed interior, out into the hardening morning light, screaming for help.

Nic Costa studied the courtyard, noting how much had been left behind after the concert, took a deep breath and went inside. This was a grander, older church than the place on Tiber Island. It had a solemn, distinguished interior, with a quiet richness of decoration. The murmur of men's voices sounded like the whispering of monks rebounding off the walls. In the centre of the nave, flanked by two high, imposing pulpits, was an ancient choir leading up to a dimly lit altar, raised slightly above ground level. A group of recognizable figures was bent low around the far edge of the structure studying something out of sight. Falcone stood upright, in expensive jeans, their neat crease visible even from this distance, and a too-white shirt. It was Sunday. Perhaps he had been called away from a social engagement Costa could only guess at. He'd been married once but that had ended in divorce years ago. Now, the gossips had it, he played the field, in fancy company too.

The cold, bearded face was creased in concentration. Costa joined Luca Rossi by Falcone's side. The focal point of this part of the church was supposed to be the small casket which lay at the base of the altar, beneath a canopy supported by delicate columns. Now another object stole their attention. In front of the coffin, surrounded by flickering candles which were almost spent, was the figure of a naked man. He lay on his side. His knees were drawn up as if crouching, his arms were extended and bent upwards, with the hands placed together in an obvious position of prayer. His eyes were open, as was his mouth, giving him an expression of mute, dead surprise, as if he had chanced upon something in the night, something that had stolen the life out of him.

His fair hair was wet and plastered to his skull. His face showed signs of a severe beating: livid dark bruises, a swollen eye and several open wounds. Around his neck was a thick nautical rope which was attached to a small rusty anchor – of a size suitable for a pleasure dinghy – now lying flat on the mosaic floor behind his back.

Teresa Lupo busied herself around the corpse. With minute care she placed a gloved finger in the mouth, leaned forward and sniffed. She wrinkled her nose and, very gingerly, took a slender arm and tried to move it. There was obvious resistance.

'Well?' Falcone asked. Standing next to him was a priest, a severe-faced man of seventy or more with a wild shock of white hair and sad grey eyes. He watched them covetously, as if the church and everything inside it was his personal property.

'Brackish water,' the pathologist said. 'The salt's pretty strong. He wouldn't smell like this if he'd been in the Tiber. Must be somewhere else. Somewhere estuarial. I'll be able to tell you more once I've got him back to the office.'

Falcone stared at the dead man's face. 'How long?'

'Several hours,' she replied. 'There's obvious rigor. He must have been placed here in the evening or early this morning.'

Rossi stared gloomily at the corpse. 'How was that possible, Father? I thought there was a concert here last night. How could a dead man be brought into this place?'

'There was a concert,' the priest answered, warming

to the unexpected politeness in Rossi's question. 'Every last seat was sold. I was here myself until one in the morning, helping to clear up.'

'Then how?' Falcone demanded.

The priest shook his head and stared at the stone floor. Nic Costa nodded towards the sunlight behind them in the open courtyard. Something large, shiny and black leaned against the far wall. 'What's that doing there?' he asked. 'Why would a musician leave an instrument behind?'

Rossi grunted, walked out into the daylight, heaved the double bass case carefully under his arm, not touching the handle. From the way he carried it the thing weighed very little. He returned to the nave and placed it on the stone floor. Falcone bent down, took a nail file out from a leather case and gingerly worked his way around the perimeter, flipping up the clasps. When he was done he threw open the lid. The case was empty. The cheap red velvet lining was soaked with water. It had a sour, salty smell.

'I still don't see,' Falcone exclaimed. 'He couldn't have moved a naked body when you people were clearing up. And afterwards the church would be locked, surely.'

'Of course,' the priest agreed. 'There are many valuable items in here.'

'Cameras?' Costa asked hopefully. The man shook his head.

Teresa Lupo waved to her men at the door to come and retrieve the body. The interior echoed to the squealing of the gurney's wheels. She came and stood next to Rossi, staring at the empty well for the double bass.

'Well?' she asked.

'Well what?' Falcone demanded testily.

'Is no one going to ask me how he died?'

The detectives looked at each other. It had seemed so obvious.

'Poor bastard was beaten up, wasn't he?' Rossi asked.

'Sure,' she said. 'I don't think that killed him, though. I could be wrong. Ask me again after the autopsy.' She took off the plastic gloves and smiled at Rossi and Costa. 'You guys are quite something, you know. I just don't get this quality of material from anyone else.'

'Meaning?' Falcone thundered.

'He was drowned,' Teresa Lupo said. 'Forcibly, in shallow water, maybe less than a metre, which would explain the amount of muddy material in his mouth. I'll be able to be quite precise with that I think. The combination of salt water and mud . . . it can't be hard to track down where it came from. He was drowned and then, for some reason, the anchor was placed around his neck after he was put on the floor there, after the candles were lit. It couldn't have been any other way because that thing isn't heavy enough to hold down a man and the length of rope is too great to have been of any use in the sort of depth I'm talking about. That's just symbolic somehow. Part of the picture we're supposed to be appreciating.'

Costa couldn't take his eyes off the priest. The man's eyes were closed. He had crossed himself and was now quietly saying a prayer.

'Father?' he asked, when the man was done.

'What is it?' the priest replied grumpily.

Nic Costa waved at the interior of the church. 'There are anchors here already. I've seen them. Carved into the columns. In the paintings on the walls. What does it mean?'

'And none of you can even begin to guess at that?' the old priest asked sourly. 'Is that what it's come to?'

Falcone eyed him unpleasantly. 'If you have some information that could help us, Father . . .'

The old man tut-tutted. 'So many professional people. So little knowledge. This is the church of San Clemente. The fourth pope of Rome.' He pointed to the tomb beneath the altar, beyond the naked body surrounded by the guttering candles. 'His remains lie there, as they have done for almost two millennia. Do you know nothing? San Clemente was martyred by drowning. He was found with the anchor round his neck.'

The man waved at the corpse on the mosaic floor, a controlled fury in his face. 'This . . . abomination is a deliberate, a direct insult to his memory. The work of a madman.'

Nic Costa wondered at that. If it was a madman it was one with a very precise theological knowledge, a very definite purpose. And, more, there was something almost akin to reverence in the violence too.

'Have you any idea who the dead man is?' Falcone asked.

'None,' the priest grunted. Luca Rossi shrugged his broad, stooped shoulders. The others in the police team looked just as blank.

Falcone's fierce gaze turned on Nic Costa. 'We're not moving a damned thing. Call her. Bring her down here. Do it yourself if necessary.'

'What?'

'The Farnese woman. I want her to see this. Before

anything is moved. I want to know if she recognizes him. I want to know what she . . . *thinks*.'

'Sir . . .' Nic Costa objected and hunted in vain for the words. What Falcone said made sense. She would have to be shown a picture of the dead man. There were too many coincidences here. Still, there were easier, less painful ways of achieving these ends. There was, it seemed to him, no practical reason to drag Sara Farnese into this grim scene.

'Why don't I just bring her to the morgue? What difference does it make?'

'You heard,' Falcone said, walking out to the court-yard, reaching for his phone.

Then he was gone and there was just Luca Rossi staring into Costa's eyes, looking shifty.

'We fouled up, didn't we?' he grunted. 'We just leapt right in and thought what somebody wanted us to think.'

It was all there, Nic Costa thought. Just waiting for them in that stinking death-filled room on Tiber Island. *I met a man with seven wives . . .*

'I guess so.' He found it hard to shake off the thought that Rossi had been expecting this all along.

'You know what?' the big man said. 'We keep thinking we're looking for facts. And that's only half the job. The other half is looking for lies, seeing them for what they are.'

'I'll do this on my own,' Costa said. 'Tell Falcone to give me thirty minutes.'

Then he was out of the door, feeling the August heat starting to fall from the sky, wondering what he was going to tell her.

Twenty

'Why did you do that?'

Sara Farnese was wearing black: casual trousers and a cotton T-shirt. She looked younger and on her guard. The press mob had yet to arrive at San Clemente but the beggars, Kosovans and Africans, were always there. Without thinking Nic Costa had handed out some money to a young black boy with wide, haunted eyes, choosing him, as always, at random. She seemed surprised they had not simply barged through the small crowd, ignoring them.

'Family habit,' Costa said. 'Twice a day, every day. Just in case.'

'In case what?' she wondered.

'In case . . . it makes a difference, I guess.' He'd never thought about it much. They were modest sums of money. The idea had been ingrained into them at such an early age. For his father this was, he thought, an act of faith, one more proof, if Nic Costa needed it, that the old man's communism was a kind of religion in disguise.

He took her by the arm. They halted outside the gateway to the church. 'Let me say something. You don't have to go through with this, Sara. Not here. We could arrange an appointment at the morgue. It may be a waste of time anyway.'

Her green eyes watched him carefully. 'Then why was I asked to come here?'

'My boss,' he said instantly, not wanting to lie since he felt sure she would know. 'It was his idea. He thinks this is more complex. He thinks we don't know everything we ought to know.'

She understood Costa's point immediately. Sara Farnese acknowledged it in silence then peered inside at the courtyard of San Clemente.

'I've been here for concerts. Have you?'

'I'm not much of a one for music.'

'What are you for?'

'Looking at paintings. Running. Making sense of things. How many times have you been here before?'

'Three. Four.'

Costa nodded, taking in the information.

She sighed, exasperated. 'Is that supposed to be significant too? Are you listening to every word I say and wondering what it's worth?'

'Not at all. I don't think anyone understands what's going on here. Except that it's obvious there seems to be some link that leads back to you. Who did you come here with, Sara? We may need to know.'

'Really,' she murmured, then pointed up the narrow street of San Giovanni in Laterano. A small electric bus was navigating the cobble stones up the hill, towards the sprawling hospital at the summit. 'Have you heard of Pope Joan? The female pope?'

'I thought that was a myth.'

'Probably. The myth says she gave birth outside a house there, on her way to take the papal crown in the

Lateran. The mob killed her and the infant when it realized what she was. Still, myth or no myth, there was an image on a house nearby, until the sixteenth century, of a woman with her breast bared and a child in her arms. Until it was torn down by the Vatican, along with a portrait of her in Siena.'

'Why are you telling me this?' he asked.

She shrugged. 'I don't know. Perhaps because I thought you'd understand. Pope Joan isn't real. She never existed. Her story is as apocryphal as that of some of the early martyrs but it doesn't matter. It's about faith. It's about how something can be fiction and true too, after a fashion. In Joan's case it's a truth about the place women are supposed to have in the world. How we're meant to be harlots or heroines. Virgins or whores. It doesn't occur to you that there might be other permutations. Some middle way in which, perhaps, we're both, or neither. Or something else altogether.'

'You sound like my father,' he grumbled. 'I'm sorry, I wasn't trying to judge you. I just feel jumpy about everything. About what's in there and why this is all happening.'

'Show me,' she said and then they walked into the dark church interior, towards the group that stood around the body, now covered with a sheet.

Falcone watched her arrive. He looked hungry for information. The smell of tobacco hung around him. There was ash on his white shirt now. It was the grey, flecked colour of his beard. Luca Rossi shuffled awkwardly on his giant feet, accompanied by some detectives Costa didn't recognize. Teresa Lupo stood at the edge watching them all, taking in everything. Costa was beginning to appreciate her presence more and more. She was honest. She had some insight, too, that was lacking in the men.

'Miss Farnese,' Falcone said, coming towards her, extending a hand. 'I'm grateful you came. This won't take long.' He looked at the pathologist. 'Please . . .'

Teresa bent down to the body and carefully pulled back the sheet exposing the dead man's face. Sara Farnese's slim hand went to her mouth. She closed her eyes and exhaled a quiet, anguished gasp, then sat down heavily on one of the bench seats. Costa was unable to prevent himself glaring at Falcone. He was relishing this spectacle, as if her grief contained within it some precious intelligence only he could see. Costa was intrigued by some small element of theatricality in her reaction too; he found himself wondering whether she was not expecting to see some other body beneath the sheet. Whether he was, in fact, witnessing her relief.

He walked to the small office that led off the nave and came back with some water, sat next to her and gave her the cup. She accepted gratefully. Falcone and the other cops watched, curious.

'I'm sorry,' he said.

She opened her eyes and stared at him. It was impossible to know whether there was some personal bitterness in her gaze.

'Why are you apologizing? I know who he is. Wasn't that the point of bringing me here?'

Falcone took a step forward. 'Of course. His name, please?'

'Jay Gallo. He was an American tour guide.'

'Address?' Falcone asked, indicating to Costa to take a note.

'In the Via Trastevere. I don't know the number. It was a cheap little apartment above the supermarket.'

Falcone paused. 'And you knew him . . . how exactly?'

She sighed and looked at Costa, as if this proved some point. 'We were both at Harvard together for a while. When he moved to Rome we renewed our friendship.'

Falcone waited, in vain, for her to go further. Finally, he asked, 'Meaning what exactly?'

'Meaning,' she replied icily, 'that for a while, a few weeks, several months ago, we slept together. Is that what you wanted to know?'

'I want to know what's relevant,' Falcone said brusquely. 'There are four people dead now. Three of them were your lovers. Where did this Gallo character fit in? Would the others have known him?'

She considered this, appearing to regard it as a reasonable question. 'No. He'd no connection with the university. Stefano never met him. Hugh came a long time after.'

'But you would have mentioned him to other people?'

'Why?' she asked, puzzled. 'What was the point? I was with Jay for a couple of weeks and then we agreed to be friends, nothing more. I haven't seen him in months. He was an entertaining man but there was something lost about him. He drank too much. He was far too intelligent to be engaged in the work he did. He was failing himself and he knew it. However amusing he could be, that kind of thing wears off pretty quickly.'

Falcone gave Costa a significant glance as if to say: see the bitch, see what she's like. The moment she's bored, the moment she has doubts, she dumps them. And now one of the names on that list of rejections, maybe a long, long list, is fighting back.

'So what do you think is happening here, Miss Farnese?' Falcone asked.

She seemed taken aback. 'I've no idea. What do you mean?'

'Why are your former lovers being killed like this? As if they were martyrs somehow?'

'I can't begin to guess,' she insisted. 'This is as inexplicable to me as it is to you.'

'And yet,' Falcone continued, 'you must know the person responsible. This is someone who is familiar with the intimate details of your private life. You see my point?'

'Everybody sees your point.' It was Teresa Lupo who intervened, risking Falcone's wrath. 'It's the way you ask. May I suggest you get some women detectives in here? You need to strike a balance between duty and prurience.'

'Thanks,' Falcone hissed. 'You can take the body out of here now, Doctor. I want an autopsy report by this afternoon.'

The pathologist sighed and called for her team. The wheels squealed across the old, stone floor. Sara Farnese watched the covered corpse being lifted gently onto the gurney, watched in silence as it was pushed out into the sun-filled courtyard. They had removed the anchor and the rope which now lay on the ancient mosaic floor.

'San Clemente,' Sara said. 'Why didn't I realize? He had that anchor round his neck when they found him?'

'As if he was another martyr,' Costa said, watching her like a hawk.

'I told you,' she snapped. 'Mostly these stories are apocryphal. In the case of Clemente it certainly is. If the person who did this knows Tertullian – which I assume he does – he knows that too. Tertullian wrote about Clemente and never once mentioned any kind of martyrdom. It's a fairy tale that was never even told until the fourth century.'

Costa tried to understand the significance. 'Why would it matter? What difference does it make whether he knows this is a sham or not?'

Falcone interrupted, smiling. 'Because it's a question of belief. We look at these acts and think they must be the work of a man with some misplaced sense of religion. In fact . . .'

Teresa Lupo, now returned to the nave and glowering openly at Falcone, interrupted. 'In fact you don't have a clue. Spare us cops practising fake psychology, please. All any of us knows is this: a man who can skin another human being is not a suitable subject for some kind of cheap Freudian analysis, however hard you try. He can surely hold two entirely conflicting rationales in his head simultaneously and never hear them rub up against each other. I told you boys last night. I tell you now. This is a man who is strong, determined and powerful. A man who has some kind of medical knowledge, or has worked in a slaughterhouse. Forget what's in his head because it's got some impenetrable logic all of its own and you'd need to be as crazy as he is to understand it. Look for the physical facts.'

Costa watched Sara Farnese's face. 'Do you know anyone like that?'

'No,' she said, looking at the long-haired woman in the white coat, grateful for her support. 'But whoever he is he knows Tertullian too. You forgot that.'

'Quite,' the pathologist agreed. 'Seems like I've got the easy job around here.' She walked away, grabbing for the cigarettes beneath the enclosed suit.

'What else do you want?' Sara Farnese asked as Lupo's team left through the outside gate.

Falcone shuffled on his feet, thinking. 'The name and address of everyone you've had a relationship with since coming to Rome.'

She shook her head. 'That's not possible. You can't ask for someone's entire private life.'

Falcone leaned towards her, so close that their faces almost touched. 'Miss Farnese,' he said softly. 'Everyone you have slept with is a suspect. Everyone you have slept with is a potential victim. We need their names. For their sakes as much as ours. Surely you can see that?'

'Some of these are married men. This is ridiculous. How would you feel if it were you?'

Falcone gave her a disagreeable frown. 'Maybe I'd feel glad to be alive.'

She had no answer. Costa touched her arm gently, wondering again about this strange chasm there seemed to be in her life. 'Sara. It's important. We can get some women detectives you can talk to. Everything will remain confidential.'

'You honestly believe that? Please . . .'

He couldn't argue. They all knew that everything leaked from the department in the end. He couldn't begin to guess what names existed inside Sara Farnese's head but it would be impossible to promise them privacy once they entered the files in the Questura Centrale. There was too much media interest already and too much money riding on any scraps of information that could be secretly gleaned from the files.

'We require this for your sake too,' Falcone said forcefully. 'Whoever this man is, he knows everything about you. Perhaps he's trying to impress you with these acts.

Perhaps they are warnings. But one thing I'm sure of. At some stage he will realize they're not having the desired effect and he will hold you to blame. At that point his next victim will surely be you, the source of his sorrows.'

She stared at him. 'Whoever this is, I am not the source of his sorrows. This is not my doing.'

'As he sees it . . . I should have put it that way,' Falcone said, in the closest to an apology his pride would allow. 'Who do you know in the Vatican?' He threw the question at her idly, as if it were unimportant. Costa cursed himself. He had told Falcone of his concerns about what had happened in the library that morning. He had no idea his vague doubts would translate into direct questions so quickly.

'What?'

'There were phone calls, between Rinaldi and some-one in the Vatican. There were indications that Rinaldi believed he was under some kind of surveillance when he entered the Reading Room, either electronically or from some person in the room. In your line of work you must know many people. It's important we have their names.'

'I've no special relationship with anyone in the Vatican.' Her face was pale and hard, a mask.

'Without some honesty . . .' Falcone shrugged. 'I fear this will go on. I can't see any reason why he should stop here. We need names. All of them.' He reached forward and looked intently into her eyes. 'We need to know everything about your life.'

'Go to hell,' she hissed.

Falcone smiled. Costa recognized the moment. He enjoyed breaking people. He believed this was the point of victory. 'Miss Farnese. I can insist on your cooperation.

I can take steps if it is not forthcoming. I can call you into protective custody.'

'Sir,' Costa interrupted, gaining the full blast of Falcone's furious gaze. 'This is happening too quickly. If we give Miss Farnese time. If I get one of the women detectives to help us back at the station.'

'If . . .' Falcone said sourly.

Costa took him to one side so she couldn't hear. 'Please. If you push her she'll say nothing. Let me talk to her somewhere else. Somewhere she can think it through.'

Falcone's hard features froze for a moment. Then he nodded at Costa. 'Maybe she needs one person she can trust. Maybe . . .'

He eyed Costa, wondering. 'There's a lot of reporters out there now. Take her out on your own. Go have a coffee somewhere and think about this. Bring her in by the back door in an hour.'

'OK.' Costa was puzzled. There was something else and Falcone was uncharacteristically reluctant to say it.

'Sir?'

'You're right,' he said, smiling. 'I've an idea. Act a little, kid. Those reporters think they've got some scarlet woman in their sights here. Let's play them along. When you go outside stay close to her. Make it look like . . . there's perhaps something between you.'

'You're asking me to . . .' Costa began to say, furious.

'I'm telling you to send out a message. I want this lunatic to see you and think he knows who's chasing her tail now. We could spend months following him around like this. It would make it a lot easier if he comes to us. Comes to *you*, to be precise.'

'Sir . . .'

'Don't worry, kid,' Falcone beamed. 'We'll be waiting. You do have faith in your own police force now, don't you?'

Nic Costa walked off without answering and beckoned Sara to follow him to the door. Outside the media had arrived in force. A mob five metres deep thronged the gateway into the courtyard, held back by uniformed men trying to keep the line intact. The moment they saw her the questions came: screamed out of the heaving mass, unintelligible in the babble of desperate voices. Nic Costa threw an arm around her and they braved the mob, moving through the cameras and the thrusting microphones, pushing forward, all the way to his small car.

She kept her face down to the ground. He held his arm tight round her shoulders and stared, unbending at the cameras, finding time to smile once or twice, time too to look at her, fondly, with an affection he didn't find hard to feign.

He remembered her story. About the female pope being torn to pieces not far from here, and how it was all untrue, and maybe that wasn't the point anyway. Nic Costa stomped his way through the pack with all the finesse he once used in a bad-tempered rugby match, holding her safe, feeling her slender, fragile body and, after a while, an arm clinging to his waist.

Then they reached the car, he made space with a few deftly aimed jabs of his elbow, and they were free.

He looked at her, pale and frightened in the passenger seat, and thought of the faces he had made into that sea of cameras, the way he had acquiesced so easily, so willingly, to Falcone's idea.

She turned to him, puzzled, hurt. 'What's happening, Nic? What's going on?'

'I don't know,' he said. 'But don't worry. I'll fix this. Somehow.'

She stared out of the window, out into the hot, airless day. Nic Costa watched and felt he was swimming in a sea of lies.

Twenty-one

Gino Fosse lived in a three-storey tower which belonged, he felt, in the pages of a Gothic fairy tale. The structure was built of honey-coloured bricks and situated on the Caelian Hill midway along the imperial thoroughfare of the Clivus Scauri. Opposite stood the sprawling hulk of the basilica of Santi Giovanni e Paolo, to which he was now loosely attached as one of the parish priests, though almost all his professional time was spent at the hospital of San Giovanni, a ten-minute walk away. It was not the same as working in the Vatican, but the Church knew best.

Fosse felt obliged to know some history of his surroundings. The tower which had been his home this last month was embedded in the Aurelian Wall, built in the third century AD and still, for the most part, an intact circle around the centre of the city. A pleasant run, one he sometimes made in a tracksuit which disguised his calling, was to follow its line unimpeded straight to the great gate of San Sebastian and onto the Appian Way.

Initially the structure had been a small Roman sentry point along the brick expanse of the defences. In the Middle Ages it had been enlarged to provide accommodation for the expanding ecclesiastical entourage of the large and powerful basilica across the square. Giovanni e Paolo, though little known to the average tourist, was, for Fosse, one of the most interesting churches in Rome. The visible shell was unremarkable, save for the Romanesque campanile which cast an afternoon shadow across his first-floor window. Beneath the church lay centuries of rich history, however, and a story which had bemused him from the moment he first encountered it.

The tale of the martyrs John and Paul was, for centuries, thought to be apocryphal by those who dared say as much. It concerned two Christian officers at the court of Constantine who, after the accession of Julian the Apostate in AD 360, refused to sacrifice to pagan gods. As a consequence, they were beheaded, along with a woman who came to comfort them, in their own house on the Caelian Hill which later became the site of the basilica.

Myth begat myth, church begat church. Centuries of building and rebuilding ensued, resulting in the formidable pile which now dominated the view from Fosse's tower. Yet, when the archaeologists – doubtless atheists to a man – came to explore the foundations of the present church they found, deep beneath it, the well-preserved remains of an ancient Roman house. And three Christian graves, with clear signs that they were the scene of much reverence from as early as the end of the fourth century AD.

Sometimes Fosse would take privileged visitors into the subterranean houses and show them the paintings on the wall. It was always a humbling experience, an unspoken sermon on the mystery that underpinned all human life, and the relentless unreliability of what the clever people in universities like to call 'facts'.

The former guard post had, since the fifteenth century, been given over to the more humble employees of the parish. The modest living quarters afforded him a sitting room, a bedroom and a tiny bathroom, all built into the first floor of the circular tower, with the ground floor used for storage. At the top was a small octagonal room which Fosse regarded as his private place, closed even to the occasional visitors who were, to his annoyance, granted entrance to the tower.

The composer di Cambio, who wrote a choral work described by the 'bad pope' Alexander VI as 'the sound that angels now make in Heaven', had lived and died in these quarters in the late fifteenth century. This obscure historical connection – which Fosse found baffling on the occasion he listened to the boring drone of the work when it was performed, on the anniversary of di Cambio's death, in Santi Giovanni e Paolo – meant the tower was on the list of ancient monuments for which permission to view could be gained by applying to the relevant office in the Vatican. Accordingly, every few weeks since his arrival he had been forced to allow some curious gaggle of sightseers, usually American, into his home, where they would bill and coo at the 'cuteness' of the place. They would then stare out of the four slitted medieval windows that gave onto the Clivus Scauri and begin, surreptitiously, to peek at their watches.

None had the wit to ask what was in the tiny space at the summit. Nor would they have gained admittance in any case; Fosse had established that this last room had no public right of view. This was part of the price of what he saw as his exile. The resulting privacy made it perfect for the purpose required when his new and urgent calling had become apparent.

It was now seven on a blazing Sunday morning. His collection of more than three hundred jazz CDs was scattered on the floor in the small octagonal tower. It was difficult sometimes to know what to play. Soon he would go to the hospital, to talk to the sick and the dying, to sit in on operations, gowned and gloved, and offer his support to the surgeons and nurses. Soon, too, he would be forced to think of other matters, of the names he had gathered, and how these lives might be taken.

While Gino Fosse sat listening to John Coltrane racing through 'Giant Steps', he felt a sense of wonder. On the walls were the photographs, the constant, nagging reminder of his duty. Here too were the tools of his new trade: the ropes; the drugs he had carefully smuggled out of the hospital for when his own considerable strength was insufficient; the nine-millimetre M9 Beretta automatic pistol he had stolen on a visit to the army hospital next to San Giovanni – he enjoyed the idea it should have virtually the same name as the cardinal's three-pointed hat; and the knives – large and small, slender and broad, all sharpened so delicately that he was able to believe there existed but a single atom at the edge of the blade, one that would slice through anything it encountered.

The hospital had need of him for the rest of the morning. But from lunchtime onwards he was free, and there was much to do.

Twenty-two

Publicity mattered. Alicia Vaccarini learned that two months after she had won the parliamentary deputy's seat for the Northern Alliance in Bologna. It took that long for one of the local rags to uncover the truth about her private life: that the former university professor was a lesbian with a string of lovers, some of whom were only too willing to talk in return for a little money. The Northern Alliance had a firm position about 'aberrant behaviour'. It did not approve. In a few brief, heady weeks Vaccarini had gone from being the fêted victor in a marginal seat to an outcast inside her own party.

When the central committee organizer had marched into her office to say she would not be chosen for re-election at the end of her term three years hence she'd complained, bitterly, 'Why didn't you ask?'

The cold, hard man had stared and said, simply, 'Why didn't you tell?'

She now had only a year left, a year before unemployment, obscurity, poverty perhaps, at the age of forty-eight. Yet Alicia Vaccarini was a clever woman, a lecturer in economics, a worker of the system. She knew how to get grants out of Brussels. She knew how to sit on committees and wait until the right moment to intervene. She had worked to ensure her future, accepting seats on a variety of bodies, judicial, municipal and even one which had overseen some preliminary discussions about the merging of the Carabinieri with the state police. There had been opportunities, compromises, particularly when she found her decisions had some sway with people of influence, interested parties seeking a certain resolution. From time to time, there had been arrangements which, under a strict reading of the law, were illegal. But these, she reasoned, were the price of political practicality. Whatever the Northern Alliance felt about her now, she had been elected with a duty, to serve those who voted for her in Bologna, and to further her own career. These were not necessarily contradictory. Vaccarini had been careful. None of the current corruption investigations came close to her, nor was it likely they would. When she had intervened she had been careful to ensure that the reward was never obvious: a favour here, a simple, valuable gift or service, or a payment abroad. She had cultivated new and unexpected friends, people who would never have come close to her had she stayed inside the cold, rigid embrace of the Alliance. And there was the irony: some of them were from quarters she would never have done business with before. On the right. On the left. In the higher echelons of the police and the security services. Even in the Vatican. The world was full of people needing a little help, and willing to offer something in return. It was pragmatic to accept these visible flaws in the façade of society and, when appropriate, to use them to one's own ends.

Still, unemployment beckoned. She had hoped for a position in Brussels: perhaps even the job of minor commissioner. Nothing had happened and the PR people she employed on a tiny retainer thought they knew why. It was the profile that was wrong. She remained, in the public eye, the lesbian from Bologna who had lied to get herself elected. True, she was bright, she knew how to navigate the system. She was, in many ways, a hard-working, dedicated Italian politician. Nevertheless the stain of her sexuality, and the way she had hidden her true self for personal gain, continued to taint perceptions. Without some more favourable press her hopes of a continued political career were unrealistic.

This was the reason, the only reason, why Alicia Vaccarini now sat at a table in a deserted Martelli's, the restaurant in the narrow alley around the corner from the Parliament building which, during the week, was the workers' dining hall for deputies, journalists and political hangers-on.

'I didn't even know this place opened on Sundays,' she said, lighting a cigarette.

The journalist said he was from *Time* magazine. Now she was here, Vaccarini realized she should have checked. There were some jokers out there. People with hidden tape recorders who tried to embarrass you into making stupid comments then selling them on to the TV and radio stations. This was an oversight on her part but an understandable one. The pranksters had low horizons; they always claimed to come from minor, regional papers, not the bigger ones in Rome and Milan where their false identities would be transparent. To say one was from *Time* was different; it was too bold a claim, surely, to be anything other than genuine. And now she was here Alicia Vaccarini could believe it too. The man was about thirty, well dressed in a casual, Sunday fashion, with a pale rose shirt and blue trousers. He had an anonymous face, handsome in a vapid if somewhat exaggerated way, with dark, intelligent eyes and a quick, slightly nervous smile. Only one thing stood out: he seemed too big for his clothes. His muscles bulged against his shirt sleeves, he held himself in an awkward, stiff fashion. He looked like someone who endured work-outs in spite of himself, endowing a body that was meant to be more slight with a physicality that didn't quite fit. And there was a smell too. Like some kind of liniment or a chemical that belonged in a hospital.

'It doesn't open normally,' he said in a measured, educated voice. 'You're witnessing the power of the American media, Deputy.'

She laughed and looked around. There was only one other couple dining on the far side of the room. 'I could almost believe that.'

'I thought you'd like privacy,' he said.

'Why?' she asked, heart sinking. 'I told you on the phone. If you're looking for some kind of dyke confession piece, if you think I'm going to pour my pink heart out in public, you've got the wrong person. That part of my story has been done to death and I'm very happy to leave it in the grave.'

He raised a glass of red wine. 'Me too.'

She joined him in the drink. It tasted good. Alicia Vaccarini realized she felt like some wine. There was nothing else to do in the city that afternoon. It was too hot to think straight. The Parliament was closed. The private work which had kept her in the city was finished. She could afford to be lazy.

'What I want is to talk about you. The real you. What

you believe. What you want to achieve. Where you see your life going after your term as deputy is over.'

'And this is going to make a story for *Time* magazine?' she asked.

He frowned and poured some more wine from the carafe. The waiter came and placed two plates of pasta on the table. 'You've got me there, Alicia. I'm a fraud. But only up to a point. Every story needs a tag. They want to do some piece about how being gay is no longer a bar to public office in Europe. I need some examples that show the real story. I need to ask the question: what would have happened to you if you'd been heterosexual? If you'd been married, with children, and put in the same kind of work you're doing now?'

'I see.'

He pulled out a small tape recorder and placed it on the table. Then he leaned over and placed his hand on hers. It was, she thought, a very powerful hand.

'Alicia. People like us have to stick together.'

Her eyes widened. 'You're telling me you're gay?'

'You're telling me you didn't know the moment you set eyes on me?'

'No. I mean yes.' She didn't know what she meant at that moment. He seemed a disconcerting person. When she thought about it she was able to think of him as gay. But it required effort and she couldn't help wondering whether this was not some trick on his part; whether he was, in truth, some kind of chameleon who could change his shape, alter his appearance at will.

He pressed the button on the tape recorder. She watched the little wheels whirl.

'Tell me about yourself. Only the things you want to

talk about. Tell me how you became who you are. What you believe in. About your religion.'

'My religion?'

'Everybody believes in something, Alicia. We just have different names for it. You came from a Catholic family. I read that in the files. You must have believed once.'

She nodded. The wine helped her remember. There had been a time when she was convinced by all those old stories, when they gave her some comfort in the lonely, dark nights of childhood.

'Of course. And then you get older.'

'Wiser?'

'I didn't say that.'

'And then you get older still, and sometimes it comes back.' He paused. 'Do you think that might happen to you?'

'Who knows?' she said lazily, feeling the wine go to her head, liking this strange young man, who was not really gay, she thought, simply very good at lulling an interviewee into believing whatever was appropriate for an easy conversation.

'Doubt is a virtue,' he said firmly as the meat course arrived: grilled lamb with artichokes. 'It's better to believe than to know.'

Alicia Vaccarini laughed. 'Quite. Are you really a journalist?'

'What else could I be?'

'A priest, I think. I could imagine you in black. Taking confession. Listening.'

He stopped eating and considered this. 'Perhaps I could be a priest. But not today. And I don't want to hear confessions, Alicia. Confessions are tiresome, whining things, surely.' He looked at her frankly. 'Confessions won't rebuild your career. Only the truth may do that.'

'Only the truth will set you free!' she said, deciding she would get a little drunk, because it was that kind of day.

'Precisely,' he said, suddenly very serious. 'Now talk, please. Of yourself. Of what you wish to become.'

The carafe was refilled. After the meat there was *zabaglione* and *grappa*, though she felt she drank more than he did. Alicia Vaccarini began to talk, more freely than she had recently with anyone, in the media or outside it, not caring what the little tape recorder heard. This odd young man, with his considerate, priestly manner, was excellent company, a sounding board who listened closely to everything she said, criticizing when he thought it appropriate, praising when he felt praise was due.

The afternoon disappeared in a whirl of one-sided conversation. When he paid the bill it was approaching four o'clock. She felt wonderful, elated, released of some unconscious burden that had been haunting her for years.

They walked outside. The heat of the day was beginning to fade. This part of the city was empty. The day was so hot it shuddered in front of her eyes. She was reluctant to return to the cramped, stuffy apartment in the Via Cavour that was her solitary home.

Her companion pointed down the narrow alley adjoining the restaurant.

'Alicia,' he said. 'It's such a lovely afternoon. I have my car here. Let's walk by the river for a while. Drink some coffee. Eat some ice cream. You're such excellent company. Would you like that? Please?'

She nodded, liking him all the more, and followed as he entered the shade of the alley, disappearing into the darkness. The alley grew dark and unexpectedly cold. There was the smell of damp in the air. Finally she saw him, standing by his vehicle. It was not a car but a small van, with windows in the back, the kind used by tradesmen. He was not smiling.

She walked up to him, wondering what accounted for the change in his face, which was now very serious, now looking at her in a way – was this distaste? – she did not recognize.

This stranger put his hand into his pocket and pulled something out: a plastic bag containing a piece of white material. There was that smell again, the one which seemed to belong in a hospital.

She wanted to run but she was too drunk. She wanted to shout but there was nothing to say, no one to hear it.

The white cloth came up to her face and the hospital smell filled her head. Alicia Vaccarini wondered stupidly why all the oxygen had just disappeared from the world then felt the blackness start to creep into her head, steadily, with a rushing, roaring sound, in from the corners of her vision, devouring her consciousness.

When she awoke, after an unfathomable period of time, she was in a small, brightly lit circular room, tied to a chair, surrounded by images: photographs and paintings, some so strange she refused to look at them, not daring to let their content enter her head. Music was playing from behind her: hard bop, fast and edgy. Someone was humming to the long complex solo, note for note.

A cloth gag was tied tightly around her mouth. Her hands were bound behind her back. Her ankles were secured firmly to the legs of her chair.

She tried to speak. The words came out as a pathetic

grunt. The figure emerged from behind her. In his right hand was a long butcher's knife. In his left a sharpening rod which he stroked quickly and professionally with the blade.

'You're awake,' he said, nodding to drive home his point. 'Good. We have much to discuss, and much to achieve.'

Twenty-three

Falcone glowered at the three names on the desk, names Nic Costa had provided in his report. He had assembled a team of sixteen for the investigation: all men. They sat in the briefing room smoking, drinking coffee, feeling uncomfortable. The air-conditioning was struggling to keep ahead of the heat. The atmosphere in the station was tense, unpleasant and desperate. They knew when they were grasping at straws.

'Is this all?' Falcone asked Costa.

'How many are there supposed to be?' Falcone had to learn that pressure wasn't the only option. There were other ways of getting what you wanted, Costa thought. Perhaps more efficient ones.

'I don't know,' Falcone grumbled. 'Do you think she's telling the truth?'

He thought about this. 'I don't think she's lying.' Sara had dictated the names very carefully over coffee, spelling out the addresses, giving a short rundown of the details of the relationships. Two of them were married. All were people she had met in some kind of professional capacity, as if she had no private life of her own at all. No relationship appeared to have lasted more than a few weeks. Most puzzling of all for Costa, she seemed non-plussed by this, as if it were normal to lead such an empty, two-dimensional existence.

'That wasn't what I asked,' Falcone complained.

'I know. What I was trying to say was that these people check out. We've spoken to them. They acknow-ledge what went on, even the married ones. They all have alibis for the period we can fix absolutely – those hours when he must have been in the church on Tiber Island. I'm not saying none of them is a suspect but they look more like possible victims to me. The way they leapt at the idea of protection certainly seems to suggest so.'

Falcone raised a heavy eyebrow at Rossi. 'Are you going along with that? He's doing a lot of the talking these days.'

'He's not saying anything I wouldn't,' the big man grunted. 'I go along with it all.'

Falcone looked at the list again. 'A judge. Some bureaucrat from the Finance Ministry. And this last one? It doesn't even say what he does.'

'Toni Ferrari,' Rossi said, reading from his notes. 'Creepy little stockbroker. Skinny string of piss. Believe me, he isn't up for this. Almost wet himself when I said he could be next in line.'

Falcone grimaced. 'What connects them? Why these men?'

'They asked her out,' Costa answered. 'She said yes.'

'Denney? Any connection there? These are just the kind of people he used to mix with.'

'Nothing that we can see or they admit to,' Costa replied. 'There's nothing like the link Rinaldi had. They've been near no judicial commission. As far as we can see they don't have any connection with the Banca Lombardia.'

'So that's it? She just meets these people, sleeps with them for a while and then it ends?'

Luca Rossi stabbed the air with his finger. 'At their insistence,' he said. 'Every one of them I talked to said that. It just got too freaky for them. She'd turn up on dates. She'd smile and talk all the way through. She'd sleep with them, and I get the impression that was no bad thing either. But it was as if there was something missing. Here. One of them said this . . .'

He searched through the notes. 'The Finance Ministry guy. He said, after a while it was like taking out some woman from an escort agency. Just impersonal. Even a man gets to tire of that eventually.'

'Guess he must have known what it was like though,' Falcone said. 'Could that be what she is? Some college professor who's a high-class hooker on the side?'

Costa groaned. 'Please. Why would she do that? The apartment's hers, bought with her own money, no mortgage, from the inheritance she got from her parents when she turned twenty-one. If she doesn't need the cash, what's the point? Because she likes it?'

'I've heard stranger things,' Luca Rossi said. 'Do you understand what's going on in her head?'

Costa said nothing.

'Check it out anyway. There are people out there who would know. What about one-night stands?' Falcone asked. 'Did she say anything about that?'

Costa hadn't pressed the point. She didn't want to go there; he didn't want to hear the answers. 'Nothing. I don't think they happened.'

'So what do we have?' Falcone wondered. 'A woman

who sleeps around casually. Nothing unusual there. A good-looking woman, someone people want to be seen with for a while. And then they get bored, or they get scared, and just fade into the background. Except one of them remains obsessed, one of them doesn't want this to end, or if he does he wants to make sure she remembers him. He'll do anything to make his point to her. Kill people. Do it in a way designed to make her sit up and take notice because it ties in with what she does. But . . .'

'She didn't finish with people,' Rossi said. 'They finished with her. All of them. Isn't that what she said?'

'Yes,' Costa admitted.

Falcone threw the sheaf of notes onto the far side of his desk. 'Then she's lying. She has to be. All of these men, the ones we know about, don't want to go near her. There has to be more. She's got to know. What about the apartment?'

Costa was lost. 'The apartment . . . ?'

Furillo, one of the men Falcone had brought in that morning at San Clemente, said, 'Nothing to go whoopee about.'

'You've searched her apartment? You did that while I was with her? That was the point?'

Falcone stared at him. 'This is turning into a serial murder investigation, kid. We don't have time for the niceties.'

'If you'd asked her . . .'

'She might have said no. And then we'd have got permission anyway. What makes you think we have time to wait around like that? Two days, four people dead. He could be back at work somewhere out there right now.'

Costa was silent. Falcone was right.

'One thing,' Furillo added. 'We found a mobile

hidden in a drawer in the bedroom. Not her normal phone. We called the number we had and checked. This thing didn't ring and it's locked by a code. Technical said they couldn't crack it. Doesn't store numbers either so we don't know who she's called or who's called her. Neat, if you want to make sure no one knows who you're talking to.'

Rossi was unimpressed. 'A phone in a drawer? Maybe it's just an old one she put away.'

'It's fully charged,' Furillo said. 'It's still got the sticker on the back saying it came from Monaco. Why would you have a phone from Monaco in your bedroom drawer?'

Falcone grimaced. 'That's it? Nothing else?'

'Nothing.'

Falcone watched them for a while and they knew what he wanted: suggestions. No one was willing to play the game. If Sara Farnese was keeping something from them there was precious little they could use to sweat it out of her.

'I'm taking her into protective custody,' Falcone announced eventually. 'Get some safe house somewhere. Not a nice one either. I don't want her comfortable.'

'It won't work,' Costa objected.

'Why?'

'Because . . .' He knew the answer. It was obvious. Falcone knew it too. 'Because she will only tell us when she wants to tell us. She won't break just because we pile on the pressure. She's not like that.'

Luca Rossi agreed. 'He's right. I've been watching that woman since we first saw her in the library. She holds it all inside and she's going to keep it there until she chooses to let it out. The tougher we make life for her, the harder it gets.'

'Then what?' Falcone demanded. 'She can't go back to that apartment. The media's camped out in the street. And she is, like it or not, potentially under threat.'

Costa thought of his father, how the old man's calm was perhaps what was needed. The house on the Appian Way had the room. There was privacy. It could be perfect.

'You're trying to drive this man to me, right?'

'The TV pictures I saw weren't wonderful,' Falcone moaned. 'Maybe they'll have something better on a different station. You could have got in a bit closer. You could have made it look more obvious.'

'Whatever. We can kill two birds with one stone. Let her stay at my father's place for a while. I can be there. If he's coming for her, he'll find out too. If you want to whet his appetite, what better way could there be? He could take his pick.'

'This is Red Marco, right?' Falcone said sourly. 'The commie with the big farm out in the country?'

'Most of which he rebuilt with his own hands if you want to know. Sir . . .' Costa was not taking that. He knew the real story behind the farm and it was nothing like the scurrilous gossip that the papers had made up.

Falcone smiled. It didn't make anyone in the room feel any happier. 'Oh, that could work. We can pump up the press with it. We can put you right in his sights. There's still time for the evening news. Is this place easy to cover? My guess is we'll get one chance with this lunatic and I don't want it thrown away.'

Costa thought of the untidy sprawl of farmland, enclosed by rickety fences. It wasn't ideal but it was manageable. 'We'll need plenty of people on the ground.'

'My, my,' Falcone said. 'I hope it's worth the expense.'

They waited.

'Do it,' he said. 'And you go break the news that she's going to be your house guest. If you're right, maybe she really will talk to one person and one person alone when she feels like it. Make sure it's you.'

'Sir,' he said.

'And Furillo?'

The detective nodded.

'Use this time productively. Go through that apartment of hers again. Go through it until you find something else. On with it!'

The team rose. Falcone looked at Costa and Rossi getting ready to leave. 'You two. We'll drop into my office on the way. There's one more thing.'

They walked down the corridor into the small, neat room where Falcone worked, Nic Costa wondering all the time how he would manage to sell this idea to her. Falcone closed the door and went to the desk. There he opened a drawer and took out a video cassette.

'This came in marked for your attention this morning, Costa. I took the liberty of opening it. Save you the trouble.'

Costa looked at the video. There was no label on it, nothing to indicate where it came from. Falcone handed it to him and nodded at the VCR in the corner. Then they watched the tape: three minutes of it, every second so gripping Costa couldn't took his eyes off the screen. When it was done he looked at Luca Rossi. The big man's face was deathly white. These were images the big man did not want to recall.

It was a composite of several scenes, culled from at

least four different cameras, and covered Stefano Rinaldi's time in the Vatican Library from the moment he walked through the main doors to the time of his bloody death, with the skin of Hugh Fairchild spread out on the desk before him. Sara had been right. He hadn't intended to kill her. The gun he held was going towards his own head. Rinaldi was trying to commit suicide on someone else's orders, someone he felt could see him through the security system and would, perhaps, let his own wife live in return. His eyes, dark, haunted eyes, caught the lens in every scene; in one, as he entered the Reading Room, he even nodded at the camera.

'So?' Falcone asked. 'What does that tell us?'

'That it was the video system he was trying to convince,' Costa said immediately. 'Not the people in the room. He checked the position of the video all the time. When he whispered to Sara he didn't even seem to notice them. He turned his back to the camera. It was deliberate.'

Falcone agreed. 'Exactly. So, rightly or wrongly, he believed someone who had access to that system would know whether he was doing the right thing or not. And?'

Costa's head was a blur. He couldn't think this through and Rossi wasn't helping. The big man was looking at him, horrified.

'Tell him,' Falcone barked at Rossi.

'Jesus, kid,' the big man moaned. 'Think about it. You've been stirring things in places we never want to go. Someone in the Vatican knows something. Furthermore, someone in the Vatican likes you. Likes you enough to send you this tape. Are they the same person? Or is it two different people working in opposite directions? What did you do after I left you yesterday?'

'I went and talked to Hanrahan,' Costa admitted. 'Why not? He knows stuff.'

'You leave this alone,' Falcone insisted. 'I talk to Mr Hanrahan. In my time. On my conditions. I don't want any more secret visits, you hear?'

Costa nodded and wondered how Falcone seemed to know, with such certainty, that he had returned to see Hanrahan again even before he admitted it.

Falcone walked to him and patted his arm. It was an oddly unfamiliar gesture. 'One step at a time, Nic,' he said. 'You've got enough on your plate with that woman. Talk to her. Make her feel at home. Make her feel you're her friend. She knows someone inside that place. Understand?'

'Yes,' Nic Costa grunted. But Falcone wasn't listening. He had turned the TV onto another news channel. It was coverage of Costa and Sara Farnese leaving the church that morning, with a voice-over story that was grossly lurid even for one of the Rome channels. The camera lingered on Sara, trying to catch her face as she ducked and turned from the pack. Then the picture turned shakily to him. Nic Costa was unable to place this moment. It must have happened accidentally. He had his arm around her, affectionately it seemed. She was clinging to his body. They looked like lovers.

In a moment that was quite foreign to him he smiled at the camera. A smile that was not his, an actor's smile, one that left little doubt as to its meaning. It was knowing, proprietorial. It said: *I own this troubled, dangerous woman, and I can do with her what I want.*

He watched himself on the TV and hated what he saw,

wondering what she would make of it, and how he could apologize sufficiently.

'Now that,' Falcone said, 'is good. That can change things.'

Twenty-four

He had given her some water and a piece of bread, allowed her to go to the bathroom, though strictly under his supervision, and he had watched, a little too closely she thought. Then he had led her back, kicked the chair across the room until it stood next to a black, upright beam, and tethered her tightly to the arms. Her hands remained bound throughout, with a loose rope around her ankles to prevent her trying to run. This was, in any case, not an option. They were in some strange medieval room, an upstairs octagonal chamber littered with rubbish: books and video tapes, CDs, clothes and, on the walls, photographs, everywhere, some of a woman she vaguely recognized.

The pictures continued to alarm her. Alicia Vaccarini refused to look too closely.

In the corner a narrow, circling staircase led to the room below, to the outside world and freedom. Some way distant, it had to be. As soon as he took off the gag she had screamed until her lungs hurt, bellowing for help, yelling murder, murder, murder. He just stood there, watching, not smiling, not angry. Waiting for the fury to subside. When she was done, when there was no more breath left in her body, he shook his head and said, 'No one can hear, Alicia.'

She had screamed again at that, until her voice went hoarse. He had hardly paid any attention, half watching the movie on the TV somewhere behind her head. She recognized the film from the soundtrack. It was Pasolini's *The Gospel According to Saint Matthew*, the arrival of the three wise men to the accompaniment of the old Negro spiritual 'Sometimes I Feel like a Motherless Child'. He seemed affected by it somehow; she wondered how to turn this to her advantage. How she might get out of the stuffy, airless tower alive.

Then he switched channels, over to one of the mainstream stations which was showing a soccer match. It was a deliberate act, one with a point. It said there was something to be done.

Gino Fosse picked up a low wooden stool, brought it in front of her, sat down and took her head in his strong, pale hands.

'You thought I was a priest, Alicia.'

She was too frightened to say anything, too confused to second-guess what he wanted.

'Well?' he insisted.

He waited. Perhaps her silence would make him angry.

'You looked like one,' she said. 'For a little while.'

'Then confess to me,' he said. 'Confess everything.'

'What do you want me to say?'

'The truth.'

He was crazy, she knew that. But there was some strong, linear logic in what he sought. If she found what that was, perhaps there could be some hope of survival.

'I have sinned, Father,' she said.

'*Don't call me "Father"!*' Gino Fosse's bellows echoed off the walls of the tiny, octagonal chamber. His face contorted with fury. She was silent. She waited, watching him make some purposeful effort to control his emotions.

'I'm sorry,' she said softly.

'Not your fault. My anger wasn't directed at you. Just talk to me, Alicia. Confess.'

The tears were starting to burn in her eyes. She racked her head trying to think of something that would satisfy him.

'I've committed unnatural acts.'

'Of course,' he said. 'And you'll be forgiven. But these are small things.'

It was impossible to know, she thought. No one was free of private vices, no one lacked a history he or she would not care to share with the world. 'Help me. Please.'

He nodded his head, understanding what she required. 'Four months ago,' he said, 'you sat on a judicial committee looking into the question of diplomatic immunity for certain people. You recall this?'

'Yes.'

'There were decisions made, votes taken. Were all of them based on fairness? Or did you seek, and get, some reward for some of your actions?'

'Denney,' she said, feeling cold.

'No names!'

'I didn't know the rest of them would vote against me. I thought . . . I was given to understand they'd received the same favours. They'd go the same way.'

His dark eyes regarded her coldly. 'Judges and deputies. Lawyers and "*public servants*".' Spittle flecked his

181

lips when he said the last. Some deep, inner hatred surfaced within Gino Fosse and she knew, at that moment, this was hopeless. He would do whatever he planned to do because his mind was made up. The rest was an act, a show for his conscience, not hers.

'I did what I promised,' she insisted. 'I can't be held responsible for other people.'

'There was a price, Alicia. For you. And for those involved. What was that price?'

'Money,' she said. 'Don't ask how much. I can't remember. Not a lot, I don't think.'

'And?'

He knew. He had to have some prior knowledge. It was a wonder to her. She had believed this had been so private. She thought of the photographs on the wall. It was possible . . .

'I was provided with some personal entertainment.'

His dark eyebrows rose. ' "Personal entertainment"? Specify, please.'

'They sent me a woman for the night. She didn't mind. What's it to you?'

His hand came out from his side and slapped her hard across the cheek.

'What's it to me?' he demanded. 'I drove her there, Alicia. I was a party to that act. I thought I understood what was happening. I didn't. Just as you understand nothing, regret nothing, feel no sense of anguish for what you've done. This man you talk about. I still can't see him walking down the street. I still can't touch him, Alicia. There was such a great cost for your favours. You took so much and gave back nothing.'

'I'm sorry,' she said. 'I'm truly sorry. If there's some

way I can make amends. If it's a question of paying back the money.'

'Money.' He stared at her, his face full of pity. 'You think it's so important. You have no idea of how pathetic you are. Or how grateful you will be to me. And soon.'

Gino Fosse stood up and walked over to the bookshelf in the corner of the room, taking out two thick photographic volumes. He came back and placed them in front of her, opening the first at a double-page spread depicting a church courtyard.

'Santa Cecilia in Trastevere,' he said. 'Do you know it?'

She tried to catch his eye, pleading. 'Gino. Let me go. I won't tell anyone. I promise.'

He frowned. He had, she thought, an actor's face. It was so mobile, able to go from passivity to deep concentration in a second, able to change shape, from plainness to a kind of warped beauty with just the shift of an eyelid, a turn of the mouth.

'You must listen. This is important. Cecilia was a family woman. The wife of a nobleman who was converted to Christianity during the persecutions of Diocletian. Her house lay beneath this church. It was here . . .'

He glowered at her. 'You're not listening. I do all this for your benefit *and you're not listening*.'

Alicia Vaccarini was beginning to sob, was unable to stop the choking noise that kept rising in her throat.

He leaned forward to make his point plain. 'She was a martyr, Alicia. She will help wash your sins clean.' He pointed at the book. 'Here in the very place she died, in the very way she went to glory.'

His finger stabbed at the image there: a virginal woman, staring peacefully out from the page.

'First, since she was a high-born woman, they tried to suffocate her in the baths beneath the house, a noble death. When that failed, they were allowed three strokes of the axe. These still did not kill her. There's the miracle. There's the proof. The senators and the patricians came to see her lying in bed, wounded, singing hymns, turning to Christ as she died before them. Afterwards they made her the patron saint of musicians in recognition of her courage. Alicia . . .'

He opened the second book and thrust it in front of her face. She did not wish to look. His strong hand gripped her hair and turned her head to the page. It depicted a beautiful white statue of the prone corpse of a young woman wrapped in a shroud, face half turned away from the beholder.

'In the sixteenth century they opened her casket,' he said. 'Cecilia was incorrupt, perfect, still beautiful in her golden robe thirteen hundred years after her death. The marks of the axe were on her neck. An artist painted her, Alicia. A sculptor made this statue which still sits beneath the altar in her church, above her house.'

'Please,' she gasped. 'Gino . . .'

He took her hand. 'Don't fear. You'll be there tonight. You'll lie in front of her, give homage to her martyrdom. And in doing so you'll make amends, you'll help me put right these wrongs that you're a part of.'

'No . . .'

His face changed again, becoming hard and determined.

'It's time,' he said and went over to one of the windows, retrieved a large pillow from a storage box, returned with it and, very carefully, placed it over her mouth.

Alicia Vaccarini breathed in through the white fabric. It stank of damp and mould. She coughed, retching. He took it away, waiting until she recovered her breath.

'This is the first part.'

The pillow came back, covering her face. She felt something wind around it, something like a rope which fastened the thing behind her head, tightly, but not so hard she couldn't inhale. Not quite.

'Good,' said a voice from behind.

The fabric grew damp and sticky with her saliva. The passage of air seemed to diminish with every snatched effort of her lungs. She gagged, gasping, and felt him tighten the pillow further around her face.

There was one last push. The thing entered her mouth, its fibres stuck to the back of her throat. She threw up bitter bile into the fetid cotton, coughing. Then the rope relaxed, the smothering stopped. Gino Fosse withdrew the stinking, vile object from her face. She fought to get clean air into her lungs, hyperventilating rhythmically as she did so.

'Good,' he said. He now held a long sword in his hand. It was well polished, with a glittering silver blade, like something out of a military museum. With no perceptible effort, holding it in one hand, he raised it to her neck and cut the flesh there in a single, sweeping movement.

Alicia Vaccarini shrieked in agony. She could feel the blood starting to run down her neck, down onto the good, cotton shirt she had chosen to wear for the lunch at Martelli's. It was a painful wound, but a light one. He was testing himself. He stood over her now, wondering about the second blow: how hard, how deep it might be.

'I beg you,' she bawled. 'I'll do anything. Just don't kill me.'

She looked into his eyes. There was confusion there. Perhaps there was some hope. He was no longer focused on her, no longer wondering how deeply he might hack into her neck with the sharp, shiny weapon held in his hand.

Gino Fosse's attention now lay on the television set on the far side of the room, behind her. There was a newscast. She could hear it. There was talk of a murder and a woman, a scarlet woman who, the reporter said, seemed to bring death, a shocking death, to everyone she knew.

He was unable to take his eyes off the set. She heard him catch his breath when he saw whatever was on the screen. He put down the sword. Then he took out a clean, white handkerchief and wiped the blood off her neck.

'I apologize, Alicia,' he said. 'I'm distracted.'

'Untie me,' she pleaded. 'Let me go. I won't tell a soul.'

He looked at her and there was pity in his eyes. 'Tomorrow,' he said, 'I'll do you justice.'

Then he was gone from the room, leaving Alicia Vaccarini to her thoughts and the image from the book: a pale white corpse, wrapped in a delicate shroud, head obscured, waiting for resurrection.

Twenty-five

Sara had swiftly agreed to stay at the house once Falcone had outlined the alternative: protective custody in some safe house in one of the city's grimmer suburbs. At Nic Costa's insistence they had watched the TV news in the station before leaving. He didn't want her to find out accidentally. He also wanted her to understand that the media would follow them to the farm, where they would be carefully herded into a well-controlled position by Falcone's men.

She took in the TV clip, and the possessive way in which it portrayed him, with her customary passivity. Costa apologized. Sara said, simply, 'It's your job, isn't it? But I don't understand why you think he'll come. If there are so many police around and the press too. It would be stupid.'

'It's a gamble,' he replied, trying to convince himself. 'I guess we're hoping he can't resist taking a look.'

This was the best he could do. Falcone was, he judged, either clutching at straws or playing some deeper game altogether.

He'd told her about Marco in the car, withholding nothing. To his surprise she'd turned to stare at him and there was something new in her eyes, a different expression, of sympathy and perhaps something more: understanding.

'What do you want me to do? How do I talk to him?' she asked.

'I don't have an easy answer for that. At least I never found one myself. Treat him as if nothing's different. I think he likes that. He likes to amuse, too, and be amused.'

She was silent for the rest of the journey. Fifteen minutes later they left the city, entered the countryside off the Appian Way, and passed through the media posse at the front gate.

Bea was at the big barn-door entrance, waiting. She wore a gaudy floral shirt and cream trousers. Her tanned arms were crossed. She seemed ambivalent about welcoming a stranger into the house.

'How is he?' Nic asked. The inevitable question.

'Hungry. Or so he says. You kept him waiting.'

'Sorry.' He glanced at Sara. 'We have a visitor.'

'So I gather.' She held out her slim hand and examined Sara Farnese frankly. 'Don't let the old devil talk you into giving him wine. Or anything else for that matter. He's sick but he's not beyond mischief. And mind the dog. He's funny with women. It's a family trait.'

There was a scratching from behind the half-closed door. A paw worked its way around the woodwork and made the gap wide enough for a small body to squirm through. Pepe saw Bea and sat immediately, emitting a low growl.

'See what I mean?' Bea asked.

Sara reached down and touched the creature's head. It watched her warily then lifted its chin, deigning to be stroked. It had typical terrier colouring: white, brown and black, now tinged with the distinct grey of age.

'You seem to be accepted,' Bea said, surprised. 'It's a rare honour. I've known that beast for a decade or more and it's only in the last few months he's stopped trying to savage me.'

Sara smiled and stroked the dog more fondly. He closed his eyes, delighted. 'Dogs are easier than people,' she said.

'This is the Costa household,' Bea replied. ' "Easy" never comes into it. Am I right, Nic?'

'No argument there.' He kissed her cheek. 'Thanks, Bea. You can come tomorrow? I don't want to press you if it's awkward.'

'I don't want to be anywhere else,' she said, and Sara noticed how she failed to meet his eyes when she said this. 'It's just selfish, I know. You can't keep me out.'

'I wouldn't dream of trying. He needs you. We all do. We always have.'

'The ever loyal servant,' she said, with a measure of bitterness. 'I'm sorry. I . . .'

She walked briskly to her car, shaking her head. Sara watched her go. She was an intense person, she thought. But Bea needed the Costa family as much as they needed her.

The dog looked at her, barked once, then turned into the house. Sara followed him inside and walked straight to Marco Costa in his wheelchair, taking his hand, smiling, full of a level of small talk Nic had never expected. While he took her bags upstairs, Marco guided her around the ground floor, the dog following on faithfully behind in his tracks. His son then did the same for the rest of the sprawling house. She was staying in

Giulia's room on the first floor, one of six, at the far end from his own. It was private, with its own bath, and, like the house itself, secure. There was only the single barn door into the farm. Marco had insisted on the authentic, bucolic design for all its inconveniences. His son was satisfied that it was a good choice for the purpose he had outlined to Falcone and surprised too to find that he was looking at the place in a different way through Sara's enthusiastic eyes. When the tour was over she followed him downstairs looking more content than at any time since they had first met. This was, he realized from what she had told him about herself, something foreign to her: a home.

Marco Costa dressed for dinner: a white shirt, impeccably pressed by Bea, black trousers and a silk neck scarf which hid the scar of an operation. The old man had combed his thinning hair carefully. The spotlights in the farmhouse kitchen made his face seem cruelly cadaverous. Nic Costa had grown up seeing his father's round, caring, persistent features at every turn of his life. They were losing their form now under the punishment of the disease. The generous skin was sagging, as if something was removing the vitality that lay beneath the surface. And this was an entirely physical ailment. His father's personality, so warm when he wished it to be, and his quick intelligence were undiminished.

The three of them sat around the table eating pasta and salad and Nic Costa was astonished to find that he was the one feeling uncomfortable. Sara and his father seemed to have come to accept each other, as if they recognized some mutual trait.

'You've a beautiful house,' she said.

'We built it,' Marco boasted. 'Most of it, anyway. All

with local stone. There's masonry here that Seneca might have touched. Forget all the nonsense the press wrote about Red Marco and his country palace. When I bought this plot no one wanted to live here and it cost me next to nothing. I don't care what it's worth now. What you see is what we created, through our own labour, with no help from anyone.'

'Oh yes,' Nic agreed. 'No arguing there. I spent five years sleeping in a bedroom without heating, next to a bathroom with no running water. We were given a fine proletarian upbringing.'

'Quite right too,' his father declared.

'Except,' Nic objected, 'I seem to recall you grew up in a nice, comfortable council apartment . . .'

'Which is why I knew what was best for my own offspring. Look at this place, Nic. It's too familiar for you to see it properly but I can still remember how much we put into it. I can look at some of the brickwork and recall your mother laying in the mortar. I can touch something you plastered, and pretty well too, when you were thirteen. You could have made a builder. Instead it's his sister who's the artisan. I'll show you her paintings later. She gets that from her mother. Whatever *he* has comes from me, I guess.'

Sara raised a glass to them both. 'I don't think either of you have much to complain about.'

'No,' Marco replied, looking at his son with an obvious measure of pride. 'I don't believe we have.'

'Drink,' the old man added mournfully, watching the red wine in her glass. 'Lost pleasures.' He looked at her frankly. 'My son tells me you never had a home like this. Your parents died when you were young.'

She shrugged. It occurred to Nic that she was never

unwilling to talk about herself. What was missing, all too often, were the details, which had to be prised from her carefully, one at a time. 'I don't recall ever living at home with them. I was at a convent school in Paris in the early years. There was an accident.'

'I can't imagine what that would be like,' Marco said.

'The nuns were kind to me. I never lacked anything. Money least of all.'

'Money and happiness,' the old man declared, 'exist apart from each other. When I was in politics I met some of the richest and most miserable men in Italy. Five minutes' walk from that door I could take you to people who are dirt poor and wouldn't exchange their lives with anyone's.'

'Money *with* happiness,' Nic said. 'I think that's the goal.'

'Really?' His father looked disappointed. 'Why? Money's something you can strive for, something you can make yourself. Happiness, in my experience, only comes from others, when they decide to give it to you. You can't force people to do that, not even with money, though there's plenty out there who seem to think otherwise. It has to be earned and that's what makes it worthwhile.'

Sara finished her wine. Nic refilled the glass. She was dressed down tonight: a blue shirt with an exotic pattern, dark trousers. She looked young, naïve almost. She was relaxed too; the hard mask she wore so much of the time was gone. He wondered about her life; why no man had come to fill it properly, and, against his own instincts, could not help but wonder what was needed for that role. There would be pre-conditions. Honesty lay at the base of any relationship. He felt that strongly, so strongly it had ruined several of the liaisons he had enjoyed in the past. To love someone demanded more than physical attraction. There had to be some closeness, some pact of alliance against the cold, inexplicable vagaries of the world. Without those any affair was, it seemed to him, doomed to be a brief, shallow ghost of passion, something Sara Farnese seemed to know well.

'Is that what a family's for?' she asked. 'To give you that love?'

'Ideally,' Marco agreed. 'I hope we did that. Not perfectly perhaps, but then families aren't about perfection. They're about trying.' He stared at Nic. 'Any complaints?'

'You made me read Marx when I was ten.'

'And the Bible would have been worse?'

He thought about this. 'Probably not. I was ten. I wouldn't have taken much notice of either.'

'So there. Where's the harm? But don't think families are some kind of magic formula for happiness. They can cure you, they can kill you too when they go wrong.' The old man saw her reaction and grimaced. 'Sorry, I was being stupid.'

'Why?' Nic asked. 'It's true. You should see some of the families I meet.'

'But the alternative,' she said, 'is to walk down the middle. You know the highs. You know the lows. I don't really. It's like being . . . incomplete somehow. You're lucky. Both of you.'

The two men glanced uneasily at each other. It had not been the most comfortable of relationships at times and each bore equal weight of guilt and resentment for some of the arguments that had occurred in the past. In the present circumstances these seemed petty matters.

There was a reckoning coming, and certain things needed to be said.

'You're right, we're lucky,' Marco Costa said, watching her wine glass enviously. 'I'm a stubborn old man who always thought he knew what was best for the world. I don't imagine that made me an easy person at times.'

'You can say that again,' Nic agreed. 'But that was never the problem. It was the fact we always lived under your shadow. We were always the offspring of Red Marco, the man in the papers, the one who made the headlines. We were never individuals in our own right. We were parts of you. I know that wasn't your intention but it's what happened and it was hard. To have parents you loved so much you couldn't quite separate their identity from your own.'

The old man laughed. 'Now I understand! You see what this woman does? Tells us something we should all have seen years ago. I bring you three up as good revolutionaries. And what do you become? A cop, an American lawyer and an artist, and you do this in order to say, "We are ourselves." Good for you, son. More power to your elbow.'

Nic smiled. It was, he thought, the first time he had ever heard his father approve explicitly of his career.

Marco raised his glass to Sara. 'And thanks to you too. For extracting this from us. You grew up in a convent. Is this the Christian in you?'

'You mean do I believe?'

'Exactly!' It was as if no one had ever asked her.

'I suppose so,' she answered. 'I go to church sometimes. I pray and it makes me feel better, though I'm not so sure I think there's a God. If there were, he would surely do something about the state of the world. That old excuse about free will isn't good enough. Still, as a way of explaining why we live, why we do what we do, it has a point. And they're very beautiful stories, some of them anyway. I always thought that as a child when they were read to me in the convent. Beauty counts. I don't know anything better.'

Marco stared out of the window, into the darkness, thinking. 'I suppose I'm meant to argue it's politics. Communism or social democracy. I don't think I have the energy any more.'

Nic felt a dark thought rising at the back of his head. 'You're kidding me?'

'No. Oh, it's not the sickness, Nic. It's just being realistic. What matters, I think, is that you believe in something, and something that's not too comfortable, something that keeps you awake at night from time to time. If that's religion, so be it. I never took you into that chapel down the road but you know the story, surely? That it was where Peter stopped while fleeing Rome, and Christ appeared to him. "Domine, Quo Vadis?" he asked. Lord, where are you going? And what did Jesus say? "To Rome to be crucified again." It's just a story, of course. That doesn't make it any the less powerful. The Church then wasn't what it is now. Peter would surely be horrified if he saw what's been built in his name in the Vatican. These people were revolutionaries. They were trying to change the entire Roman state, and the world after that. They weren't persecuted for no reason. Their beliefs were dangerous, treasonable. What the story of Quo Vadis is about is not giving up, not turning round when you're in trouble. Remembering that people have made sacrifices to get you where you are. Sometimes the biggest sacrifice of all.'

He closed his eyes briefly. Nic wondered if he was in pain. 'I haven't told you this before,' he said. 'But that was why I bought this plot of land. Because it was so close to that chapel. I thought it would serve as a reminder in the hard times, and it did. You know something else? If I'd been alive then I would have joined them. I would have been a Christian too. Maybe things will change sometime and people like me will take to it again. I don't know, but I do know we all need some kind of faith.'

'What's yours now?' Sara asked carefully. 'The same as you always believed?'

'That's a dead faith,' he answered. 'It killed itself before any of us ever had the chance to understand if it would work.'

He looked at his son. 'My faith rests in my children. This one in particular. One day Nic will find his calling. Perhaps in the police, where he'll cast out all those crooked bastards who give this country a bad name. Perhaps elsewhere. I don't know but I have faith it will happen, even if he doesn't believe it himself.'

There was a knock on the door.

'I'll get it,' Nic said. 'There are too many confessions for me tonight.'

They watched him go to the front of the house, take his police pistol out of the shoulder holster that lay on his carefully folded jacket, and gingerly open the door latch. There was an exchange of low, male voices.

He came back and said, 'Someone needs to see me. Outside. He doesn't want to come into the house. There's a guard by the door. Keep it locked. I'll let myself in. You don't have to wait up.'

Marco Costa nodded at the dog. 'Don't worry. We've got protection.'

Sara laughed. Nic looked at the two of them and the animal, its head cocked to one side, peering at him. He tried to understand why they should be so comfortable in each other's company. Then he mumbled an excuse and was gone.

'Did I make him feel awkward?' the old man asked, feeding the rest of his food to the dog.

'A little, I think,' she said. 'There's a conversation he needs to have with you. He can't do it with me around.'

Marco Costa's shoulders rose. A dry laugh emerged from his throat. 'Sara. Without you around we would never have spoken like that at all. That was the frankest talk we've had in years. You were the catalyst. We're both grateful.'

She was flattered by his compliment. 'I did nothing, but if that nothing helped I'm glad.'

He nodded at the bottle. 'Now I'll have some wine.'

She snatched it away from his grasping hand. 'No.'

'Whose house is this, girl?' he demanded. 'For pity's sake. You can't refuse a dying man a glass.'

'Convince your son of that, not me.' She started to clear the table of the plates, the glasses and the wine. 'If he doesn't want you drinking, he's got a reason.'

'I suppose a cigarette's out of the question then? It's medicinal.'

'Medicinal cigarettes?'

'These ones are. All the way from Morocco. Or Afghanistan if you prefer.'

She tut-tutted and loaded the dishwasher. 'Are you serious? Your son's a policeman.'

'It eases the pain. Really it does.'

'No!'

'Jesus,' Marco Costa moaned. 'Relax. There are no medicinal cigarettes. You know you're the first woman he's brought back that I can't wind around my little finger. What irony.'

Sara returned with a bottle of mineral water and poured some for both of them. 'I don't believe I quite fit that picture. I'm not here under the same circumstances, am I?'

The old man's face hardened in mock anger. 'So, there's something wrong with my son, is there? Not intellectual enough for the likes of you? You should hear him talk about painting. About Caravaggio. That's one legacy I left him. He knows a rebel when he sees one, and he knows a hell of a lot about him.'

She didn't blush. 'I'm not rising to the bait, Marco.'

'Ah. You're thinking he looks down on you for all this publicity.'

She sighed. 'And why shouldn't he? I thought I led a normal life. Now I'm painted like some . . . creature.'

'Pah! The press. If you listen to what they say you'll go crazy. You know what you are. He knows too.'

'Quite. It still shocks him. I see it on his face from time to time. Perhaps he's right.' She toyed with her glass. 'I like being on my own. I don't feel the need to be close to anyone. I can take men, I can leave them. It doesn't bother me.'

'Oh, please,' he groaned. 'The young. They think they invented everything. My dear, I grew up in the Sixties. Can you begin to imagine what our lives were like then? What you think of as promiscuity? Nothing. Nic's mother and I, we went through that in the first five years of our marriage. Talk to Bea about it if you like. She was there. I'm amazed the kids don't remember some of the things that went on.'

She thought of Bea, who said so much without uttering a word. Bea, who would not leave the old man's side. 'Perhaps they do and they're scared to show it.'

'Perhaps,' he acknowledged.

'Bea still loves you nevertheless. You do realize this?'

His face contorted in astonishment. 'What? You can see this? You, who has never met either of us until today? And saw her for, what, just a few minutes in any case?'

He had a point but she was certain of this. Even in the brief time they had met, Bea's devotion was obvious. 'Yes, I could see it. She loves you and regrets it was just a fleeting thing. And there you have the proof. The legacy of your infidelity. And that's nothing?'

'Defeated by your own argument,' he declared. 'I said Bea was there. I never said we were lovers. By the time Bea's feelings for me became apparent – men are deeply stupid on these matters as you doubtless appreciate – Nic's mother and I had realized that way of life was a waste. It had become unimportant to us. We were married, we were lovers but we were friends, allies too. All the other people were a distraction for us. We became monogamous because we wanted to, not through a need for propriety. Who's to say the same won't happen for you?'

'It won't,' she said with some certainty.

'If it does, it's in the future and none of us can see there, Sara. Not even a clever university professor. Mind you, I meant what I said about Nic. He has something in him if only he'd let it out. He has that anger, the same anger I felt, even if he keeps it well hidden.'

'He's afraid.'

'Of what?'

'Losing you.'

'All men fear their fathers' deaths. It's the moment you see your own mortality face to face. You witness a part of yourself dying with them.'

She went back to the counter and poured a glass of wine for herself, then one very small one for him.

'There's more to it than that, Marco.'

'Again? You know this?' he asked, a little angry. 'You, the convent girl who never had a family?'

'I can see what he feels. He's a transparent person in some ways. There's some part of him that's wounded already, in preparation, waiting for the real hurt.'

He grasped the glass of wine, took a tiny sip then pushed it away. 'Then it's time he grew up. We try to be their rock, you know, but even the rock goes in the end. You have to find your own.'

She listened. There were voices a long way off. One was Nic. He sounded angry.

'You know what I thought he would be?' Marco Costa asked. 'What I really feared him becoming when he grew up?'

'I've no idea.'

'A priest. It used to keep me awake at night. Not that he ever expressed any interest. There was just something in his manner. I was a politician. I tried to change big things, not help little people, individuals. You couldn't do both. And frankly I was no good at it. Nic has that gift. When he talks to you he sees you, no one else. He looks right into you, hears things you daren't even say to yourself. And here's another thing. You have that too. So I guess it's not a question of upbringing. Maybe you're both psychic. I don't know.'

Sara understood immediately that he was right. Nic had that talent. It was what had drawn her to him from the first. He seemed to possess the same internal emotional bruises.

'You're not drinking your wine,' she said.

His old eyes glittered and she saw a glimpse of a different Marco Costa then, a younger man, who was surely handsome in his prime, with a sharp, mischievous sense of humour. 'I didn't want the wine. I just wanted to see you pour it.'

A tea towel flew across the room and landed on his lap.

'Bea warned me. You're a wicked old man,' Sara Farnese declared.

Marco Costa laughed. They looked at each other, wary of the intimacy that had grown in a single night, an intimacy based on some unspoken, perhaps unrecognized, mutual need.

'Will you stay long?' the old man asked, trying not to sound as if he was pleading. She was a warm and human presence in the house, not least because she behaved as if there were nothing wrong with him at all. 'Bea is a friend, and a better one than I deserve. But the old require young people around them. We need to suck the vitality out of you like vampires.'

'As long as I'm welcome.' She had turned away from him so Marco Costa could not see her face. The old man watched this solitary woman and remembered what his son had said earlier in one of their brief conversations touching the case. There was a part of Sara Farnese that was beyond reach, a secret part that defined her. Nic believed it was there that the riddle of these bizarre deaths lay. Marco Costa had no way of knowing whether this was true. All he understood was that he did not envy the young any more, not Nic, not Sara Farnese. They had yet to place their hands into life's flames. They had yet to acknowledge their existence. Not Sara Farnese, though, the old man thought. She had been burned already, and in ways he could not begin to comprehend.

'Will you sit with me?' he asked. 'And listen to some music?'

'Of course,' she said, smiling warily.

Marco Costa pushed his wheelchair over to the hi-fi unit and found the CD. He put on Dylan, played loud, singing 'Idiot Wind' and was amazed that back in 1975, when he first heard this scream of rage and pain, he wondered what the hell it was all about.

Twenty-six

Luca Rossi's white face was miserable in the moonlight. The visitor he had brought along was refusing to come to the house. He wanted to meet Nic outside the farm, under the eye of the police team stationed there but out of earshot. Rossi explained this in a low, mournful voice as they walked.

'You should be asking yourself what a man like this is doing here, Nic,' Rossi said firmly. 'Why don't they leave us alone?'

He knew the answer and didn't want to say it. Falcone was right. Hanrahan was involved in some way, perhaps on behalf of the elusive figure of Cardinal Denney.

'What harm does it do to talk?' Nic asked.

Rossi grimaced as if to say: you never learn. The harm is you just don't know who you're talking to.

Hanrahan stood beyond the almond tree by the rickety wall that formed the perimeter of what once was a sheep field. He was half illuminated by the headlights of a black Mercedes with Vatican number plates parked some twenty metres away. Costa recognized it as one of the city's pool cars, familiar symbols of authority. An anonymous driver sat behind the wheel, the light of the

203

radio reflecting on his wan face. Hanrahan wore a dark overcoat in spite of the heat and was smoking a cigar. The stocky Irishman stared at the cops around him until they dispersed, Rossi with them. Costa walked over and took the hand that was offered.

'Nice place,' Hanrahan said. 'All yours one day, I guess. A big house for a cop.'

'What do you want?'

Hanrahan stared at him. 'A little gratitude wouldn't go amiss. I took risks sending you that tape, Nic. There are people who'd be less than pleased if they knew what I'd done.'

'Thanks,' he said curtly. 'Is that good enough? It was all too late. We had another body by then. We knew Stefano Rinaldi wasn't the one.'

He shrugged. 'I was just offering a little something. I wasn't to know what would happen in the meantime.' Hanrahan pulled out a pack of cigars, took out a half-smoked stub, and offered him one. Costa shook his head.

'Clean-living boy,' the Irishman said cheerfully. 'That's what they all say about you. And now you've got that woman living in your house. How's that going? I saw her on the TV. She's an attractive piece of work. Quite a private life too. I saw that trick you played, pretending there was something special between the two of you. Do you really think anyone would fall for that? With all these cops around?'

'Who knows?' He didn't like Hanrahan. The man was too indirect. Talking to him was like juggling with eels.

'Perhaps you could take a shine to her. Anyone could, I imagine. Though I can't help wondering what would make an intelligent, attractive woman behave like that.

I'm a single man by choice. Young people. It's just laziness. All these empty lives. Why does it happen?'

Costa waved the stinking cigar smoke out of his face. 'I'm asking one more time before I go back in. What do you want?'

Hanrahan frowned. 'You don't like small talk, do you? It's a shame. You'll never make a diplomat. It's important to learn how to deal with people. Going straight to the point is not necessarily the best way. You have to learn about nuances. You have to be patient.'

Costa looked at his watch then glanced back at the house. Hanrahan waited, knowing he wouldn't walk away.

'I gave you something. It was a gift. The next one doesn't come for free.'

'The next one being what?'

Hanrahan threw the cigar on the ground and stubbed it out with his toe. 'A name. Maybe the name you're looking for. I don't know.'

Costa blinked back the fury rising in him. 'Let me make sure I understand,' he said slowly. 'This is a man who has killed four people and you know who he is? You think you can bargain for that? I could get you arrested right now for withholding information and throw you in jail until you talk. I could tell those reporters round the corner and let them sweat your ass off.'

'But why would you do that?' Hanrahan asked, bemused. 'I wouldn't say anything. To you. Or to the press. Where's the gain for any of us? And besides it's just a name. I don't know if it's useful or not. I just think it would be . . . productive if you talked to him.'

'Jesus, Hanrahan. What if someone else is killed?'

'It could be the wrong man. Who's to know?'

'You make me sick. Haggling over something like this.'

Hanrahan sighed. 'You're so young. I thought I was doing the right thing going to you, not through Falcone. Perhaps I made a mistake. Perhaps I should just let you go your own way. Whatever that may be.'

'I can get Falcone here in ten minutes if that's what you want.'

The Irishman scowled. 'No. I don't think so. You haven't even asked the obvious question. What's the point?'

Costa gripped the Irishman's dark coat in his right hand and pulled the man to him. 'I asked the question. It was the first thing I said. "What do you want?" Remember?'

Hanrahan released himself from Costa's fist and raised a conciliatory hand. 'Apologies. I forgot. You don't do small talk. Let's get straight to the point then. There's a man in the Vatican who needs his freedom and a particular kind of freedom at that. I require you to look the other way when I ask. Nothing more.'

'Denney? You're not serious. You think you can trade for that?'

Hanrahan looked surprised. 'You can trade for anything.'

'A cardinal of the Vatican? You don't need us. You can let Denney go yourself. There's a helipad behind those walls, isn't there? Get him out that way. Don't waste my time with this.'

'Nic.' Hanrahan looked disappointed. 'If it were that easy don't you think it would be done by now? Even if the cardinal were predisposed to leave like that, and he isn't, probably with good reason, we couldn't make it look as if the Vatican approved his departure. There are too many . . . strings attached. All he would require is discreet free passage to the airport, say. We could organize a private plane there. You'd just turn a blind eye for fifty minutes, no more.'

'Are you asking for this on his behalf? Did he send you here?'

'Not exactly. His life's going through a little turmoil too right now. People he thought were on his side are starting to desert him. He's an old man. Confused. A little scared. Don't believe everything you've heard about him. He was a good priest once. You should know what the press are like better than most. Do you think every word they wrote about your own father was true?'

Costa glanced back at the farmhouse, wondering what was going on there. 'My father isn't a crook. From what I hear Denney is.'

'So you know he's guilty? You're judge and jury in this too?'

'No. I'm a cop. I hand him over to people who make that decision.'

Hanrahan laughed. 'And you the Italian? Here, where nothing's ever black and white. Can you hear yourself talking?'

'I can. And one more thing. What if Denney has something to do with these murders? Maybe I'm letting go of a material witness. Or worse, someone who's involved.'

Hanrahan's bluff manner disappeared immediately. 'Nic, I swear to you. The cardinal has nothing to do with this. He doesn't even know I'm here. I'm just trying to grease a few wheels for all of us. You with your problem, me with mine.'

Kill two birds with one stone. The Irishman was so like Falcone. He tried to discern some unease on Hanrahan's rugged face. 'So Denney doesn't know Sara Farnese?'

'Why the hell should he?' Hanrahan answered, shrugging his stocky shoulders. 'You mean that call to the Vatican? Let me tell you. There are forty people working off that same switchboard, for lots of different officials. So someone answered, "Denney's office" by mistake. You ring again and you could get mine. It doesn't make him part of this any more than it does me or the other people who get their messages taken that way. But I've been looking at some of those we've had working there. And maybe – I don't promise this – but maybe there's something there for you. Nothing to lay at Michael Denney's door. Just a name, that's all.' Hanrahan caught him with a dark, intent eye. 'Maybe there's a little interesting history. But it doesn't come for free, my boy. I don't have to lift a damn finger to help you. Remember that.'

Nic Costa took a few steps away from him and looked down the dirt track. The other cops were smoking underneath the old carob tree that marked the farm boundary. They looked deeply bored. It was insane to think they could draw out anyone like this. Falcone was clutching at straws.

He came back and looked at Hanrahan. 'I'm not convinced.'

'To hell with it then. What else am I supposed to do?'

'Fix a meeting. Me and Denney. Inside the Vatican, naturally. Whenever, wherever he pleases.'

Hanrahan's eyes sparkled. 'Oh! Is that all?'

'That's all for now,' Costa said and turned to go.

'Hey.'

He felt a strong hand on his arm.

'Are you serious?' Hanrahan asked. 'You really want me to book an appointment between some junior Rome cop and a cardinal of the Catholic Church, a man you people can't wait to throw in jail? How do you think I'm going to sell that to him?'

'Tell him I want to talk about religion,' Costa said. 'Tell him I'm thinking of converting.'

Then he walked off to the farm without waiting for Hanrahan's answer.

Twenty-seven

She was sitting by the fireplace, next to the old man, who was asleep in his wheelchair. Sara put a finger to her lips and indicated to Costa to come to the foot of the stairs.

'You were gone a long time.'

'Sorry.'

'Was it worth while?'

'Possibly. I can't talk about it, Sara.'

She frowned, disappointed. 'I understand. I gave him the tablets he asked for. He was very animated for a while. And then . . .'

She looked down.

'Thanks for being so kind to him. He can be quite a handful at times.' He meant that. She had gone out of her way to amuse the old man, and in doing so revealed something about herself too.

'It was a pleasure,' she said. 'I mean that. Nic . . .' She seemed a different woman, he thought. Somehow his father had relaxed her, given her some perspective. 'He loves you deeply. He's worried about you. About how you'll cope.'

'*He*'s worried about *me*?'

'Of course. Why would he worry about himself? He knows what's going to happen. He accepts it.'

She was right. Sometimes he allowed himself to be led into blind alleys.

' "I met a man with seven wives . . ." '

'I'm sorry.'

In the low yellow light of the farm, dressed simply, unaffected by events outside, as if this place were a sanctuary, she was extraordinarily beautiful. He was grateful for her presence. But this was all a mistake. The man would never come to the farm, not with so many cops outside. And she, unconsciously perhaps, was beginning to work on him. He would be sleeping a few steps away from her tonight. Already he was wondering what she looked like in bed, how it would feel to touch her skin.

'Distractions,' Nic Costa said by way of explanation. 'Everywhere.'

She shook her head, not understanding. 'Goodnight,' she said and, before he could move, took his arms and kissed him gently on the cheek.

He watched her go up the stairs, then, for the first time in many a year, walked into the kitchen, took down the ageing bottle of *grappa* that sat there and poured himself a tumbler of the thick, colourless liquid.

Twenty-eight

Only thirteen hacks and TV people braved the night in the roped-off area which the police had set aside for the media. For a while they passed around beer and cigarettes, knowing there would be no action until daylight, and maybe not then either. The cops were keeping this woman to themselves. Maybe, the word went, one of them had good reason.

Just after midnight they were woken by a noise. A newcomer arrived, on foot it seemed. Denis Renard was wide awake; he wasn't drunk. The paparazzo from the French celebrity weekly had already decided he would be the first to get a decent photograph of Sara Farnese. In the darkness he glowered at this odd figure coming out of nowhere, asking questions, soliciting help as if he deserved it.

'Where you from, friend?' he asked.

The man shone a torch in his face. He wasn't big but he looked powerful in a way, not the sort to mess with.

'*Time* magazine,' the man said.

Denis Renard rolled over onto his front and swore into the dry grass. It was the ones who lied that you had to watch. *Time*. As if this was their kind of story. He knew a chancer when he saw one. This was a rival, maybe, with a little digital snap camera in his pocket, looking to fix something. He was trouble, to be watched.

The paparazzo set the alarm on his watch to 6.22: sunrise.

When it rang the man was gone. Denis Renard cursed himself. He was going to be first to get a picture of the woman. No one would stop him. Not even some faker from '*Time* magazine'.

Twenty-nine

Nic Costa rose at daybreak knowing he had to run. It was an addiction. When he ran he felt in control of himself. There was a stillness that came with the constant effort and the onset of exhaustion, a solitude which sometimes produced the most extraordinary insights. He had solved a case once, an awkward and violent domestic tragedy, one morning at six when he raced along the bank of the Tiber near his apartment, beneath the shadow of the Castel Sant'Angelo. It was a source of satisfaction, of consolation. Whatever Falcone might think of him leaving Sara briefly, he needed it now more than ever.

The house was still. The sun peeked above the eastern horizon intent on searing another August day. He wore shorts, a white T-shirt and the battered trainers that had survived the last two months, a record. Nic Costa quietly let himself out of the front door and walked down the drive to where the police cars were parked. The shift should have changed at midnight. He might not know the men who had now come to guard them. He steeled himself for an argument, then halted. Luca Rossi was in the first Fiat saloon glaring at him through the window.

Only one other cop in the adjoining cars was awake and he showed little interest in what was going on.

The big man got out, stretched, yawned and then said, 'You've got to be kidding me, Nic. Today of all days.'

'You should be home. Time for bed.'

'Yeah. And what's for me there? Too late to start drinking. I can sleep in cars. I've done it before.'

It was all a lie. Nic Costa understood what the big man was doing: staying there to look after him. He was touched and a little ashamed Rossi felt he needed the attention.

'Let me repeat myself,' Rossi said. 'You're not even thinking about this.'

'Team motto, Uncle Luca. Run or die.'

'You mean run *and* die? We're setting you up as a target here, kid. Don't make it too easy for him.'

Costa spread his arms wide, pointing down both sides of the narrow dirt track that led to the farm entrance. 'Oh, come on. Just up and down the track. Where's the harm? What's going to bite me? Mosquitoes?'

'Don't do it,' the big man pleaded. 'Just go back inside. Drink some coffee. Be patient.'

'Uncle Luca . . .'

The big man felt his heart sink. He knew it was pointless to argue. 'I am not your fu— Oh, hell, what's the point? Why do you do this to me?'

'I've got to run. I've got to get some space inside me.'

'Shit,' Luca Rossi sighed. 'How far? How long?'

'Just a little way. I won't even make it to the public road. I'll stick to the drive, that's all.'

'OK,' Rossi grunted. 'But I've got no one who can

keep up with you. And if you're not back here in ten minutes I start screaming. Understood?'

Nic Costa grinned and opened his arms wide.

'No hugging, no funny stuff,' the big man said forcefully. 'You got your own way, didn't you? Now let's have it done with.'

Costa laughed and was gone, down the track, kicking up dust, glad to feel the cool morning air in his face, glad that, for a few minutes at least, he could put the complex mix of problems in the farm into some kind of perspective. He thought of his father and how much the old man had enjoyed the previous night. He thought, too, of Sara Farnese. It had given her pleasure to be such good company. That seemed a rarity in her life. He could only speculate what she would be like if it happened more regularly.

He'd lied to Luca Rossi. The track wasn't long enough. He needed to pound the public road for a while too, as fast as his powerful legs could take him. The hard basalt stone that paved the surface of the ancient highway was part of his childhood. Once, when he was thirteen, after a row with his father, he had half jogged, half sprinted all day until he was ready to drop. Some fifty kilometres from home, exhausted, he had called the farm from a village bar. The old man had come cheerfully to fetch him and laughed off the whole thing as a grand adventure. They'd been closer after that. His efforts had somehow marked him out for the old man. Giulia was too scared to argue with him, Marco, being the eldest, too smart. Neither would have countenanced that kind of escape and Nic knew, from the moment the car arrived and his father had stepped out grinning from ear to ear, that this denoted some change in the nature of their relationship. It didn't become easier, just closer in some unspoken, mysterious way, as if they shared part of the same mind.

He spotted the press pack down the road, put his head down and sprinted past them. They scarcely gave him a second glance. It was early. All the associations were wrong too. They were looking for a beautiful woman and a smartly dressed cop, not a sweating runner in a tattered T-shirt and grubby trainers beating his way down the road. He allowed himself one look back to make sure no one was coming, then kicked hard and headed into the scrub. There was a narrow path of rock and dust that led behind the farm. He could take that, double-back around the house and surprise Luca Rossi by appearing out of nowhere.

The morning was turning out to be glorious, full of light and beauty. He put on some speed, dodged beneath a couple of olive trees, writhing and gnarled like old men, sprinted hard then stopped. The back of the farm was less than fifty metres away from this position. He could see into the windows. In the guest bedroom he could just about make out Sara moving around. She wore a scarlet shirt, nothing else. He felt guilty watching her like this but it was hard to stop. Every time they met, her actions had been shaped by the presence of others. Seen like this, she was, perhaps, the person that lived inside the hard, fragile shell she showed to the outside world. It worried him. He was becoming obsessed and not just by her beauty. There was something beneath the surface of Sara Farnese he wanted to see, to touch, and to know.

He breathed deeply, getting back his strength, leaned forward and placed his hands on his knees. It had been a good idea, whatever Uncle Luca thought.

A voice behind him, a hard voice, with a foreign accent, said suddenly, 'Smile.'

The sweat went cold on Nic Costa's skin. He turned. The man was skeletally thin and entirely bald, with a black shirt and trousers and staring blue eyes. He had a large SLR camera in his hands and was about to bring it up to his face.

'Who the hell are you?'

'Press.' He fired off a couple of shots then moved to improve the angle.

'This is private property. I want that film right now.'

'Fuck you,' the photographer hissed from behind the lens.

Nic Costa sighed. It was so obvious. He'd seen the trick many times. They'd try to make you mad just to get a better shot. A fist raised to the lens made the picture. Passive people didn't sell.

'OK,' he said. 'Fire away.'

He stood upright, folding his arms in front of him and smiled, a big, cheesy smile, like that of a teenager out for the day.

The photographer grunted. This wasn't what he wanted.

'Do I get paid?' Costa asked, then stopped. Someone else was coming. One of the team, he guessed, and about time too. They were supposed to be watching the perimeter. They should never have let the photographer get this far.

He peered at the figure walking rapidly up the track. He was about thirty, powerfully built, with a striking face and dark, straight hair. The check shirt and loose jeans didn't fit properly. The black spectacles he wore seemed out of place. Costa didn't recognize him. But the photographer did.

'Not you?' the paparazzo yelled. 'Hey. This is my find. You fuck off back where you belong. Back to . . .' He made a sarcastic quote mark gesture with his fingers. '*Time* magazine.'

The man in the checked shirt said nothing. He was staring beyond both of them, staring at the house. Costa said, 'You've both got to get out of here. Before there's trouble.'

Then he followed the gaze of the one in the checked shirt. His eyes were fixed on the window. Sara Farnese was there, watching this odd confrontation, as if she were trying to make sense of it.

There was a noise from the photographer, a gasp of surprise and hurt. The checked shirt had pulled a flick knife from somewhere and had stuck it into his ribs. The wounded man was stumbling to the ground, his hand clutching his chest as if he were trying to stop his life running out onto the dry, rocky ground.

Nic Costa watched him, watched the check shirt change his focus, away from the paparazzo, first to the distant figure of Sara and then to him.

Sometimes you fight. Sometimes you run.

'The blood of the martyrs . . .' the man said and took a swift step towards him.

Costa didn't move, finishing the sentence for him, 'Is the seed of the Church.'

The man stopped a couple of metres away, puzzled, watching. His eyes narrowed behind the ill-fitting glasses. This was not part of the plan.

'None of it's true,' Costa said. 'I never touched her. It was all a game. To get you here. And it worked.' He opened his hands, a calm, conciliatory gesture. 'Let's call it a day, huh? This place is crawling with police.'

The man looked around him, amused, as if to say: *really*? Something was wrong. They should have been here already. They should never have let him get this far.

He roared, coming forward with an unexpected turn of speed, the knife, now red, held firm in his right hand. Nic Costa feinted to one side, dodging the power of the attack, and began to sprint. There was no way he could reason with this man any more. He needed to get out of there, to distract him away from the wounded photographer, to bring in the rest of the team.

He dashed through the thorny scrub, feeling it rip his thighs, then breathed deeply, thought of nothing but the speed in his legs and leaned into the light morning wind. He'd taken no more than four long strides when something fiery and painful bit into his shoulder.

Nic Costa's foot struck a hard, solid object. He fell onto the dry, brown ground, slamming his head onto a rock, dragging at the thing in his back. The blade was lodged deep. He grasped the handle and felt like screaming, in pain and anger. He should have been able to pull it out and get back to running away from this deadly lunatic who seemed to have risen from the rocks of the parched scrubland.

He stumbled drowsily to his feet, anxiously scanning the dead farmland.

There was a figure on the shimmering horizon, approaching fast.

Sometimes you fight. Sometimes you run.

And sometimes, Nic Costa thought, his head reeling into concussion, you had no choice at all.

The dark shape grew larger. He wondered what else

the man carried in his armoury, wondered where the rest of the team were. A cop didn't deserve to die like a saint. It seemed inappropriate, somehow, almost profane.

Nic Costa slumped to his knees, feeling his consciousness begin to fade.

Then there were voices. Loud voices. Shouting. Two people only, and one of them familiar. One of them – the word came easily in his present state; he felt no shame in thinking it – cherished.

He lay prone on the hard, arid earth, feeling the darkness begin to swamp his mind, listening to Sara Farnese. It sounded as if she was begging for his life.

Thirty

Alicia Vaccarini spent the night tethered to the chair against the upright wooden beam in the curious octagonal chamber where Gino Fosse had left her. There had been a sound outside only once; the noise of a drunk going home, singing. She was gagged. She was tied. There was nothing she could do, nothing she could hope to achieve. He would return soon, she knew, and then there would be no more delays. This madman believed, in some strange way, that he was doing her a favour. The manner of his 'apology' left her full of dread. There was no avenue for persuasion, no prospect of clemency. He was set upon this path, and was distraught that something – something on the television – had disturbed his well-planned sequence of events.

She had slept, for how long she could only guess, and woke when daylight began to filter into the room through the narrow, slitted windows. There had to be people nearby. There had to be someone who would come, she believed. Even in August, when the heat had depleted the streets, this was still Rome. The city was alive beyond these crumbling medieval walls. The guards would soon be opening up offices in the parliament building. Secretaries would be delivering mail. Staff at the small neighbourhood café where she normally drank her morning *macchiato* would be wondering why she was absent. Alicia Vaccarini was a woman of habit. There would be those who noticed her absence. By lunchtime, she believed, someone would question it. She had been due to attend a reception for a visiting party of Brussels bureaucrats at ten. It was unknown for her to miss such events. She was diligent. She had nothing else to do.

So by two, three at the latest, there would be someone checking her apartment, discovering she had never returned home the previous day. The police would be involved. Questions would be asked, with no ready answers.

She tried to convince herself there was hope in this slow, muddled series of small discoveries. It was impossible. He would be back and when he did he would achieve what he wished. He would be anxious to be done with her and move on to whatever came next.

The book was still open on the floor. She refused to look at it. The patron saint of musicians deserved to be a brighter, happier figure, she thought. Not a white marble corpse lying in a shroud, with three visible wounds on her neck. Alicia Vaccarini had only one, and it was shallow and ceased to bleed soon after Fosse had raced from the room. One wound was enough, she believed, and closed her eyes, wondering if there was somewhere, within her, the ability to pray. It was a time for desperate measures.

Then there was a sound from downstairs. Her heart leapt in hope. She heard footsteps rising. Familiar ones: determined and heavy. She closed her eyes and wept.

When she opened them Gino Fosse was standing in front of her looking confused. He was wearing a checked shirt covered in dirt and torn at the front. His mouth hung open as he gasped for breath. She didn't know what to make of him, was unable to decide whether his odd appearance was good or bad. Then he started to speak, a rapid-fire babble of insane nonsense about the Church and the perfidy of women. The phone rang. It was on a sideboard next to the window opposite her. He walked over and picked it up. She listened intently. There was a shade of subservience in his voice. It was the first time she had ever noticed it. He seemed so confident, so capable of acting individually, most of the time.

He went quiet, his head fell down. This was bad news. She closed her eyes for a moment and prayed someone would come, that soon there would be the sound of the police beating down the doors to this odd monastic prison.

'No,' he said insistently down the phone. 'It's impossible. You can't ask that. Where will I go?'

He went quiet, listening. His shoulders hunched over and his face contorted with grief and fury. But he would do as he was told, she thought, and there, perhaps, lay salvation.

'*Shit!*' he yelled.

He threw the phone on the floor. He kicked it across the carpet. She watched as he dashed around the tiny, airless room, snatching at curtains, ornaments, anything he could lay his hands on, smashing these objects to the ground, screaming obscene nonsense.

They'll hear, she thought. Someone knows. Someone is coming. *And they will hear.*

He went behind her. She felt cold. Two clammy hands came around her neck and clasped her cheeks. He turned her head to look up at the disgusting, frightening photographs on the ceiling, photographs she had avoided up to that point. They were black and white. The women in them looked back, their faces immobile, as if they didn't care or wanted to wish themselves out of the frame.

'See what happens,' he murmured into her ear, half crying. 'See what's done and can't be undone.'

Her bladder failed and a warm stinging stream ran down her legs. The hands moved again. The gag relaxed. He untied the knot at the back of her head and let the gag fall from her. Alicia Vaccarini moaned, pleased she could breathe easily again.

Then he came back around her once more and she looked into his eyes. He'd changed again. This was a different person, one full of conviction and determination. His hand came up suddenly and slapped her across the face. She yelped. The hand swept backwards, his knuckles hard against her lips. She could taste blood. She could sense something new: an intense, personal hatred for her.

'Whore,' he hissed. 'You're all the same. The doorway of the devil. You know that?'

'Please . . .'

'Shut up!' His fist came up again, hesitated. She got the message. She was quiet.

He wiped his mouth with his hand, thinking. She watched him, silent. It was beyond protest, beyond pleading. The decision now was his, and he was crazy, violent one moment, repentant, or at least uncertain, the next.

'They're coming,' he said. '*Here!* To my home. *My* home.'

She spoke very quietly, very calmly. 'Don't make it any worse than it is.'

He stared at her, wondering. 'It could be worse? How?'

There was some light in his eyes. Some kind of doubt. There was room for her to work. 'I can help you,' she said. 'I have friends. I can tell the police you've been kind. That you didn't mean it. We all make mistakes.'

'We all burn in Hell.'

'No,' she said. 'That's an old story. Even the Church doesn't believe that any more.'

'Then they're stupid.' He sighed. 'I'm sorry. Truly, I'm sorry.'

She breathed deeply for the first time in hours, finding a flicker of hope in his apology.

'It's all right,' Alicia Vaccarini said. 'Everything will be all right.'

His face was so odd. In some light he would be handsome. In another, not hideous but exaggerated somehow, like a figure from a medieval painting.

'You don't understand, Alicia. I'm sorry because I can't do you justice. The church in Trastevere. The means of your death, a holy means. Something which could help wash away your sins. Save you perhaps. All of this is impossible now. They're coming to take away my home. They think they can trap me. They're very, very stupid.'

'It can work out. I can help.'

'Perhaps.' He was thinking. He was as rational now as he had appeared in the restaurant. Something occupied him. He went over to the pile of jazz CDs strewn on the floor, sifted quickly through them until he found what he wanted, then put it on the hi-fi. The sound of a high, sweeping electric violin filled the room. Then he came back to her.

'Have you ever watched a man smash a brick with his hand, Alicia? The martial arts place I go to. They show you how to do that. They teach you the secret.'

'No,' she answered quietly, not wishing to excite him.

'The secret is you don't try to hit the brick. What you aim at is something imaginary a little way behind it. That is what you're trying to destroy. You get the result you want by focusing on that hidden place, by making that your target. And in doing so you smash the brick. Do you understand?'

'I think so. Could you untie me, please? I'm very stiff. I need to go to the bathroom.'

He shook his head, annoyed she appeared to miss his point. 'This is important, Alicia. Our true goal's beyond. It's not something that we see. What we do along the way, what we touch, what we destroy, is irrelevant. It's the end point that matters. Being able to see it with your inner eye. To know you'll get there.'

She looked at him, not liking what she saw. 'They'll be here soon. It would look best if they didn't find me like this. You can understand that, can't you?'

'Of course,' he said and walked behind her. The earth began to shift. The chair moved through ninety degrees as Fosse tilted it forward until Alicia Vaccarini was on her knees, head hanging down, eyes fixed on the worn, stained carpet.

She waited for his touch, waited to feel him working on the rope. It never happened. Gino Fosse came back to stand in front of her again. This time he was holding the sword, the bright, glittering sword that had cut her once already.

'Jesus Christ.' She looked at the blade and felt the

breath disappearing from her lungs. 'Don't,' she whispered.

But Fosse wasn't even noticing. His eyes were on the chair to which she was tied and the space that lay beyond her neck.

He walked to one side of her. Only his ankles were visible: white socks in black trainers. She heard the sound of the sword cutting through the hot, dank air of the room and a strange memory came to her from a history course long ago: Anne Boleyn going to her death at the hands of the Calais swordsman, a bitter kindness on Henry VIII's part, to save her from the conventional executioner's axe. The man had been brought in for the occasion because of his reputation. The sword had a clean, deadly efficiency impossible with the axe. He'd hidden the blade beneath the straw, stood behind her, listened to her last words, then decapitated the disgraced queen with a single blow.

She could hear it: unseen, the silver blade dashing at her back as her executioner made his practice strokes. Then there was silence. She could picture him drawing it to his shoulders, turning in a deadly forceful arc.

Without thinking, she lifted her chin and forced her eyes shut. She didn't wish to see a thing. She didn't want to think of the blade missing her neck, smashing into the back of her skull.

In the curious practicality of the moment she recalled something further of the history lesson: Anne's last words, 'To Jesus Christ I commend my soul'.

It was impossible to say them. It would be an insult, she thought.

The music ended, then looped back on itself. The wailing violin began to dance again.

Thirty-one

San Giovanni, once a refuge for fourth-century pilgrims, was now a modern hospital that sprawled through countless buildings covering a vast parcel of the Caelian Hill. The complex stretched from the old narrow road that led to the church of San Clemente across to the traffic-choked modern highway that fed streams of cars, buses and trucks into the piazza from the south. Only minutes away too was the Clivus Scauri, where Falcone and his men were engaged in the discovery of a further victim and the disappearance of the priest who once, albeit briefly, worked the corridors of the place where Nic Costa now lay on a table in a small cubicle, his head hurting like hell.

Luca Rossi and Sara Farnese had only just argued their way into the room. They sat on the bench seat watching the nurse bandage him, watching the way he listened to the doctor talk about concussion and how, all things being equal, he ought to spend the day in a ward just to make sure there were no lingering after-effects. The knife wound was minor. The knock to his head when he fell and hit the rock had left a livid but compact blood-filled bruise on his right temple. Still, Nic Costa was alive and maddeningly ignorant of the reason for it. He waited for the doctor to go away, then turned to the big man.

'I don't like the look on your face, Uncle Luca. You took him?'

'We wish,' Rossi replied miserably.

Costa was wide-eyed with amazement. 'Christ. What more do you need?'

Sara Farnese looked at her feet. Rossi glowered at him from across the room. 'Hey, kid. Don't get precious with me.'

'There were how many men there?'

'*Enough!*' The big man's flabby white face turned an odd shade of half-angry pink. 'Eight. Maybe ten. Think about it. They were there to protect the farm. Which was where you were supposed to be. None of them knew you were running around doing this crazy stuff somewhere else. Falcone is going to tear the skin off my back for letting you go out there. Except, of course, it wasn't even where I thought you were going to be. Remember the deal? You stay in the drive? Where we could be close by?'

His head was painful, confused. He did remember now, and Luca Rossi was right. He'd no one to blame but himself. He remembered, too, the sight of Sara at the window and the terror on her face.

'I'm sorry, Luca. I was an idiot.'

'Yeah, well . . .' The big man cast a glance at Sara next to him. 'You survived. No thanks to us. And we've got a name. And another body. Enough there for Falcone to get happy about or crucify us with, depending on his mood.'

'I'll check myself out. I have to go there.'

'Nic, the doctors . . .' Sara began to say.

'This one's even less pretty than the others,' Rossi

grumbled, taking it as read that Costa would leave hospital. 'What can you do?'

He moved his shoulder and was pleased by the small amount of pain that resulted. 'It's not bad. Besides, Luca, you need me. I saw this man, remember?'

Rossi looked at the woman again. Costa couldn't work it out. There was something he disliked about Sara Farnese. It was so powerful he seemed to hate even sitting next to her in the hospital cubicle.

'Doesn't matter that you saw him, Nic. Weren't you listening? We've got his name. Miss Farnese here provided it once we'd got you into the ambulance. Seems she had it all along.'

His head hurt even more after that. She was staring at the white wall, intent on nothing. Her hair was tousled. It made her look different. Maybe there hadn't been time for her to do anything else. She'd just left the house with him, unable to put on the mask she normally wore to keep the world from touching her.

'I've got some calls to make,' Rossi said. 'Your father decided to stay at home once the ambulance people said you'd be fine. I'll let him know things are OK all the same. I'm outside when you want me. It's two minutes away, max. They can take her some place else. Falcone says the protective custody thing is still on. I guess you won't want her back at the farm so they're making other arrangements.'

He patted the pack of cigarettes in his pocket. 'Smoking time too.' Then he was gone from the room, out into the long corridor illuminated by cold fluorescent lights.

Nic Costa pushed himself upright off the hospital

table. The cut in his shoulder was minor. His head would get better. It was all a matter of time.

She still wouldn't look at him.

'Thanks,' he said finally.

Sara turned. Her eyes were scared, astonished too. 'What?'

'I don't know what happened out there, Sara. But you stopped him. Thanks.'

Her head moved from side to side, her long, unkempt hair shifting slowly around with the motion. 'I just saw him from the window, Nic. I knew something was wrong. When I got there he ran away. I imagine he was scared everyone else was turning up. He didn't want witnesses.'

That was a lie. He knew it for sure. He'd heard them talking.

'You spoke to him.'

'Of course I did! I screamed at him to stop. What do you expect?'

'No.' His memory was hazy yet there was something fixed there: he recalled the tenor of their conversation. 'You spoke to him. He answered back. It was more than that. You knew who he was.'

'Enough to know his name. He used to hang around the Vatican Library when I was there. We'd talk sometimes.'

'You didn't . . .' There was no easy way of asking.

'What?' she answered, furious. 'Sleep with him? No. There are men in Rome who've been denied that privilege. I hope that doesn't come as too much of a shock.'

'I'm sorry.'

'Oh, God.' She shook her head, eyes closed, miserable. 'I'm the one who's sorry. You don't know what you're saying. I saw him. I yelled at him until he went.

Then as soon as he was gone I yelled until the police came. For you and that photographer. He's worse than you, they say. He'll be in here for some time.'

It was possible she was right. He could have imagined the entire exchange.

'Someone else is dead?'

'So they say.'

'You know him?'

She picked up her bag and put it on her knee. 'I think I should leave. They want me to stay somewhere else. They say they're sending another police team to pick me up.'

Costa got up off the table and walked, a little shakily, across the room. He sat next to her on the bench, very close. He wanted to make a point: that she couldn't chase him away so easily.

'Do you know him?' he asked again.

The old Sara looked frankly at him, unafraid. 'It was a woman.'

He thought about the bold, unabashed way in which she said it.

'So did you know her?'

'I think I slept with her once. Is that what you want to hear?'

'You think?'

'No. I did. They showed me a picture. She was a politician apparently. I slept with her a few months ago. I can't be certain. I don't keep that kind of diary. I apologize. It happened once. It was her idea. Not my kind of thing really.'

He sighed. She could still shake him, even though he knew this was what she intended.

'I don't understand any of this, Sara. I don't

understand why you do it. I don't understand why you never gave us her name.'

She laughed, a dry, deliberate laugh, one that was supposed to make him hate her. 'You're so old-fashioned, Nic. You and your father. I love him. Really. I could talk to him for hours because it's like talking to someone from another time. But the world's not the way you two imagine it. Maybe it never was. You ask me why I never gave you her name? What makes you think I knew her name in the first place? This was just one night. That's all.'

It made no sense. It couldn't be the whole story. 'But why?'

'Because . . .' She had to hunt for the answer. 'You've your kind of love. I've mine. We're different. What happened satisfied me. Then it's gone, with nothing lingering, nothing to go stale. No awkward attachments. No bitterness, no pain.'

'So it's not a kind of love at all?' he said without thinking. 'And it isn't gone. Something stays behind. Something that may go wrong. Then people get screwed up. Sometimes horribly.'

Her eyes grew wide. 'So this is my fault?' she demanded angrily. 'You think I'm to blame for what's happened?'

It was a stupid thing to say in a way but she had misread his point. 'Not for a minute.'

He stood up, trying to convince himself he didn't feel too bad. His head was clearing rapidly.

'I knew you wouldn't stay here,' she said. 'Why can't you just leave it alone?'

He watched her get up and collect her bag, organize herself for whatever lay ahead.

'It's what they pay me for.'

'No they don't. No one pays you to risk your life.'

'Next time I'll be more careful.'

Sara Farnese stared into his face. Then she touched his cheek gently with two slender fingers. It was a deliberate act, one he could not mistake.

'Nic,' she said carefully. 'If you asked, would they take you off this case?'

The question threw him. 'I guess so. But why would I want to do that?'

'Because I want you to? This is about me. There may be things you'll find out that I don't want you to know. Things that will make you loathe me.'

'I'm a cop. They give you drugs to make you unshockable.'

'It's not a joke.'

'I know. Don't worry about it.'

She glanced at him, uneasy. 'Then you'll ask for something else?'

'Are you kidding? This is shaping up to be the biggest thing of my career. What would I look like if I backed out now? I don't give up on things. Not just because they might be hard or awkward or make me face decisions I'd rather avoid. That doesn't get you anywhere.'

'It makes life easy,' she said.

'It makes life dull and boring and . . . perhaps pointless even.'

She nodded. 'I thought you'd say that.'

'Thank you. Now, you face a decision. I have to go back to the team. You can stay in this safe house of Falcone's. Or I can make the case for you to go back to the farm. Not for my sake, you understand. It's my father. He enjoys your company. You seem to enjoy his.'

She didn't recoil from the idea. He was glad. 'Will he agree? This awful boss of yours? I don't like him. He's too . . . hard.'

'Falcone thinks that's what's required of him. If I ask him to let you stay I can't see why he'd object. Let's face it, your security can't be much at risk. You met this man. He didn't harm you. Did he?'

'No,' she said quietly. 'And your safety?'

He'd thought about that already. 'I'll be more careful. Besides, I don't think he'll come back somehow. It's as if he has an agenda. I wasn't really on it. Also I told him the truth. That we just set this up for him, the idea that something was going on between us. I told him it was all a lie.'

Was that the way a psychopath behaved, he wondered? Being so picky about who he killed? A chill, dark thought ran around Nic Costa's head. What if this lunatic had seen him there on the ground, spared his life, then wondered afterwards: what was the point? Would he make the same choice again? Or did you just let the innocent off the hook once and then, the next time, think . . . to hell with it?

There was a sound outside in the corridor. Luca Rossi poked his big white face around the door and looked pointedly at his watch. Costa waved at him for one minute more. She waited until the big man was gone, then said, 'You'll find him, won't you? He's sick. He needs help.'

'We'll find him.' He hesitated, wondering whether he dared ask. 'Sara?'

She didn't like the tone of his voice. She knew, he guessed, what was coming.

'Yes?'

'Are there more names we ought to know? Are there more people like this woman? People who aren't names, just faces?'

'A few. Not recently. I don't know who they are. I don't know how you could reach them.' She said it with such conviction. He wanted to believe her.

'There's a man in the Vatican. Cardinal Denney . . .'

'Nic!' She was the real Sara again. He could see the tears starting in her eyes. 'Is this you talking? Or the policeman? How am I supposed to know who I'm dealing with when you do this to me?'

'You mean the answer would be different depending on who I was?'

'Not at all,' she replied immediately. 'I mean that I want to understand what your interest is. Whether you're asking as a friend. Or because you think it's your job.'

'As a friend.'

'I don't know him,' she insisted. 'Whoever you are.'

Thirty-two

The apartment they gave him was on the third floor of a poky residential building adjoining the Vatican Library. It was unfit for a junior clerk, let alone a cardinal. That it was available at all was significant. Accommodation did not just materialize out of thin air in the Vatican. This was a pre-ordained punishment by the state, one that must have been planned weeks, if not months, before. The perfidy of Neri and Aitcheson was just part of the act. Perhaps Neri had worked in concert with someone on the political side. There was no way of knowing. Only one plain fact consoled Michael Denney: they could never abandon him altogether. If he was handed over to the Italian police or anyone else he could incriminate any number of men in Europe and America. Three present Italian cabinet ministers were deeply in his debt alone. The European Commission was full of his placements. He numbered Lloyd's names and syndicate members of the New York Stock Exchange among those who had, in the good times, been the grateful recipients of any number of generous gestures, from the provision of company for the night to a well-placed inside tip. These were all items he would willingly have traded over the past few months as he attempted to buy safe passage out of the Vatican by any number of different means. It was a disappointment that he had failed, but the power of these weapons remained undiminished. He was grateful, too, that he had declined Neri's whispered hints that the mob could find a way out for him. With hindsight, placing himself in the hands of Neri's friends could have proved the most dangerous option of all.

Now they would all wait, hoping he would die of boredom perhaps, or take a gun and put it to his temple, solving the problem for everybody. It was a poor reward for a lifetime's service. Nevertheless, Denney was a practical man. He could appreciate their reasoning. Trying to rebuild a new Banca Lombardia from the ashes was a desperate venture and one which, in all honesty, was designed more to elicit his own freedom than enrich anyone he could persuade to come along for the ride.

Denney had known the risks and the costs all along. Thirty years ago he had changed from being a loyal and caring servant of the Church to an agent of the Vatican state, part diplomat, part financier. The red, three-cornered biretta of his position soon began to gather dust in the closet. Someone had to do this, he reasoned. The Church was a family, but the Vatican was a nation. He knew from the start that it needed to be defended. Over the years, as he became more worldly, he came to appreciate, too, that it needed to safeguard its interests, to earn money, and, in the final analysis, to deal with the Devil when it suited him. He had come to believe that there was no room for sentiment or misplaced ethics. He never once asked himself whether the young Michael Denney would have thought otherwise. Secular matters made him a secular man. He was not unwise. When he guided Banca Lombardia by pulling Crespi's strings, he had never directed money straight into the coffers of crooks. There would always be a circuitous route, one which would allow him to feign ignorance of the ultimate destination. That, at least, was the idea. Now he knew better.

He had become a material man. He had taken up the reins of commerce and come to understand that there were, on occasion, grey lines between what was legitimate and what was not. He had discovered, too, another side to himself, that his spare, ascetic looks turned the heads of women who, from time to time, offered relief from the stresses of his chosen career.

If, in the end, the venture was a success any peccadilloes would soon be forgotten. When the numbers turned wrong, when scapegoats were sought, it was different. Had three key investments, two in Latin America and one with Russian partners in Spain, delivered the profits he expected, Cardinal Michael Denney knew he would now be a fêted member of the Vatican hierarchy, perhaps expecting further promotion. But the numbers were already looking sour on the day he watched, shell-shocked, as those two planes plummeted into the World Trade Center. The risks were cruelly balanced in the worst possible directions: technology, which was already suffering; some emerging East European economies; and the supposed safe haven of reinsurance. The markets and the staggering global economy cheated him of his prize. The small fish down the food chain began to complain. Lombardia was forced to suspend trading. Then the police and, eventually, the FBI began to take an interest, started to peer through the complex entanglement of financial records – shell companies, obscure trust funds, phoney bank accounts – that stretched around the world.

There were rumours about his personal life. No one regarded him as a priest any more, but the office of cardinal still belonged to the Church. The hint of affairs and the certain knowledge that he loved wine and fine restaurants were matters which bore little weight in the good times. When excuses were sought, they became ammunition in his downfall. Once, he received invitations to some of the most elite dining rooms in Rome where he was a welcome guest who would not always return to his own bed at the end of the evening. Once he was on first-name terms with the finance ministers of several Western nations. A nod from Denney, an expression of interest, could breathe life into a venture struggling to raise capital. He had power and influence and reputation. Then, in a short year, it was gone, accompanied by a whirlwind of vile rumour. Now he was a friendless prisoner trapped inside the tiny, close community of the Vatican, knowing his life would be in jeopardy if he stepped beyond its walls. From this point on it would be a struggle to get even the smallest favour – a meal sent in from a restaurant, a few cleaning trucks to sweep away the media mob from outside a friend's door.

The apartment had a single bedroom, a tiny living room, and a bathroom with a rusty cubicle shower. An ancient gas hob stood in the corner of the main room, perched above a miniature fridge. The place overlooked a dead, grey courtyard full of trash bins. The air-conditioning rattled and wheezed in the cruel August heat and still did little to ameliorate the temperature. Without asking, they had moved in some of his possessions: clothes, books, a handful of paintings. Perhaps Hanrahan hoped it would deaden the blow. The canvases seemed out of place inside these meagre quarters. Denney, who had once loved art, thought he might never look at them again. He was sixty-two and in reasonable health, though mentally he increasingly found himself prone to fits of doubt and depression. He should have known what was coming. No one, that week, had addressed him as 'Your Eminence', an honour to which he was still entitled. No one but Brendan Hanrahan and he found little comfort in that.

Denney knew the stocky Irishman only too well. Hanrahan belonged in the dock as much as any of them. Somehow he possessed the skill and foresight to see the storm clouds gathering long before Denny had – and failed to pass the message on. Hanrahan was a survivor and, in a way, still loyal to an extent, perhaps for the most basic, selfish reasons. It was in his interests to see that Michael Denney remained out of the hands of the police. That doubtless explained the private request for a meeting. Denney looked at his watch. A few minutes later there was a knock on the door.

On time, as ever, Hanrahan let himself in and bowed. 'Your Eminence.'

'I don't know why you bother with that, Brendan. No one else does any more.'

'That says more about them than it does about you.'

'Maybe.' Denney was a slender, fit man with not an ounce of flab. Now his once handsome face was lined by worry and age. He wore a grey suit with no ecclesiastical trappings. He had long ago given up hope of resuming a role in the Church in Italy. He would never wear the cloth again until he was free of Europe, anonymous, with a new name, somewhere near home in Boston perhaps, where a man might disappear for a while and learn how to make others forgive. There was no redemption for him in the Vatican. If he were to recover himself that would have to occur elsewhere, in the close Catholic neighbourhoods of his youth.

'Well, Brendan. These are interesting times. Is there news?'

The visitor sat down in the chair opposite the sofa. From outside the window came the noise of drilling. One of the workmen had told him why. They were improving these modest apartments, one by one. The work, and the racket, would go on for months.

'The woman politician. Vaccarini. The one who voted for you on the committee. She's been murdered.'

Denney's face fell. He looked grief-stricken. 'Good God, man. What are the police doing?'

'Looking for him. He tried to murder one of theirs. After that he killed her. At his home. The house we gave him, if you recall.'

The cardinal was aghast. 'Who?'

'Please,' Hanrahan said harshly. 'If I'm to help we must be frank with each other. There can be no mistake any more. I warned you. I said . . .'

'I know what you said!'

Hanrahan waited for him to recover his composure.

'I'm sorry,' Denney groaned after a while. 'You're absolutely sure of this?'

'It has to be. The police are in the place. Fosse is gone. They've no idea where. Neither have I. Do you?'

Denney leaned forward and folded his hands on his lap, rocking slowly on his chair – a habit he had more and more these days and one which emphasized his age. 'Of course not. Where can he be, for God's sake? He's not a man of the world, is he?'

Hanrahan considered his answer. 'I wouldn't say that. I took a very good look at Fosse's file. He did many interesting things before he worked here. He was attached to the Italian Olympic squad for a while and seems to have been a proficient athlete. He was chaplain to the National Theatre in Palermo and even persuaded them to let him appear in a Pirandello play while he was there. Not bad for a farm boy from Sicily.'

'So what?' Denney grumbled.

'So he sounds pretty resourceful to me. Educated beyond his standing too. And he seems to have a very clear idea of what he wants, what his plan is.'

Denney knew where this was leading. 'Which winds up with me? Is that what you're saying?'

Hanrahan frowned and looked around the apartment, as if he were noting how humble, how undesirable it was. 'I don't know. It's possible.'

'Why would he want to kill me, Brendan? Aren't there enough people with that in mind already? Do you have any reason for Fosse's interest in the matter?'

Hanrahan took a pack of cigars out of his pocket and lit one, letting the stink waft over into Denney's face. 'Something to do with the Farnese woman, perhaps? I don't expect you to give me details of your own personal life but I see the logs. I know who comes and goes in this building. Fosse has a grudge. He is, I think, a little like a tinder box. It takes very little to spark the flames and when they're alight, well . . .'

The Irishman waited for a response. None came.

'This is not, Your Eminence, a complete surprise now, is it? There was plenty of trouble before. He's quite a history. That matter here which necessitated his removal from your staff. What was it exactly? I was away at the time and the records are unclear.'

'Does it matter?'

'Perhaps.'

'He was overfond of the wrong kind of women, Brendan. He was warned many times. He ignored those warnings. It's not an uncommon fault.'

Hanrahan frowned. 'So we rewarded him with a rather fine home and a new job. Even though he did, I believe, threaten you publicly then. Your dismissal of him was, I hear, rather fierce.'

Denney's head rocked from side to side. 'I lost my temper. I'd put my trust in the young fool. He betrayed it. So he was upset at losing his post? He never mentioned Sara Farnese to me. Fosse was a troubled priest deserving of sympathy. I've no idea why he's behaving like this now.'

Hanrahan stared at his fingernails in silence.

'Do you think he could get in here?' Denney asked. 'Don't we pay you people for protection to save us from that kind of trouble?'

'Of course you do. And you get it. But Fosse is . . . different somehow. He's not an ordinary priest. He's not an ordinary murderer either. He has reasons, motivations, I can't begin to understand. Or rather ones which I lack the information to clarify.'

Hanrahan paused to give his revelation some weight. He had only just come off the phone with Falcone and even he was shocked by some of the detail. 'He beheaded Alicia Vaccarini. Quite extraordinary. I know for a fact he's seen files on everyone connected with your . . . ventures too. Names, addresses. Details of meetings. There were photographs in that place of his. Extraordinary photographs. You wonder about their purpose.'

Denney's sallow face turned the colour of granite. 'Why are you telling me this? Do you think I scare that easily?'

'No. But I think you need to know what kind of game we're in now. What we're up against. You've fallen from grace, Michael, and what's done is done. You can never go back. That charade you played this afternoon can never be repeated.'

Denney cast him an accusing glare. 'And you knew it wouldn't work all along?'

'I hoped against hope. One does in these circumstances. I try to help, Michael.'

'Then get me safe passage out of here. Fix it and I'll go.'

'To America? You think it's safe there? The FBI would meet you off the plane.'

'I've friends,' Denney grunted. 'People in Washington who can keep those hoods in their place. The FBI won't even call. Don't forget who I am, Brendan.'

'Who you were, Michael. These are changing times. I wish I could help. I've tried. Believe me.'

'Try harder.'

The Irishman held his big hands open. 'With what?'

Denney recognized the move. 'What are you asking for?'

'Leverage. Something I can bargain with.'

'Such as what?'

'The file on Fosse. Some information on his background. People he might turn to in Rome. I have most of that already though I'm sure there are some details you can add. He worked for you after all. They will want to know why you fired him. What happened after that.'

Denney grimaced. 'You think that's going to work? I've paid close to two million bucks out of my own pocket in bribes these last six months. I've sweetened politicians. I've done things I never thought I'd even consider to try to get my way out of here. Some of them make my skin crawl. None of it worked. You think they'll do this for a file?'

Hanrahan's blue eyes flashed in anger. 'Do you have a better idea? I'm looking for solutions. No one else is.'

'Sure, sure,' Denney grunted, trying to calm himself down. He didn't have many friends left. He needed this unfeeling, slippery Irishman.

'The truth is,' Hanrahan continued, 'I don't know of any other options right now. Let me make it clear, too, that even if this succeeds I doubt you'll get this open one-way ticket you fancy. The best we can hope for is that they'll turn aside just long enough to get you out to the airport. That's all I need.'

Denney stared at him, astonished. 'Are you serious? You think I can just hop into the nearest cab? You heard Neri. That psychopath would probably do the job himself. You know the kind of people out there. They make Gino Fosse look like an amateur. It's impossible. Get me some quiet escort all the way to the States. I don't intend to walk naked beyond those walls.'

Hanrahan acted offended. 'We'd have people to look after you to the airport. We're not complete incompetents.'

'I never suggested you were.'

'No? Well anyway. If you want the police to be your bodyguards then think again.' Hanrahan cast his eyes around the apartment again, pausing at the paintings, which seemed to amuse him. 'Consider your position, Michael. Think about what you've become. For that kind of treatment you need friends. You've none. Except me.'

'Thanks,' the cardinal said with bitterness.

'I was trying to put this into some perspective. Nothing more.'

'No friends? We'll see about that. Get Falcone in. He'll still talk to me.'

Hanrahan scowled. 'No. I've already spoken to Falcone. He won't deal any more, not in person. He won't come anywhere near you unless he has a set of handcuffs ready. All the favours have been called in. All the phone calls go unreturned. Everyone can smell failure on you, Michael. Maybe they can smell death. No one wants to be touched by that stink.'

Denney pointed a finger across the room. 'Don't try to make me the scapegoat here, Brendan. Don't let your masters try that trick either. I wasn't in this alone. I wouldn't be the only one to suffer if they throw me to the wolves.'

Hanrahan took a deep breath then issued a disappointed sigh. 'Now that, Your Eminence, is the kind of stupid talk I don't ever want to hear. That is the kind of talk that makes me think I'm wasting my time with you, Michael. That perhaps I'd be better off leaving you to rot in this dump, just waiting for the day you can't stand it any longer. Then what do you do? Put on an "I Love Rome" T-shirt and hope you can mingle with the tourists until you get to Fiumicino? Is that *really* what you think? Because if it is I have news. You'd be dead before you even got on the bus. Maybe it would be some of those people who think you owe them good money.

Maybe it would be Gino Fosse for whatever reasons he feels he has. Personally I'd prefer the former. It's just a gun, that's all. Gino . . . well, he's skinned a man, he's drowned a man, he's beheaded this woman you thought was in your pocket. What's he got saved for you, Michael? Is he going to nail you to a cross? Or has he been in that church just down the road from his apartment? You know, the round one with all those wonderful martyr-doms on the wall? He must have been there. Where else would he get these ideas?'

'From living,' he grumbled. 'From being a part of this nightmare.'

'Now that I don't believe,' Hanrahan said quietly. 'Or perhaps . . .' He considered the question carefully. 'Perhaps that's what Gino Fosse is trying to tell us. That by appreciating our mortality we inform these brief lives with a little perspective. It's an interesting intellectual point, I agree, but I'd rather avoid a direct involvement in the rhetoric. Fosse makes his case in a such a forceful way. Besides . . .' Hanrahan paused over his words, deter-mined to express himself precisely. 'Rain or shine, it's always a season for the dead, isn't it? Only a fool forgets that. I've no time for fools, Michael. Nor have you.'

Denney shivered in the stifling air of the tiny apart-ment. He was scared, Hanrahan could see that. But what the Irishman didn't know was that there were much bigger things to be frightened of. Denney was still a Catholic at heart. The faith had never deserted him entirely. There was a judgement coming, one in which his transgressions would no longer be hidden. He had to escape. In America it was possible he could find the courage to open his heart fully in the confessional. In America he could become another person.

'What do you want me to do?'

'Meet one of Falcone's colleagues. A junior one, who thinks very highly of himself, with only a little reason. Talk to him. Offer the files on Fosse. Then leave the rest to me. I will try to negotiate a price that gets you out of here. Then keep your head down and pray.'

He nodded. 'If that's what you want. I suppose I have no choice.'

'None,' Hanrahan agreed.

'Tell me, Brendan. How many more names are on his list?'

The question surprised Hanrahan. 'A few, or so I've heard. Sara Farnese seems to have been an active woman, if that's the right word. You won't see her again, will you? That would make my life too difficult. I can't protect you against yourself.'

'No,' he agreed softly. 'I won't.'

'Good. This is an opportunity. We mustn't waste it. I don't know if another will arise.'

Denney looked up at him, desperate. 'The police have these names from her? They'll warn them. The others. I don't want any more deaths on my conscience.'

Hanrahan glowered at him from the chair opposite. He made no effort to disguise his contempt.

'I've warned the ones who want to listen myself. For what it's worth.'

Denney felt like shrieking. 'It has to be worth something, Brendan. For pity's sake.'

Hanrahan got up, stretched lazily and cast him one last, backward glance. 'Spare me your concern, please. We both know this is about you. If you run, Michael, it all comes to an end in any case. Can't you see that's what he's doing? He's sending you a message. He's saying he'll go on killing until you flee and give him a chance to kill you. If he finds you on the way, then that's OK with him. If you manage to escape then it's finished anyway. He has no more reason to do what he's doing. Either the police catch him or he saves up for a fare to Boston or wherever you plan to run and hide. End of story. And no more corpses in Rome.'

Denney closed his eyes wishing he couldn't hear any of this.

'Don't talk to me about your conscience. Don't even dare.' Hanrahan's voice rang off the walls of the meagre apartment. There was a kind of judgement there, and one which Denney found hard to bear. 'This is not about conscience. It's about courage. It could be ended so easily. So would you care to take a walk with me now, Your Eminence? It's a fair day, a hot one, true, but I wouldn't be anywhere else except Rome on an August morning like this. There's not so many tourists. There's a breeze coming down the Tiber. We could get out from behind these walls. We could stand in the shadow of the castle. We could sit on the street and take coffee. I could buy you lunch in that old restaurant in Trastevere, the one where we used to sit in the garden, the one where the lamb's so good you just pick it up and eat it with your fingers. Then we could walk, anywhere we felt like and wait to see what happens.'

Denney heard the Irishman cross the room, felt his hand on his shoulder.

'Well, Michael.' Hanrahan demanded. 'Will you be coming out with me or won't you?'

'Get the hell out of here,' Denney hissed.

'I'll arrange for this kid to come at four.' He patted

Denney hard on the head. 'I take it you have no conflicting appointments?'

Denney said nothing.

'Good. And I'll call beforehand. You'll say what I tell
you to. Nothing more, nothing less. I'm putting in a lot
of work on your behalf, Your Eminence. I'd hate to see it
fucked up just because you can't remember your lines.'

Thirty-three

Nic Costa didn't know where to begin. Teresa Lupo was on her hands and knees carefully examining the sprawling blood stain which marked a good metre or more of the grubby carpet. Falcone and some detectives he only half recognized were on the far side of the octagonal chamber carefully going through the drawers of a small desk, scrutinizing every piece of paper it contained.

On the ceiling and upper walls were scores of black and white photographs, badly developed, roughly cut and taped to the crumbling plasterwork. Whatever other talents Gino Fosse possessed, he was a dedicated and skilful peeping Tom. The pictures were taken through half-open curtains, with a long, telephoto lens. They were grainy, squalid, intrusive. Most of the people in them were unknown to him. But Rinaldi was there, in three sets of shots, each with a different, unidentifiable woman. The other cast members were only half-seen: a woman, bent over the spread-eagled legs of a bored-looking hooker with blowsy hair, a fat, whale-like man whose mountain of white flesh tumbled onto the skin of the figure slumped beneath him. The pictures could have come from some porn magazine touted in the sex shops around Termini Station. The missionary position was largely absent. Several photos showed women gagged, hands bound behind their back, eyes staring blankly at the white shape heaving over them. Fosse had taken his time, photographing from every angle he could find.

Then he moved along the wall and saw what he knew, with some dread, was bound to be there. She was naked, on her back, legs wide open, waiting for a man who was only just visible, sliding towards her across the floor. It could have been the fat man in the other picture. He found it hard to judge. The location looked like an expensive apartment. A hotel maybe, since the bed had that clinical, just-made look that spoke of housemaids and room service. It was the first in a series. In others she was made to crouch in a vulgar sexual position, looking over her shoulder as if inviting the unseen viewer. There were grainy close-ups of her breasts and her abdomen: gross, intrusive pictures, almost clinical in their detail.

It was important, he thought, to scrutinize these images closely in order to understand what they had to say. There was no question of prurience. He found it impossible to look at them without feeling he was living on the edge of some waking nightmare, a world in which all the normal rules of human behaviour counted for nothing. He examined those in which her face was visible. She seemed detached, somehow, perhaps even drugged. Sara may have come here willingly but she did not wish to be a party to these games. Or was he being naïve? Her life was alien to him. Perhaps he really was, like his father, simply out of date. Perhaps it was not so unusual to meet a stranger, decide casually to have sex, and then play these bizarre, dark games in front of the prying camera. Terror and ecstasy sometimes walked hand in hand. Nic Costa was lost for answers.

He was still staring at the photographs when a hand touched his arm. It was Teresa Lupo, who looked a little less crazy each time he saw her. She was taking off her gloves. She seemed concerned.

'What do you say, Nic?'

'Nothing. It's beyond me. Rinaldi I recognize. The rest . . .'

She nodded at the body bag. 'The woman's over there. Most of her anyway. You know what I find most interesting? These aren't pictures of the protagonists. He's not trying to capture them at all. What he wants is the partner. The hooker. Or whatever they were.'

Teresa threw the gloves into a plastic bag, sniffed and let down her black hair which was tied in a rough, child-like pigtail. The act made Luca Rossi glance covetously at her from across the room.

'He kept plenty of souvenirs too.' She pointed at a couple of the photographs which showed Sara's clothes on the floor beside her naked body: flowered pants, a bra, and a loose, flowing dress. 'Look.'

She pointed to what was an untidy pile of underwear thrown into the corner of the room, so much it must have come from several different sources. 'He's a collector, I think. I just took a brief look but you can match some of those things with the photographs. This is a very tactile man. He needs some physical evidence to remind him of what he's been up to. Maybe he creeps in and steals them. Maybe he's best friends with some creep at the laundry.'

He couldn't stop looking at the photographs. 'He's crazy.'

'Never mind him. Think of the women. At least the

one woman we know. Look at the facts,' she said, pointing at a series of overlapping prints. They showed Sara
lying on the floor, neck uncomfortably upright, face to
the distant camera, staring towards the lens. The man was
scarcely in the frame. 'What do you see?'

'A naked woman in an uncomfortable position. I
don't get it. I don't understand what motivates Fosse.'

'It turns him on, I imagine. But look at the woman.
Some answers are there. What message is she sending
out?'

'She just seems . . . passive. As if it's happening to
someone else.'

Crazy Teresa groaned. 'Call yourself a detective. Are
there any signs of arousal? Are her nipples erect? Is she
opening her legs for whoever she's about to screw?'

He pulled down the clearest of the prints and peered
at it. 'No. Like I said, she looks passive.'

'You've got to extract as much as you can from this.
You get erect nipples for a variety of reasons. Arousal's
just one of them. Cold. Fear. Think about it. This woman
isn't feeling any of those. What does that mean?' She
waited. He said nothing. 'It means she's naked, possibly
with a stranger, and she's not that bothered. She's not
even half afraid. If I were a detective what would that
make me think? Why would a woman behave like that?
She knows this game. Maybe she's played it before. She's
practised.'

'That can't be true.'

'Look at it, Nic. Dispassionately.' She stared at the
pictures again. 'I could almost convince myself she knows
the camera's there. But I guess that's going too far.'

It was. It had to be. He was unconvinced by what she

said and that was not simply because he didn't want to believe it.

Teresa Lupo's big hand patted his good shoulder, hard. 'Alternatively, dear boy, she is very comfortable with strangers. I give up. Now excuse me. I need to write up some notes.'

Luca Rossi wandered over, discreetly touched her backside, then went to stand by Costa. 'How are you feeling, kid?'

'Fine.'

'I heard the woman's still going to stay with you. Is that wise?'

'Why should it be unwise?' Costa snapped.

'Hey. Will you stop biting my head off? Someone tried to kill you this morning because of her. In case you forgot.'

Costa cursed himself. It was unlike him to take out his unhappiness on others. 'Apologies again. But why shouldn't Sara stay with me? You people know how to guard the place now. I promise I won't play hooky any more. Besides, I think she's still got things to tell us. In her own time. When she feels she can trust someone.'

The big man grunted. 'I'll take your word on that.'

He nodded at the body bag. 'You hear who this is?'

Costa shook his head.

'Semi-famous lady. Alicia Vaccarini. Parliamentary deputy for Bologna. She hit the press when she turned out to be a dyke and the party bosses disowned her. Remember?'

'Vaguely,' he lied. Reading the papers was never one of his strong points.

Rossi eyed Falcone who was sifting through a pile of new photographs found under the desk. 'And he thinks he's got an idea why she was on the list too. Come on. Let's join the fun.'

Falcone shuffled through the set of prints someone had found in a tiny darkroom downstairs, built into an alcove. These weren't peeping Tom shots. They were taken in the tower, of women who'd received personal attention from Gino Fosse. In the pictures they were bound, exposed for the lens in a variety of sexual positions. Most looked scared, and two of them showed signs of violence: bruised eyes, cuts on the mouth and nose. None of them, however, was deemed worthy of display in the small octagonal room in the tower, which seemed odd. As if Fosse drew more inspiration from the snatched photos than the ones in which he was directly involved.

'He raped them,' Rossi observed.

'Really?' Falcone wondered. 'So why didn't any of them complain? We don't have anything on this man.'

'Who is he?' Costa asked.

One of the detectives he didn't know said, 'Gino Fosse. Priest at the hospital up the road for the last month. Before that he worked in the Vatican. This place is a Church property. They leased it to him at a peppercorn rent. That's as far as it goes. We're talking to the Diocese but they say they just got handed him by someone from on high. Got told to put him in here, look after him, get him a nice quiet job, keep him out of trouble.'

Falcone looked at the pictures. 'He had bad habits. Perhaps they were trying to hide him away for some reason. Perhaps he'd done this before.'

The detective shrugged. 'If he did I doubt we're going to find out about it. I've put in the calls. No one's ringing back. I'll tell you one thing though, he liked jazz.

The place is full of CDs. He had one track on loop when we turned up. Sense of humour, huh? It must have been on when he did it.'

The man held out the case: a picture of a dapper violinist sitting in a gorilla's open palm, and the title, *King Kong, Jean-Luc Ponty Plays the Music of Frank Zappa*.

'The track in particular,' he said, 'is called "How Would You Like to Have a Head Like That?"'

The morgue team heaved the body bag onto a gurney and lugged it to the narrow stairs. 'Alicia Vaccarini,' Falcone said. 'I met her once. She was on a couple of police committees. Cold bitch.' He glanced at Costa. 'Why her do you think?'

It couldn't be avoided. 'Sara Farnese slept with her. A one-night stand just like this Fosse character. Which is why she never mentioned either of them.'

Luca Rossi whistled. 'Jesus. How many other things has that woman got hidden inside her?'

'She says there were others like that. No names. She never knew them.'

Falcone put a hand to his silver beard and stared out of the slitted window. 'At least we know where Fosse is getting some of his information from. Peeping through windows, following her around.'

'Not just her,' Costa objected. 'There must be ten, twelve different women in these pictures.'

'Right. Let's show their pictures around. Specially to vice. See if anyone knows them. Let's see if we can identify any of the men too. They might appreciate the warning. Look for some link between Fosse and Denney too. It has to be there. Vaccarini certainly had one.'

She was, Falcone said, a player in political circles, with

no small amount of influence. Earlier in the year she was on the committee that looked at changing some of the diplomatic immunity rules for the Vatican. The same one that Rinaldi gave evidence to. Interesting or what? If that vote had gone the right way, Denney could have walked onto the first plane home unimpeded by the authorities, ready to disappear. Was this coincidence? Or was this the fundamental reason behind the deaths? In which case, how was Sara Farnese involved?

The men looked at each other. They knew when a case was slipping away from them. There were too many loose ends, too many roads to nowhere.

'This is turning bad,' Falcone said, glowering at Rossi. 'We missed our chance this morning. You . . .' He looked at Costa. 'You're fit to be here?'

'No problem.'

'Go back and see your friend Hanrahan. He's been on the phone hinting that maybe Denney will let you into his apartment for a talk. Could be they have something else to bargain with. And Sara Farnese. You still think she should stay at your father's house?'

'If that's what she wants.'

'To hell with what she wants,' Falcone snarled. 'Get something out of that woman. She's running rings around us, you in particular. Find out what the hell she's been dabbling in because this is more than just some nasty by-product of casual sex. She's been screwing the wrong people. Maybe someone with a cardinal's cap for all I know—'

'She denies knowing Denney,' Costa interjected, feeling weary with the man's relentless badgering.

Rossi wrinkled his fleshy nose in distaste. 'She denied

having any other lovers until one turned up without a head.'

'Just talk to her,' Falcone said. 'Don't stop until she says something. And here's a question for all of you. Just where does a runaway priest hide in Rome, for God's sake?'

'Somewhere we can't touch him,' Rossi said. '*That* place.'

'Don't be ridiculous,' Falcone sneered. 'This Fosse character is just like Denney now. They gave him some kind of chance. He threw it away. They won't want him near them. He's here. In the city. Someone knows. Someone can tell us. Get the papers onto it. Is there a photograph of him here?'

'Nothing,' someone said. 'We've got fingerprints. That's all.'

'Find some. Costa can give you a description for a photo-fit.'

Rossi scribbled out a note and gave it to one of the junior cops.

Teresa Lupo bumped into the gathering, gave them all a schoolgirl smile, fluttered her copious eyelids and said sweetly, 'I've got DNA. If anyone's interested.'

Falcone took one step back from her and said, 'What?'

There was one final package that hadn't gone on the gurney, a black plastic bag like a heavyweight supermarket carrier. She had it in her grasp and, with gloved hands, opened the sealed top for a second look. The men watched as she withdrew the head of Alicia Vaccarini tenderly, held it by the severed neck and turned the dead politician's features around to face them. Luca Rossi breathed deeply and went to the window to stare out at the Clivus Scauri. A couple of the others joined him.

'Sorry, boys,' Teresa said with a grin. 'This is all for your benefit, you know.'

She held the short hair, allowing the head to dangle freely, then opened the mouth with a plastic prong, looking inside, peering into the throat. Even Costa, not the most squeamish of men, felt something churn in his stomach. Then she put the head back in the bag, called one of the team over and passed it to him.

'Well?' She beamed at the cops. 'Just making sure I don't say anything premature. Does anyone here want to know exactly how she died? Or am I just along for the ride and your charming company?'

Falcone lit a cigarette. The men were grateful, even Nic Costa. The head stank of meat and blood and the smell seemed amplified in the cramped, overheated room. 'We're listening,' he said.

'Listen well because there may be questions after,' she said, walking to the wooden pillar in the centre of the tower. 'You boys are causing so much work for me right now I'm going to have to call in extra budget. If I have to go through the inquisition to explain that, you can too.'

She walked to the window side of the beam, smiling as the men scuttled out of the way. 'You've seen the sword.'

'Oh yes,' Rossi agreed, his back still turned but listening to every word.

'Interesting weapon. Slim. Medium length. Not a stabbing sword. More the kind of thing used on horseback. Not what the hoi polloi would think of when it comes to decapitation but then, what do they know? They just think: head needs to come off, call for the axe. Stupid. Messy. Inefficient. You know how many times they get the whole thing off in one go? One out of ten maybe. Usually they're hacking at it like some dumb peasant trying to get a chicken ready for dinner.'

Without a word Rossi crossed the room and started to march down the stairs, fumbling at his cigarette pack all the time.

'A sword is the smart executioner's weapon,' she continued. 'This man knew his stuff. He'd done his research. There's a picture in the cathedral in Valetta, *The Beheading of John the Baptist*. Our young running friend here will know it, I guess. The work of Caravaggio on his travels, when he was avoiding the law. I'll be surprised if the main man here hasn't seen it too. You've got the Baptist on the floor already dead. His neck's almost entirely severed by a sword not dissimilar to this one. And over him stands the executioner, hiding, for some reason, a dagger behind the back. Which he needs for the final cut. The blade gets through the spinal cord, you see, but tends to leave behind a flap of skin that you have to snip through to get the whole thing off. Look . . .'

She pulled out a small package from the bags of evidence and opened it. There was a tagged knife there: a kitchen implement with a broad sharp blade which was stained black with dry blood.

'Exactly the same thing,' Teresa said with an undisguised note of triumph.

Even Falcone was lost for a suitable remark.

'The question is,' she continued, 'which saint was it that he was trying to emulate here? I mean, so many died by losing their heads. Is this really like the man we have come to know and love? Is this what he intended all along? Surely not. Otherwise why go to the trouble of San Clemente and skinning that poor bastard on Tiber

Island? This destroys his continuity somehow. And here's one more thing.'

She was mocking them, Costa thought. She was relishing every moment of it.

'Isn't anyone going to ask me the time?'

'Well?' Falcone demanded.

'Three, four hours ago. Couldn't be more. He did this *after* he tried to take out our small athletic friend here. And he did it in a hurry. Conclusion? Boys, boys! You're the detectives here. I'm just a butcher's girl with a postgrad degree. But to me that says: someone rang him. Someone said, do your worst then get your crazy butt out of there before the cops come down.'

They watched her stroll happily down the stairs. There was a look on Falcone's face that Costa recognized. He was thinking on his feet.

Falcone turned to one of Teresa's assistants, Di Capua, a tubby shapeless student-type face with long, lank hair. 'How many possible DNA samples do you have in all?'

'Here? You want me to count them?'

'And the rest?'

'Skin. Blood. Bone. We could keep the lab going for a week.'

'So what are you doing with it?'

'Right now? Keeping it cool. We just haven't had time.'

'Make time. Get samples from every one of those people we're guarding too. The ones the Farnese woman named. I want to know if any of them has been near these places. Understood?'

'You're the boss,' he said.

Then Falcone crossed the room and pointed at the

pile of spent women's clothes. 'Put these in too. Just for luck. I want to know who's been doing what with who here.'

Finally, he returned and took Costa to one side. 'When you meet Denney,' he said, 'there's something I need you to do. It may sound odd but just do as I say.'

'Sure,' Nic Costa agreed. And it was odd, very odd indeed.

Thirty-four

The address he'd been given was a couple of hundred metres from Termini Station, above a Chinese restaurant. It was the worst place Gino Fosse had ever occupied, worse even than the farm he dimly remembered from his childhood, before the church school in Palermo. They'd fixed it for him. They'd told him where to run and he did, so quickly he only just remembered to snatch a few CDs and the player along with some more important belongings. They'd told him too to keep quiet, stay inside for a few hours, until the police got less jumpy, less observant.

There was money waiting for him. There was someone to act as go-between: a red-haired foreign girl who could have been no more than nineteen. She said she worked tricks around the station back-alleys, took her clients into the adjoining bedroom, where he imagined her performing her work with a brutal, brief efficiency, and then sent them quickly back out onto the street. She'd fetch food for him. She'd act as a liaison with the people outside. At one on that stifling afternoon she sat down on the one spare chair in his bedroom and looked fetchingly at him. She was pretty after a fashion: big brown eyes, an alert, alluring face, a ready, open smile.

But her skin was flawed by pink blemishes and her teeth were crooked and discoloured, like two rows of pebbles from a grimy beach. She wore a skimpy red halter top and a glossy plastic miniskirt in fluorescent lavender. When she perched on the seat she opened her legs to show him there was nothing underneath. He thought of Tertullian and what might happen next. Then, when his head just got too full to think of anything else, he nodded at her, sat on the bed and let her come down on him, just daring to touch the back of her head as she went about her work, trying to force from his mind the picture of another scalp beneath his fingers that morning.

He wondered if she was familiar. When he was doing the cardinal's business, when he was ferrying women to and fro across Rome, using his camera at every possible opportunity, he met all sorts. She could have been one. Most of them were hookers. Most of them were classy. A few straddled the borderline. It depended, he guessed, on the taste of those that Denney was trying to please. And one fitted no such category. One was just beautiful, so beautiful that, on occasion, Denney would see her alone himself, leaving Gino Fosse to wait downstairs in the apartment block, like some miserable cab driver, imagining – there was no preventing it – what was going on in the bedroom above.

She never spoke when she was in the car. She never said anything after a visit, whether it was to Denney or someone on his list. She simply sat there as lovely and serene as a portrait in a church.

Then things got bad with Denney and Gino Fosse was only driving occasionally, when there was no one else for the job or the destination was too delicate.

A month ago, in disgrace for nothing more than a

rough encounter with a hooker, he'd been exiled to the place in the Clivus Scauri. They had given him the ridiculous and mind-numbing task of comforting the dying and the bereaved in the hospital at the top of the road.

And he'd begun to change, begun to understand that he was becoming something else. It started two weeks before, in the dark echoing belly of San Giovanni in Laterano, taking a break from the weary round of visits in the hospital. In front of him was the papal altar with its ornate Gothic baldacchino. Behind a curtain, the history books insisted, were the heads of Peter and Paul preserved in silver reliquaries. He stared at this hidden space wishing he could see into it. From his childhood in Sicily to his present unhappy state in Rome the Church had enfolded him constantly, warming his nights with its comforting promises, easing his mind when the demons – and demons there were, real ones with horns and gleaming teeth – came to him and forced his hand, made him mad and bold and violent. One needed imperfect people in the world. Without them the Church would lose its meaning. Everyone would go straight to God and learn nothing, feel nothing, along the way. Peter and Paul were no strangers to anger and deceit. One had denied the Lord not once but three times, the other was a persecutor of Christians, a supreme, cruel servant of the Roman state. And now they were saints. Now their mummified heads sat in silver caskets in a hidden partition of the canopy that stood before him.

Gino Fosse would recall this moment for the rest of his life. It was here, in the black maw of San Giovanni, that something wormed its way into his soul, wound itself around his neck and whispered in his ear what he already half suspected: *he was a fool and worse*. It spoke of what he had done on the sweaty bed in the medieval tower on the Clivus Scauri. It taunted him with the bright, vivid memories. It reminded him of the sinful ecstasies: the warmth of a woman panting on his neck, the feel of her flesh against his as he writhed and moaned above her. And it asked: where, in all this delight, is the sin? Where, in all this feverish, mindless conjoining of their bodies, was there room for the old, dead myths passed down by generations of men whose primary purpose was to serve themselves?

There were no heads in the canopy's space. Or if there were, they belonged to some hapless corpses which had been appropriated for the sake of the Church. Peter and Paul were distant shadows. If they lived, they may never have come to Rome. If they were martyred, their remains were now dust on the wind, particles inhaled and exhaled by black and white, young and old, Christian, Muslim and atheist, everywhere. They weren't hiding inside an ornate metal container in some vast, overweening basilica in Rome.

He was deceived. And if they tricked him about this, then what else was true?

He found himself sweating. His head ached. His eyes felt heavy. When he looked down at the ground, to make sure it was still there, it seemed to shift beneath his feet like water moving in a slow and relentless swell.

They lied. Every one of them.

He was amazed it had taken so long for him to see through their deceit. Gino Fosse burned with anger and shame at that moment and there was scarcely a waking second afterwards when these bitter, acrid sensations abated. Then, later, there was the ultimate revelation, in a smaller, darker place, with the Irishman's dank, tobacco-stained breath in his ear, bringing a new and terrible kind of sense and order with it.

It was in San Giovanni that he began to lose the faith of his childhood and that was worse than anything he could imagine, worse than going blind or becoming a cripple. In a few, terrifying moments he was transformed. He became an outsider, a man beyond the Church that had been a kind of parent to him for as long as he could recall. From this point on he would begin to live outside the normal bounds of humanity.

Yet a faith remained, hidden, silent, waiting for him to recognize it. Later, when that occurred, Gino Fosse would know he was not alone. In his soul there was a profound, inexplicable certainty. For all their trickery, there was a God, one Peter and Paul knew and the modern world had forgotten. Not the God of bureaucrats and basilicas. Not the God of love and reconciliation, the comforting face of Jesus hanging over a child's bed. The true God still lived on from the Old Testament, a supernatural deity, angry, vengeful and hungry, ready to punish those who betrayed him. This God would become a constant presence inside Gino Fosse's head, his one bulwark against a cruel and shallow world. From time to time he spoke, offering the promise of eventual redemption. He accompanied him when the work began, wakeful and watching in the church on Tiber Island, on the shore of the dead river, in the upstairs room where the sinning bitch Alicia Vaccarini would take her first step on the road to deliverance.

And he took them to his bosom, even the vilest. The bloody harvest served its purpose. They were, against their own instincts, snatched from the darkness to his side.

Fosse thought about this as the red hair bobbed beneath his hand. One day it would be his turn and he would go willingly, knowing his sins would be washed clean. This was a world of shadows, an unreal, transitory place of stinking bodies and vile physical couplings. He was a part of it, and a part of him too. The reconciliation of these two was under way.

She moved more rapidly. He felt the heat rise and pushed her away. She went to the sink. He listened to the sound of her there. It seemed an act as commonplace as brushing one's teeth. This woman's body had been subverted for a purpose. He was surprised by the realization that she was not to blame.

'What are you called?' he asked across the room.

She turned and looked at him, puzzled. 'You want to know my name?'

'Is that so odd?'

'You bet.' Her voice had an odd tinny quality, as if she struggled with the soft vowels of Italian.

'Well?' he insisted.

'Irena.'

'Where are you from?'

'Kosovo,' she answered, a little nervously.

'Orthodox? Or the other?'

'Neither,' she said sharply. 'Why do you want to know?'

'Just asking.'

'Where I come from you don't ask that. Good people don't. Just the ones looking for someone to kill.'

'I'm sorry.' There was a lifetime of fear and grief inside her. He could see it behind her pretty, blemished face.

'My name's Gino,' he said. 'I won't hurt you, Irena. I just want you to do something for me. Here . . .' He pulled out a sheaf of notes from his jacket pocket. She stared at them. It was big money for her, he guessed. They had been generous and he'd robbed Alicia Vaccarini's purse too. 'What do you make in a day?'

'A hundred and fifty. Two hundred sometimes. Maybe more.' She toyed with her hair. 'Don't get to keep it. I'm not what you'd call top-class goods.'

There was something else inside this damaged half-child. Something still young, still unspoiled in spite of everything. 'Looks don't matter. It's what's in here –' he patted his heart – 'that counts. And you don't look bad either.'

'Thanks.' The pebble teeth shone wanly in the afternoon sunlight streaming through the window.

'Here's three hundred. You get this every day you're with me. In return, you don't do any tricks. You just do what I say.'

She came over and took the money. There was a stupid, puzzled smile on her face.

'If I do some tricks we get more money.'

He took her arm, gently. 'No tricks.'

She smiled. 'OK. It's fine by me.'

'Now. Go get me a phone book. I want some wine too. Red. Sicilian. Some bread, cheese. Whatever food you like. I don't care.'

'Sure,' she said, grinning. 'And when I come back we'll have fun. I'll show you things. Things you don't get in Italy.'

A black angry look rose on his face. She took a step back. 'If you want . . .'

'If I want,' he repeated.

She scuttled out of the room quickly. It was almost two hours before she returned with what he asked for.

Surreptitiously he stood next to her, letting the smell enter his nostrils. He expected a stink to her, of sweat and something else he recognized, and a guilty look in her lost eyes. There was nothing. She looked at him, smiling, then, for no reason at all, kissed him on the cheek.

'What was that for?' he asked.

'Being kind.'

She lived in a lost world too, one in which an absence of cruelty counted as gentleness. She was a part of a greater mechanism, small, unimportant. She was, in a sense, very like him.

Thirty-five

Nic Costa and Luca Rossi stood in the Via di Porta Angelica, watching the Swiss Guards kicking their heels in the private entrance to the Vatican quarters opposite. Only three days before they had been in St Peter's Square routinely seeking out bag-snatchers. It seemed a lifetime ago. The city had turned strange and deadly since. Their own relationship had shifted towards sourness too and, it seemed to Costa, that stemmed from more than his new-found assertiveness. The big man was unhappy, deeply unhappy, and reluctant to explain why.

Rossi cast an evil glance at the blue uniforms across the street, then complained, 'If you hadn't had that damned scanner stuck to your ear none of this would have happened.'

'None of what?' Costa asked, dumbfounded. 'You mean those people would be alive? And all the world would be sweet and peaceful? All because I left the scanner at home?'

'Maybe,' he grumbled. 'Who's to know?'

'Right.'

'I'll tell you one thing, kid. You wouldn't have that hole in your shoulder and a face that looks like you've been head-butting the wall all day. And you wouldn't have that woman stuck in your father's house, messing up your imagination all the time.'

'That's crap, Rossi.' He heard the harshness of his own voice and how he used the big man's surname. It was all so foreign.

'Yeah, it's crap. Here's some more crap too. I talked to a couple of criminal friends of mine early today. Asked them if the name Cardinal Michael Denney meant anything. You know what? I was right. It's not just us that gets twitchy every time we hear about him. There are whole brigades of bad bastards out there itching to get their hands on him. Except they don't really want the conversation side of things. They just want to tear the heart out of his chest and leave it somewhere for the rats to gnaw on. He messed up some important people very badly and they don't take kindly to that sort of thing. Are you listening to what I'm saying? There's a bounty on him, kid. You could probably pick up fifty thousand dollars or more if you handed him over to a couple of thugs in dark glasses right now.'

Costa pointed to the gate. 'So why don't they just walk in and do it? We stay out because we have to. It's not like it's a fortress in there, except where the boss lives. They could go in if they wanted.'

'Get real.' Rossi was shaking his head, looking at him with contempt. 'You don't understand a damned thing, do you? These people who want him, they're all good Catholics to a man. Sure they kill. They maim. They steal. They sell people stuff that ruins their souls. But they think of themselves as honourable men. They've got rules. They don't even kill cops unless they have to, though judges, that's a different thing. They've got a code and it says that place in there's safe. As far as Denney's concerned he's living in some mink-lined sanctuary as long as he's behind those walls. He'd just better not step out, that's all. Or if he does, he'd better be gone from here real quickly and surface some place else looking nothing like he did before.'

Costa felt tired. His shoulder was aching. A vein was pumping through the bruise on his temple. 'So what?'

The big man leant down into his face. 'So we take care, Nic. We watch what we say, what we do, who we trust. This is a complicated world.'

'I'll bear that in mind.' Costa looked at his watch. 'Right now I have an appointment. I'll catch you tomorrow.'

'I can come along,' Rossi suddenly offered. 'No problem. I don't mind.'

Costa couldn't fathom it. 'You heard what Falcone said? He wanted me there, alone.'

'Yeah. I heard what Falcone said. I can still come. We're supposed to be partners, aren't we?'

But they weren't. Something had happened to open up a gulf of mistrust between them.

'I appreciate the offer, Uncle Luca. Don't get me wrong.'

The big man snorted as if he was expecting the rejection. 'Sure. Nice to be appreciated. Well, you just go do what Falcone wants, and make sure you do it to the letter. That's why we're here.'

'Luca? What's wrong?'

The flabby, bloodless face fell. Luca Rossi looked lost. 'Nothing. Everything. This stupid job. You. You more than anything, if you want the honest answer.'

Costa was silent. He felt hurt and responsible too somehow.

'When this is over, Nic, I want a change. Maybe they can give me a job pushing paper somewhere. I'm sorry. I lied. It's not just you. It's this line of work. It depresses me. It follows me everywhere. I want to sleep at night. I want to sit in a park and not notice the needles on the ground. I want to go for a walk and never wonder why some creep is standing by a car on the other side of the road, handing stuff out to kids who happen by. Most of all I want to meet women who talk about their clothes and where they shop, not about whom they dissected that morning and what they found in his gut.'

'If you date a pathologist . . .'

Luca Rossi sighed. 'Yeah. Point taken. I'm stupid. Sorry. Sure you don't want to reconsider my offer?'

'And get ourselves into deeper shit with Falcone?'

'Sometimes,' Rossi said, 'you have to be your own man.'

It sounded like the kind of thing his father would say.

Rossi waited until he saw there was going to be no answer. Then he turned on his heels and shambled off towards the metro station and the long journey back to his apartment in the suburbs. Nic Costa watched him go, asking himself what he could do to repair this breach. He wasn't ready to lose Luca Rossi just yet. He needed some pillars in his life. In the brief time they had known each other, he had become convinced this sad, big man could fit the bill somehow. Partly because they could, he thought, learn to lean on one another from time to time.

Disconsolate, he looked at the gate into the Vatican. Hanrahan was there, in a dark suit, watching him from across the road. Nic Costa remembered why he was here, threaded his way through the pedestrians, sweating in their shorts and T-shirts, wandering down to the piazza, and, for the third time in three days, found himself in a foreign country.

Thirty-six

They walked along a narrow road running parallel with the main public street to the south. The tall buildings on either side cast some welcome shadow on the pavement. The place was deserted. The crowds and the visitors were elsewhere, in St Peter's and the grand piazza outside. These were the administrative quarters of the Vatican state, with a few blocks set aside for residences.

Hanrahan looked him up and down. 'You've been in the wars.'

'Nothing to worry about.'

'I'm glad to hear that. I'm glad too that you took my offer of last night seriously. You'll find me a good friend, you know. I've a little influence beyond these walls. I know people that don't cross your path ordinarily. You never know when I might be able to help.'

Costa looked sceptical.

'Now, now,' Hanrahan continued. 'A friendship has to be based on some kind of exchange. Otherwise it's not friendship at all. It's just one person using another. This is the oldest kind of relationship in the world, Nic. I give you something. You give me something back.'

'Something you owe me by rights anyway, if I'm not mistaken.'

Hanrahan opened the door to a grey block that could have been an office building. 'But you are, Nic. I don't have to give you anything. Please remember that. It's most important.'

He walked inside. The Irishman followed. They were in a dark, narrow stairwell with simple stone steps leading up. Costa's surprise must have shown on his face.

'Now I know what you're thinking. You're thinking, what's a cardinal of the Catholic Church doing living in a dump like this? Do you know something? Our man here's asking himself the same question too.'

'And the answer?'

Hanrahan held his arms open wide. 'We all pay for our transgressions in the end. What more can I say?'

They went up to the third floor. Hanrahan rang the bell. Costa watched an eye glint at the spy hole, heard two sets of chains rattle, then saw the heavy wooden door fall back to reveal the slim form of Cardinal Michael Denney. He looked more like an old matinee star than a churchman. Denney had a fine, chiselled face that was still handsome in spite of the lined cheeks and the wrinkles at the corner of a straight and humourless mouth. His lips were grey and thin, his teeth when he briefly smiled were white and perfect. He had a full head of straight, silver hair cut unfashionably long so that it hung over his ears and his collar. He was a tall man with the slight stoop that came from perpetually looking down to the people he was addressing.

'Come in,' he said in an educated American accent.

Nic Costa walked through and found himself in a modest apartment, meagrely decorated save for a few expensive-looking paintings that were, he imagined, Denney's own. Then he looked more closely and saw one that was familiar: a copy of Caravaggio's *Martyrdom of Saint Matthew*, the same canvas that had caught Luca Rossi's attention as they left San Luigi dei Francesi. There was a threadbare three-piece suite, a low table in front of the sofa, and a small desk covered in papers. The two main windows were too small. Even on this bright, dazzling day Denney needed the extra illumination of a standard lamp to be able to work at the desk. The place was minuscule, smaller even than his own home. Denney had surely come down in the world.

'It's all a single man needs,' Denney said, watching the way Costa took in the room. 'Can I get you something to drink? A beer maybe?'

'Nothing.'

Denney picked up a bottle of Peroni and swigged from the neck. He was wearing a cheap grey sweatshirt and jeans. Costa found it hard to think of him as a churchman at all, least of all a cardinal. 'You don't mind if I do. Damned hot today. Don't worry about Hanrahan here either. Never seen him touch the stuff. Worried your guard might drop, eh, Brendan?'

The Irishman sat down in one of the chairs. He looked ready for business. 'Drink and work don't mix in my experience, Your Eminence. And I tasted enough of it when I was young, thank you very much.'

'See?' Denney said with a grin. 'The perfect servant of the Vatican. Brendan here's a true diplomat, son. Not a made-up priest like I was. He understands this place better than anyone.'

Hanrahan shot him a savage glance. 'May we get down to business now?'

'Sure.' Denney sat down heavily on the sofa, spreading his long legs wide in a way Costa associated with Americans. 'So, Mr Costa, what have you got to give me?'

'What do you want?'

'Safe passage,' Denney said instantly. 'Just a car to the airport with a blue light on the top, not flashing, I'd like some privacy. And a nice convoy back and front to keep any unwelcome spectators away. My colleagues here would rather I was gone. I think there are plenty of others outside these walls who feel the same way. To be frank with you, it would make me happy too. I've a fancy to go back home. There's some little places I knew back in Boston when I was a kid. There are some people who'll help me start anew if I ask them right. Thought I might change my name, get a life back. Not a lot to ask.'

Hanrahan was watching him avidly, as if judging every word, and making notes on a pad.

Costa wondered what there was to play with. 'Cardinal, I can tell you there are three judicial warrants in preparation for your arrest right now. The moment you step onto Italian soil any number of people, not just me but the Finance Ministry and the tax people too, have a duty to arrest you. I don't know how I can even begin to address that kind of demand.'

'So why are you here?' Hanrahan asked. 'If you've got nothing to offer, what's there to talk about?'

He thought about the long briefing he'd had from Falcone. It was precise and definite in its terms. 'What I'm authorized to say is this. If you cooperate with us on the Gino Fosse case, turning over every item of information you possess, I can guarantee that you will be placed somewhere secure, pre-trial and after, if there's a custodial sentence. You've plenty of friends.'

Denney snorted and looked out of the meagre windows, disgusted.

'No one wants to see you in jail,' Costa continued. 'Not least because I don't think we could guarantee your safety there. It would be somewhere comfortable. Somewhere you could have access to the people you want to see.'

'Jesus,' Denney snapped. 'Do you think I don't have that much here? I'd just be swapping one prison cell for another. Don't you understand? I don't want your protection. I don't want to talk to the judiciary. There's plenty of government people here wouldn't like that either. I just want to disappear back where I came from.'

Costa was unmoved. 'This isn't a parking ticket you're asking us to tear up.'

Hanrahan sighed and closed the notebook on his lap. 'I apologize, Your Eminence. I've wasted your time. I thought these people were serious. Clearly I was wrong.'

'No,' Costa insisted. 'We're serious about treating you fairly. About keeping you alive too and that may not be so easy. From what I hear I don't think you could just fade away into the back streets of Boston and lose these people. They're persistent. They're angry. They want your blood.'

Denney stared at his long thin hands. He had the fingers of a pianist. For all his dignity he was beginning to look like a broken man.

'Gino Fosse is dangerous, violent and unpredictable,' Costa continued. 'He's killed four people that we know of and caused the death of one more. He could be out there right now working out how to kill someone else. I can't bargain your freedom from justice against finding a man like this. You must understand that.'

'Justice?' Denney went over to the desk, opened a drawer and took out a file. It had Fosse's name on it and an official Vatican stamp on the cover. Hanrahan watched him, worried.

'Look,' he said. 'Fosse was some junior employee who worked for me. I fired him when he got out of hand. Everything anyone knows about him is here in his personal record. From the moment he went to school till last week when, as far as anyone knew, he was doing a routine job in the hospital. It's got the man in here. It's got his problems too. I never knew about them at the time we took him on. I swear that. But I've checked since. He was never someone we could be proud of. Still, the Church looks after its own. As much as it can. Everything's here. You're telling me that's not worth a bean?'

Costa eyed the blue folder anxiously. 'I didn't say that. I offered you preferential treatment. I offered you security. You wouldn't be getting that if you were some working-class hood from Testaccio. You still have to answer for what you've done. I can't avoid that.'

' "I can't avoid that"?' Denney repeated. 'You're sitting in judgement on me? Let me tell you something, son. I know what I've done. I know what others have done too. We all get judged sometime, and not by some bent and stupid judiciary either.'

Nic remembered Falcone's instructions. 'Can I have that beer now?'

Denney looked puzzled. He walked to the corner of the room, opened the fridge and came out with two fresh ones.

'*Salute*,' he said.

Costa waved the bottle in his face. '*Salute.* Oh, and go to hell. This man's killed. He'll kill again and go on killing until we stop him. How can you ask for something in return? Is that what it means being a Catholic these days? Is that where your conscience lies? In your own self-interest?'

It was worth a try. He was tired of Denney's tricks. He was sick of Hanrahan's silent, oppressive presence.

Denney said nothing and stared at his hands.

'See that picture,' Costa said, nodding at the painting on the wall. 'What's that doing here?'

Denney looked at the Caravaggio. It sparked some interest in his face, as if he had forgotten it existed and was grateful for the reminder. 'Old times' sake,' he said eventually and left it at that.

Costa wondered whether to take the risk. There was nothing to lose. It was a good copy, a third size or so. The figure of the murderer, sword in hand, half-naked, and bathed in the same light of Grace that fell on the dying Matthew, prone and bleeding on the ground, dominated the centre, raging at the martyr. Onlookers fled from the scene in terror. Only one face, half-hidden in the shadows, was still, and keenly curious, with that familiar, pained expression, one that Nic Costa had recognized and understood since his father first told him the story.

'Let me tell you something.' He stood up and beckoned for Denney to join him. 'You know who this is?'

He pointed to the bearded figure almost lost in the shadows.

Denney let out a low murmur of pleasure. 'Hey, I remember that now. What is this? A cop who knows art?'

'I'm curious. That's all. So who is it?'

'Caravaggio. It's his self-portrait, putting himself into the scene.'

'Why?' Costa asked.

'As a witness. As a sympathizer.'

'And as a participant too. Look at his face. Isn't he asking himself why he has to paint this scene? Why he's partaking of Matthew's blood as if it were some sacrament? And, most of all, why he's creating this drama out of his own head in the first place, since none of it has any historical authenticity. What he's saying is: we're all involved, we're all part of the story, whether we recognize it or not.'

'Nice sermon,' Denney said, nodding. 'You missed your calling.'

Then he went back to his chair and picked up the bottle of beer. Costa followed him, wondering whether he had made his point.

'I meant that,' Denney observed. 'You're an unusual young man. Do you get many cops in church these days?'

'I just go where the paintings are. There's nothing religious in it.'

'That may be true, I guess. Or at least you could think so. To be honest I haven't looked at that picture in years. You forget what's important sometimes. You take it for granted. I loved that place when I first came to Rome. It seemed to me to be what being a Catholic was all about, much more so than . . .' He waved a hand in the direction of St Peter's. 'Hey. I'd better watch my mouth. That right, Brendan?'

The Irishman shuffled uncomfortably on his seat.

'To hell with it,' Denney said suddenly. He threw the folder on the table. 'Take the thing. No price. No deal. Just tell your man Falcone I expect him to think about what that's worth. Think of the risks I'm running letting private Vatican files out of this place. Then, maybe, he should consider doing me a favour in return.'

Hanrahan leapt from his chair and tried to grab the file. Denney's slender fingers went down on the cover. 'No, Brendan,' he said firmly. 'My mind's made up.'

'Jesus, Michael,' Hanrahan pleaded. 'Give him that and we've got nothing left to bargain with.'

'I don't care. I don't want any more deaths on my conscience. Let them have it.'

Hanrahan swore, then returned to his chair. 'Well, that concludes our business, I think. Quite what else there might be to discuss is beyond me now.'

Costa looked Denney directly in the face. 'Do you know Sara Farnese?'

'Who?' He didn't even blink.

'The university lecturer in the papers. The one who seems to have sparked this.'

'Ah.' Some recognition rose in Denney's sallow face. 'I did read about her.' He shrugged.

'Is that a yes or a no?'

'You're an insistent little bastard, aren't you?' Denney observed dryly.

'Like I said. Just curious.'

He sniffed. 'Well, you don't need to be that curious to know I've had a taste for women in my time.'

'I was asking a specific question,' Costa insisted.

'Do you have a picture of her? The ones in the papers didn't jog my memory.'

'No. I gave you her name. Sara Farnese.'

'Names?' He smiled at Hanrahan. 'He thinks names are important, Brendan? What kind of people are the police recruiting these days? Liking art I can understand. But this *naïveté* . . .'

Hanrahan stared miserably at the folder and said nothing.

'Let me be honest with you, son. When a man like me wanted a woman, I got one sent. I can't afford affairs. Long-term relationships. All those things are just too messy if they go wrong. So if the mood took me, I'd get someone to place the call. Understand?'

'Does the mood still take you?'

Denney's head moved from side to side. 'You're getting personal. That's out of bounds.'

'So you're saying that if you met her it was because she was a hooker.'

'Your words not mine. *If* I met her. And that's an end to it.'

'OK,' Costa said. 'Do you mind? I need to go.'

He walked into the small bathroom and turned both taps on full. Falcone had suggested the toothbrush or a comb if there was no alternative, though it could have alerted Denney to what was going on. Instead, Costa rifled through the waste bin. There, beneath a spent shaving foam canister, was what he wanted: a paper tissue with a tiny blood stain, doubtless from shaving, on the edge. He picked it up and placed it inside a plastic bag, then hid the thing in his pocket.

The two men weren't even looking each other in the eye when he returned.

He picked up the folder, waved it at Denney and said, 'Thank you. I'll pass on what you said.'

Denney nodded. Then he and Hanrahan watched the young cop walk out of the door.

When they heard his footsteps die away on the stone staircase below, Denney turned to the Irishman. 'Well?'

'A good job, Michael,' Hanrahan said. 'I couldn't have done better myself. I'll have you safely out of here. And that I promise.'

Thirty-seven

By seven that Monday evening the case of Gino Fosse occupied most of the resources of the Rome state police. More than thirty officers were on duty guarding the men Sara Farnese had named as former lovers, all of whom had now been swabbed for DNA and the samples passed, along with that illicitly taken from Michael Denney, to the big police lab near the river. A team of four had been assigned to go through the personnel file from the Vatican which Nic Costa had brought back to the station.

Nothing looked promising. Fosse was raised in Sicily by peasant farmer parents. At six he had gone to board at a local Church school. His parents rarely visited. His record there was one of promising academic achievement and persistent, violent misbehaviour. Falcone pointed out a significant event: when Fosse was nine he'd been found torturing a young cat in a wood by the school play-ground. The inspector got one of the detectives to track down a retired teacher who knew the boy. The details were revealing: Fosse had skinned the animal alive then nailed the corpse to a tree. A year later there was another case. A stray dog was tethered to a set of railings, doused in petrol and set on fire. Fosse denied all knowledge.

No one believed him but, if they had proof, none came forward with it. He had, said the former teacher, an intense curiosity in one particular field of study: the lives and, most of all, the deaths of the early martyrs.

He grew older and discovered new interests. At the age of thirteen he was reported for a serious sexual assault on a schoolgirl. Two years later he was reported for an almost identical offence. Both cases were dropped, for no obvious reasons.

Five years later he entered the seminary. From that point on he had occupied a series of junior positions in Palermo, Naples, Turin and finally Rome until joining the administrative staff of the Vatican five years before. Falcone set men calling the cities where Fosse had worked before, talking to the local cops and any priests they could persuade to come to the phone. They soon picked up a picture, as much from what was not said as the details they gleaned from the reluctant parties on the other end of the line. Gino Fosse was constant trouble. In each job he'd been moved on for some misdemeanour. In Naples he had been accused of sleeping with prostitutes in his own parish. In Turin money had gone missing and he had become involved in a fist fight with the senior detective who had been assigned to investigate the loss. There were darker rumours too, all unproven, of sadistic sexual encounters. Yet he was never charged, never dismissed from his position. Fosse floated from post to post, falling apart after a few months, often with disastrous consequences. Still he made steady progress towards Rome, towards the Vatican and the pinnacle of Church bureaucracy. Finally he found himself in the job he had occupied until only a few weeks before, working on the clerical staff for Denney, typing, phoning, driving.

'So why does he keep on going up and up like this?' Falcone asked Costa.

'I don't know. Maybe they try to keep people in the fold.'

'Bullshit. Look . . .'

It was a single-page report someone had gleaned from the anti-Mafia squad: six years old and scarcely the stuff of scandal. It said that a young trainee priest, named as Gino Fosse, with the details of his parents' farm attached in parentheses, had stayed at the home of one of the city's most notorious Mafia bosses for three months while attending studies in a nearby college.

Falcone tapped the page. 'Friends. Look at that. He knows the people of old. He's a house guest of the biggest hood in Palermo.'

'And they could ease his way in the Church? They could get him off the hook when he walks into trouble?'

'Are you serious? How long have you been a cop, kid? These people can call the Quirinale Palace direct and ask if the president's at home. That's not the issue. The real question is, why? Why keep some farmer's punk out of jail? Why keep him groping up the slippery ladder like this? Do they really think he's cut out for better things?'

That was surely impossible. Fosse looked like a dangerous loser, a liability for anyone to have around.

Falcone dashed the folder on the desk. 'And I'm supposed to let that bastard in the Vatican go for this? Hanrahan honestly thinks he can trade for Denney's freedom with a bunch of personnel records?'

Costa had been thinking of Denney ever since he left the apartment. The man seemed desperate but defeated too, as if he were waiting for some unknown fate to overtake him. He wanted to escape the gloomy prison the authorities had made for him. Costa doubted there was much joy in the prospect either, or much hope of redemption. Even when he talked about home, about Boston, he seemed downcast, as if he knew it was a pipedream.

'Perhaps that's all they have. They're clutching at straws.'

'Now that,' Falcone replied, 'I do doubt. You must never take them at their word. Hanrahan least of all.'

'So you'll tell him there's no deal.'

'He can sweat until tomorrow. Then we'll see.'

Tomorrow, he nearly said, there could be another corpse. And Michael Denney still screaming to get out of that dismal apartment.

He tried to think straight and found his eyes closing, the drowsiness taking over. Falcone's hand on his good shoulder jolted him awake.

'It's been a long day for all of us, specially for you. Go home, Nic. Talk to that woman. Try to make more sense of this than I can. Come back in the morning and tell me how it all fits.'

'Are you sure?' The inspector's sudden amiable mood took him by surprise. He was dog-tired. All the same, there was so much happening. He hated being anywhere else.

Falcone looked him up and down, something not far from sympathy on his face. 'I'm sure you're no use to me here. And I don't want to be bawling you out for anything else today. It may just make me feel guilty. It was your own damn fault Fosse nearly killed you yesterday, no one else's. That doesn't stop me feeling bad about it. So no solitary running, mind. That partner of yours is pissed off enough as it is. As am I. Hey . . .' Falcone patted him on his good shoulder. 'On your way. You earned a break.'

Nic Costa looked outside the office door. Beyond the glass Luca Rossi was bent over the computer, stabbing awkwardly at the keyboard with a big index finger.

'Rossi wants out,' he said without thinking, then cursed himself. It was the big man's prerogative to break this news.

Falcone seemed unmoved by the idea. 'I know. He told me. People get like this in the middle of a bad case. Don't think anything of it. Don't take it personally.'

'But it is personal. There's something about me that bugs him.'

'Age. You're getting older. You're starting to want to be on top. He's just feeling everything winding down. His life's a pile of shit. He's got no future. He's looking for someone else to blame.'

Costa was incensed. 'That's unfair. Luca's a good cop. An honest cop. He'd do anything, for you, for me, anyone on the force.'

'Yeah. But he's *spent*, kid. Just a burnt-out case and I've got no room here for people like that. When this is done he can ship out and lick envelopes or something. Or take the pension and go drink himself to death in Rimini. Who's to care?'

'Me.'

Falcone's face turned sour again and creased with disgust. 'Then you're an idiot. One of these days you've got to decide whose side you're on. The winners or the losers.'

'You're going to say that when some young buck comes in and thinks you're a loser? Sir?'

'Not going to happen,' Falcone said emphatically. 'I

go when I choose to go. Look at him. Four years older than me. That's all. Do you think anyone could believe it? He's just run to seed. No use to anyone. He's no power over himself. A man has to possess that. If he doesn't, somebody else will take it from him or, worse, he just gives up on everything and blows with the wind. That's what your friend's doing and he doesn't even care much where it takes him.'

Costa stood up and walked out of the room not wishing to hear another word. He passed the big man at the desk and patted his huge shoulder gently. 'Good-night, Uncle Luca.'

Two puzzled watery eyes looked up at him. 'What's wrong with you, junior?'

'I'm tired and I want to go to bed.'

He snorted. The sound was like a walrus choking on something. Costa was pleased. It was good to see he could still raise a laugh in the man.

Then Luca Rossi's face turned serious. 'Don't let her tuck you in, Nic. Not just yet, eh?'

He walked down two flights of steps, out into the open air. The night was humid and oppressive. There was scarcely anyone on the street. The usual bum was occupying his usual position by the café the cops used round the corner next to the station car park. He was hunched on the street, head between legs. He stank to high heaven.

The familiar, bearded face looked up as he walked by. Costa stopped and reached into his pocket.

'Why do you do this?' the bum snapped, half drunk already. 'Why the hell's it always you.'

'Does it matter?' he asked, surprised. 'It's just money.'

He had an ageless face. He could have been thirty or

twice that age. He was, Costa understood this, lost already. The money made no difference. It went on drink straight away, only hastening the inevitable. 'Not for you it isn't. For everyone else it's just small change. They don't notice me. I like that. Not you. With you I have to earn it. I have to talk. I have to act grateful. You know what I think?'

He felt dog-tired. His head hurt. 'Tell me.'

'This is for you. Not me at all. This is just a little ointment for your conscience, huh? A little something to help you sleep at night.'

Costa looked at the miserable figure on the ground. He held out a hundred-euro note: ten times the usual amount. The bum's eyes glinted in the gloom. 'Want it?'

The tramp held out his hand.

'Fuck you,' Nic Costa said, then put the money in his pocket and walked into the car park, only half hearing the slurred stream of curses directed at his back.

It was the first time in years he'd never made that second gift. Falcone had made his point.

Thirty-eight

Thirty minutes after an exhausted Nic Costa left the station Falcone looked up from his desk to see the familiar figure of Arturo Valena waddling towards him across the office. This was only the second time he had seen Valena in the flesh. The first was when the television presenter had been paid to MC a police awards ceremony, a job he had undertaken with a swift, efficient professionalism that almost merited the huge fee he pocketed with little grace afterwards.

Falcone had found the appearance of the man fascinating. He was one of the most familiar figures on Italian television. He interviewed everyone: politicians, film stars, entertainers. He had a big, handsome face and a gruff, booming voice that had a permanent question mark inside it, as if asking, perpetually, 'Really?' Officially he was forty-nine, though rumours suggested this was one of many myths surrounding the man. Valena had been born into dire poverty in Naples, probably at least fifty-five years before, working his way up through minor jobs in government and public relations until he was given his chance to try his hand at broadcasting. It was, Falcone now thought, the same kind of relentless progress Gino Fosse had made from his peasant farm in Sicily, perhaps aided by the same kind of friends. Once Valena had established his position as the leading commentator for one of the most successful private channels, he never hesitated to criticize government policy and, on occasion, question whether the fight against 'crime' did not infringe the rights of the individual. He had dabbled with politics himself, sitting on a variety of committees, and made no secret of his right-wing views. The one-time Naples gutter kid had become a mover and shaker in the higher echelons of social life in Rome, and had married a minor countess too, a severe-faced woman rolling in money who preferred to spend most of her time on the family estate in Perugia.

And it was all an act, one which could only be sustained on TV. The camera flattered his exaggerated features, the clever lighting hid his fast-expanding belly. The rigorous preparation for each interview, the ever-ready autocue and his cultured on-screen sensibility, which was more that of the actor than the journalist, all served to hide the real man from the public. Falcone had seen this at the awards ceremony, when Valena made the mistake to hang around long enough afterwards for people to talk to him and come away disappointed by what they found. Valena lived behind a mask and fought to keep everyone from peering round the sides. Close up, in unrehearsed conversation, he was exposed for the fraud he truly was: inarticulate, snappy, unconfident. And physically repellent. The man was a famous gourmand who had sponged his way around the city's finest dining rooms for years. Now he was paying the price. His waistline had expanded enormously, enough for the magazines to notice. In the last few months they had nicknamed him

'Arturo Balena' – 'Arthur Whale' – and started running a series of pictures to hammer home the point. There were snatched shots showing him at the table, with *foie gras* and worse on the plate, alone, eating like a pig. There was a series, too, of him around the swimming pool of a hotel in Capri, with an unidentified blonde. He lounged on a sun bed slowly cooking under the sun, his over-ample flesh turning an unattractive lobster colour. The spectacle had sold many, many magazines. Valena, unwisely, had complained to the authorities and pleaded for the editor of the rag to be prosecuted under the privacy laws. The result was predictable. He was now on the paparazzi's A-list of people to be photographed at every possible opportunity. They stalked him on scooters. They invaded the restaurants where he ate alone, in a single darkened table at the back. Arturo Valena had become fair game for a media sensing a figure on the brink of some spectacular, public downfall. The ratings for his nightly chat show were in decline. There were rumours that he might soon be dragged into an endless and messy civil court case about the misuse of state funds by bent officials who had bribed the media for favourable coverage. He was on the cusp of a cruel descent from the starry heights.

Falcone opened his desk drawer and took out a set of copies of the photos found in Fosse's room. There was a big, pale fat man in some of those. You never got to see his face but it could be the same man. He opened the door to the office and watched Valena collapse, sweating, into a chair.

The TV man looked terrified. His dull brown eyes were bleary and liquid. His chest heaved hard with laboured panting.

'I want protection,' Arturo Valena said, between

snatched gasps. 'You hear me? I only just got back from doing a show in Geneva. I read on the plane what this crazy bastard did to that poor bitch Vaccarini. He's after me next. You hear it?'

Falcone gave him a glass of water and smiled, hoping to calm him down. 'Please,' he said. 'From the beginning.'

'To hell with the beginning,' Valena spat back at him. 'I've got to be at the Brazilian Embassy in forty-five minutes. Can't avoid it. There's an exhibition opening and I need to be there. I want protection, you hear me? Or do I have to ring upstairs and get someone else to make you listen?'

Falcone pushed the phone across the desk. Valena glowered at him. 'What?'

'Call. Whoever you like. They'll just ask me to decide anyway. In case you hadn't heard, Mr Valena, we have every officer we've got on this case. Most of them are looking after people who have given us good reason to spend some time with them. You'll have to convince me you fit that category.'

'Idiot!' Valena yelled. He was sweating profusely. A bad smell, of perspiration and fear, was starting to permeate the little office.

He picked up the phone and started to make the calls. Falcone watched him, knowing what would happen. Arturo Valena understood he was on the slow drift downwards but had yet to appreciate how far he had already progressed. There would be no coming back. The future held only obscurity and perhaps some disgrace to fill it.

He tried six people, five of them senior men within the police department, the last, in desperation, a government minister. Every one of them was 'busy'.

After the final rejection he slammed the receiver back on the hook and buried his head in his hands. Falcone wondered if he was going to start to sob. Valena spared him that. The man was simply drained, left helpless by some inner terror.

'Mr Valena,' Falcone said calmly, in a pleasant, comforting voice. 'All you have to do is talk to me. I'm not saying we can't help. I'm just saying I need a reason why.'

The big, exaggerated face looked up at him. 'What do you want to know?'

'The Farnese woman? You're saying you had a relationship with her?'

'No,' Valena replied grimly. 'I wouldn't say that. I screwed her. That's all. And it wasn't a lot of fun either. At least when you got a real hooker they try to fake things a little. She didn't even make that effort. Lousy bitch. I don't know why she bothered.'

Falcone nodded. This was progress. 'You hired her? From an escort agency or something?'

'Are you serious? Did I come in here to be insulted? I'm Arturo Valena. I don't hire hookers. I don't have to.'

'I'm not hearing anything that helps me here,' Falcone said icily. 'Why don't you just go home, Mr Valena? You've got a big house here. You've got money. Hire yourself a guard if you're feeling scared.'

The man's face went white. 'A guard? With that lunatic out there?'

'I need more. How did you meet her? What happened?'

Valena closed his eyes. 'She was a gift. She was a reward. She was a prize. Call it anything you like. Someone wanted something. She was a few coins they left on the plate afterwards to try to tip my hand.'

'Who? What?'

'Huh?' Valena grunted. 'I've got one man out there wanting to kill me already. You honestly think I should make it two?'

Falcone shrugged. 'It only takes one though, doesn't it? I mean, what does it matter? If you tell me, I can put a couple of cops by your side. If you don't, you can walk out there right now on your own.' He paused, watching the man, noticing that there was something dead in his eyes. 'It's nothing to me either way, Valena. I hate your fucking programme. It stinks. You stink. And you're stupid enough to think you still carry some weight around here. The only weight's that tyre around your belly. Don't you get it?'

'Bastard,' Valena murmured. His head hung down once more. 'Bastard.'

'There,' Falcone said, smiling. 'Now that's out of the way. May we get down to business? Please?'

Thirty-nine

The police car had delivered her to the house late in the afternoon, where she was greeted by Bea, who left almost immediately, saying little, unwilling to look her in the eye. Something had changed at the farm, something between Marco and Bea. It was not simply the story on the news and her own direct involvement in it. Bea seemed nervous, somehow, as if expecting the slow, ordered life of the place to change.

Sara showered, slept for a while then changed into casual clothes to watch the television with the old man. When the latest bulletin came on he immediately switched channels. She insisted he go back to the newscast. He sat in his wheelchair, squirming, as the macabre details of Alicia Vaccarini's death were disclosed alongside stock footage of the deputy, smiling, looking happy at some public function. When it was over, Marco Costa said nothing.

She walked into the kitchen. Out back, close to where Gino Fosse had almost murdered Nic, a crow danced across the yellow scrub that led down to the Appian Way. Sara Farnese watched its black wings flapping over the dusty ground. There was a handful of police at the gate.

Marco Costa joined her and they sat around the table, drinking coffee. The city and its terrors seemed to exist in another world.

'Did you know her?' she asked eventually, desperate to break the silence that had come upon them.

'Who?'

'Alicia Vaccarini.'

'Ah.' It was an act. His mind never roamed, even when he was tired. 'We met once or twice. She seemed a pleasant woman. Vaccarini was after my time, you understand. One tries not to get personal in politics. I'd like to think I had friends across the spectrum, regardless of party. But the Northern Alliance . . . they never were my type. Those petty-minded bastards treated her very badly. So she liked the company of women? So what? Does anyone care these days?'

It was a pointed remark, designed to make her feel comfortable. 'You don't need to say that for my sake, Marco. It was a stupid thing to do. I didn't enjoy it. I never want to do it again.'

His lined, grey face peered at her. 'You mean that was all it was? Curiosity?'

'Yes,' she replied, knowing that he thought she was lying.

He shook his head. 'I never understood that idea. That you should try everything once. Where do you draw the line? Isn't there always something else untried along the way?'

'I said it was a mistake.'

'I was making a general point, not a personal one. You should never assume everything pertains to you, Sara. That's what children think. It's always seemed to me that life is about focus and depth. Something like your academic world perhaps. You presumably think it's better to know a lot about a little than the reverse?'

The university felt as distant as the city. So did the work, which seemed a part of another person, someone she no longer understood or even, perhaps, liked.

'Of course.'

'Then that's how I feel about most things,' Marco continued. 'I'd rather just make a good job of a few things and leave the rest to someone else. It makes sense, to me anyway.'

She looked around the kitchen, wondering if she should fill the silence by preparing a meal. There was good olive oil and balsamic vinegar for the dressing. He pushed his wheelchair forward and put his hand on hers, bidding her to stop.

'But that's easy for me,' he said. 'I was brought up that way. It was natural. For you . . .'

He put down the coffee cup, wondering whether it was correct to continue. 'I'm sorry, Sara. It's not my business. But I have to say it. I don't understand. Nic doesn't either. That doesn't make it wrong. It just makes it hard. No one's judging you. No one's thinking the worse of you for what happened. They're just . . . puzzled. That's all.'

'And you think you deserve an explanation?' she said coldly.

He retreated, feeling he had come too far. 'Not at all. You don't owe anybody anything. It's your life. To do with as you wish.'

'I know.'

'It's just that I find it hard to believe this makes you happy. You're so smart. You're good to be around.'

Her green eyes opened further. She was, he saw, surprised.

'And you don't know that, do you?'

She went to the fridge and poured herself a glass of Verdicchio dei Castelli di Jesi from the Marches. The wine was young and fragrant. Marco watched her taste it, his face a picture of envy.

'It's easy for you,' she said finally. 'It comes naturally. I can't just learn.'

'And why not?' he demanded. 'Are you the only person who ever grew up an orphan? I couldn't begin to understand how difficult that is. No one would wish it on another. But you should never think of yourself as some fixed, unchanging point in the universe. None of us is that. Not me. Not Nic. We're always changing, sometimes for the worse, sometimes for the better. The person you were when these things happened is not the person you are now, surely?'

'And you think that you know either of them?' She said it too harshly. There was disappointment on the old man's face and she was shocked to discover this made her feel guilty.

'I think I know one of them better than she might give me credit for,' he said.

She poured a second glass of wine and offered it to him. Marco Costa laughed and pushed it away from him.

'Now you're playing games with me,' he said. 'I don't want the wine, Sara. These drugs they give me they make everything seem the same. What I want is the old taste, the one I remember, and that's impossible. That will never happen. I can't get that back. So what would be the point?'

She poured the Verdicchio back into the bottle and gave him some water instead.

'Don't wait until it's too late,' he said. 'Regret's a small sour thing but it can poison you for years. You saw Bea when you left? How was she?'

'Confused, I thought.'

'Not surprised. I asked her back here for dinner with us this evening. What you said last night made me think it was the right thing to do. It's easy to take people for granted, all the more so when you've known them for a long time. We're lazy creatures, looking for the soft option.'

'So you asked Bea for her sake?' she said, half scolding.

Marco Costa smiled, accepting the rebuke. 'No. I admit it. Mine too. She's a beautiful woman. I can't believe I stopped noticing. I can't believe I forgot that life requires the occasional surprise. And this is a special occasion now I come to think of it.'

There was the sound of cars outside. She could hear the voices of the distant cops on the gate. Then the doorbell rang. The old man looked at her expectantly. She went to open the door and was, for a moment, made giddy by the perfume of flowers, bouquet upon bouquet, in the arms of two pleasant-looking middle-aged women chattering wildly, looking ready to go to work.

Forty

Rossi was three hours past the end of his shift when Falcone collared him. He could tell from the smile it wasn't good news.

'Overtime,' Falcone said.

'That's voluntary, I imagine?'

'You're going to be in the company of a star. You should be paying me.'

Rossi had seen Arturo Valena walk into Falcone's office. He couldn't stand the man. 'Jesus . . .' he groaned.

'Piece of cake. The guy needs taking to the Brazilian Embassy in the Piazza Navona. There for half an hour, no more, then you see him home. I'll send someone else to take over around eleven.'

'How kind. He's another one on the list? Another one she never told us about?'

'Seems so.'

Rossi shook his head. 'Such taste . . .'

Falcone scanned the office, looking at the men on duty. 'Shame Costa's gone home. I could call him back.'

Rossi knew what game he hoped to play, winding the kid up with another ex-lover she'd forgotten to mention.

He was having none of it. 'Are you serious? The kid's half dead.'

'True. But he needs to learn. You know that, don't you?'

'Learn what? All the old tricks we know and love so well? Maybe he thinks that's not such a good idea. Maybe he's right.' Rossi was tired of Falcone. He couldn't give a damn about the job any more.

'You don't fit in here, Rossi. Just three days and it's so obvious.'

'Now should I be offended by that? *Sir?*'

Falcone looked out of the window of his office, thinking, calm, as always, in these situations. 'It doesn't make much of a pension at your age. You should have stuck it out longer.'

'There's more to life than money. Can I ask you one thing?'

The silver beard nodded.

'Just take the kid off this case. It's beyond him and he doesn't realize it.'

'Seems to me,' Falcone said, 'he's done pretty damn well. Found out more than you, to be frank.'

'Yeah.' Rossi wondered how far he could go. 'Found out lots of things that just seemed to be sitting there waiting for him, huh? I just don't want to see him damaged. Do what you like to me. I won't have that. Understand?'

'Get the hell out of here. Take Cattaneo instead.'

Rossi groaned again. In three days he had already come to learn the dull little man from Bologna was the least popular detective in the division: slow-witted, boring and an incessant talker.

'The sooner you're gone, the sooner this all becomes someone else's problem.'

'And the kid?'

'I'll think on it.'

'Sir,' Rossi grunted and walked to Cattaneo's desk to break the news.

'Arturo Valena?' Cattaneo was in his mid-thirties, single and without vices. He bought his suits, shirts and shoes in threes from Standa because he got a discount that way and it removed the needless task of deciding whether to choose something different each day. His shift had started one hour before, which meant he was just bursting with energy to expend in useless conversation. 'You mean *the* Arturo Valena? The man on the box?'

'Just don't ask for an autograph,' Rossi said. 'I don't think I could take it.'

'Oh, come on,' Cattaneo complained. 'It wouldn't be for me, you understand. My brother's kid. He just loves the guy.'

'Your brother's kid is how old? Twelve?'

'Eleven.'

'And he watches Valena on TV?'

'We all do.'

'Sweet Jesus. The poor bastard's marked for life. Can you walk and talk at the same time?'

Cattaneo scowled, picked up his jacket and followed Rossi to the door, where they joined Valena and went downstairs to the car. The detective from Bologna talked every step of the way. Before they'd even left the building, Rossi could see from the TV man's eyes that he loathed Cattaneo too.

Forty-one

She was sleeping. It made Gino Fosse feel odd. She'd made love to him on and off for two hours, never asking what he wanted, always knowing somehow. Irena was now curled next to him on the cheap, hard bed. With her mouth half open she looked younger, almost a child. The red and blue neon signs outside the window flashed repeatedly and cast lurid beams across her head. He touched the marks they made. She had soft, clean hair. It was fragrant, enough to be noticeable amid the smells of sweat and sex that filled the room.

He'd never slept with a woman before, not like this. They always came and went. He'd not known what it was like to close your eyes and find them still there when you woke up. It was unreal somehow, like a scene from some dream that would be shaken from his head in an instant. Then she stirred, her eyes opened, she saw him and smiled.

Unasked, Irena leaned up to his face and kissed him softly on the lips.

'You're crazy,' he said.

'Why?'

'Acting like this. Like we're ... together or something.'

She touched his dark hair, let her fingers curl against his cheek. 'What's wrong with that?'

'You're just a hooker. And I'm just ... nothing.'

Her lips formed a pout and he was sure now: she could have been no more than seventeen or eighteen. 'Doesn't mean you can't love someone, does it? Where's it say that?'

Somewhere, he thought. In the books they wrote. It didn't come from God. Even the old God, the cruel, hard one, understood the imperfections in the clay he'd once shaped. They were part of the journey each individual had to take, one that was unavoidable though so many people tried to ignore it. She was right there: there was nothing to say either of them should be denied a thing.

'How much money have you got?' she asked.

'Why?'

'We could go. We could get out of this hole. We could go to the coast, Gino. Someone told me it was nice there. All clean and fresh and none of this crap to ruin us.'

He found himself laughing. 'You *are* crazy. And what do we do when we get there?'

'Screw.'

The neon painted its colours on her hair again. He couldn't stop himself laughing again for a moment.

'And then?'

Her small, perfect shoulders shrugged. She grinned this time. He didn't mind the bad teeth, he decided.

'Whatever. We just roll, Gino. We just take it as it comes ... and *roll*.'

He thought about it. They gave her to him. She knew their faces. She would receive a visit from the police sometime. It wasn't difficult to guess what their solution would be.

'I never ran anywhere before. I never had that option.'

Her face lit up with surprise. 'You mean you just do as you told? They say this. They say that.'

'These are big people, Irena. I'm just so small.'

Her hand moved stealthily and took hold of his penis. It lay in her fingers, rising, hardening. 'I wouldn't say that.' Her fingers moved. 'Let's do it, Gino. Let's go. Anywhere.'

He felt his breath begin to catch. He wondered how many times they had made love. His head felt fuzzy, unfocused.

The phone rang. Gino Fosse pushed her away from him and turned to get it. She looked at the sheets sulkily as he spoke. It took a good three minutes. Someone was telling him what to do.

'Got to go,' he said when it was through. He started putting on his clothes. Then he looked in one of the bags he'd brought, a big one. She'd taken a peek when he was in the bathroom, wondering if there was money there. It was just junk. Theatrical make-up. Stage props. Crazy stuff. And something at the bottom. Something grey and metallic she didn't want to think about, didn't want to see.

Gino Fosse sat down on a thin wooden chair by the neon-lit window, thinking, not taking any notice of her. Then he got up, ordered her off the bed and snatched the crumpled, stained sheet off the mattress. She sat down on the bare divan and watched him.

'We could catch a train,' she said, half-pleading. 'We could go anywhere. We could be in France or Spain.'

He picked up a pair of scissors and began stabbing at

the sheet. When he was done he bent down and touched her hair. 'But we'd still be what we are now, Irena. You can't run away from yourself.'

'So you want me to go work some tricks while you're out?' she asked petulantly. 'Or do I sit here like some stupid girlfriend waiting on her man?'

He seemed shocked by her reaction. She wanted him to stay. Gino Fosse reached into his pocket and pulled out some money. 'Go buy some champagne. Tomorrow, I promise, will be a special day.'

Her face brightened. She was attractive, beautiful after a fashion. But she was stupid. This wasn't about him. It was about her finding some rock she could cling to, something that could improve things a little.

She kissed him on the cheek. He could smell her rotten teeth.

Gino Fosse walked out into the stifling night with the bag on his arm. The air was acrid with traffic fumes. He strolled down one of the grimy back alleys that led from the station, thinking. There were drunks and hookers and dope dealers.

And a small, dark van with a man by the side. He was in uniform. He looked as if he'd had a few drinks himself. Fosse walked towards the vehicle. He recognized what it was now. There was the sound of animals moving in the back. The dog catcher still had his pole, with the noose on the end, in one hand. He held a bottle of beer in the other and waved it unsteadily in Fosse's direction.

'What a job,' he said with a slur in his voice. 'What a stupid, boring job. You know how many times I got bitten by these miserable mutts today?'

He hadn't killed an innocent person before. But he knew now: there was no such creature. They all shared in the guilt. They all partook of the shame. It was weakness to exclude them.

'How many?' he asked.

The man held up three fingers.

'I'm sorry,' Gino Fosse said and took the knife from his pocket. The blade caught the moonlight. A shaft of silver flashed in the dog catcher's face. Abruptly sober, he took one look at the man in front of him, turned and ran with a sudden turn of speed. Fosse watched him race frantically down the street, debating whether to follow. There was a low whimper from inside the van. He peered through the barred window, open to the air at the rear. The vehicle stank of dog crap and urine. Several pairs of eyes stared back at him. The animals growled. It was too much effort to give chase, he thought. There were better, more profitable, avenues to pursue that evening.

Forty-two

When Nic Costa arrived home he thought, for a moment, that he had stepped back in time. The house was alive with voices: his father, Sara and a laughing Bea who, when he walked through the door, was playing with the dog as if some unexpected peace pact had just been signed. There were flowers throughout the downstairs rooms: roses and chrysanthemums, dahlias and sprays of lurid irises. The scent hung heavy everywhere. Sara and Bea drank champagne. Marco stuck to mineral water. In the kitchen two women, hired hands for the night, were putting the finishing touches to an extravagant cold buffet, the kind of meal his mother had once prepared so well. Plates of cold grilled vegetables, glistening with olive oil, were going on the dining table alongside scampi and lobster, *bresaola* and a variety of cheeses. He had to close his eyes for a moment to ensure this was not some dream. When he opened them again his father sat in front of him, in the wheelchair, still grey and cadaverous, but wearing the broadest smile Nic could recall for many months.

'Why're you looking so damn fed up, son?'

'I just . . .' he stuttered. 'Did I forget a birthday?'

Marco waved a hand at him, then motioned for one of the women to pour a glass of champagne. 'Do you always need a reason? Isn't it possible I was just bored with being miserable? It's so enervating after a while. And all this crap out there. Your work. Sara . . .' Marco cast a glance back at the women chatting in the living room, the dog at Bea's feet. 'Whatever the facts tell you, Nic, I think she's a good woman. She just doesn't realize it herself.'

'I know.' He hesitated. He didn't want to break the spell. 'That's what makes it so hard to understand.'

'Bullshit!' Marco declared. 'How can you understand someone until you get to know them? You fret about things too much. You want everything wrapped up all nice and tidy before you'll deign to touch it. Relax, Nic. Make the most of things while they're still there.'

He picked up a glass of champagne and raised it to his father. '*Salute!*'

'And to you, my son. There . . .' Marco cocked an ear. 'You know that sound?'

Women chattering. The dog yelping at their feet for attention. Voices ringing off the plain stone walls of the farmhouse. He knew what his father meant. 'Yes.'

'How many years since we heard that racket in here? Eight, since you were the last to leave home? A house needs the noise of people or it starts to die. That's what I've been missing all this time. I'm going to record you all secretly and play it back when you're gone. Do that and you could fool yourself into thinking you'll live for ever.'

Nic Costa was unable to take his eyes off the women in the other room. Sara looked so calm, so lovely. Bea, too, was transformed, as if being invited back to spend some social time with Marco was the greatest compliment she could receive.

'And Bea?' he asked.

'She deserved it. That's all. I'm an idiot, Nic. You should know that about your father. I was never good at seeing things in other people. That was your mother's talent. It's where you got it from.'

The four of them sat down as couples around the dining-room table and admired the feast. Then the two women from the agency lit the large, antique candles Marco had insisted be set up throughout the ground floor and turned down the electric lights. He paid them, with much thanks, and they were gone. The farmhouse was now lit like a canvas. There were deep shadows where the guttering flames failed to reach, and rich, natural colours, the ancient timber table, the subtle red of the curtains, the ochre of the walls, in the idle beam of the waxy light.

'A toast!' Marco declared. 'You were right, Nic. There is a birthday. But whose?'

He looked at Bea and Sara. They had no answers. 'I give up.'

Marco raised his glass to the dog. Baffled, Pepe placed his paws on the old man's knees and was rewarded with a slice of dried beef. 'To him, of course. We bought the dog three months after your mother died, when he was eight weeks old. By my reckoning, that makes him ten today and I shall brook no arguments. Least of all from him.'

'The dog!' Sara repeated. Nic did the same and enjoyed the hard cold taste of the wine in his mouth.

'And the wisdom of dogs,' Marco added. 'Which surpasses our own if only we knew it.'

Bea cast a doubtful eye over the creature staring lovingly into Marco's face. 'Now *that* requires an explanation.'

'Surely not. Think of us. Consumed by worry about events beyond our control. Forever watching the clock and wondering what tomorrow brings. What concerns a dog? The present, only. Will he be loved? Will he be fed? He's no concept of tomorrow, no idea that any of this comes to an end. All he cares about is the here and now and he cares about that passionately, more passionately than any of us could imagine.'

'That's a kind of wisdom?' Sara wondered.

'Absolutely,' Marco insisted. 'Not our kind, but one that serves a dog very well. There's a lesson for us too. You don't remember, Nic? That little scene after we got him?'

Nic toyed with some buffalo mozzarella and refilled the wine glasses. Marco was now taking a little alcohol. 'Don't embarrass me with childhood stories, please. That's the cruellest trick a parent can play.'

'Not this one. It's informative. A man should always be ready to be informed.'

He sighed. 'And it's about?'

'Life and death,' Marco replied, amused. 'What else is there?'

Forty-three

It was impossible to move for bodies. Every tourist in the city seemed to have migrated to the Piazza Navona. Rossi scanned the ocean of blank faces, grateful that Valena had been smart enough to dash straight into the embassy building and not linger to sign autographs or attract the attention of the paparazzi. The small-time crooks were out in force, attracted by the prospect of stray handbags and easy pickings among the crowds. Rossi recognized a couple in a single sweep of the square. He'd seen two uniformed cops on duty – no more. It was a disgrace. The hucksters were just working the hordes of visitors with the usual set of scams: cards and cheap gifts, invitations to 'night clubs' and simple, sly theft.

'I like it here,' Cattaneo said. 'This is what living in Rome's all about.'

The big man scowled at him. 'It's a dump. It's Disneyland.'

It wasn't really. He knew enough history for that. In daylight, when it was half empty, the place was beautiful. It still followed the oval outline of the old Roman stadium that preceded it. He could just about imagine chariots racing round the perimeter. There was the big fountain of the four rivers by Bernini, who seemed to have built half of Rome. The piazza didn't bug him. He could almost like it. The people were the problem. They were just too loose, too relaxed to help him keep his mind on the job when he was this tired. If Gino Fosse wanted to attack the jerk from the TV – if he felt like just walking up to him on the steps of the embassy as he left and pumping a gun in his face – there was no way two cops could stop him. The one consolation, Rossi thought, was that this wasn't the man's style. It was too plain, too prosaic. Every time he killed someone Fosse made a statement about himself, one that said: *See me? I'm different, I'm smart, and I can send you to Hell in ways you never even dreamed of.*

'Will you look at that?' Cattaneo gasped in delight.

The fake statue artists were out in droves. Rossi could see at least eight of them, each covered in make-up, perched on an upturned crate with a few simple props, trying to get a little cash out of the tourists. It was honest, he guessed. The first time he'd seen the trick, years before, it was quite amusing. Then they appeared everywhere and soon ran out of subject-matter. At that moment there were two Statues of Liberty, one Mona Lisa, one strange, fluorescent alien and any number of classical Roman figures in togas, a couple with scrolls in their hands, all standing stock still in the square trying not to blink. The nearest, who was no more than three metres away, had painted himself a powdery white, splashed the same stuff on what looked like a grubby bed sheet, thrown the cloth around his shoulders and was now pretending to be Julius Caesar or somebody. No, Rossi thought, that was wrong. He had a full head of hair and a young, half-handsome face. Caesar had to be bald.

He needed a laurel wreath. This was just a chancer trying to make some quick money. Maybe he was supposed to be Brutus, though his hair seemed a little long for that. There was one other point Rossi had got wrong too, he realized. It was about more than just standing there not moving a muscle for minutes on end. At some point you had to drop the guard. You had to let the people in the crowd know it was part of the game – by winking or even touching them – because that was the trigger that made them reach into their pockets. If you never moved an inch they'd just walk on. This was meant to be entertainment, after all.

Rossi stared at Brutus. This moron didn't even get it. He really didn't move. The whole act was just plain shoddy, unconvincing. He'd be hustling for a metro ticket before long, hoping to turn his gauche inexperience into sympathy.

Cattaneo tapped his arm. 'Now that Mona Lisa. She's a looker. She'll get all the money.'

He watched the figure in the black dress, standing with her head in a gold-painted frame just a few metres along from Brutus. 'It's a man,' Rossi said. 'I arrested him for picking someone's pocket once.'

'You're kidding me?' Cattaneo gasped. 'You mean he's a queer?'

'No,' Rossi replied, exasperated. 'Don't be so damned literal. This is what he does. It doesn't make him queer.'

People always got that wrong, he thought. Appearances were deceptive. Sometimes they were meant to be that way. The idea nagged at him but he felt too tired to examine it any further.

He looked at his watch. 'Where the hell is the creep? An hour he said. It's been at least . . .'

Rossi couldn't remember when Valena had walked up the marble steps of the embassy into the reception. It just seemed a long time ago.

'It's been fifty-eight minutes,' Cattaneo said. 'He's not due yet.'

Rossi swore under his breath, hating the precise little bastard by his side. Then he looked at the door. Valena's fat frame was waddling through it, brushing aside anyone who stood in his way.

'Looks like his timing's as bad as mine,' the big man said. 'Tut, tut. He could have spent a hundred and twenty more seconds inside with the glitzy people.'

'Yeah,' Cattaneo agreed, and then found himself staring at Rossi's broad back as the older man walked over to greet Valena.

He stood on the steps, looking nervous. He had food stains down the front of his white shirt. He smelled of drink, champagne probably, Rossi guessed.

'What kind of service is this?' Valena demanded. 'You're supposed to be looking after me every second I'm outside.'

'Apologies,' Rossi said, noting that Cattaneo had caught up with him now. 'We didn't want to cramp your style.'

'Idiots!' Valena bellowed. His eyes looked a little too wild. Rossi wondered if there was just alcohol rolling around inside his fat frame. Maybe he'd added a little white powder in there to help things along.

'Your car awaits, sir,' Rossi said with a wave. The two men watched him roll along ahead then Rossi cursed himself, caught up with the man and walked by his right, as he was supposed to. His head wasn't working properly.

It was just plain exhaustion. Cattaneo did the same on the other side. They picked up pace towards the far side of the piazza where Rossi had left the car. Then Cattaneo put a hand on Valena's arm. The TV man stopped, his head revolving right and left. Really out of it, Rossi saw. There surely was something floating around his fat-filled veins.

'Do the honours,' Cattaneo barked.

'What?' Rossi thought he would hit the man one day. He was just too infuriating.

'Look. He's good. Give him something for Christ's sake. Here . . .'

He threw some coins in front of the astonished Valena. The living statue, the one who looked like Brutus but with hair that was too long, smiled and caught them in a cheap black hat. He was holding it, fingers over the rim which was held tight in his very large thumb, panning for money.

'For the love of God,' Rossi declared and still found himself reaching in his pocket for money, wondering about these instant reactions and why you never questioned them.

Brutus was still on his crate. He was smiling like a loon. He was terrible, Rossi recalled. It was a crime just to give him money.

The big man pulled out a few coins and dropped them in the hat. It was odd. The statue wouldn't stop smiling like that, as if this wasn't about money at all.

'Enough,' Rossi said, looking around for the uniformed men, discovering that once again they were never there when you needed them. 'You don't get a cent more. You just beat it now or I start to get mad.'

Brutus bowed his head, still smiling. Luca Rossi suddenly felt his spine go cold. There was something familiar about the face. He knew it somehow, not well, but enough to make him think it deserved attention.

Forty-four

'As I said,' Marco continued, 'we bought the dog in sad circumstances. I don't even recall what gave us the idea. We scarcely even spoke about it.'

Nic shuffled on his seat, feeling uncomfortable. These were memories he didn't want revived. The past was difficult, painful. From time to time it pricked his mind unbidden, it pointed the way to the future. Sara watched him, saw how he felt. Her fingers briefly touched the back of his hand.

'And there I was one day. Talking to this man with a dog for sale, spouting nonsense, not knowing what questions to ask, whether this was a good idea at all. He was an old farmer with a little smallholding down the road there, a surly bastard who looked at me as if I were an idiot. Which I was, in his eyes, I guess, but this was all new to me. All he kept repeating was, "It's a dog." As if that said everything.'

He shuffled in his wheelchair, thinking of what should come next. 'I brought him home in my jacket. He peed and crapped in it on the way. The first night he cried, constantly, and none of us slept.'

'That I do remember,' Nic interjected.

'And the second night he cried a little less. By the third he was sleeping, in the kitchen there, starting to make it his home. There was just Nic and Giulia with me then, you understand. Young Marco was at college already. We were three damaged, angry people, full of hurt about what the world had done to us. Full of some stupid, blind fury over a loss that made no sense. And here was a dog, demanding we keep him alive, we love him, we give him so much attention, night and day. And what did you do, Nic?'

'I gave him it,' he said. 'So did Giulia. So did you, less than the rest of us, if you want to know, though it was still you he always saw as the boss. Some things never change.'

Marco shook his head. 'It was just age. He loved you then. If he had the brains to remember, the strength to play those games all over again, he'd love you in the same way now.'

The old man was right there. Nic had spent hour after hour with the dog, on walks through summer fields full of flowers and the humming of bees. In these lovely, lonely places he would talk to the animal as if it were a human being. They were inseparable. Then he'd grown older, and so had the dog. Time had worked its cruel trick once more.

'One day,' Marco said, 'I came home. It was just before Nic left school for college and that worried him, I think. But there was something else too. You remember?'

He did and he wished he could stop the old man saying it.

'I remember. Is this really . . .'

'Nic was almost as upset as the day his mother had died and it was over this. He'd come to think about the dog, an animal which has a natural lifespan of – what? – ten, twelve, perhaps thirteen years? He'd come to realize that one day, a day not that far distant, Pepe would be gone. Not in a human lifetime, but in a canine one, which seems so short to us. And he thought what? Come, Sara. You're the psychic, you tell us.'

She looked at Nic, wondering if it would embarrass him. It was so obvious. It was understandable too. 'He thought it was pointless. Owning the dog. Growing to love him. Growing to adore having him around. Knowing all along that one day he would die, and so soon.'

Marco watched her closely. 'And is he right?'

'I don't think there's a right or wrong for a question like that,' she replied cautiously. 'I can see his point. I can appreciate why one would think that way.'

'There, Bea! Behold the young. What have we done to bring them up like this?'

The older woman stared at both of them, amazed. 'And you both think this? Sara? Nic? I'm no dog lover. Even that damned animal can see that. But you must take what joy you find, while it's there. Not go worrying about a tomorrow that might never come.'

'And that,' Marco said, banging his glass on the table, 'is the wisdom of dogs.'

'Which is ignorance!' Sara declared. 'Surely you can see that? A dog has no comprehension of time. Of seasons. As far as it is concerned life is like a light switch, either on or off.'

'And isn't it?' Marco demanded, teasingly.

'No.' She looked at Nic for support.

'I agree,' he said. 'It's a bad comparison.'

'What you mean is,' Bea suggested, 'they never read

Ecclesiastes. A time to be born, and a time to die; a time to plant, and a time to pluck up that which is planted.'

'A time to love,' Marco continued. 'And a time to hate; a time of war, and a time of peace. You're right, Sara. An animal knows nothing of the seasons and that's what defines him. Are we that different? It was the knowledge of our mortality that informed all those early Christians buried along that old road out there. Today we make death the uninvited guest who sits in the corner, in perpetual darkness. We pretend he doesn't exist until finally he proves us wrong and then we are shocked – we are offended! – by his presence.'

Nic waved a defensive hand at him. 'Point taken. I understand what you mean.'

'Not at all!' Marco insisted. 'That was aimed at me more than you, son. I've let this damned thing wear me down so much I took the opposite view. I thought there was nothing but death around me. A time to plant, a time to pluck up that which is planted. This is a farm, remember? Until this blasted disease we fed ourselves from those fields. We turned the land, we grew, we harvested. And look at it now. Bare, barren earth. And for what reason? Because I forgot. Because, like a child, I believed I was the world and without me nothing existed which is, I think, the greatest sin a man can commit.'

There was silence. The mood of the evening pivoted around Marco's confession, and each of them knew it could easily disintegrate. Then Sara asked, 'What was this like as a farm?'

'Wonderful,' Nic replied, smiling, grateful that she had chosen the moment. 'We could grow anything then. I remember . . .' His head filled with the recollection of artichoke heads nodding in the breeze, tall rows of tomatoes, verdant clumps of *zucchini*. 'I remember how green it was.'

'Why do you think he eats what he does?' Marco asked. 'He gave up meat when he was twelve. Said there was no point.'

'There wasn't. And what we grew was ours. It came from us.'

Marco wheeled himself to the front door. They followed, watching as he unlatched the huge slab of wood, threw it open and turned on the floodlights which illuminated the front of the farm. The cigarettes of the men at the gate winked back at them like tiny fireflies. The earth stood arid and solid under the harsh lamps.

'And the best part,' Marco said, 'was the unexpected.'

Around now, he said, they would plant the black Tuscan kale *cavolo nero* for the winter. Sara watched the way his eyes glittered when he spoke about how they were his favourites for the very reason most people would avoid them: their sluggish, steady growth, from seedlings at the waning of summer, through the lean, cold winter months, reviving again, to give nourishment, in the spring. This was a rebirth of a kind, a token that the world began anew each year, whatever happened. A seedling planted in the earth in July knew nothing of the future that would embrace it when the warmth returned the following Easter – that is, if it survived the winter. This was a peasant's faith, and one that Marco Costa loved, the fundamental belief that the seasons always returned and good husbandry would be repaid. It was inevitable that the chain would be broken. Some years the crop would fail. Some years the gardener would fail to return to tend the land. Nevertheless, it was the act itself which mattered: the planting, the nurturing, the tilling of the soil.

There had been no winter crop that year. Marco's faith had failed him, crushed by the disease.

She watched the old man eyeing the earth. 'I want to see things growing there again,' he said. 'Tomorrow . . . I'll send for help.'

Sara looked at Bea and the two women exchanged glances. 'What's wrong with us? We can dig. We can plant seeds.'

Marco laughed and waved a dismissive hand at them. 'This isn't work for women.' They screeched at him.

'Peace, peace,' Nic said. 'They can start in the morning. Later, when I've time, I'll do my part too. You can just sit and watch and bark orders.'

'It has to be done properly,' Marco insisted.

'It will be,' Nic replied. 'I promise.'

They looked at one another and fell silent. The storm never broke. Marco had made his point.

The old man sniffed the air. 'There's autumn inside that heat,' he said. 'You can smell September on the way. I love the autumn. The colours. Sitting round the fire, burning a few chestnuts. I wouldn't want to be anywhere else when the leaves start to fall.'

Nic walked behind him, placing a hand on his shoulder. Marco's fingers gripped his. Nic felt his eyes begin to sting and was grateful for this moment.

'Old reds like me don't believe in Hell,' Marco said. 'But if I did, do you know what it would be? A place where nothing grows. A place where no one knows the seasons. God save us all from that, if you'll pardon the expression.'

Forty-five

Rossi cursed himself. It was so obvious when he thought about it. They'd found just one blurry picture of Gino Fosse and here, he now knew, was the same face, covered in white powder trying to pretend to be a statue. He grappled inside his jacket, trying to get the gun out, yelling at Cattaneo, yelling at the TV jerk, telling them to get down, to keep out of the way because Brutus wasn't Brutus at all, he was some crazy, bloodthirsty priest who didn't know when to stop. At least Cattaneo seemed on the ball then. He dragged Valena into the massing crowd by the scruff of his neck. Rossi turned and watched the two of them tumble into the mass of bodies then fell back, trying to follow them.

His hand felt greasy. His mouth went dry. By the time his fingers reached the butt of the weapon Brutus had leaned forward on his crate. The hat had fallen from his hands, Luca Rossi's few coins were rolling on the ground making a precise, musical sound oddly audible over the animal racket of the crowd. Maybe the metallic chink of the coins was, the big man thought, the last thing he'd ever hear.

Then the swarm of people closed around him and

Rossi was fighting to clear his head. Shoulders jostled him. Tourists yelled abuse. He held up his gun, high above the mass, trying to make them see some sense. Not knowing why – not even understanding whether this was a conscious action – he fired a single shot into the air and sent some small slug of lead flying out of Bernini's piazza, spinning wildly towards the bright moon set in a black velvet sky.

Someone nearby screamed. He saw a woman's bulbous, gaudily made-up eyes and they reminded him of the look he once saw on a bull as it went into the slaughterhouse.

'Luca!' It was Cattaneo yelling. He held Rossi by the arm. Valena was firmly attached to the other. Luca Rossi felt like a jerk. He'd always hated Cattaneo. Always thought him a loser. And here they were, rolling around inside some steadily panicking mass of people, not knowing where they were going or what was on their trail.

Cattaneo was barking something into the radio. Rossi raised his hand again, let the gun pump upwards once more. It felt good. It felt like a statement, something even a warped priest with blood on his hands and a penchant for women's heads might begin to comprehend. Then a big figure in a Stars and Stripes T-shirt pushed hard into him. Rossi felt the breath disappear from his chest, a sharp pain rising underneath his ribs. The strength left him, just for an instant. It was enough for the gun to slip from his grip, out from his fingers, tugged down by the nagging force of gravity into the sea of stampeding legs at his feet.

Rossi bent over, gasping for air, noting as he did so that some space appeared to be growing around him.

When he had his senses back – as much as he could muster – he pulled himself upright. Brutus was there, smiling in front of him, with a semi-circle of scared tourists at his back. He looked like a bit-part actor suddenly thrust into the limelight. He had something in his hand, something small and light and deadly.

Luca Rossi stared at it, saw Cattaneo racing to his side. He said, simply, 'Shit.'

The weapon shrieked once, jerked back in Fosse's fingers, then changed direction, just as Rossi's sight was beginning to fail him and a thick, stupid pain started to cloud his ears.

The last sound was thunder repeating itself, a muffled, echoing roar through which Luca Rossi wished to make some final point, about living and dying and what ought and ought not to be accomplished. Except it was impossible. Something stole away his thoughts, left him helpless, unable to speak. There was a hand on his shoulder and he knew it was Cattaneo's. The idiot was dragging him down to the hard stone ground of the piazza. He fell with an extraordinary, irresistible momentum, down towards the red pool running into the cracks of the cobblestones like a sluggish river, growing, turning into a flood.

Gino Fosse stood back, wiped his mouth with the back of his hand and looked at the two stupid cops prone on the ground, not moving. The crowd was going wild. They were screaming, fighting to get away from this white figure, his fake toga now stained with the splash-back of Luca Rossi's blood.

Only Arturo Valena didn't run. The fat TV presenter stood there, cowering, unable to move, alone in a circle being created by the fleeing bodies around him.

Fosse walked up and held the revolver tight against Valena's sweating temple.

'Come with me,' he said. 'Quickly, by my side. Right now.'

Valena nodded.

A minute later the dogs had company.

Forty-six

She stood outside the main door, beneath the vine veranda, marvelling at the evening. The heat of the day had dissipated. Fireflies now danced through the twisting shapes of the olive trees that crouched on the moonlit horizon. The champagne had been followed by white wine, then red. They were all quite drunk, even Marco. It was as if the house had infected them with its spirit, as if its rich, hidden memories had woken from some dream and come to inhabit them. The coming day would exorcize these happy ghosts. She knew that had to happen. Still, Sara Farnese was grateful for the fleeting gift they had each received at Marco's prompting. The timing was welcome. The nightmare of the city was still real. There were hardships and trials ahead but they were not insurmountable. There was hope. There was the possibility of redemption in the light which shone in all their faces that night.

Bea took Marco to his bedroom and did not emerge again. Nic, perhaps to cover his embarrassment, had dragged the sleepy, stiff Pepe out for a final walk around the grounds. Sara could hear him talking to the men at the end of the drive: slow, lazy chatter, not the whispered, feverish talk men had when things were going wrong. They all deserved a respite from Gino Fosse. It wouldn't last. That was impossible. Yet even the shortest break seemed like a miracle. It gave her space to think, to breathe. Here, beyond the grip of the city, safe in the cool darkness of the farmhouse, surrounded by people who didn't judge her, didn't look at her as if she were a different kind of creature, Sara felt briefly content in a way she did not wish to analyse.

Marco himself had said it: nothing stayed the same. The world was in flux, always. This was its gift; this was its burden too.

She stepped onto the dry, hard ground and kicked at it with her shoe. It was impossible to believe anything could grow in such conditions. She knew nothing about gardening. Bea was probably just as ignorant. But with Marco's guidance, which would, she felt sure, be exact and exacting, something would take root here. It would become fertile and one day bring forth produce, though she knew she would never be there to witness it.

Nic stepped out of the darkness, from behind one of the few living things near the house, an old, wizened almond tree. The leaves rustled lightly in the breeze. He looked happy. She was glad, for him and for Marco. Something had passed between them, some unspoken pact, that night. There was no news from the policemen at the gate. Perhaps the distant city was quiet. Perhaps Gino Fosse slept easy, the demons gone from his head, if only for a little while.

The dog stepped forward, cocked a leg and peed profusely on the trunk of the tree. They laughed.

'The wisdom of dogs,' Sara said.

Pepe came to sit tamely at their feet. 'Or the

ignorance,' Nic answered. 'He doesn't know what lies ahead. He doesn't understand what there is to anticipate.'

'And because we do that makes us wiser?'

'I think so. Not happier perhaps.'

The dog's eyes closed behind dry, wrinkled lids. He looked old like that, she thought. He looked like Marco: grey and wasting.

'It's not enough for them to be alive,' she said, patting the old fur. 'They need to live. Happy birthday, Pepe.'

The dog stared at them both then fixed its gaze on the door with a firm deliberation.

An awkward silence fell between them. Sara turned and let them in. The dog ambled across the threshold, found its bed in the kitchen and curled its frail body into a lazy apostrophe.

She watched the animal settle, knowing Nic couldn't take his eyes off her.

Forty-seven

The dog catcher's van was parked inconspicuously outside the church of San Lorenzo in Lucina in a small piazza north of the parliamentary area where Alicia Vaccarini had dined with Gino Fosse the day before. The site had been associated with the martyr Lorenzo since the fourth century though a temple, probably to Juno, had existed here long before, its columns, crowned by medieval capitals, re-used in the dark portico that gave onto the square. The delicate illumination of the piazza now outlined the plain triangular pediment and the Romanesque bell tower, much like the one on Tiber Island, behind. In spite of its location next to the Via del Corso, the church retained a modest, fetching dignity. Gino Fosse was unable to forget the place for entirely different reasons.

This was, he knew, where the cycle began, where the doubts which first rose in his head in the dark belly of San Giovanni hardened, became real and demanded action. One week ago to the day Brendan Hanrahan had phoned him, sounding amiable, sympathetic, wondering why Denney had reacted so ruthlessly to what was, in truth, a minor infraction. Hanrahan suggested they meet, take a short tour of the city, visit some places which would, he believed, intrigue him.

Thirty minutes later the Irishman pulled up outside the tower in the Clivus Scauri inside one of the black Mercedes Gino Fosse knew so well. Then, as a chauffeur drove them around the city, the Irishman introduced him to Lorenzo's tale. In the van with Arturo Valena screaming pointlessly to the howling of the dogs beside him, he could still recall the moment the poisonous worm locked its jaws hard into his soul. Perhaps Hanrahan had noticed it. The Irishman missed very little. Perhaps he had wanted it there, feasting.

It was a scalding, airless day, the first to give a hint of the heat wave that was to come. Hanrahan ordered the driver to take a circuitous route passing the Villa Celimontana, the public park close to the Clivus Scauri.

'The man has a terrible temper sometimes,' he confided. 'Denney, I mean. I imagine he blames it on the stress, Gino. But we're all under stress now, aren't we?'

He had dead eyes, a dead face. Gino Fosse knew why they used him to fix things. Nothing was beneath Hanrahan. He was relentless, patient, forever planning.

'Note the fountain,' Hanrahan indicated as they rounded the park entrance. He had admired the stone boat with its generous water spout, uncertain about Hanrahan's intentions.

'An old priest from Limerick took me on this tour when I first came to Rome. Now I wish to return the favour to you. To take you through an entire episode of our glorious history, Gino,' Hanrahan declared. 'I'm a bureaucrat, not a churchman, so pay attention and forgive any errors, though I think I know this story well enough to be true to it throughout.

'Let's imagine,' he said, in the manner of a teacher, 'that today is August the sixth in the year of our Lord 258. The emperor is Valerian, no friend to the Church at all. Lorenzo, a Spaniard and one of the six Christian deacons of Rome, is standing on the grass over there handing out money to the poor, money he has gained from selling some of the Church's gold. Valerian has heard of this, decided he wants to wet his beak too, and demanded that Lorenzo show him the remainder of the Church's rich treasures so that he may claim his imperial share.'

Fosse had not been sleeping soundly. The incident which led to his banishment from the Vatican continued to puzzle him. He had behaved no more badly before. Hanrahan was right. The punishment seemed out of kilter with the crime.

'For three days Lorenzo has assembled a crowd close to where the fountain now stands and is giving out alms. He's surrounded by the poverty-stricken and aided by supportive fellow Christians. When Valerian's soldiers come and ask him for the emperor's gold, he gives them not a penny. Instead, he points to the assembled crowd and declares, "See! Here is the treasure of the Church." '

'Sounds like he was asking for trouble,' Fosse observed.

'Quite,' Hanrahan agreed. 'And he got it.'

He pointed to the Palatine passing to their left, on the opposite side of the road. 'Had we time, we could still follow Lorenzo along every stage of his impending martyrdom. He was dragged through the Cryptoporticus passage, up there, which you may walk today, to a trial, the verdict of which was already decided. We could go to the church of San Lorenzo in Fonte, in the Via

Urbana, see the cell in which he was incarcerated and the fountain he used to baptize his fellow prisoners. After that we could visit San Lorenzo fuori le Mura, built over the humble chapel Constantine himself erected to mark the martyr's burial place. In San Lorenzo in Panisperna, close by, we could stand on the site of his death and admire a vivid fresco of him receiving the martyr's reward, though this is a work that's perhaps a little too realistic, I think, for a young man's taste.'

Hanrahan was wrong there. Gino Fosse found these strange depictions of martyrdoms fascinating. He had spent hours in the church of San Stefano Rotondo, not far from the Villa Celimontana, watching the workmen renovate the startling images on the walls there. These pictures spoke to him, saying something he could not quite understand. On the martyrs' lips, as they endured their agonies, there was some cryptic eternal secret they could share across the centuries if only he knew the key.

When they reached San Lorenzo in Lucina and fought their way through the lazy crowds of shoppers into the small church in the square, Hanrahan had stood him in front of Reni's *Crucifixion* and asked what he thought. Fosse was indifferent. It seemed, he said, somewhat romanticized, unreal. A man would not die on the cross quite so prettily. Hanrahan had grinned with pleasure and pointed out the monument marking the grave of a French artist Fosse barely knew, Poussin. 'Another romantic,' Hanrahan declared. 'You know Caravaggio?'

'Of course,' Fosse agreed. 'He's wonderful. He paints real people.'

'Quite,' Hanrahan continued. He kicked the Poussin monument. 'This idiot derided him for his "partiality for ugliness and vulgarity". By which he meant, of course,

Caravaggio's wilful attempt to portray humanity as it was, not as seen through a pair of rose-tinted spectacles. We mustn't fool ourselves into thinking we're more than we are, Gino. Caravaggio was a thug and a lunatic and he knew it too, just as well as he understood his genius.'

He had agreed and Hanrahan had led them into the Fonseca chapel where the Bernini busts sat like frozen decapitated heads on their plinths. They then returned and spent a few minutes in silence on the hard seats in the nave.

Finally, Gino Fosse asked the inevitable question. 'What happened to Lorenzo?'

'Dead, of course,' Hanrahan said with a mock mournfulness.

Fosse was in no mood for black jokes. He was mildly disturbed. He had been looking into a small side chapel which contained a strange, glinting object. An elderly man was on his knees in front of the iron railings which separated it from the nave. He seemed intent on the odd, metallic frame beyond the bars. Then something had moved there. A rat, he was sure of it. And, in the shadows, a half-visible figure too, dressed in a dark-red cardinal's robe, looking much like Michael Denney. A man who may, in some way Gino Fosse could not quite envisage at that moment, be some kind of martyr too.

'Of course he's dead,' he said. 'But what happened?'

Hanrahan stood up. Gino Fosse followed him to the bars of the side chapel, standing next to the praying man, his head hurting. There was no mistake now. A rat was moving underneath the altar, scampering in and out of the light. At least it appeared to be alone. The figure in red was gone and he knew it was simply some strange creation of his imagination.

'When Lorenzo failed to find any gold the authorities were very cross. All the normal punishments seemed somehow inapposite for a crime of this nature. So he was sentenced to be roasted to death over a slow fire while strapped to an iron grille so that he was, very gradually, cooked.'

Fosse watched the shining eyes of the rat gleam from the shadows.

'What?'

'You heard,' Hanrahan said. 'Think of Tertullian. The blood of the martyrs . . . Lorenzo was among the bravest, which is why he's named in the canon of the mass. Several senators converted on the basis of his courage alone, believing that God must have spared him the true agony of his martyrdom, since he was in good humour throughout the entire ordeal. The poet Prudentius later wrote that he laughed and joked for the duration, telling his torturers at one point, "I'm done on that side; turn me over, and eat." '

The kneeling man rose and walked away, cursing under his breath.

'The grille is preserved,' Hanrahan said with a sudden dramatic gesture. 'There. You may admire it.'

He followed the direction of the Irishman's arm and saw the cruel iron structure in its enclosure, finally realizing what it was.

Gino Fosse had checked out this story afterwards. Hanrahan was being truthful, after a fashion. The gridiron was, some believed, a later invention. Prudentius was not born until eighty years after the event. In all probability, Lorenzo had been beheaded like most of those who figured in the early, bloody history of the Church. Perhaps all the martyr stories he had heard in

Rome – Bartholomew carrying his skin, Lucy with her eyes on a plate, Sebastian shot full of arrows – were inventions too. There was no way of knowing and never would be; no archaeologist had dug up the evidence, as they had in Santi Giovanni e Paolo. Everything was conjecture, dependent on faith; without it Lorenzo became simply a character in a fairy story, a player in a fourth-century tale from Grimm designed to cow the gullible into submission.

Then Brendan Hanrahan leaned over and whispered in his ear, the close, hoarse whisper of a man in the confessional. The words burned in his head. The rat scuttered across the floor in front of the altar once more. In his mind's eye – and he knew this could not be real – Cardinal Michael Denney really did lie on the rack now, over a slow flame, like that of some country barbecue, grinning at them both and laughing through a dead mouth, asking, 'Am I done yet? Are any of us done yet? Will *she* be here soon? Is *she* getting hungry too?'

It had occurred to him that there were so many stories concerning instant conversions, from Paul onwards. The Church revelled in them. Yet there must be some counter-balance to these: events, sights, sounds, perhaps even an odour that destroyed a lifetime's faith in an instant. How many Catholics walked into Belsen and walked out atheists? How many, on a more mundane level, felt some darkness enter their soul while walking down the street, put one foot in front of the other and found their previously held beliefs were gone for ever? That they had lost twice over, spending half their life in ignorance and the rest in the solitary despair of knowing there was no salvation and never had been?

He looked again. There was no cardinal roasting

slowly on the rack. Only the rat, running on the iron bars, bright eyes glittering back at him in the darkness.

A rat could steal away the last few remnants of your faith, snatch it from your mouth, then shred it to pieces with its sharp, sharp teeth, slowly, silently in some dark, dusty corner away from the sight of man. It was always the small things, the unexpected things, which would kill you.

Recollecting all this with a grim precision Gino Fosse shook his head, wishing the memories would disappear for ever. They clouded his judgement. They stole from him his determination. There was no time for thinking, only action. He'd killed two cops, something he'd never envisaged when this began. There would be repercussions. This was, he thought, the precursor to the end. Events were circling around him like crows eyeing a coming meal. Within the next twenty-four hours everything could surely be accomplished. It was a welcoming thought. He was growing tired of the game. He was impatient for the inevitable resolution.

How quickly that happened depended on what he did next. Denney had proved himself a stubborn man, unwilling to run, to let himself be exposed to risk, in the face of the most severe provocation. There had to be a final exertion, a turn in the savagery none of them expected.

Gino Fosse had rubbed off the white make-up, as much as he could. He wore his old clothes again: jeans and a black T-shirt. He was sweating like a pig. The night was unbearably close. The city felt like an oven. He felt conspicuous, as if the darkness was full of eyes, glittering rodent eyes, greedy human ones, glancing feverishly in his direction. He stuck his head outside the van window.

The piazza was empty. A few lone figures wandered down the Corso, past the shuttered shops and the flashing neon signs in the windows.

He picked up the sack of keys he had stolen six days before from the administration office in the Vatican when he called to pick up the rest of his belongings. He sorted through them until he found the set marked for the church. He had reversed the van so that the rear door was tight against the locked entrance into the building. No one would see Arturo Valena being dragged inside. Behind those heavy wooden doors, in this deserted part of the city, no one would hear what then ensued.

Forty-eight

They stood in the corridor on the landing, unable to find the words. It was quiet downstairs now. The house was silent, filled with some strange happiness, an oasis of sanity hidden from the sight of the hard, bleak world beyond the gates. Sara thought of the other times; how she had allowed herself to be used, how her own desires were always secondary to theirs.

Then, gingerly, she walked up to him and looked into his eyes. Was there fear in them? Perhaps, but not doubt. He had stepped beyond its reach. Something had happened in the old farm that night, moving them all: Bea, in her search for love before it disappeared, Marco in his quest for some meaning in this fast-diminishing period of life which had been left to him. She, too, had been touched by their closeness, their frank questions and answers. This was so unlike the world she had inhabited before. Here no one asked for anything except her presence and understanding. This small, enclosed universe – and Nic Costa – now existed for her satisfaction, to do with as she wished.

Sara Farnese reached out, touched his hair, waiting, mouth tentatively open, for his kiss. He hesitated. She brought her lips up to his, felt his response, letting her tongue wander into his mouth, touch the wetness there, feeling the hard outline of his teeth. His hand came behind her back, strong, determined, and moved below to her thighs, gripping them. In a single powerful movement he lifted her from the ground. Her legs wound around his waist. She tore at his hair, kissed him hard and deep.

Then he carried her purposefully into the bedroom, let her legs slip to the floor and slowly, nervously, with no small wonder, they undressed each other, coming to stand naked by the bed, breathless, full of anticipation.

Again he hesitated.

'Nic,' she whispered.

His dark eyes tried to look inside her, beyond the surface he scarcely knew. 'And tomorrow?'

'Tomorrow I plant seeds for your father,' she said without a moment's hesitation.

She looked at the bathroom and the small marble shower in the corner.

'Here,' she said, taking him by the hand.

He followed her into the cubicle. She turned on the water, letting it run down on their heads, soaking their hair, stone cold at first, then lukewarm.

He laughed.

She took the liquid and began working it into his soft white skin. His head came down to her neck. His lips closed gently on a nipple. Her face arched upwards, teeth clenched, charged by a new and sudden determination in his grip. She felt his hardness, reached down, let her fingers run up and down its length and leaned back against the cold wet tiles, opening her legs, guiding him.

For a minute, no more, he entered her, making a few

measured strokes, shallow at first, then gradually deeper until she clung to him, hand tight in the back of his head, legs wrapped around his back.

She sighed, anguished, as he withdrew. Nic led her to the bed, watched as she spread herself across the white coverlet, beckoning. He was thinking about where to begin, what to consume first. His head went down, his teeth suckled briefly at her breasts and moved on to probe her navel. Her breath caught and shortened to brief snatches. This was new to her. In the past she had always been the one to serve, who sought to deliver satisfaction. Nic was determined to deliver that gift to her. His tongue licked lower, pressed beyond her hair, found her widening, warm crevice, entered fully, writhing inside with a powerful, muscular intent. She held his scalp, forced him down further into her, arching her back, wishing she could open herself so wide he might be consumed in the rich fleshy dampness of her sex. Then, with a certain, relentless rhythm, he began to work upon the smallest, sweetest part of her, raising its tumescence until her head had lost all reasoning, her mind knew nothing but the fiery delight he brought. And at this last gasping moment he revealed another secret too: his little finger sought another entry, pressed insistently from a second direction so that these secret, private doors to her ecstasy became a single coursing torrent of wild and shapeless pleasure.

When her shrieks gave way to panting he paused, rising from the bed to peer at the pale, lovely body on the sheets, as surprised by himself as he was by her. She laughed, wiped away the sweat from her brow with the back of her hand, then cupped his face with her hands. His fingers moved across her cheek. She sucked greedily on the tips, tasting herself on the skin and the nails. He moved onto her. She lifted her legs, placed her feet around his back, gripping him, tugging him, demanding more, taking him into her with anxious fingers.

He hesitated again, waiting in front of the unfolding entrance like an uninvited guest unsure of his welcome. Then she held him more tightly and the game ended. In the small bedroom of the farmhouse off the Appian Way, where Nic Costa turned from man to boy, where his personality was forged, through happiness and pain, the oldest ceremony of all was enacted with joy, enacted again and again until a sated exhaustion took them into a sleep undisturbed by dreams, untainted by the memory of a fallen world beyond the open window and the vine-twisted veranda.

Forty-nine

Arturo Valena stumbled out of the back of the van, grateful to leave the dogs behind. He sniffed the petrol-stained breeze from the Corso hopefully, then screeched in terror and pain as Fosse fetched him a hard blow on the side of the head with the butt of the gun.

That was a mistake. Fosse was shocked by his careless-ness. He'd half hoped the fat man would fall to the floor unconscious, making what came next easier. It was stupid. He should have realized this before the attempt. Valena was too heavy to be manhandled around a quiet piazza just a few yards from a street that still had its stragglers, even after midnight.

Fosse watched the fat man reeling in pain, wondering whether to run perhaps, and forced himself to think. Then he hit him once again, in the same place on the head but with a little less force, waved the gun in his face and hissed at him to go to the church railings. He had the keys in the small shoulder bag he'd brought with him from the van. He knew the place: where the light switches were. And where to find the instruments for the rest of the artistry.

Valena complied, shambling the few metres to the

entrance. Fosse fumbled at the lock, opened the gate, and pushed the terrified man through into the gloom of the portico. In the space of a minute he had unlocked the door to the church, sent Valena in and set the lights to low.

They stood in the nave, Fosse unable to detach his attention from the small chapel on the right which Brendan Hanrahan had revealed to him. Somewhere beyond the low, glittering frame of the iron grille a tiny voice squeaked. Fosse wished he could see them, not just hear their scuttering in the dark corners: tiny feet running, going nowhere, just like him. In his mind's eye he could imagine their yellow rodent teeth, ready to snatch away his soul the moment he faltered. He could picture their bright eyes glittering, the colour of polished jet. In those black pupils stood another universe, a black one that went on for ever, in time, in every direction, an endless place that could swallow up an entire world and still leave space for millions more.

Valena was trembling, holding himself by a pew. His face was a waxy yellow under the lights and there was an unmistakable flicker of hope there. His abductor had hesitated. Something had spooked him. Perhaps there was a chance.

'What do you want?' he asked, his voice husky with pain. 'Money?'

'Just you,' Fosse said flatly.

Valena's piggy eyes glistened, damp and pathetic. 'I never did anything to you. I never hurt anyone.'

'It's the not doing that counts,' Fosse said. 'You can go to Hell just as easily for your omissions as your deeds. Didn't they tell you that? Didn't you even begin to suspect?'

Valena fell to his knees, put his hands together. 'I'm just a stupid old man,' he pleaded. 'What do you want with me?'

'Your life.'

'Please . . .' His voice rose with that, turning almost into a squeal. It sounded like a rat. It sounded like the end of everything.

'Don't pray to me. Pray to God. And pray for yourself.'

The fat man sobbed. His hands went more tightly together. He closed his eyes. His lips moved, fleshy, blubbery lips, a mouth that had once caressed Sara Farnese. Gino Fosse knew that. He'd been the driver that night. He'd taken the pictures. It was one more stain to erase, one more station of grief along the way.

He reached into the shoulder bag and took out the pack he'd stolen from the hospital. The hypodermic was ready. The liquid sat in the barrel. He walked behind the praying Valena and stabbed him hard in the upper arm. The fat man got up, screeching.

'What are you fucking doing?' His eyes were burning black coals, full of hatred and pain. 'For the love of God . . .'

'Be grateful,' Fosse said. 'Hope it lasts.'

They danced slowly around each other for a while. He wasn't letting the fat man make for the door. Eventually Valena's eyes started to turn dull.

'What?' He swayed once. Then his pupils rose, went upwards into his head. His large frame collapsed like a building that had suddenly lost its foundation. Gino Fosse looked at the pile of humanity that lay on the floor, no more than ten metres from Lorenzo's altar.

The drug was the easiest option. There was much

preparation to be done to achieve the required effect. This would be the last before the final deed. He knew that somehow.

He bent down over the unconscious Valena and began to tug at his clothing. Five minutes later the TV man was naked on the tiles of the church. He'd pissed himself at some stage. Fosse was disgusted but not surprised. Ordinary men feared death, failing to understand the need for the transformation. They lacked the sense and the courage to greet it smiling, welcoming its inevitable embrace.

He turned Valena to face the small altar in the chapel. With no small amount of effort he dragged the iron grille into the nave. It was cold and shiny to the touch, polished for centuries, a perfect instrument alive with its past. Perhaps the story of Lorenzo's death was apocryphal. To Gino Fosse it seemed irrelevant. So many people had come to believe in it that this elaborate construction of iron, with its curlicues and its flamboyant grating, became what they imagined: the gateway to Paradise, the ultimate redemption. Even Arturo Valena deserved that.

Gino Fosse fetched the kindling, the charcoal and the petrol and decided, at this point, that he must cease deluding himself. He'd learned enough in the hospital to understand how long the shot would keep Valena unconscious. It was fifteen minutes, perhaps twenty, no more. Arturo Valena would not sleep his way to judgement.

Fifty

A noise woke her: the sound of a dog barking from some distant farm. He stood at the window, with his back to her, staring out into the blackness of the night, silhouetted against the moon. She looked at the clock on the stand. It was nearly two.

'What's wrong?' she asked softly.

He didn't even turn round.

'Nic? Look at me.'

He sighed and returned to sit on the bed. In the cold light that fell through the window his face wore the same hard expression she had seen when they first met. This was serious Nic, tough Nic, a man who preferred duty over passion. A man who feared anything that might disrupt an ordered, logical world.

'I'm sorry,' she said. 'It was too soon. I should have stopped myself.'

He stared down at the sheets and said nothing.

She took his chin with her hand, made him look at her. 'Don't sit in judgement on me.'

He scowled. It wasn't a pleasant look. 'I'm not. It's me. I didn't want this to happen. I promised myself I wouldn't allow it.'

'And I made you? Is that it?'

'No. Of course not.' He meant what he said, though there was no comfort in his sincerity. 'But that doesn't make it right.'

'It felt right to me,' she replied icily.

That touched him. He reached out and held her hand. 'It felt right to me too. But Sara . . .'

The words ran dry. His reticence annoyed her. 'What?'

'I don't know you. Not really. Just a side of you. There's still something missing, something important in your life you don't want me to see.'

She withdrew from his grasp. 'Haven't you seen enough?'

'No. Because what I know doesn't add up and that just makes everything worse. I don't believe it's the real you. Maybe not even a real part of you either. There's something else. Something you won't disclose. Something you're keeping from me, still, and I can't bear the thought because without that piece of knowledge I feel I don't really know you at all. It just . . . tortures me.'

'Listen to the cop inside you talking. Am I supposed to be more frank after you've screwed me?'

'No!' His voice almost broke. She recognized the truth in what he said and despised herself for doubting him. Nic was honest, too honest perhaps.

She came closer to him, put her hand to his face, stared into his eyes. 'I'm sorry. That was just the fear in me talking. This is hard for me too, you know.'

There was doubt in his eyes. 'Is it? You've a capacity for keeping things inside. I never learnt that.'

'I asked if you'd come off this case for me. I begged. You still can.'

'It's impossible. This is my job. It's what I do.'

'Then maybe this is what I do too. Maybe this is who I am. Just someone who sleeps around and then goes on somewhere else, not remembering, not caring. What's wrong with that? Is it a sin just because you don't think that way?'

He shook his head. 'No, it's a sin because you don't. This person you're trying to paint for me is someone you created and I need to know why.'

'Trust me. You don't need that.'

He put his arms around her shoulders. He kissed her lightly on the mouth then stroked her soft hair. 'I woke up with the taste of you. I can smell you in my head. Don't take this lightly. It doesn't happen to me.'

The first sign of dampness appeared at the corner of her eye. He wiped it away with a finger and placed the tip in his own mouth, tasting the salt of her, as if it were some precious fluid.

She closed her eyes. The tears ran freely down her cheeks. He knew himself to be on the verge of some new discovery and felt disquiet at his own insistent curiosity.

'Tell me,' he murmured.

She wiped her face with her arm then gathered up the sheet around her, ready to leave the room.

'Tell you, Nic? I'll tell you. I promise. When Michael Denney is out of the Vatican and gone from Italy. There. Is that what you want to hear?'

It was the last response he was expecting. No words formed in his head, only thoughts and images of Sara with the old, grey man trapped behind those distant walls in the city.

'No,' he said finally, with a bitterness which surprised him.

She got up from the bed, clutching the sheet to her body. 'Then I'm sorry, but it's true. And you'll hear nothing more from me, not a word, until that's happened.'

He gripped her arm, refusing to let her go. She forced his fingers from her wrist. His head was working overtime, a whirl of ideas, connections.

'Is that all I am?' he spat, shocked at his own unfamiliar fury. 'Just another random fuck in the night like the rest?'

There was the coldness in those green eyes again. Nic Costa knew he'd broken the spell with his own stupidity.

'You sound like you're back on duty,' she whispered.

He was furious. He wanted to strike her. 'Maybe I am. Maybe I should have stayed there all along.' The cop in him was waking. He took her by the arms and forced her into the bedside chair. 'Let's talk then. Like we're supposed to. Did you sleep with Rinaldi to get that expert opinion to go Denney's way? Did Denney ask you to do that?'

Her eyes were fixed on the dead, dull tiles.

'OK. Don't answer. Either way it doesn't matter. It explains something. And the American, Gallo. He never knew Denney at all. We found nothing to link them. What happened there?'

His mind raced in the silence. 'You used him. Denney needed something. A messenger perhaps. Someone to take a package some place, pay someone off maybe. You slept with Gallo to get him to do favours. Denney didn't even specify him by name. He just asked you to find the right person. Was that what happened with the Englishman too? He was something big with the EU. Did that make him useful to Denney as well?'

'Hugh Fairchild was my lover,' she hissed. 'He came to me for what I am. Don't judge me with your guesswork.'

'He was a married man looking for a warm bed in a strange town. I'm not guessing. I'm just working my way towards something that makes sense. I believe . . .'

'Believe what the hell you like.'

She got up, pushed brusquely past him. He watched her slim figure disappear through the doorway, into the corridor, towards the room at the end of the house, torn by his own warring emotions. He wanted to know; he didn't. She was right. This was all guesswork. It still left so many questions unanswered.

Nic Costa lay back on the crumpled bed clothes, still damp from their bodies, and closed his eyes, wondering if he could sleep. His head filled with such possibilities. His mind ran with images he never wished to imagine. Beyond the window, in the hot darkness, owls called through the night. He could hear, far off, the chatter of the men on the gate, their radios crackling in the darkness, alive with some news from beyond this small, cherished haven, safe from the depredation of the city. He felt a fool. He'd let Marco's magic, and her sudden gift of a startling, physical ecstasy, steal away his concentration. Gino Fosse would surely not be sleeping. There was a cycle in motion beyond this fleeting sanctuary his father had tried to create. It would not be broken yet.

He thought of Michael Denney again, pushing aside the insidious vile images that wanted to rise inside his imagination.

Then, after a fashion, he slept until the phone woke him with a start. He looked at the clock. It was now nearly six. Almost three hours had disappeared in some jumble of a half-waking nightmare.

He listened to the voice on the phone, Falcone's familiar cold monotone, and was immediately dragged from his anguished reverie, back to reality.

Fifty-one

The livid stain of a new dawn was breaking over Rome as
Nic Costa drove along the deserted road, towards the
looming, illuminated shape of the gate of San Sebastiano.
There was scarcely a soul on the streets. The city seemed
to have died in the dry August heat. It was hard to
imagine life ever returning.

Then he pulled onto the main road that led through
to the Lateran and on to the police station. As he did so
the phone rang.

'Where are you?' Falcone barked.

'On my way to the Piazza Navona.'

'Don't bother. He's been busy again. Meet me in the
Corso, the church on the little piazza, halfway along. You
know it?'

'Yes.'

Falcone paused for a moment. Then he asked, 'Did
you get anything out of her? Anything we can use?'

'What?'

'The woman. That was the idea. Remember?'

'No,' he said, wondering how much Falcone could
hear inside his voice. 'Nothing.'

He heard the familiar bitter sigh.

'Oh well,' said the voice on the line. 'And me with two men dead. The bastard's going to pay for that. Nobody kills cops in this town. Not my men.'

He couldn't find the words. Falcone seemed more offended by the personal affront than the loss of Rossi and Cattaneo.

'He was my friend,' Costa said. 'He . . .' The words wouldn't come out. He had to fight to stop himself pulling into the side of the road and falling apart.

'I know,' Falcone acknowledged. 'He was a good guy underneath it all.'

Even at that point Falcone had to make some judgement. Costa wondered why he worked with the man, why he did as he was told.

'One more thing,' Falcone ordered. 'Don't eat breakfast. Even Crazy Teresa couldn't smile through this one.'

He thought about that, recalling the evening the three of them spent together in the restaurant in Testaccio, in what seemed like another lifetime. There were other reasons, ones Falcone couldn't imagine.

'Hey. A question,' Falcone added. 'You come from farming stock. How many brothers and sisters you got?'

'Two.'

'You ever meet another peasant family smaller than that?'

Costa was baffled by the question. 'I don't recall.'

'Think about it. Farmers breed kids like they breed livestock. They need them to make the whole thing work.'

'So?'

'So where's Gino Fosse's siblings, huh?'

He recalled the file. 'Fosse didn't have any. He was an

only child. Maybe the mother had a medical problem or something?'

Falcone's dry laugh echoed in his ear. 'We got someone to talk to the local doctor about that. You're right. According to him she was barren. So what happened there? A miracle?'

He was headed for the big junction in the Lateran square. Here the traffic was starting to get heavy: trucks and buses hustled each other for position at the lights. He felt his concentration fading.

'No such thing,' he said, then turned off the phone. He didn't want to hear Falcone any more. He didn't want to think about Gino Fosse's family background. There was a picture in his head: of Sara beneath him, naked, a half-musical sigh emerging from her lips. The taste of her returned, a physical entity in his mouth. Somehow, and this made him feel ashamed, it even obscured the image of Luca Rossi, the big man, who was now dead on some slab in the morgue.

Fifty-two

He stopped a little way off from the church and watched the circus growing in the piazza. The media pack was out in force beyond the railings. He couldn't blame them. Valena was a celebrity, a fading one too, which, in some strange way, made the story even better. He was beginning to recognize the reporters now. These were some of the people who'd doorstepped the farm until the hunt had moved on. One, a woman with one of the seedier dailies, caught sight of him and walked over. She was about thirty, pretty, with fiercely hennaed hair and a determined face.

'How's the back?' she asked. 'I heard he cut you up pretty badly.'

'You heard wrong,' he snapped.

'Look,' she said, unmoved by his aggression. 'It's just a job. You're doing yours. I'm doing mine.'

'They don't match.'

'Really? How many hacks have you seen on corruption charges recently? Nothing personal but we're just looking for some socially acceptable reasons to justify felling a few trees. We tend to hunt as a pack and it's not a pretty sight, I know. To be honest it's a little like attending a meeting of gargoyles anonymous most days. We're not crooked. Neither are you from what I hear but you're not exactly standard issue.'

To her surprise he didn't take it badly.

'Greta Ricci,' she said, extending a hand. He shook it quickly. 'I'm sorry. Mornings are not my time. This is the big one, isn't it? Arturo Valena. What a way to go. And those two poor cops last night.'

'There's no point in asking me. You probably know more anyway.'

She lit a cigarette. He waved away the smoke. 'No problem. I wasn't after anything. It's all running away from me anyway. One of the TV bastards has got something up his sleeve. I can tell from the smug look on his face. One more fuck-up and they'll have me off crime altogether and writing make-up advice or some such shit. I have this anarchical idea that somehow reporting's all about digging stuff up. Whereas what you're really supposed to do is suck up to the big people, your people, the politicians, then take down notes when they feel like leaking something. If I'd wanted to be someone's secretary I'd have worn a shorter skirt and learned how to type properly.'

Costa was interested. 'What do you think he might have?'

'Search me. The way this story's been running it could be anything. Craziest job I've ever worked on. But I'll tell you this. There's something up with the Vatican. I heard him calling the media people there, all quietly so he thought none of us could hear. He's asking for something from them. God knows what. I mean, this Fosse guy was a priest, sure. All the same, you can't blame them for what he's done, can you?'

He shrugged. 'I can't imagine the connection.'

She sucked on the cigarette, stared at him, knowing he was lying, then handed over a card. 'Listen. If you ever feel like leaking something . . .'

He put it in his pocket. 'I thought you were against that.'

The woman looked him up and down. 'From you I think it would be different.'

He nodded and said, 'I have to go. *Ciao.*'

Then he crossed the piazza, pushed his way through the crowd, ignoring their questions, showed his ID to the uniformed men on the gate and walked into the church.

There was a stink there, an odd mixture of burnt wood and meat. The forensic team was gathered around a low metallic object upturned on the floor, next to a pile of ashes. A thin wisp of grey smoke still worked its way upwards from the embers in the middle of the nave. The body was gone. He was glad of that, after Falcone's warning. In the far corner of the church, penned in by two uniformed cops, stood a straggle of dogs undergoing slow and careful examination by another of the forensic team.

Teresa Lupo was on a bench not far from the metal grille, her back to him, hunched, miserable. Nic Costa walked over and sat by her side. She'd been weeping.

He took her hand. 'I'm sorry, Teresa. I should have been there.'

Her damp eyes turned on him, full of sorrow. 'Why? So you could die too? What's the point of that?'

'Maybe . . . I don't know.'

Her mood changed from grief to fury in a second. 'Maybe it would have been different? Is that what you mean? Don't fool yourself. I talked to people who were there. This ... monster just popped them, as if he were putting down an animal. He'd have killed you. He'd have killed anyone who stood in his way. That's what he's like. It doesn't mean anything to him. None of this does. It's as if it's all a game. Or as if he's in hell already and thinks this is the way he's supposed to behave, like he's handing out punishment to anyone who deserves it.'

'Luca didn't deserve it. He was a good man. He was ...' His own eyes began to sting. 'I could have learned a lot from him.'

She pummelled at her nose with a handkerchief then squeezed his hand. 'He's in the morgue right now. I've got to go back for the autopsy after this.'

This sudden practical turn shocked him. 'You don't have to do that. Get someone else.'

'What?' She looked surprised. 'Nic, this is my job. In any case what's on that slab isn't him. Not any more. I've dealt with enough bodies over the years to know that. When they're gone they live in just one place. Here ...' She tapped her lank, dark hair with a strong finger. 'He'll be there a long time. I liked the stubborn old bastard.'

'He felt the same about you.'

'Yeah,' she said, with the hint of a smile. 'I think he did too. He didn't call me Crazy Teresa, did he? Not behind my back.'

'Never.'

'Liar.'

He grimaced. It was hard to shrink from the truth when she turned on the heat.

'It was just that you scared him sometimes. Not because of who you are but because of him. Because he didn't like ...'

He fell silent.

'What?'

'He didn't like having those feelings. They disturbed him.'

'Seems to go with the job,' she replied, staring at him. 'Tell me. Is that why you all do this? To get the excuse you want?'

'I don't follow.'

'Oh, I think you do. You tell yourself you're like this because of what you do. But is it just faintly possible there's another reason? That you pick this stupid profession because it allows you to be what you are and never have to take the blame?'

'Yeah,' he grunted, thinking that she could have been talking to herself. Teresa was a quasi-cop. That much had become obvious over the past few days. What turned them on, turned her on too. 'That's right. You see through us all.'

Her hand touched his knee. The tears stood big in her eyes now. 'I'm sorry, Nic. I'm so sorry. I'm just lashing out because it feels good, except it doesn't. I didn't mean it.'

He folded his arms around her, felt her over-large body against his.

'Don't apologize,' he said. 'Anyway, you're right.'

She wiped her streaming nose with her sleeve. 'Maybe for Luca. You . . . I don't know. You want to do something, don't you?'

'Do I?' he asked mournfully, not wanting an answer. He nodded at the activity across the nave. 'What happened here?'

'Someone had a barbecue. Let the dogs in to clean up afterwards.'

'Jesus.'

'It was that TV creep, Valena. Ask your boss. Falcone's livid, which I guess ought to impress me, except that it's weird. You'd almost think this was about him, not two dead cops and God knows who else. Seems to think he knows all the answers too. When this is over, Nic, I'm taking a break. Maybe I'll go back to the university, teach for a while. I don't mind the work. Truth is it's the best there is. It's just the people. Falcone in particular. He's . . . I don't know. Luca loathed the man and I trust his judgement. Let's leave it at that.'

He said nothing. It was unwise to be drawn.

'How's she doing?' Teresa asked.

'Who?'

'Sara Farnese. She's still staying with you, isn't she?'

'She's fine,' he said automatically.

'Fine?'

He wilted under the ferocity of her gaze.

'Nic. Whatever she is, and I sometimes wonder if you're even mildly qualified to judge, she is not "fine". Look at what's happening here. Look at what someone's doing because of her.'

'You sound like Falcone. It doesn't mean it's her fault.'

She sighed, exasperated. 'I didn't mean it was, not for an instant. I meant that she knows this is to do with her. She feels responsible to some extent, however much she may try to hide it. She's not "fine". And one other thing. She slept with Valena apparently. She never told us about that.'

'She said there were some others. She just didn't know the names.'

The look on her face was just a couple inches short of contempt. 'She didn't know the name of Arturo Valena?

The moron was on the box every night. In the papers too. Where does she live, this woman of yours? In a convent? Except when she's out screwing?'

She waited for an answer. Nothing came. Then she watched the team working on the iron grille, watched the men examining the dogs for traces of Arturo Valena's flesh. It was all pointless. Everyone knew what happened. A lunatic stepped out of the dark and death followed in his shadow. No, that wasn't enough. There was a reason behind it all. There had to be.

'I've got work to do,' she muttered, and joined the team with the dogs.

Nic Costa felt as if his head would burst. He was exhausted. He was confused. Then he heard a commotion at the door. Falcone walked in, flanked by some cops he recognized only by sight. Costa knew the investigation was moving away from him. Now the big man was gone, now he was reduced to little more than a bodyguard for Sara, Falcone had brought in a larger, more experienced team. He wondered what could be left for him to do.

Falcone caught his eye and waved him over. He was carrying a briefcase and Teresa Lupo was right. He wasn't himself. His eyes refused to meet Nic Costa's at first. He looked lost, distraught, furious.

'How's she doing?' he asked. 'Crazy Teresa. I heard they were an item.'

'Pretty cut up.'

'Join the club. Jesus. How dare this asshole touch my men? Does he think there's some kind of equivalence between them and dirt bags like Valena? I'll put the fucker down myself if I get the chance.'

'Wouldn't help.'

Falcone glowered at him and there was a little of his old self in the expression, asking: *is that so*? He took Costa to one side. 'You watch TV?'

'Not a lot.'

'You should. It's good sometimes. Going to get better too now that fat jerk's not preaching at us every night.'

Falcone barked at the team to start questioning forensics and anyone they could find living in the vicinity. Then they walked outside, into the fast rising heat and Falcone opened the door of the police Mercedes, ushering him into the passenger side and sitting next to him.

'Where are we going?' Costa asked. 'Do you know where Fosse is?'

'No idea. Be patient.'

Costa nodded at the door of the church. 'No time for patience.'

Falcone shrugged. 'Show a little trust, kid, we're almost there. Remember what I asked you? About Gino Fosse's family?'

'Of course.'

'Yeah,' Falcone looked at his watch. It was just coming up to six. Then he flipped open the cover of the little LCD screen in the dashboard, switched off the navigation system and tuned into the TV channel. 'Well, watch. After that you can go and see Rossi's sister. Act sympathetic. We don't want to get sued.'

'His sister?' he asked, furious with himself that he didn't even know Rossi had a relative in the city.

Falcone read his reaction immediately. 'He didn't tell you? They lived together in some apartment out near Fiumicino. Go talk her down from whatever state she's in. Tell her I personally guarantee the bastard who did this is going down for good. After that . . . take the day off. Go spend some time with that father of yours. Go fishing. I don't care. You're not going to be around when Denney runs. I want people with some real time under their belts.'

He said nothing, hating himself for the way he took this. Then the news came on. They extended the newscast from five minutes to fifteen. Valena's dreadful death led the bulletin. Costa listened to the details they gave.

'Is that right?' he asked.

'Should be. I gave them the briefing myself,' Falcone replied.

'You didn't hold anything back?'

Falcone scowled. 'What's the point? We know who we want. I could put him in the dock today without a scrap more evidence.'

'But we don't know why.'

Falcone put a finger to his lips, gave him that cold smile, then pointed to the screen. There was a stock picture of Michael Denney there, and a recent photo of Gino Fosse too. He listened to the newscaster, amazed. Then he turned to Falcone.

'The DNA? That's why you wanted something from his apartment? To prove this?'

'The DNA report doesn't come back until this morning. That was the idea but I didn't need it anyway. A little bird behind those walls started to sing for me. I've got documents. I've got pieces of paper that are proof, just as much as some stupid lab test.' Falcone smiled. 'Gino Fosse is Denney's son. We still don't know who the real mother was. But he was taken from her at birth and given to that couple in Sicily. Denney's managed to hush it up for years.'

Nic found it impossible to think. Nothing made sense. 'Why leak it to the media? What does it mean anyway?'

'I want that crooked bastard. I want him out of that place where he's sitting pretty, looking out of his window, thinking nothing can touch him. If we let him run from there anything can happen. If we cut a deal I'll stick to it. As long as the rules stay the same. But if the son comes in, that's different. We get him too and take the father in for protection. Because that's what this is all about. That's what Gino Fosse is trying to say. That he keeps on killing until he gets the one he wants. His old man.'

It was wrong. It was impossible. 'But why? Because he was fired from his job?'

'Are you serious? Sara Farnese was the old man's woman. She slept with these people – Vaccarini, Valena, some of the others, because Denney told her to. It was her attempt to get him safe passage out of that prison of his. She slept with Rinaldi. He tried to fix the judicial commission. Vaccarini the same. She slept with Valena. Four months ago he came out on that show of his arguing for wider diplomatic immunity in the Vatican on the grounds – get this – that the Church needed protecting in a godless world. You think maybe Sara Farnese performed a few favours on the fat fucker afterwards? The Englishman . . . I don't know. Maybe he was trying to swing something for Denney with the EU.'

He remembered her insistent denial of just a single accusation. The Englishman was her lover, he realized. A liar and adulterer. But he was unlike the rest. That much, Nic Costa now believed, was true.

'Maybe he was just standing in the wrong place at the wrong time,' he said.

Falcone nodded, surprised that Costa agreed with him

so readily. 'It doesn't matter any more. If Denney runs, they're both out in the open. Maybe I'll let the cardinal get on the plane, maybe not. Doesn't matter. If he makes it to America we extradite him anyway.' He shook his head, as if the game was already won. 'And Gino Fosse, he stays here. He's ours the moment he steps out into the sun and if he so much as sneezes I'll shoot the bastard myself.'

Falcone waited for Costa's reaction. 'You're quiet. Aren't you going to tell me I've got her all wrong? That she didn't know Michael Denney? This can't be true?'

'I don't know anything any more.'

There was a pained grimace on the inspector's tanned face. 'Say that again. You should watch the eight o'clock news. Take a break. Buy yourself a coffee and enjoy the fun. You have to stage these things with the media. You don't give them it all in one chunk or it just goes to waste. Come eight they'll have another little item to add to the public's knowledge about His Eminence Cardinal Denney.'

The triumph in his voice was muted. There was a despairing note of bitterness behind it. Leo Falcone felt the loss of Rossi and Cattaneo, more deeply than Costa would have expected. 'What else?'

Falcone reached for his briefcase on the back seat of the car and took out an envelope. He opened it and thrust the contents onto Costa's knee. It was a black and white photograph of dubious quality, taken from some distance judging by the flatness and the grain of the picture. A telephoto lens from slightly above the subject, perhaps, shot through a window. It showed Denney in a grand apartment, the one, Costa guessed, he used to occupy by right, before they threw him into the rat hole where he sweated now.

Denney stood with his back half turned to the camera. He wore a white shirt and dark trousers. His grey hair was neatly groomed. Sara Farnese faced the lens, smiling, a wonderful, open smile, full of love, an expression he'd seen for himself the previous night. Her arms were around Denney. She was coming forward as if to kiss his cheek or his neck. Sara and Denney would soon be one, her body merged with his. She held him, tightly, in a way which brooked no mistake. It was impossible to fake. This was the two of them engaged in a loving, close embrace. A prelude to what? He looked again and knew. Denney's right hand was already reaching for the curtain at the apartment window. In a few seconds the two of them would be snatched from sight.

The photo had the same grainy quality as the ones they'd found in Fosse's flat. It wasn't hard to guess where it came from.

'Where are the rest of the pictures?' he asked.

'That's all I have,' Falcone replied. 'Look for yourself. He's getting himself a little privacy. This is the Vatican, after all. What do you want? To see them in bed?'

Something still nagged at him. 'Where did it come from?'

Falcone scowled and looked at his watch. 'Come on. You've figured that out, surely?'

He had. He just didn't want to admit it. 'Fosse took it. Just like he took the others. He kept the ones of Sara, of the other women, for his own purposes. Really he was there to provide backup. To make sure that if they didn't bend from the favour, they'd bend from a little blackmail.'

'Precisely,' Falcone said, pleased with Costa's analysis. 'Fosse drove for Denney. He was the chauffeur on these little night-time escapades. For the Farnese woman. For the more conventional hookers Denney used too. He hung around peeking through the curtains with his lens while they got on with their work.' He paused for effect. 'They knew what was going on. She knew.'

Costa thought of her face in the pictures in the Clivus Scauri. The way she was looking towards the lens. Falcone was right but Teresa Lupo had seen this first: Sara was party to the trick.

'She knew,' he agreed. 'And Denney thought this was all his doing. He never realized Fosse was working on the side for someone else too. Maybe giving them the same information. Spying on Denney as well.'

He looked Falcone in the eye. 'Who was that? Who's pulling the strings? Hanrahan?'

'Hanrahan's just a servant. Like me. What does it matter? We've got what we need. At eight o'clock these go public. Match that up with the news about Fosse and I don't see how the Vatican can continue to hold him. He's an embarrassment. He's a visible scab they'll want rid of.'

Costa put the photograph back into the envelope.

The older man took it and said, 'If you breathe a word of this to anyone before it appears I'll have your hide. And I mean her in particular. This is all beyond you now. I don't want any more accidents, understand? So you just talk to Rossi's sister then sit back, get some rest. You look like you need it.'

'Accidents?' he demanded, his voice rising, some red stub of anger beginning to fire in his head. 'I lost a partner to this lunatic. I want to be there when he's taken.'

Falcone looked offended. 'Hey. Gimme a break here. I got two dead cops squatting on my conscience. I don't want your skinny hide added to the pile.'

This was the limit, this was the moment. Costa reached into his jacket pocket and took out his police ID card.

'Fuck you,' he said and threw the thing into Falcone's lap, then got out of the car, out into the fast rising heat of the morning.

Fifty-three

She walked out to the gate at seven and spoke to one of the cops. It was easy to get what you wanted with a smile. The man took her money, looked a little puzzled, and drove off to the nearby nursery. It wouldn't be open yet but he was a cop. He'd bang on the door till they came.

Then she stayed near the lane, mutely watched by the other policemen, trying not to think, trying not to expect too much from the day to come, waiting. Half an hour later he returned with the plants housed in a battered cardboard box. There were three sets, each wrapped in damp newspaper. She looked at the seedlings of *cavolo nero*, little taller than an index finger. It was hard to believe they would grow through the coming harshness of winter, thriving in the cold and damp, becoming stronger each day until, in spring, they would be ready for harvest.

Sara walked back to the house and found Marco and Bea on the porch drinking coffee. He sat happily in his wheelchair, Bea at his side. She thought about the expression on his face. Marco finally looked at peace with himself. He'd lost the impatient energy, the need to make some kind of point at every opportunity which she had noticed since the moment she stepped into the farm-house. The internal, gnawing need to settle accounts had been resolved, for the time being at least. There had been a debt to be settled, she thought, and one he'd forgotten, which only made things worse. In a sense he looked older, wearier, more resigned. Perhaps these were steps along the way, stations of love, of insight, which needed to be passed. This was the luxury – and the agony – of a lingering death. It gave one the time to consider, to make decisions. It contained, too, sufficient space for both regret and, with a little luck, reconciliation.

Bea stood up and took the box from her, smiling at the slender green forms that lay inside.

'You remembered?' Marco said, amazed.

'Of course.'

He laughed. 'It was the wine. I didn't mean you to do this. You can't really want to get down on your hands and knees and plant these damned things. What for?'

Bea patted him on his grey head. 'I thought we'd agreed. Because it's a farm, silly man. Things should be growing here. It looks barren otherwise.'

Marco scanned the arid, yellow ground. He gazed at both of them. 'I'm a fool, aren't I?'

'You're a man,' Bea said.

'Well, at least I won't be grubbing around planting something no one's going to look after come the winter.'

'They'll grow,' Bea said. 'I promise.'

He harrumphed, though there was still an amused satisfaction in his eye neither of them could miss. 'What's happening to my life?' he asked, then shot Sara a glance. 'You heard from Nic?'

'He left early,' she said, not committing herself. She understood they knew where she had spent the night.

Perhaps Marco and Bea had heard them. She'd no idea how much noise they had made. Her time with him, in his arms, astride him, touching his hair, feeling him inside her, all this now seemed like a dream. They had parted on bad terms. It was her fault. She knew this and she regretted hurting him. Nevertheless there were boundaries that had to be established. She wondered whether she would ever see Nic Costa again. Whether he would even want to see her. The future rose ahead like a mist, full of so many formless possibilities.

'We should watch the news,' she said.

Sara saw the expression cross Marco Costa's lined face, followed the way he looked at Bea. It was something bad. It had to be.

'I did,' he said. 'While you were down at the gate.'

'I need to know . . .'

'No you don't. Not right now. All that would mean is that we'd have to watch you go through the agonies again, Sara. This is not about you. These people aren't your responsibility.'

'You know that?' she replied coldly.

'We know enough,' Marco answered.

'Please tell me.'

They glanced at each other. Bea nodded.

'He shot two cops dead last night,' Marco said grimly. 'One of them was Luca Rossi, Nic's partner.'

She closed her eyes.

'Then he killed someone else,' Marco continued. 'Arturo Valena, the man from the TV. They're saying . . .' He hesitated. 'They're saying all sorts of things, to tell you the truth. They're saying this priest they're looking for is the son of that cardinal the papers are writing about.'

'I need to see this . . .'

His hand went out and held her as she passed him. Marco was still strong. This surprised her.

'No,' he insisted. 'It's just there to drive you crazy. *There is nothing you can do.* Are you hearing me? Leave this to Nic and the rest of them. It's their job. Not yours.'

'I have to know.'

His old face examined hers. He was a clever man. She understood that. Nic must have found out at an early age what she knew now: it was impossible to keep a secret from him when those sharp, intelligent eyes turned on you.

'No you don't,' Marco said, and let the rest of the sentence hang in the air. She knew what he left unsaid: *you don't need to hear because you know already.* It was, she admitted to herself, this that interested her: finding out how much they had discovered, using that information for her own ends.

Marco picked up one of the sets of plants and examined it, touching the stalk, feeling the tender young leaves with his fingers.

'These are good,' he said, looking at her. 'They're a little late but never mind. It's just a matter of care and attention. Don't plant them together too tightly. You'll need to water them in well. Sara . . .'

She did what he wanted. She looked into his face.

'The tools are in the outhouse over there. You should dress down a little, both of you. I want this done with care. When you're finished, then we let the rest of the world in here again. But not before, please.'

He knew everything, or thought he did. She could see this in his face.

'And when Nic calls? When he comes round?' she

asked, aware that she was already thinking about how soon she could get away and make the phone call.

'I think Nic will be pretty busy today, to be honest with you.'

'When isn't he?'

Marco had the answer already: she wouldn't be there. She would never have to face the possibility.

'The ground needs a little preparation,' he said. 'I'll teach you how.'

Fifty-four

Michael Denney sat at the low coffee table in the little apartment, opposite Hanrahan, trying not to look at the TV. The picture of Sara, her bare-sleeved, comforting arms around him, filled the screen. It seemed even more fascinating for the news programmes than the images of Arturo Valena's body being taken from the church off the Corso. What irked Denney most was that he couldn't recall the moment. He'd seen so little of her recently. He missed the time they spent together. It infuriated him that someone could have spied on them and not left sufficient clues for him to place the occasion.

'Who the hell took it, Brendan? You?'

The Irishman's lugubrious features met his angry gaze. 'Chickens come home to roost. You sent Fosse out to take those bedroom snaps for you. Don't blame me if he didn't know when to stop.'

'I thought Fosse was working for me.'

Hanrahan sighed and said nothing. Denney thought hard. He hadn't seen her like this in more than a month. That meant they had decided to throw him to the wolves long before he had tried, and failed, to resurrect the bank.

'You're an ungrateful man, Michael,' Hanrahan said.

'I've watched your back in this place too long. I've risked my own reputation, perhaps more than that. And what do I get in return? Your misguided anger. Your lack of trust.'

'I'm sorry.' It was possible Hanrahan was offended by the suggestion. Or perhaps it was just part of a broader, more subtle act than Denney had appreciated. 'I'm not myself right now. It's just the thought of Fosse spying on us like that. Did they really think I deserved that?'

Hanrahan stabbed at the TV. '*Deserve?* Michael, I told you so many times she would be your nemesis. And there she is. Plastered all over the place. In every newspaper too when they get the chance. A cardinal of the Church and the woman they've been painting as some loose whore all week. What do you expect?'

'A little understanding,' Denney grumbled. There was no point in telling this icy Irishman about the need for love. It was inexplicable, incapable of being reduced to plain and logical analysis. Hanrahan didn't believe in mysteries. He wanted only hard, unbending facts around him. He never noticed, never felt, the holes these hard, inhuman certainties made in a man's life.

'Don't blame anyone else now,' Hanrahan warned. 'No one made you start seeing her. No one else forced you to use Gino Fosse as a bagman on these night errands of yours. This is your doing. Not mine nor anyone else's. If you must indulge in these black secrets – bribery, black-mail for God's sake – don't go blaming others when they creep out into the light of day.'

'And you think I don't know that?'

Hanrahan grimaced. Denney looked at his grey, emo-tionless face and knew there was more to come.

'Maybe. Maybe not. You're a man prone to whimsies,

Michael. It's odd, given the job you used to do. I would have expected a more practical nature.'

'Like yours,' Denney said without thinking.

'I like to think of myself as a reasonable man. One who helps keep the wheels turning.'

There was a time they had been together for a conference in Dubai. A financier had provided company for them both. It was a ritual, a gift it would have been impolite to refuse. He'd watched Hanrahan with the woman. She was beautiful, a tall Cypriot girl with perfect English and a ready smile. It was the only occasion on which he had seen the Irishman uncomfortable, incapable of controlling the world around him. He had left before the dinner was finished.

'And never being touched by anything, eh Brendan? Living on your own. Running other people's lives. You're not like me. You could get married. You could do what you like. Instead you just scheme and scheme. For me. For anyone that pays.'

Hanrahan's thick black eyebrows rose.

'I gave you good money to fix things, Brendan. You were supposed to help me put the Banca Lombardia back on track.'

Hanrahan scowled. 'I can't raise the dead. That idea didn't stand a hope in hell from the moment you first suggested it.'

'And you never thought of saying so.'

'I'm a servant. Have you forgotten?'

'Who doesn't know who his master is.'

'Oh, but I always remember that. You were the one who forgot. You were the one who overstepped the mark because you just couldn't resist, could you? It flattered your fulsome ego, dining with all these politicians.

Having these women at your beck and call. You lost sight of yourself and drowned in your own arrogance. Don't take your own faults out on others.'

Denney nodded. There was truth in Hanrahan's words.

'But at least I've lived, Brendan. I'm not convinced you can say the same. Do you really believe the world begins and ends at your fingertips, man? Or are you just frightened of it all? Scared to death that a little love might steal away your powers? That you might be like Samson and wake up one morning to find your hair on your pillow. And suddenly you're just the same as the rest of us: weak and dependent on others. Is that what scares you? That you might lose your strength and someone will come looking for revenge? Because if it is, I must tell you what you are. An emotional coward. A man who fears what's inside himself and takes that fear out on the world.'

There was hatred in Hanrahan's eyes. Denney knew he had hit the spot. It gave him no comfort.

'To be honest,' Hanrahan said very carefully, 'none of this matters any more, Michael.'

'It matters, Brendan. Tell me now. Do you think we'll be judged one day? All of us? Or is that just one more piece of whimsy?'

'I think there's plenty who would like to judge you now.'

'And who are they? I've wasted my time in this dump, fearing them. Fearing you. What can they do except steal away what little of my miserable life's left?'

Hanrahan shifted uncomfortably on his seat. 'I wouldn't value that too lightly, Michael. Think of what happened to Arturo Valena and the rest.'

Denney looked around the apartment. It seemed smaller, more dismal than ever. He was unable to believe he had allowed himself to be talked into being some voluntary kind of captive here.

'Terrible ends,' he agreed. 'But you know the problem with spending your days afraid of dying? What you really end up fearing is life itself. You wind up hoping no one knocks on the door, no one comes close. You die anyway, it's just that you don't notice it happened a long time before you stopped breathing.'

Hanrahan closed his eyes as if he weren't listening.

'Tell me, Brendan. Do you believe in anything?'

'I believe in keeping our little piece of the world in order. Protecting it from those who'd destroy it.'

'Isn't that what Pontius Pilate said?'

'You're talking like a churchman, Michael. That's something you're not.'

'Say it then,' Denney spat back. 'Let's hear what you came here for. Because it wasn't to pass the time.'

'You're out,' Hanrahan said flatly. 'Today. By noon, it must be, or they'll send someone in and throw you onto the pavement, I swear it. I've argued till I'm blue in the face but it's no good. What with these pictures. The proof that Gino Fosse is your boy. The woman. They're scared there's more to come, Michael. And let's face it . . .' Hanrahan's emotionless face fixed on Denney. 'There is.'

Denney felt trapped in the small, airless room, felt as if his head might explode. 'Meaning?'

'Meaning I've known a lot about you for a long time, Michael. It wasn't that hard. You cover your footsteps well, but you're still an amateur. Now it's beyond my powers. When they turn and say, "Is this all?" I won't lie for you any more. That time's past.'

Denney folded his arms and rested back on the chair, thinking. 'So who's casting the first stone then? Just for interest's sake. I'd like the names. I'd love to know how many people in this place would survive having someone spying on them night and day, seeing everything they do.'

Hanrahan pulled a half-smoked cigar from his jacket pocket and lit it. The strong, vile smoke began to fill the room.

'Think of someone. Put him on your list. I tried my best, but not with much conviction, to be honest. They're right. You're too much of an embarrassment now. We have to wash our hands of the stain of you before it leaves a mark on the rest of us. There'll be a private plane back to Boston. Someone can help you there if you need it. We can give you a new name. A place to live where they won't find you, with a touch of luck. But . . .' he waved his hand at the world beyond the walls of the apartment, 'this part of your life is past. You can't return to Rome. You can't be Cardinal Michael Denney any more. If you stay in Italy, even under a false name, someone will find you. Maybe the police. Maybe some people with other ideas. Either way, you don't want it and we don't want it.'

It was what he expected but still the words smarted. 'So I'm reborn. I become Joe Polack and work on some factory line in Detroit. Is that it?'

Hanrahan shrugged. 'If that's what you want.'

Denney's pale face became suffused with red. He wished he could keep the anger away. 'Damn it, Brendan. *I want what they owe me.*'

The Irishman laughed. The sound made Denney miserable; it emphasized how alone he truly was. 'Everyone wants what they're owed, Michael. That's the problem, isn't it? All these debts to be paid, and so many of them to people none of us would like to know.'

'You'll take me to the airport.' He tried to make it sound like an order, not a question, but the words failed to come out right.

Hanrahan scowled then slowly shook his head. 'No. We can't afford the publicity. In America things can be different. There we can be more subtle. But for now we need to make it plain. At eleven the press department plans to issue a statement. I can show you a copy if you like. It will say you've decided to resign your office for personal reasons and intend to take up a new life outside the Church, beyond Italy. No more than that. We will brief the press privately, of course, and set some clear water between the Vatican and yourself. That must be done. You're a pariah. We'll make it clear we've been concerned by your actions, by the rumours about your personal life, for years, but these last revelations, which were, of course, new to us, proved too much to bear. You'll become the prodigal son, Michael, one we must send out into the world to atone for his sins. Except you'll never return, naturally. We'll not meet again after today. You're making the rest of this journey on your own.'

Denney couldn't believe what he was hearing, couldn't comprehend how Hanrahan took such obvious pleasure in torturing him like this. 'And what am I supposed to do, exactly? Call a cab and wait for one of those crooks to join me in the back? Do I look suicidal,

Brendan? I'd rather walk straight to the nearest policeman and ask him to take me in.'

Hanrahan laughed again. 'And how long do you think you'd last in prison? If you got that far. Don't be naïve. The police can't save you. Maybe even we can't save you in the end. You've gone so far. You've offended so many people, given them such a wealth of ammunition to bring you down. Oh, to hell with it . . .'

He scanned the apartment, wrinkling his nose. 'Don't pack much, Michael. Tell us what, if anything, you wish to keep and I'll see it's done. Bear in mind, though, that most of your possessions are attached to the office you held until this moment and remain our property. Anything that is truly personal you may mark and I'll send on later.'

Denney nodded at the copy of the Caravaggio. 'The paintings are mine.'

'That I doubt. But you're an accomplished thief. I'll send them on, perhaps.'

Michael Denney wasn't listening. His eyes were fixed on the couple at the focus of the canvas: the dying Matthew and his assassin, both bathed in the compelling light of grace.

'Now you won't be thinking of yourself as the martyr in all this, Michael, surely?' Hanrahan asked lightly. 'That would be a little rich, I fancy.'

Denney hung his head and whispered, 'Christ, Brendan, don't enjoy it so much.'

He looked up. The Irishman's eyes now held him in a fixed, concentrated stare, full of contempt.

'You confuse pleasure with duty, Michael. You always have. It's the root of your problem. Don't hate me, man. I've performed one last favour, for old times' sake. Two men will meet you outside the gates at twelve. A couple of Rome cops. They'll take you to the airport. Off-duty as it were.'

'Two men?' Denney asked. 'Do you want me dead?'

'If I wanted that do you think I'd have gone to all this trouble on your behalf? Not that we haven't discussed it, you understand. There are those who thought it would have been the . . . cleanest solution.'

Michael Denney closed his eyes. He could picture them talking, somewhere else, in a private, secret room, somewhere in this tiny, insular state which had, in the space of thirty years, turned from a kind of heaven into a cruel, unbending prison. Perhaps they met weekly. Perhaps they had more information, more pictures, tapes. And they'd been planning, for how long? Wondering how to dispose of him, safely, cleanly, with the minimum of fuss. Wondering where they would find a trigger, the catalyst who could flush him out of his lair. Time and fate had finally provided that, but not by chance.

He pointed an accusing finger at Hanrahan. 'You told him, you bastard.'

The Irishman said nothing. His eyebrows rose a fraction.

'You told Fosse about us. You set him against me, thinking that would be a swift end to it. You never guessed what he'd do instead. All these other people, Brendan. Alicia Vaccarini. Valena. Those poor bastards Falcone sent out to watch over him. Don't you feel the slightest sense of guilt?'

Hanrahan drew himself up in the chair, preparing to go. 'You're rambling again, Michael. All wars have their casualties. The trick is making sure you're not among them. Do yourself a favour and focus on that.'

Denney rose quickly from his seat, crossed the room and brought his hands to the Irishman's throat. Age and agility were not on his side. Hanrahan was on his feet in an instant, knocking his arms away, standing there ready to fight if need be. He had big fists and they were now half raised. Denney tried to remember who he was, who he still would be in his own head, whatever they did to him.

'Anger's such a wasteful emotion,' Hanrahan said. 'You should have spent more time dealing with yours, Michael, and a little less beneath the sheets.'

'Get the hell out of here,' Denney hissed.

'Midday,' Hanrahan said. 'I'll come to make sure you're gone. Don't worry. The press will be elsewhere. You'll leave in privacy.'

He extended a hand, waited, then withdrew it. 'You must place a terribly low value on your life, Michael.'

'What makes you say that?'

'Because I've saved it so many times. Here I am saving it again. And not so much as a word of thanks.'

He looked at his watch. They had their arrangements. He'd no idea whether they still held. Michael Denney closed his eyes and prayed for the call.

It was two minutes late but it came.

Fifty-five

Costa rang the doorbell of the apartment. It was on the third floor of a modern block a couple of kilometres from the airport, just off the main road. You could hear the traffic constantly but it was still better than he'd expected. In the few days he'd known Rossi he'd built up a mental image of what the man was like beyond work: unkempt, disorganized, solitary. He thought he'd be living in some dump closer to town. Instead here was this neat apartment block with geraniums on the staircases and the smell of good home-cooking floating out of the windows of the adjoining homes. He wished he'd noticed more about the man. Teresa Lupo had seen something else there. His own detachment had prevented him noticing, though he couldn't help but ask himself whether this was what Rossi really wanted.

A slender middle-aged woman in a plain blue blouse and black skirt came to the door. Her hair was greying and cut severely short. She stared at him through a pair of black-rimmed glasses. He didn't feel welcome.

'I'm from the station. I was Luca's partner.'

'Really?'

'I came to say . . .' She didn't look as if she'd been

crying. If anything she was full of fury. '. . . how sorry we all are. We'll do what we can.'

'Too late for that, isn't it? Hell, I'm not his sister. Come in.'

She threw open the door and he followed her along a hall decorated with paintings of flowers. It led into a sunny living room. In the corner, seated in a plain wooden chair, was a stocky woman in her early thirties. She was dressed in a nylon housecoat. Her face was pale and flabby, recognizably similar to Rossi's. She had long black hair flowing down her back and shoulders, like a schoolgirl's.

The woman looked at him as he entered, opened her mouth and made an unintelligible noise. It sounded like the moan of a wounded animal.

'Nic Costa,' he said, extending a hand. 'I worked with Luca.'

She made the noises again, only this time they were more prolonged, more agonized.

'Maria's deaf and dumb,' the older woman said. 'I'm her care worker. I used to spend time here when Luca couldn't cope.'

She turned to Maria Rossi and began signing with a quick, ready fluency.

'I didn't know,' he said. 'I didn't even know he had a sister, let alone any of this. I can't believe we never got around to talking about it.'

'Don't be too hard on yourself,' she replied, and began signing again. The woman in the chair nodded and smiled at him. 'That was Luca for you. I offered your condolences by the way. I made some small talk.'

'Thanks.' This was all so unexpected. He had no idea what to ask, what to offer. 'How bad is she?'

'How bad does deaf and dumb get?' the woman snapped. Then she cursed herself and went to the window for a moment, staring out at the motorway. 'I'm sorry. Don't take it personally. I've been working with Maria for five years. Ever since Luca took her out of the home to try and look after her himself. After a while I came to realize you don't just end up caring for one person. It's both of them, and lately, to be honest, it was him. He was a complicated man. A good man. Not that it ever made him happy.'

'Why didn't he tell me? I wouldn't have let him work all those hours. Last night . . .' He couldn't say it. Rossi's presence in the Piazza Navona was coincidence. Falcone could have sent any of them on the same job. No one was to blame except the man who killed him.

'What do you think?' she asked. 'He was ashamed of her?'

'No.' That was impossible. 'Perhaps in some way he was ashamed of himself, for not being able to make things better. I only got to know him recently. There was something . . . Luca wasn't happy inside his own skin. Maybe that's part of the job.'

She looked at him, seeming to approve of his answers, then went over to Maria, sat down next to her, smiling, and put an arm around her shoulders. 'I think you're right. He told me one time he kept waking up in a fury, mad that he couldn't do anything else for her. I don't think he was making it up.'

A flurry of signs brought a brief smile from Rossi's sister and then half a sob.

'She can't lip-read. Always found it too difficult. It means it's easy for me to lie.'

Costa scribbled out his home phone number. 'If she

needs anything, call me any time. We can help with
money. There's a pension. I know it's no comfort now
but tell me what she needs and I'll see to it.'

The woman looked at the piece of paper and sighed.
'She needs her brother back.'

Costa's face fell. The woman closed her eyes, ashamed
of herself.

'I'm sorry,' she said. 'There's nothing you can do.
Maria has to go back in the home. She can't look after
herself. That's the only place she can get full-time care.'

He understood how Rossi felt.

'It's OK,' the woman continued. 'She's not going to
be worried about that. She has friends there. She used
to visit anyway. It's just . . .' She had to wait until she
could continue. 'She'll miss him. We all will.'

'I know.'

He looked at the small, tidy apartment. There were
images of flowers everywhere.

'They're Maria's,' she said, noticing his interest. 'It's
what she does. She's deaf and dumb. She's not stupid.
Nor was he.'

Costa walked over and looked at a small oil painting
of a single hyacinth bloom: vivid blue hues against a
yellow background. She'd seen Van Gogh. The work was
full of life and happiness. She'd found something that
eluded her brother and had, perhaps, fought to share it
with him.

'If you want,' the woman said, 'I can show you his
room. Perhaps there's something there you'd like. To
remind you of him. A photograph. I don't know. He had
a lot of stuff.'

'I didn't know him that well. But I know someone
who'd appreciate it.'

She led him down the corridor. Rossi's bedroom was small and looked out of the back onto a car park. The dead smell of stale cigarettes hung in the air. There was a single bed, neatly made, a desk with a few tidied papers, an office diary and a swan-neck lamp. A corkboard on the wall was covered in little yellow notes and photographs. Costa looked at them. They were dates for outings: trips to the sea at Ostia, meetings at the hospital, coach tours into the country. His sister was in every last photograph, smiling throughout, on the beach, at a fancy-dress party, eating at a country restaurant. Luca made her happy. That was his gift.

There was only one with Rossi in it. The two of them were pictured seated in a long open-topped Bugatti 57 in a vintage car museum somewhere. Rossi had his hands on the steering wheel. Maria laughed from the passenger seat. He looked like a different man, someone in control of himself.

'That was before he had the breakdown,' she explained.

'Was he always like that?'

'No,' she answered with a bitter laugh. 'He was always on the brink, to be honest. For as long as I knew him.'

He touched the photograph. 'I can't take this. It belongs to her. It's too precious.'

'It's my photograph. I was on the trip. I can get another made. Take it.' She looked around the little room. 'He hated me coming in here. It was his secret place, I think. Somewhere he liked to hide on occasion. Still had to be cleaned though. I'll leave you for a while.'

She walked out, closing the door. Nic Costa sat at the small, neat desk and looked out of the window, out at the rows of cars and the apartment blocks running away from the motorway. This was a life he could never have associated with Luca Rossi: an ordered existence with responsibilities no one in the department could have guessed at.

He opened the desk diary and immediately felt guilty, ashamed. It was apparent from the moment he looked at the page that this was where Rossi put the other side of himself: the black and gloomy side that always threatened to lead him to the edge. The writing was unbalanced: sloping and too small. There were doodles, tiny scribbles that could have been the faces of demons. And a small line of doggerel, one Costa knew by heart . . .

> *As I was going to St Ives*
> *I met a man with seven wives.*

He read more. This was the private place where Rossi took his inner fears for a walk and everyone was in there: Falcone, Teresa Lupo, Sara, everyone. No one was spared. No small detail went unrecorded. He wasn't surprised Rossi kept the care worker out of the room.

Costa read two more pages then tucked the diary under his jacket, went back into the living room, said a polite, curt goodbye and was gone.

Fifty-six

'You made a sound. When . . .' He was reluctant to finish the sentence.

She laughed at his embarrassment. It was mid-morning. The traffic outside made a low roar. Gino Fosse had returned at eight, showered, slept a little, not disturbing her. Then she had woken him slowly, gently, touching his strong, naked body with keen fingers, arching over him, letting her breasts fall into his face until his teeth fastened on a nipple and she felt his growing interest stir against her legs.

'When you what?' she asked. They were still locked lazily together, she above him, rolling gently, feeling his physical presence subside.

'You know.' His eyes went dark for a moment. There was so much inside him she didn't understand. Where he went to all night. What he did. Robbing, she guessed. It wasn't such a bad thing. Needs must. But if all he did was steal, why would they want her to look after him like this? Why would they demand, so insistently, with threats only barely concealed, that she had to call them every time he left and tell them everything they'd discussed?

'Say it,' she ordered.

The pinkness in his cheeks, the result of their mutual exertions, flushed a little brighter. 'When I came. You felt it.'

'Of course.' She laughed. 'What do you think?'

She threw back her hair. Her teeth glinted dully in the fierce morning light. There was a sheen of sweat on her soft, young skin. 'Those others. I make them wear something. But you're special, Gino. You're safe. With you I want to feel when it happens. Not that I wouldn't know anyway. I'm good. Aren't I?'

'You're good,' he agreed. 'Why? Why me?'

She peered frankly straight into his eyes. 'Because you didn't expect anything. Because you were gentle.'

There were so many mysteries for him here. He'd never wanted Irena, not in the beginning. Then something had changed, in him, not her.

'What do you feel when it happens?'

She thought for a moment. No one had asked before. He saw this in her face and felt some small, warm surge of pride to think he was the first. 'That there's something of you just blooming inside me. Something that could stay if I wanted it to. Stay and grow. Become a child maybe.'

His face went white. Abruptly he withdrew from her, shrinking back under the damp sheet. She hated to see him like this, the sudden shock, the strange, internal grief that seemed to be masquerading as fury.

'I told you,' she said, stroking his matted hair. 'With the others I make them wear something.'

He refused to look at her. She wondered once again what he did, thought about the curious smell on him when he came back that morning. A stink that suggested he'd been near cooked meat.

'But it won't happen, Gino. It can't.'

He looked into her pale, young face, struggling to make sure she told the truth. 'I got pregnant once back home. You can go places. You can get rid of the problem before it arrives. They made a mess of it. I can't have kids, not ever. I just make them wear these things so I don't get their diseases. But I can dream. We can both dream if we want.'

He let her fingers run down his cheek, play with his lips. She bent down and kissed him, hard, in a dominant way.

'Families kill you,' Gino Fosse said. 'Families tear your life to shreds.'

'Sometimes,' she agreed. 'What else is there?'

He was unable to think of an answer.

She leaned into his ear, her breath hot, gasping the way she knew he liked. 'When you come inside me I feel something warm and alive, where it's supposed to be, as if you were bleeding out your life for me, Gino. I take your gift and it sits there, wondering, making me grateful.'

Not once, not in any of the brief, aggressive encounters he recalled from the past, had he considered the idea that this was a mutual event. The act had always been about his own efforts to achieve some brief, cathartic satisfaction. It had never occurred to him that there could be pleasure on the other side too. *You're the doorway of the devil.* That was what Tertullian had said and he'd always interpreted this literally, that a woman was the receptacle, an unfeeling, unresponsive place into which he could cast his lust.

He looked around the room. It was grubby. Their clothes lay on the floor. His bag, now depleted of most of his tricks, sat on the stained carpet. All that was left was the gun and some ammunition. It had to be enough.

'Tell me about yourself,' she said. 'Tell me about your family.'

He looked at her with those cold, dead eyes and she wished she could keep her mouth shut sometimes.

'Why? What do you want with them?'

'Nothing.' His anger could annoy her. It was a reasonable question, not the kind he ought to resent. 'I want to know about you. I want to hear what they did to make you this way.'

'I was this way without them,' Gino Fosse said. It was foolish, dishonest, to pretend anything else was to blame. No family, no colliding set of events had made him what he was. He recalled the fat TV man roasting on the grille, thought of the look of terror in his eyes. This was no one's doing but his. It was a conscious, deliberate act with a specific purpose in mind. Just like skinning a live cat had been twenty years or so before. The dark seed had been growing inside him all along. It just needed someone to nurture it.

Before the work began he'd stared for hours at those haunting, grisly depictions of martyrdoms in the churches, watching the saints meet their fate, wishing he could hear the words on their lips. But they were different. Arturo Valena screamed nothing but curses in his agonies. Alicia Vaccarini went weeping, unenlightened. He tried to remember the Englishman, losing his skin, tied to the beam in the church on Tiber Island, tried to decode the noises that issued from his gagged throat. And the Rinaldi woman, so stupid, so baffled by what was going on. These were now distant memories. What happened that day was not his doing alone. Hanrahan had set the arrangements. The Irishman had spread his net wide, culling so much information, from tapped phone calls, Fosse's own illicit photographs, stolen items perhaps. He knew names and dates. He was a constant voice in Fosse's ear. Even so, there was no blood on Hanrahan's hands. He may have suggested the means but it was Gino Fosse who used them.

Then there were the cops. Hanrahan would never have sanctioned that. He had his limits.

'What do you do?' she asked. 'When you go out of here? Who are you, Gino?'

He scowled at her. She should have known better. She was in enough danger as it was. 'Don't ask.'

'I want to know!' she pleaded.

He closed his eyes, wishing she wasn't there. The end was so close. This distraction was the last thing he needed. And this revelation too: that she felt him inside her, that two people could touch one another in such a strange and intimate fashion. This was, in its way, a momentary, mystical epiphany just as shocking as the glittering eyes behind the altar in San Lorenzo in Lucina. This threatened his resolve. This made the world seem a different place.

He stood up, went over to the bag and took out the gun, brought the weapon back to the bed and placed it in her hand. 'I bring deliverance,' he answered. 'To people who deserve it.'

Her pretty face cracked at that. Her fingers refused to grip the gun. She seemed terribly young again, and scared. It occurred to him that she knew what a gun could do. He thought of where she came from. Maybe she had personal experience.

'Why?' she asked, handing him back the weapon.

'I told you. Because they deserve it. Because their sins cry out for vengeance.'

Not the cops though. They got theirs for free.

She wiped her damp eyes with her forearm, like a child.

'Come with me,' she said. 'We could run away.'

'Where?'

'The coast somewhere. Rimini. They say it's nice.'

He thought of the sea, the endless sea, and the way the blue tide washed away everything.

'I'd like that,' he said.

He walked over to the bag and took out an envelope. It was full of notes. He counted out all but a handful and gave her the money. She stared at it. There was so much, more than she could ever have imagined.

'I'm not finished. I've one more piece of work to do. Irena . . .' He leaned forward and kissed her on the forehead, surprised by his own tenderness. 'You must leave, right now. In two days' time. Rimini. Be on the beach. I'll see you there.'

Her chin hung on her naked chest. He wanted to feel she lied, too, lied about feeling his warm, sparking presence inside her. *You're the doorway to the devil.* Tertullian was right. He had to believe that. If he didn't he could never be the Gino Fosse he knew, the one he understood, the one with a goal, a mission. This Gino had heard the rats chattering in San Lorenzo, had dared the anonymous, shrivelled heads in the Lateran to speak their true names.

There was no choice. He clasped her hand, making her fingers curl tightly around the money.

'Go,' he ordered and handed her the cheap champagne. 'Take this and we'll drink it together.'

Her eyes were wet. She didn't dare call him a liar.

He watched her pack her few things, waited as she walked out of the door, not looking back. Soon now, he knew, the phone would ring. Soon there would be a new deliverance.

Fifty-seven

The office was empty apart from a couple of cops shuffling papers at the far end, out of earshot. Falcone had gone on from San Lorenzo in Lucina to organize the cover for Denney's departure. He had teams throughout the city and more at the airport. Almost every man in the department was on the case, except Nic Costa, who now sat at Luca Rossi's old desk, drinking bad coffee from the machine, trying to clear his head. Throwing his ID card at Falcone had helped. No one asked for it at the station anyway. Now he thought of himself as a civilian again, a state he barely remembered, he was surprised and interested to discover his mind could go to places that some inner restraint prevented it visiting in the past.

There were footsteps across the big, bare office. Teresa Lupo was approaching, a folder in her hand. She looked dreadful, older than her years. He wondered if anyone would ever call her Crazy Teresa again.

'Thanks for coming,' he said.

'You caught me on the way out. Got some papers for Falcone. What do you want?'

'Just to talk.'

She took a good look at him, trying to judge his

mental state. 'I have to do the autopsy on Luca this afternoon. If you want to see him, it would be best now.'

'Seen enough dead people for a while.'

She sat down and put her folder on the desk. 'Me too. And I never thought I'd say that.' She was puzzled. 'What are you doing here, Nic? Falcone's throwing every man he's got onto the street.'

'I guess he doesn't want me around. I'm supposed to deal with the loose ends over Luca. Contact the pension people. Do whatever you do when a cop gets killed.'

She shook her head, baffled. 'There are civilians who do that for a living. He doesn't need the poor bastard's partner to get involved.'

'I don't mind. He had a sister. Did you know that? She's deaf and dumb. Luca took her out of the home and looked after her.'

He took the photo out of his pocket and passed it across the desk.

'What?' She sighed. 'He never mentioned a thing.' She ran her hand across the photo, as if there was some of his presence still there.

Then he threw across the book. 'Luca kept notes too.'

She opened it and stared at the contents. 'Who'd have thought a big man would write like that? It looks like a girl's hand or something. One screwed-up individual. And all these tiny doodles. Jesus. Poor fucked-up man.'

There were scribbled headings with dates and times. It was a kind of diary, but one driven by Luca Rossi's head more than actual events.

'It's what he was thinking,' Costa said. 'I just spent the best part of an hour inside his mind and I'm damned if I can get out again. It begins the day after that accident on the motorway, when he thought he was losing it.

It's . . .' he hunted to get the right words, 'a little insane, to begin with anyway. Some of it I just don't understand at all. Rossi really thought he might be going mad. Then you come into it. Then Falcone.' He stared at her. 'Then me. It wasn't meant for public consumption. You don't have to take it personally.'

She flicked through the pages. 'He thought I was sweet? No one uses that word about me. Never.' Then she turned the page and went quiet.

'It's OK,' he said. 'I'm not offended. Read it out. Maybe it will make more sense that way.'

' "Kid Costa".' She spoke softly, even though the office was as good as empty. ' "V. clever. V. naïve. Why the hell me?" What does that mean?'

'Go on,' he said. 'It doesn't end there.'

A few pages later Rossi returned to the subject and didn't mince words. She was surprised by the venom in the dead man's words. She didn't realize Rossi resented being Costa's partner so much. He seemed offended by Nic's innocence and, in particular, the way he had dealt with the Vatican.

'I don't want to look at this,' she said, putting the diary down on the desk. 'It doesn't do anyone any good. It's just Luca rambling. Doesn't mean a damn thing.'

'You think he was mad at me?'

'Maybe,' she admitted. 'Or mad at himself. I don't know.'

'You haven't read enough,' he suggested. 'He was mad with Falcone. He genuinely didn't understand why the man was leaning on me like that. Luca thought I was taking too much on myself and not asking enough questions. Maybe he was right.'

'Don't resent a dead man, Nic. Luca liked you. He

told me so himself and that means more than any crap in some stupid diary.'

'No! I don't resent him at all. I just kick myself for failing to see what he saw. He didn't understand why Falcone kept putting me at the front of everything. Letting Sara stay at the farm so readily. Pushing me to pretend we were having some kind of relationship. As if . . .'

It could be wrong to take this further. He was aware of her intense, concerned attention, aware too that he didn't want to involve someone else in his own troubles.

'I don't like what I'm hearing, Nic.'

'Then forget it once I've said it. But I have to ask, Teresa. Why me? Why not someone with more experience?'

'You did your best.'

'That's not the point. I did what I was told. I always do, without question. And I should have been asking more questions. I should have made Luca want to say all this to me direct instead of putting it down on some piece of paper he thought no one else would ever see.'

He took the diary and turned it to a page near the back. The tiny handwriting was even more extended here, as if Rossi was scribbling down his thoughts in a frantic rush. He stabbed his finger at the point in question. She took the diary and looked at the passage, trying to interpret the scribble.

' "Rinaldi: dope in the bathroom. And they missed it! Message on the computer, appointment with the killer. And they missed it! Are we lucky or what? And this: someone from the Vatican phoned that morning to make the date. Fosse? No. He was in exile. Who?" '

She looked at him and he wasn't wrong now. Teresa Lupo was scared.

'It was the obvious question and I can't believe I never asked it. Gino Fosse couldn't have made the arrangement to meet Rinaldi. He was banned from Denney's office more than a week earlier. The way Rinaldi behaved in the library, looking for the video cameras, suggested there was some accomplice. This surely confirmed it, and makes it look like someone with access to Denney's office. But we let our heads go somewhere else. We got taken up by events and never stopped to think about what was really happening.'

'You had a serial killer on your hands. You knew who he was. Nic? What else do you expect?'

'And something else,' he said, ignoring the question. 'I checked. Before Falcone sent us round to Rinaldi's apartment the place had been searched by six experienced men who know scene of crime inside out. You see what Rossi's asking himself here? How come they missed two such obvious and crucial pieces of evidence?'

'People screw up. It happens all the time.'

'No,' he insisted. 'Not like that. It's too convenient. Rossi knew all along.'

'So why didn't he say anything to someone?'

'Who to? Me? He tried to, I think. But I wouldn't listen and look what he says in the diary. He didn't think I could handle it directly. He thought that, if I suspected the truth, I'd take it too far, start screaming for justice instead of doing what he thought was right: keeping quiet, keeping my head down. He wanted to protect me as much as he could. Could he tell Falcone? Think about it. If Luca was right, the reason the search team found nothing in Rinaldi's apartment was because *there was nothing to find.* Someone, Hanrahan maybe, put it there later. And then Falcone sent us round to find it. What interpretation do you think Luca put on that?'

She was beginning to look around the room, making sure no one was eavesdropping. 'Too much. You've got to look for simple answers. They always tell you that.'

'You've got to look for answers that work. Do you believe Gino Fosse is doing all this on his own? Just ticking off a list of Sara Farnese's lovers for the hell of it? Surviving in the city without any help?'

She was silent. It was too much to accept. There had to be someone else.

'I'll take that as a no,' he went on. 'So let's move on to the next point. Do you believe this is even about Sara Farnese at all? If he's so pissed off with her, why didn't he kill her when he had the chance? The two of them spoke, remember, when I was lying half conscious on the ground. She somehow persuaded this lunatic to let us both live. Have you worked out how?'

'No.' Her face said it all. It was ridiculous that they should both have survived.

'There's only one answer. Because I didn't matter. Neither did she except as some kind of trigger for his actions. A trigger someone knew how to pull. How?'

'I don't know. He's psychotic, Nic. You saw those pictures. He's sexually obsessed with her.'

'That's it? No. Someone made him like that. Deliberately. And then they set us on his tail knowing the direction we would take because it was a direction they had already laid out in advance.'

It was the only explanation that made sense, but even so there were gaps. 'And that destination was Michael Denney, all along,' he continued, thinking about the man in the Vatican, with the Caravaggio copy on the wall of his poky little apartment, desperate for a life beyond those walls. 'I picked up the fake appointment with his phone number attached to it. I brought him into this case just like I was supposed to. Luca was trying to tell me all along the whole thing stank. Now Falcone has the man wriggling on the line. He's got the evidence that's forced the Vatican to eject him.'

His head was spinning, trying to comprehend the possibilities. 'And it can't just be Falcone.'

She reached out and touched his hand. 'You're going too far, Nic. Take some advice. The world isn't black and white. Sometimes you have to look the other way. Leave this alone.'

He stared at her. 'I don't like "looking the other way". It's not why I came here. Think of the people who want Denney dead. A few politicians. A few *mafiosi*. A few people who worked alongside him in the Vatican. They know each other anyway. Luca understood that. I was too stupid to listen. Fosse is loose in the city, a crazy priest who's never, as far as we know, had to fend for himself for one day of his life. Someone's looking after him. Someone's providing him with weapons and money presumably. Falcone couldn't do that. The risk would be too great. I doubt it would come from inside the Vatican either. But there's plenty of criminals who could help. We keep trying to fool ourselves this is just one lunatic working his way through a list. It's not like that at all. This is a concerted, organized campaign. Three distinct sets of people, each with their own agenda, working together to get Michael Denney on the run because that will suit them all. I just walked right in and did what they wanted. Now Luca and some other poor cop are dead and Falcone's walking round with something on his face you could just about mistake for guilt.'

She glowered at him. 'Don't judge people without the facts. Not yourself. Not Falcone either. It was Gino Fosse who murdered these people. Whatever took him there. All of this is conjecture. Luca just had doubts, that's all. There's no evidence. Just a lot of inconsistencies.'

'Inconsistencies,' he repeated. 'You're right. Here's the biggest. Why did Gino Fosse start in the first place? He was bad material, but there's nothing to suggest he was a killer before. What was the trigger?'

He recalled the picture on the TV: Sara Farnese with her arms around the old man. 'They were lovers, I guess,' he continued. 'Sara and Denney. I know she denied it but they were anyway. Gino Fosse knew her through his work in the Vatican. He knew she was sleeping around somehow but not with Denney, not to begin with. When he found out . . .'

He waited for her to interrupt, in vain. 'He what? Went "crazy"? That's all it ever comes down to and it isn't enough. Gino Fosse is crazy, I don't doubt it. Everything we know about these killings confirms that. But it still doesn't tell us why it began.'

He thought about Sara. She was an extraordinary woman. It was not just her beauty. There was some luminescent quality that made him need her, made him feel that her presence provided some form of completeness for his life. Gino Fosse could have felt this way. It would have been easy. Still, it wasn't enough to kill for.

'None of this makes sense,' he said. 'The way she slept with these people. Fosse's reaction.' He recalled the tiny tower on Tiber Island, with its smell of meat and blood.

And the cryptic message that was still running round in his head.

'I'm an idiot,' he said. 'Even Gino Fosse told us this wasn't all it seemed. That's why he wrote those lines on the wall. He was laughing at us all the time. He knew we'd look the wrong way. He was taunting us all along.'

She looked into his eyes, not liking what she saw there. 'You want some advice? Just go home. Pour yourself a drink. Read a book or something. Falcone's put you out of this for a reason. There's nothing more you can do.'

He reached inside his jacket, pulled out the service pistol and put it on the table. It was a Beretta 92FS semi-automatic, the matt black police workhorse they all carried. The fifteen-round clip was full. He'd fitted the extra sight aid on the end of the barrel to make it more accurate. Not that it made much difference. Nic Costa was a lousy shot and knew it.

'So you're going to take on the world with that?' she demanded.

'I went into this job for a reason.'

'They all do, Nic! Luca probably said the same thing when he joined. Falcone too. Then you see the world for what it is. You learn to bend, before you break.'

He touched the black metal. 'Bend enough to conspire in a judicial murder? Because, if I'm right, isn't that what's going on here? Falcone doesn't plan to arrest Michael Denney. He just wants to step aside when some hood moves out of the shadows and does the deed. What's the betting Fosse never makes it out alive either? What does that do for Falcone? One more feather in his cap. He gets to close all the options on the case, put a few corpses in the morgue he feels belong there, and probably pick up some money on the side. Is this the first time? Did Luca know that already? Am I the idiot around here? The only one who doesn't know what's going on?'

She didn't argue and that gave him his answer. Perhaps Luca Rossi had even spoken about it.

'The gun won't do you any good,' she said.

'I know. I was just going to hand it in. I quit. I threw my card at Falcone this morning. Enough's enough.'

'Wonderful,' she groaned. 'I imagine that really made an impact. How many men do that to him in a week do you think? He adores that kind of thing. You can take it all back, Nic. Think of it as part of the initiation.'

'Initiation?' he asked, astonished. 'Into what? A world of compromises? A world where you're willing to cut deals with crooks, of all kinds, because that's the easiest way to get what you want?'

'There are people who'd say that's just being pragmatic.'

'I know,' he said. 'Falcone. Our man in the Vatican. The people it suits to think that way. Not me.'

'So what do you think you can do?'

'Something. Maybe.' The words sounded lame as he said them. 'Try to make sure this crap doesn't happen again.'

'And if you're wrong?'

'Then I look a fool. So what's new?'

She closed her eyes. 'Is there anything I can do to dissuade you from this madness?'

'Doubt it,' he shrugged.

'You're a stubborn kid.'

'I'm twenty-seven years old. I'm not a kid. Not any more.'

She pulled out a pack of cigarettes and lit one. The

smoke curled out towards the open window, out into the smoggy heat of the morning. 'No,' she agreed. 'You're not. You know what worried Luca most about you? He didn't understand why you couldn't let things go. Why you just hung on like a terrier when any rational person would just say enough's enough. Luca knows what Falcone is. We all do. Listen to me well, Nic. That doesn't make him a bad cop. This has all gone wrong for him now but you don't think for a moment he would have countenanced any of this if he knew his own men would get killed, do you?'

'I don't know.'

'I do,' she said firmly. 'And he doesn't take money either. In his book, he's as honest as they come. He just happens to think the ends justified the means. When you think that way, sometimes it all goes horribly wrong.'

He thought about that. She was probably on the ball. He could see the pain etched into the inspector's bitter features. 'So what if you're right? Doesn't bring Luca back. Doesn't put me on his side either. Blame my old man. It must be in the genes.'

'Oh, God.' Teresa Lupo looked at him then picked up the folder in front of her. 'Hell, let's live dangerously together. Here . . .'

She took out two one-page reports and put them on the table, turned towards him.

'What's this?' he asked.

'You wanted a reason why Fosse did what he did. You wanted a trigger. There it is and it isn't anything any one of us could have guessed. Even Falcone I think, though someone else knows because they must surely have used it.'

He looked at the pages. They were both DNA analysis

reports from Fosse's home in the Clivus Scauri. It took him a little while to understand. When the revelation came it was, somehow, a relief too, a final and welcome piece of the puzzle falling into place.

He checked his watch. In ninety minutes Michael Denney would get into the car that would, surely, take him to his death. Then a memory entered his head: of the day he stood outside the church of San Clemente, with Jay Gallo's drowned corpse inside, listening to Sara tell the tale of the fake Pope Joan and how she was torn to shreds by the mob once they understood her true nature.

Teresa watched him, waiting for his response. 'We just assumed what they wanted us to assume all along,' he said. 'That she was Denney's mistress, sleeping with these people to try to help him. We never began to think there could be some other explanation.'

'No,' she said, with some regret. 'Not that one.'

He ran his fingers across the report. His head was fighting to get all this straight. There were so many answers here if he could put his finger on them. Explanations that tied up everything, and left Sara as much a victim as anyone. 'This couldn't be some mistake, Teresa?'

'DNA doesn't lie. Sara Farnese is Denney's daughter. Gino Fosse's sister. Non-identical twins. I checked their birthdays through the driving licence records. Same day. Him supposedly in Palermo, her in Paris. God knows where in reality, but they're twins. There's no other explanation.'

He remembered what she told him about growing up in a convent in Paris. While she was surrounded by nuns, Gino Fosse must have been fostered on two Sicilian peasants, then shipped off to Church school as soon as he was old enough, perhaps because his true nature was already apparent. All the while Michael Denney had kept tabs on them both. Somehow he had managed to bring both close to his side, never telling one about the other. Perhaps he judged Fosse was too unstable to handle that knowledge. Perhaps the old man just liked playing these games. Whatever. He wanted his family near. Nic Costa could only guess at the reasons.

'She's doing this because he's her father,' he said, seeing the pieces fall into place. 'She knows the trouble he's in. She knows he's frantic for a way out. So she's sleeping with anyone he tells her to, letting Fosse take the pictures, just to give him some hope, a chance maybe. And none of it works. In fact it just makes things worse because someone's been watching the games Gino Fosse has been playing. Someone with a reason to get Denney out of there. So this someone tells Gino who she really is, knowing this is the trigger. Gino realizes Denney's been . . . pimping his own sister and using him to make the delivery. Getting him to take pictures of her. Christ . . .'

'That would piss me off,' she said. 'And I'm halfway normal. Nic?'

She watched him, worried. Costa seemed lost in his own world of startled shock.

'Nic?'

'I can't just sit back and let this happen.'

He picked up the phone and dialled the farm. Marco answered. He sounded happy, almost young.

'Is Sara there?'

There was a pause on the line.

'What do you mean?' Marco asked. 'She said she called you and checked it was OK.'

'Checked what?'

'She wanted some things from her apartment. Bea drove her there half an hour ago. She said she'd make her own way back.'

He swore, then snatched the gun back from the table.

Fifty-eight

It was an hour before noon and the weather was starting to change. Clouds of tiny flies hung in the humid air, as if held there by some electrical charge from the angry grey sky. The pressure was rising. It gave Teresa Lupo a headache. Looking at the tense, absorbed faces on the street she knew she wasn't alone. She had pumped a couple of plain clothes men on the street. They disclosed that an unmarked police car with two detectives inside would draw up at a small rear gate of the Vatican, some way north of the public library entrance, and pick up Michael Denney at midday. The media had been thrown off the scent by one more carefully placed leak. They had stationed themselves in the Via di Porta Angelica, a ragged mass of reporters, photographers and TV cameramen, squabbling in the baking heat. Teresa Lupo had seen them as her car took her to Falcone's lair, a long, plain khaki van sprouting antennae which was now parked just off the large square of the Piazza del Risorgimento, close to the bus stops. From here, she guessed, Falcone could jump into a car and follow Denney all the way to the private jet at Ciampino, waiting for Fosse to emerge from the shadows and do what was expected of him.

She wondered where they would let the lunatic loose. Not at the gates of the Vatican, surely. If Denney died there, the outcry against the State and the Rome police would outweigh the gain from his death. Nor was the airport an obvious option. They could hardly ask a man who had once dined with presidents to walk alone across the runway, bag in hand, waiting for his fate to overtake him. Some other eventuality was in hand and she was determined to find it.

Falcone looked up from the row of radio operators stationed at the communications desk and asked, sourly, 'What the hell are you doing here? We've got no corpses for you. No customers at all.'

She held out the folder with the reports inside. 'I have the DNA results from the Fosse place. I thought you'd like to see them.'

He was watching a computer screen with a digital map of the city on it. A red marker winked from a street round the corner. It was, she guessed, some tag on the car that Denney would take.

'We know all we need to know.'

'No you don't.'

He glared at her, annoyed. 'You've something to tell me?'

'I'm just a lackey. I deliver messages.'

He looked at the offered papers, refusing to touch them. 'Well?'

'Gino Fosse is Denney's son all right. But Sara Farnese isn't Denney's lover. She's his daughter. She and Fosse are non-identical twins.'

He was astonished. 'That's impossible!'

'It was all there on the DNA from Fosse's place. They

found menstrual residue on that underwear. Hers. We could match it with the photographs.'

The tanned face wrinkled in disbelief. 'Are you sure?'

'Look at the reports. Look at the dates on the birth certificates. There's no other possibility.'

'Jesus.' He seemed genuinely shocked. 'That place is just full of secrets. Hanrahan should have told me. We will have words. On that and other matters.' His face was lined, his eyes dead. Falcone looked terrible, damaged by events.

'Does it make a difference?' she asked.

'Not that I can see,' he replied, shrugging. 'So Denney's an even bigger bastard than we thought. Whoring his own daughter to try to get himself out of that place. Imagine sending your own flesh and blood round to sleep with that fat creep Valena. And the rest of them . . .'

'Imagine being the kind of woman who'd agree to that.'

'Family,' he muttered. 'There's no comprehending those ties sometimes.'

Falcone seemed pensive for a moment. She felt like pushing it. 'Or imagine being Gino Fosse,' she continued. 'Discovering the woman you've been driving around on these engagements, the woman you've been photographing, staring at on your wall, this woman's your sister. Who told him that? Who pulled that trigger?'

The dead eyes held her. Falcone really didn't know, she realized. He'd been fooled as much as everyone. 'Search me. I don't care any more. It's irrelevant.'

'Irrelevant?' she asked, exasperated. 'Whoever did this is as culpable as Fosse himself.'

'Stick to forensics. Why are we having this conversation?'

'Prurience.'

'That's my job. Not yours. And as for this . . .' He picked up the folder and waved it at her. 'I don't want to see a word of this in the media. Not for as long as you can stop it leaking out of the station. I don't want anyone seen in some kind of sympathetic light. They're all losers. Understand? The story that the Farnese woman is his mistress stands.'

'But it's untrue. It paints her to be something she isn't.'

'Fine! So she just whores herself around to a handful of influential jerks who might be able to do her father a favour. That puts her in a more favourable light? Here . . .'

He snatched the report off the desk, glowered at the type on the page then tore the thing to shreds in front of her eyes, walked to an open window of the van and dumped the pieces out into the hard light beyond the glass.

She folded her arms and shook her head at him. 'My. I am so impressed.'

'Enough. I want no more of this. And no more of you.'

'I'd like to stay. I'd like to observe. That's an official request.'

'Refused. You . . .' He nodded at one of the plainclothes men working the radio desk. 'Show Crazy Teresa to the door.'

She was just a little shorter than Falcone but she had some bulk on him. Teresa Lupo took one step towards

him, leaned in, close to his face, and noted the way he
drew back. Then she jabbed a finger into his chest.

'You should never piss off a pathologist,' she said carefully. 'You know why?'

He said nothing.

Because in your line of work, Falcone, being someone with your manners, your warped sense of integrity,
and your kind of friends, it is just possible I will one day
find you on my table. And for that . . .' she ran a finger
down the side of his tanned cheek, pressing it like a
scalpel into his flesh, 'I would be delighted to set aside
a great deal of time indeed.'

The dark face turned a touch paler.

'Out,' he snapped.

She turned and left, stopping by the short metal
external staircase, exchanging glances with the uniformed
man there. He seemed vaguely familiar. They all did.
Over the years she must have met almost every cop in
Rome. She offered him a cigarette. He shook his head.
He was bored. He was like all the uniforms, she guessed,
just manpower for the day, a bunch of innocents who
could be persuaded to check how shiny their shoes were
when the time came.

'So you're going all the way to Ciampino?' she asked.

'Right,' he grunted. 'The long way round.'

'I'm sorry?'

'You didn't hear? The big man wants to make one
final stop in the city. A sentimental journey. We go there.
Then we take him to the plane.'

'Sentimental journey,' she repeated, and then they
talked a little more.

Three minutes later she began to walk towards the

river, back towards the hulking shape of the Castel Sant'Angelo, frantically punching the buttons on her phone, wondering if she could get there before the sky broke and brought with it the mother of all storms.

Fifty-nine

Michael Denney packed his belongings into a small, expensive flight case covered in airline stickers: three shirts, three sets of trousers, a couple of jackets, some underclothes. Then all the money he could persuade the Vatican Finance Department to release from his bank account in cash: $50,000, another £30,000 in sterling and €5,000. It was interesting, he thought, to see how easily they relented once he started to make the right points. Though he'd hardly touched it these past two years, Denney remained a man of considerable wealth. A good half was inherited from family in New England. The rest came from more unusual sources: gifts, commissions, fees. Bribes, if he were being honest with himself. The people with their hands on the purse strings knew that as well as he did. When he pointed out the problems that could ensue were his money to remain inside the Vatican – awkward questions about hidden accounts, calls from the left for the sequestration of funds – they were quick to sign the release. The balance of his wealth, close to $12 million spread around various institutions, would be remitted to a variety of banks across the Atlantic according to his mandates. Redemption and comfort were not, he thought, incompatible. He was only reclaiming what was rightfully his and he felt happier looking into the misty times ahead with some hard cash in his pocket.

There were two passports in the case: one from the Vatican which would, they said, be confiscated once he arrived in Boston. The second had an old photograph, from the days when his hair was sleek and black, one which made him look like someone completely different. The battered dark-blue jacket wore the familiar silver eagle. It had been a long time since Michael Denney had felt like an American citizen. The passport was, technically, out of date but, as a precaution some months back, he had let a contact he knew work on it, changing a few details. Now it looked valid, which meant he would not have to throw himself on the mercy of the consular service, pleading like an illegal immigrant. It would take him a while to get used to the idea of being American again. There was much to be learned in the months and years to come. But with money, and a US passport, there would be opportunity.

He looked around the apartment, imprinting the picture of it on his mind. It was memories like these that could keep you alive in the black days, knowing that some of the humiliation lay behind. Then he checked his watch. He was due at the rear entrance in thirty-five minutes. It would take a good ten minutes to walk there, through the private gardens, praying that everything he had been told about security inside the walled state was true. Denney was inclined to believe them. It would be too embarrassing to have a mishap on their own territory. The real dangers lay outside.

Denney looked at the painting that dominated the

cramped main room. That was one belonging he hoped to see again. There were memories behind the original which he did not wish to lose. For a moment he was lost in the precise and savage detail, held by the monstrous, lunatic assassin raising his sword high, ready to deliver the final blow to the saint who lay dying on the floor, hand reaching upwards for the palm branch of martyrdom offered by the angel. And there, in the background, Caravaggio's concerned face. Denney had always fancied himself as a spectator, one who looked on, caring yet detached, though never ignorant of one's responsibilities. Both murderer and martyr were victims in this painting, he thought, and he had no great wish to fulfil either role in his life. Matthew had been chosen, had offered himself willingly. And his killer? He remembered the conversation that began it all thirty years ago. How he had talked with the pretty young nun when they met in the church. She had railed against the man's cruelty, the savage anger in his face, asking how he could commit such a deed. He had asked the question which came into his head from nowhere: how could Matthew be what he was without his nemesis? Didn't the murderer deserve some of the credit too for delivering to him his apostle's fate? Wasn't he just as much a part of God's will as Matthew? Wasn't Caravaggio's stricken face in the background there to implicate us all in the act, and the artist in particular for his brutal imagining of it? Just as the young cop had said . . .

This was a cruel world, one in which breath could be stripped from the living in an instant.

Recalling that moment now, he remained unable to define what prompted the thought. Yet the consequences were so profound. Everything that followed, public and personal, stemmed from that moment. It was to prove the instant the young Michael Denney was touched by the world beyond the Vatican. It was a turning point, a step along the great journey, towards sin and worldliness.

He accepted now that he could never return to what he was. He knew too he could never leave the city without seeing the original once more, touching those memories that meant so much.

The bell rang. Denney was dismayed to find the sound made him jump. He walked to the door and squinted through the spyhole. Hanrahan stood there alone.

'Come to say goodbye?' Denney said, with a degree of cheerfulness, as he let the dour Irishman into the room.

'If you like, Michael. I want to make sure you're gone, to be honest.'

Denney nodded at the canvas on the wall. 'When I'm settled, Brendan, I'll be on the phone to you. There are things of mine here. You'll send them on. I'll pay for storage. You'll put that in good care.'

Hanrahan looked at it and sniffed. 'You think it's worth it?'

'I believe so.'

'It's in this church of yours, Michael. Is that correct?'

'The first church I ever worked in in Rome. I never told that young policeman, but it's true. The place is full of memories.'

'And now you expect us to leave you there for a few minutes, on your way to the airport?'

Denney stared into Hanrahan's grey face. He would not be cowed by this man. 'I won't run, Brendan. You'll make sure of that.'

'Oh yes. But why?'

There was a light in Denney's eyes. Something Hanrahan hadn't seen in a long time. 'For my own sake.'

'It's the woman, I imagine,' Hanrahan answered. 'The nun from Paris, Sister Annette. I read the files. You followed her there for a little while. Just for some bedtime games. All for a nun at that?'

Denney hesitated before replying. Just the thought of her painted such pictures in his head. 'She was the most beautiful woman I ever met. We opened each other's eyes for a little while. Life requires a few mysteries. Otherwise why would we need a God at all?'

The Irishman scowled. 'Abelard and Héloïse is a pretty story, but what a price they paid.'

'Still, they were alive, Brendan. You can't begin to imagine how these things happen, can you? I pity you for that. It makes you a small man.'

Denney closed his eyes. The memories were so vivid he felt he could touch her still. 'I made love to her for the first time in that place. First time I made love to a woman at all. I was a late starter. It was in a small ante-room off the nave. You could lock the door, do whatever you wanted. No one ever knew. We'd go there five, six times a week, take off the clothes they made us wear, become something else. What we were meant to be.'

Hanrahan's chill stare said it all.

'Don't look at me like that, Brendan. This is something you can't understand, something you've never experienced. When we were in each other's arms there I swear we thought we were in Paradise. I felt closer to God than I've ever been in my life and there's no blasphemy in saying it. I never wanted that to end. Then . . .'

'Then you followed her to Paris and she fell pregnant. You could have left the Church, Michael. You could have been with her. The coward in you always comes out in the end.'

Denney refused to rise to the bait. 'I was a coward, but not in the way you think. I wanted to do just that. She couldn't face the ordeal we both knew that would entail. The wrath of our families. Being cast out as sinners. I was a coward because, when the Church found out, as they were bound to, I acceded to them without a fight. I let them rule us both.' A picture entered his head, of Annette naked, lying back on the old cushions of a battered sofa, removing the crucifix from her neck, a shaft of light cutting through stained glass into the dusty hot air of the storeroom, her lovely face full of anticipation and joy. 'What happened in that room was no sin, Brendan. It was a holy thing. It was what was supposed to happen. If only you could understand it.'

One memory followed another. His grey face winced at the remembered pain. 'They let her keep one child provided she pretended it belonged to someone else, someone who didn't care a damn. Imagine having to face that decision and I was nowhere in sight, I was banished. Do you take the girl? Do you take the boy? None of this was my doing. These are the cruel ways of the Church. Sometimes they make my sins seem like mere transgressions. And then . . .'

He recalled the last time he visited them both and the way the sickness was dragging the light from her eyes.

'My family had more influence. I was saved for greater things. They put my worldliness to other uses.' He took one last look at the apartment. 'Sometimes these past few days I've wondered how much are we born to be what we become and how much are we made that way? What would have happened if we'd said to hell with them and got married? Would I have made a loyal husband? A good father? Or would I have become what I am now in any case? A devious old fraud desperate to save his own skin? It's the former I know, which is the worst of it. You see, Brendan? I don't need you to judge me. I can do that for myself, better than any save one.' Denney noted the Irishman's embarrassment with amusement. 'And now I've made you my confessor. How very awkward for you.'

Hanrahan coughed into his hand. 'We've twenty minutes to wait, Michael. When the time comes I'll carry your bag and you can follow me.'

Denney stood his ground. 'And the painting?'

'I'll keep it till I hear.'

Sixty

He waited in front of the Pantheon watching the crowds of tourists struggling in vain to find some shelter from the heat inside its vast, shady belly. It felt as if there was a fire beneath the world. The fierce humid heat was working its way to some catharsis. The sky was darkening, turning the colour of lead. From somewhere in the east came a rippling roll of thunder. A speck of rain fell on his cheek with only the slightest touch of gravity, as if it had materialized out of the soaking air.

Gino Fosse had saved these clothes for the last moment. They were his own this time: the long white alb almost touching the ground which he'd worn when he took his first mass in Sicily. It was gathered at the waist with a cincture. In one deep pocket was a CD player and headphones. In the other rested the gun.

A tourist, a young girl, pretty, with long fair hair, asked for directions to the Colosseum.

'Buy a map,' he snapped and she wandered away, puzzled, a little frightened perhaps.

He looked at the looming, lowering sky. A storm was on the way, a bad one. The city streets would run deep with rain. The people would race for shelter in the cafés and bars. The short, humid summer would come to a sudden climax and still the city would not be washed clean in the flood that followed.

Man was born evil and waited for the events that purified him. There was no other way.

He pulled out the CD player, put on the headphones and listened to the music. It was Cannonball Adderley live playing 'Mercy, Mercy, Mercy' with Joe Zawinul on piano. It sounded like a spiritual, like a sinner praying for redemption.

Gino Fosse sang the refrain out loud as he walked: *Da-da-deedle – deedle-deedle-dee.*

By the time he reached the church the sky was black. He walked inside and took a bench in the darkness, watching the way the light was beginning to fail beyond the windows, waiting for a familiar shape to walk through the door.

Sixty-one

Greta Ricci stood with the rest of the pack outside the main Vatican gate, eyeing the Swiss Guards in their blue uniforms, steadily becoming more and more convinced someone was playing them for fools. The men on duty looked half bored, half amused. She couldn't believe for one moment that the event they were expecting – an event that would make the news bulletins throughout the world – was about to happen here, in front of two dumb-looking would-be cops. The Vatican surely had other plans. Maybe they were using the helipad at the back, unseen. Maybe they were taking him out of one of the small exits in the wall which led to the Viale Vaticano at the rear, or putting him on a private train at the Vatican Station, behind St Peter's.

She was with Toni, the dumb teenage photographer from Naples who had been attached to her side since the story began. He was never the most fragrant of youths at the best of times. Days and nights of constant door-stepping and itinerant sieges had given him the odour of a street bum. Which Greta Ricci believed she could have handled were it not for his manifest incompetence. Toni was six feet tall and extraordinarily well built. His strategy for getting the best picture comprised waiting for the moment then fighting his way to the front of the pack and elbowing himself into position for the shot. It lent, she was forced to admit, a certain graphic immediacy to his work which almost always appeared, with some justification, to have been taken from the inside of a brawl. But it made him useless as a journalistic colleague. He looked for nothing except the emergence of an opportunity. He had no flair for creativity beyond the raw muscle of the snatched shot, no talent for seeing that pictures must sometimes be made, not merely captured. He was a chimp with a rapid-fire Nikon, hoping that somewhere among the scores of frames he squeezed out of it a memorable image would emerge.

Her mobile phone rang. She scowled at Toni, eyes fixed straight ahead, staring at the two smirking guards at the gate.

'Don't,' she ordered, stabbing a finger into his back, 'look away for an instant. Understand?'

He nodded. He didn't have a sense of humour either.

'Ricci,' she said, walking away from the herd to get some peace and a little silence. Then she walked a little faster, a little further, when she heard who it was.

'Nic? Where are you?'

'Doesn't matter. Where are you?'

'At the main gate. Where they're telling us to be to get the best view. Not that I believe a word of it.'

'No.' He kept it short and direct and made sure she agreed, first, to the preconditions. Just her and a photographer. No other people in the media. He couldn't take the risk.

'You think I'd invite someone else along to my own party?' she asked, then hastily scribbled down the details that he gave her, looking all the while for the nearest cab rank.

When he rang off she walked back into the media pack and physically pulled Toni out from close to the front of it, ignoring his screeching objections all the time.

'Shut up!' she hissed when they were close to the edge.

'Why? What gives?'

She looked at the faces around them. Interested faces. They were hacks. They had the same instincts she had. They knew when someone was trying to pull a stunt of their own.

She dragged him into the shadow cast by the high Vatican wall.

'I got a tip-off. Somewhere we can get a picture of Denney, all to ourselves.'

'Where?' he asked suspiciously.

The cameramen liked to hunt in packs. It was safer that way. She knew he'd tell them somehow, just a little later so that he got first pickings.

'Never you mind. We just find a cab and get the hell out of here now.'

'What? And let those bastards loose on whatever happens next? You want to get me fired or something?'

'I want to get the story,' she hissed.

'Well you go off and get it. If everyone else is here, then here is where I stay. If you want to change that, you ring the picture desk and get them to tell me.'

'Moron,' she muttered. 'Give me that spare camera you carry.'

'No. It's company property.'

She stared up at him. 'Give me the camera, dimwit,

and I will, when they realize what a screw-up you've made of this, do my very best to let you keep your job.'

He thought about it. Maybe there was a little insurance there.

'It's idiot-proof,' he muttered, handing the compact over. 'So you should know how to use it.'

'Moron,' she repeated, and strode quickly off towards the Piazza del Risorgimento, looking for a cab, noting, as she did, the long khaki van covered in antennae close to the bus stops, wondering why she had failed to see it before.

Sixty-two

It was a black Mercedes with darkened windows in the rear. Michael Denney looked through the windscreen: two men in dark suits sat in the front, anonymous behind sunglasses.

'Do I tip them, Brendan?' he asked.

The Irishman carried the small case to the back of the car. Then he looked around. The street was empty. It seemed to meet with his approval.

'I can carry my own luggage,' Denney said, watching Hanrahan begin to open the boot.

'If you choose.' Both men looked at the case. It seemed so small, so insignificant.

'Have a good journey, Michael. Call me when you're settled.'

'Of course,' he said, and extended a hand. Hanrahan looked at it.

'Come on.' Denney laughed. 'I'm not a leper. And you've got what you want, haven't you? No embarrassing revelations. No more scandal.'

Hanrahan took his hand and pumped it in a summary fashion. 'Call.'

'Yeah,' Denney replied as he started to climb into the passenger seats, taking the case with him. 'If I don't just disappear into thin air.'

Sixty-three

He abandoned the car in the street and dashed through the thickening rain, looking for her, knowing she would be trying to hide. Nic Costa had no idea what was driving Michael Denney to the church but he felt sure his daughter would join him there. Teresa Lupo's news had cleared his head. He could begin to see a direct, linear connection linking her actions now. When he had time to sit down and think it all through he would see more. For now that was a luxury. The truth seemed apparent. She was intent on joining Denney in his flight from Rome, unaware of the fate Falcone had in mind for her father.

The crowds milled around the back streets of the Pantheon, trying to escape the slow, greasy rain. He pushed hard through them, ignoring the curses he got in return, praying she was not already inside. Then, in a narrow alley a minute from the church, he saw her. She wore a neck scarf over her hair and had the collar of her light raincoat up to her face. She was huddled in a doorway, avoiding the rain, avoiding a decision too, perhaps.

He ran across the cobblestones and faced her, holding out his arms, barring the way. Her green eyes were dark in the half-light of the coming storm. They refused to leave the pavement.

'Sara,' he said, gently taking her by the shoulders. 'I know.'

'Know what?' she murmured, pulling herself away from him.

'There's no need to pretend any more. I understand.'

She detached herself from his hands and leaned back against the damp, grimy wall. 'Don't, Nic. I'd rather not hear this.'

He hesitated. These were big ideas. There was so little time. 'The labs have been looking at evidence. About you. About Gino Fosse. You're Denney's daughter, not his lover.' He made sure to see the effect of what came next. 'Gino's your brother. Did you know that?'

She groaned. 'Can't you ever stop prying?'

'There are people dead, for God's sake. It's not done yet. Did you know about Gino?'

'Yes.' She sighed. 'Michael . . . my father told me some weeks ago. He thought it unwise to tell Gino as well. He couldn't handle himself. Michael wanted me to know for my own sake. He only told me he was my father last year. Before that I just thought he was a friend from the convent in Paris. Someone who administered the estate of the people I believed were my parents.' She turned her face towards the wall, fighting back the tears. 'You can't imagine the joy I felt when he told me that. There was a part of me alive, outside myself.'

'A year ago. Exactly when he began to realize he needed help to get out of that place.'

Her green eyes stared into his and he wondered what emotion was there: love, pity, hate? Or a little of all three.

'You only think you understand what's happening, Nic. Stay away from me.'

'No. There's more. Someone else knew what was going on. When they found out about Gino they had the weapon they needed.'

'What weapon? Gino is . . . what he is.'

'Perhaps. But he was primed. I know it. Pretty soon I may be able to prove it too.'

'What?' Her head went from side to side. Her eyes were wild. 'What are you talking about?'

'This was what they wanted all along. Your father dead. Everything began from that. Gino was just a tool they used to try to make him run. I know what he was doing for Denney. Driving you to those people. Taking pictures for blackmail if he needed it. Then handing them to Denney who used them to try to get his freedom. What Denney didn't know was that he was being watched all the time too. By someone who eventually told Gino who you really are. That was what drove him over the edge. He realized what Denney was doing to his own sister. That's what we've been chasing every step of the way.'

He was unable to guess what she was thinking. 'Who would tell him that? Why?'

'Denney's former friends. Crooks. Maybe some people in authority too. Maybe all three. Why? Think about it. He could put them all in jail. He's stolen from them. They want to feel safe. Maybe they want payback.'

'Nic!' she said, despairing. 'Don't make this worse than it is. He's leaving. It said so on the news. They're letting him go back to America. He'll be out of every-one's life there.' She paused. 'Including mine. I just want to see him before he goes. That's all. He's made this arrangement so that we can say goodbye.'

She looked at him in a way he'd forgotten. It was the expression she wore when they first met, the one full of suspicion and doubt. The one in which he was a cop, nothing more. 'I suppose you know that anyway.'

He held her hands, not knowing what to say, wanting to believe her.

'You know what I did for him?' she asked.

'Yes.'

'He's my *father*, Nic. I thought I could help. The person who did all that . . . it wasn't me.'

'I know. I knew all along. I just couldn't work it out.'

She wouldn't meet his eyes. It was, he thought, embarrassment. 'Was I supposed to say no? What wouldn't you do to save Marco?'

He didn't say a word. She understood his answer.

'You mean Marco would never have asked, would never have allowed such things to happen? You're right. The trouble is, most of us aren't trying to be perfect like you and your father. We accept we're flawed. We do our best to cope with that.'

He touched her face, gingerly. 'What's done is done. All I care about now is what's ahead.'

'I have to see him,' she insisted. 'Stay away, Nic. You don't have to do this for me.'

'If I stay away, he's dead. This isn't just about you either. I've lost a partner. I don't forget things like that.'

She looked down the alley. The rain was starting to fall steadily now. The crowds were dispersing into doorways. 'Leave me alone with him. Just for one minute. After that . . .'

'I can't. It's not safe.'

'What is?' she asked. 'Nic, this church is where he met my mother. *Our* mother.' She waited to see his response. 'It means something you can't begin to appreciate. Something that doesn't concern you.'

He turned away from her, scowling.

'Are you jealous of him?' she asked. 'That we're close in spite of everything?'

The words hit home. 'Maybe. Baffled too. I don't know how he could do this to you.'

'He was at his wits' end. He needed my help. He was dying behind those walls. You didn't see it.'

'This was about help?' he asked bitterly. 'He keeps his existence secret from you for years. He reveals it only when he needs you. Is that an act of love?'

'No, desperation. Sometimes love grows out of despair. He wasn't the only one who felt that way. I was alone. I've been alone all my life. I told you, Nic. We're not perfect people. We never will be. I didn't have a family around me like you. I knew when he told me about my mother, about the choice they were forced to make . . . I knew I'd do anything for him. Anything.'

'And you still will?'

She looked him frankly in the face. 'Do you think it was easy for me? Sleeping with these people? Knowing I was being watched . . . used.'

'Then why do it?' He couldn't keep the note of disapproval out of his voice.

'I'll never make you understand. We're too different. My father's a frightened, vulnerable man. He's wronged people. He's wronged me. In a way I can't explain that made it all simpler. I could either abandon him, or I could . . . do what he wanted and hope one day he'd be free. I did what I did for both of us. To set him free. To restore to my own life something that had been taken from me. Given the same choices again I'd make the same decision. What's one night with a stranger if it brings your own father back from the dead?'

'You're right there,' he admitted. 'I don't understand.'

'Don't do this to me. You're as frightened of a world on your own as I am. That's one thing we do have in common.'

He didn't argue. He didn't even want to think about it.

'I want him safe,' she insisted. 'And Gino too, whatever he's done. He doesn't deserve this.' She looked down the street. 'You think the church is where they . . .' She couldn't go on.

He scanned the street, looking for someone, anyone, he knew. There were just tourists, skulking in doorways. Perhaps they were there already. 'Falcone agreed he could go there. It's insane. In the circumstances. He wouldn't go along with the idea without a reason.'

'What can you do?'

'Something, maybe.' It wouldn't be easy. He was on his own. He'd no idea whether the calls he'd placed would work. Or whether they'd been intercepted. 'I don't know, Sara. If it's Falcone, some enemies he's made among his own people, some crooks from outside too . . .'

She was silent. It was impossible for him to guess what she was thinking.

'I've talked to some people I can trust,' he replied, trying to understand the situation himself. 'My father's spoken to some of his contacts too. I can't guarantee this will work. I know I can't just walk away. Luca's dead because of what they did. If they get away with killing your father they get away with everything.'

His mind was, she knew, made up. 'You don't have to be there.'

'I don't have a choice.'

It came so suddenly. She reached forward, took his face in her hands and kissed him. He tasted her mouth. It brought back such memories. For a moment Nic Costa's head was lost in recollections of delight.

'I wanted to tell you,' she whispered. 'I despised myself for not having the courage. Don't hate me for this. Please . . .'

When she looked at him like this Nic Costa knew he was lost, knew there was no point in protesting.

'When we get there, when it's safe, I want a minute with him, Nic. Alone. That's all. You have to give me that. You have to trust me.'

His fingers gripped her soft, fine hair. 'I could never hate you.'

'He's my father. He's all I have.'

She kissed him again, hard. He wanted to hold her for ever like this, locked tight against each other, perfect, safe, until all the world went quiet.

'You have me,' he said.

The taste of her filled his head. He was lost in her anguished beauty.

Sixty-four

The church was in a medieval lane that ran from the Corso Rinascimento, by the side of the Piazza Navona, into the square of the Pantheon. Years ago the city authorities had raised the pavement at each end and turned it into a dark, narrow corridor for scurrying pedestrians who walked in the shadow of the high Renaissance buildings on both sides.

The unmarked police car crossed the Tiber into the dawdling traffic of Vittorio Emanuele, the drivers arguing about where to park. Michael Denney sat in the rear and closed his eyes, listening, thinking. Then he turned in his seat and looked around him. It was impossible to judge, but somewhere in the snarl of traffic winding its way out of the Vatican there had to be others. For a moment he thought he glimpsed a Fiat saloon with the brown face and silver beard of Falcone in the rear. Then it flashed past, slipping away over the river in front of them.

He listened to the plain-clothes men getting nowhere nearer a conclusion then said, 'Just park in Rinascimento. It's closest. I won't be long. You're police. I guess you won't get a ticket.'

The two sets of sunglasses looked at each other. One

of them, the man in the passenger seat, turned and asked, 'You're sure you want to go to this place at all? We can take you straight to the airport if you want.'

The driver swore under his breath, hissing at his colleague. The bass roar of approaching thunder rattled down the river and shook the roof of the over-chilled car.

'I'm sure,' Denney said. 'This is my church. No one knows it better. And it's arranged, isn't it? I wouldn't want to get you boys into trouble.'

They were quiet after that. As they passed the Oratorio dei Filippini the sky suddenly darkened and thick black rain began to fall, slowly at first, as if uncertain of its intent, then in heavy, driving columns that rebounded from the pavement. The city looked like the bowl of some fantastic fountain designed by a drunken Bernini. The driver turned on his headlights. It was now as gloomy as night. He screwed up his eyes and looked for the turning. Denney patted him on the back, guiding, giving advice. The black Mercedes pulled in at the end of the lane, Denney looked along into the black cavern which led to the church, seeing nothing but people racing for shelter from the deluge.

He tugged his jacket around him, took hold of the suitcase below their line of sight, and said, 'Ten minutes. Are you coming?'

'We'll see you to the door,' the driver answered. 'They said to let you have some privacy inside. One way in, one way out of that place. So I guess we trust you. Let's face it.' The black glasses peered at him. 'Where are you going to go?'

His companion was silent, looking out at the downpour in the street. Neither of them seemed much minded to remove the sunglasses in spite of the weather.

'Where indeed?' Denney replied, patting the driver on the back before opening the door and stepping out into the rain, holding the case out of sight as best he could, hiding it with his body. The two cops followed and immediately dashed under the paltry shelter of a nearby building.

Michael Denney stood his ground for a moment. The rain left his grey hair drenched in seconds. He didn't care. He was free in Rome for the first time in over a year. It made his head feel light. It was a delight beyond anything he could ever have expected. He looked around him. He was the only human being not trying to escape the deluge from the gloomy sky above. It would be so easy to walk away, to try to escape. But the two cops were young. They could soon retake him. And, as they said, where would he go?

He walked along the lane, in the centre, not minding how wet he got. They dogged his footsteps from a distance, dashing from place to place to avoid the storm. Finally he reached the door to the church. Denney closed his eyes, remembering her, trying, too, to remember himself all those years ago. This was a time when he understood a little of the word 'love'. So much had been lost in the intervening years.

'Ten minutes,' he yelled through the rain. 'You're sure you won't join me?'

'Absolutely sure,' the one who'd been in the passenger seat bellowed back. The driver struggled with a cigarette. The flame of his lighter looked like a tiny beacon trying to hold back the night. Two successive claps of thunder burst over their heads, with a sudden torrent of rain. They pulled their jacket collars into their necks and leaned hard into the wall, staring at nothing but the black stonework with water streaming down its face.

Michael Denney smiled at both of them then stepped inside, turned hard left and walked into the small vestibule. It was, as he had hoped, empty, and just as he remembered it. Even the old sofa, where they'd made love so many times, was still there. He walked to it, touched the ancient, dry fabric, remembering the feel, the smell of her, all those years ago.

'I was a fool,' he said softly to himself. Even so, a small inner voice said, she was dying already. As they coupled with such ecstatic delight on the dusty, old sofa, the worm of sickness was beginning to turn somewhere inside her. Had they married, she would still be gone, in the same space of time, leaving him with two children to raise, no career, and an exile from his own family.

It would have been worth it, Michael Denney thought. Just for those few short years. Even so, a part of him said that what had happened was for the best. The route of his life forked in two possible directions in this place, and bitterness lay down both. At least there was a part of her still in his life now, though she was not undamaged, for which he was entirely to blame.

'I'm still a fool,' he said. He put the suitcase on a chair and opened it. Then he took off his jacket, removed the long priest's surplice and pulled it over his head, letting the black gown fall down towards his ankles. He went into the case again, came out with the hair colouring and carefully dabbed it on his silver head, rubbing in the dark dye, running it through his locks with his fingers, wiping his hand with a cloth when the job was done. He looked at himself in the mirror. His hair had an unnatural sheen to it. Apart from that and a few extra lines he could have been the priest he was more than thirty years before, working the poor, deprived Irish areas of Boston. An anonymous man. One who hardly merited a second glance.

He smiled at this image of himself. Then he looked up at the boxes on the wall which had, as he hoped, not changed in three decades. Methodically, working quickly, knowing there could be no delay, he began to turn off the lights in the church, one by one, leaving the circuit covering the vestibule till last. Finally he threw that switch too and San Luigi dei Francesi fell into darkness. From beyond the door he heard noises: cries of surprise in the interior, fear perhaps, and a loud report, like a bulb bursting. Or perhaps a gun. A few people made for the door immediately. The storm had gathered over the city by now, he guessed. There would be so little light. Caravaggio would have recognized the scene.

When he walked out into the nave it was illuminated only by the spare, warm candlelight of the offerings in the chapels. Something was happening. There was fear in the darkness. Then it occurred to Denney he had forgotten one thing. The circuit for the meters on the paintings was separate from the rest. He had left it turned on. Sure enough there was a round, rich sea of light on one of the canvases: *The Vocation of Saint Matthew*. It reflected on the image and threw back a waxy yellow tint onto the confused faces of the visitors who had gathered in a line to admire the work.

Then the ancient mechanism worked its way through the coin. The switch was thrown. Night consumed the belly of the church, only partly rent in places by the guttering flames of the votive candles.

From somewhere came a scream. He began to move, praying she would remember his brief and precise instructions.

Sixty-five

Gino Fosse had listened to Cannonball Adderley twice, all the while watching the people come in and out of the church. There were more than there should be. It wasn't that much of a tourist attraction. They had men there. Men pretending to look at the paintings on the walls, men pretending to pray. Michael Denney was nowhere to be seen. He knew him so well. He could recognize that distinguished silver head anywhere. It lived in his imagination twenty-four hours a day. He looked at his watch. It was ten minutes past midday. Torrential rain sounded like drumbeats on the roof. The light beyond the windows was now a dull, threatening grey. He let the music come to a stop and knew he couldn't listen to one more note. With a muttered curse he tore the headphones off and stuffed them back into the pocket of the white tunic along with the CD. Then he thought about the act, almost laughed, took the things out and put them on the pew beside him. There was no more need for them.

He removed the gun from his pocket and held it under the cover of the bench ahead. The metal was soon hot and clammy in his grip. 'Mercy, Mercy, Mercy.' The melody still ran through his head, sparking pictures in his mind: of Michael Denney dead. Of Sara, naked, staring mutely back at him as he thrashed over her, limbs spread-eagled in the shape of St Andrew's cross, one simple question in those sharp green eyes: *Why?*

'Because I thought you were like the rest,' he whispered, seeing her now, on the floor of the tower room in the Clivus Scauri, recalling the way she hardly fought, the shock in her expression. 'I didn't know.'

Not until Hanrahan whispered the truth in the darkness of San Lorenzo in Lucina, with the rats' eyes glittering from behind the iron rack. From that point on, everything seemed a swirling, unreal dream.

He thought of his own end: a crouched, huddled figure, the white alb stained with red, the gun still pointed at his own temple. This was one final deliverance. He wasn't waiting for them to get around to it.

'Where are you?' he said to himself in a low voice racked with tension.

The rain was bringing in too many people. They struggled through the door, most unaware of where they were, what they might see. The church was simply a refuge for them. He thought about that idea: it was what he'd always wanted it to be. He'd been cheated of that experience, by his father, by his own nature too.

'Where *are* you?'

Gino Fosse looked at the door and caught his breath. She was walking through the entrance, leading the little cop, the one he'd nearly killed a couple of days before. They were striding into the nave with no fear, no caution on their faces. It was impossible. He blinked to make certain this could be true. They were heading for the paintings now, over to where the small crowds had gathered. Were they looking for him? Or were they looking for Michael Denney? He racked his mind to try to find some answers.

One small certainty made sense. He rose from the bench, the gun tight in his hand. His voice rose to a roar. '*Sara!*'

Her eyes met his across the nave. The little cop watched him intently. He didn't even move a hand to his jacket. They shouldn't have been there, either of them.

Then the lights failed altogether. The electric bulbs died. He'd been staring straight at them, into the pool of light around the painting: the image of the naked madman murdering the prone Matthew on the ground, sword raised, ready to deliver the final blow.

'*Run!*' he bellowed, and raised the gun, firing a single shot into the black air.

There was still some light. A few bulbs remained lit in an adjoining alcove. People huddled there, terrified, waiting. He staggered towards them but before he could get there even that was snatched from him. The wan lights failed with a clatter as the meter swung the switch. The image of Matthew, in his medieval costume, staring at the biblical Christ, asking 'Why me?', faded to black.

Fosse loosed off two more shots into the air. A woman began screaming hysterically close by. As his eyes adjusted to the velvet gloom and the random sea of tiny candle flames that now shed the last illumination on the scene, something brushed past him, something black and fast-moving, a man who never spoke a word.

He swore and lunged to catch the fleeing figure. There was nothing there. Everything eluded his grasp. Everything was denied him. He stumbled forward again, colliding with terrified bodies in the darkness, yelling every last obscenity he could think of, screaming his father's name, begging the black maw of the nave to give up his body for vengeance.

He stumbled against a pillar, banged his face hard against the stone. A warm, sticky stream began to flow from his nose. He tasted blood on his tongue.

'Bastard!' he screamed and let off another shot.

Something else collided with him, taking away his breath, almost bringing him to his knees. He recognized what it was: the iron railing that ran in front of the altar, the same kind of worked metal on which Arturo Valena had died screaming. He felt his way along it, towards the tiny sea of candles. The dark, glittering eyes, human this time, looked back at him in their reflection, scared, scattering as he approached.

'Bastard!'

A hand came to his shoulder, turning him. Gino Fosse lashed out with the butt of the gun, missing, and found his arm thrust briskly aside.

The pool of light from a few guttering candles revealed the man's face. It was the little cop. He held Fosse's gun hand high above them. It wouldn't be hard to overcome him, Fosse thought. He didn't look right for the part he was trying to play. But then perhaps none of them did.

'I didn't come for you,' Fosse hissed. 'Get away. Take her with you.'

A face came out of the darkness. She looked at him, serene, controlled, unafraid, which was, he thought, stupid.

'You have to run,' he said. 'They'll kill you too.'

'Gino,' she answered, and a slim hand came and touched his face. He shrank back, unable to comprehend what was happening. 'Come with us,' she said. 'Don't do this.'

He needed her gone. He didn't want to face her. Her fingers moved against his skin.

'It's not your fault. You didn't know who I was. I should have told you.'

'Too late for that.' Gino Fosse shook his head, wishing he could get the pictures out of his mind. 'Too late!'

'I forgive you,' she said. She seemed so calm. He wanted to believe her.

The little cop's grip was relaxing somewhat. There were people moving nearby. He wanted to catch their faces. He needed to see that silver head running away in the darkness.

'It's what they want,' the cop said. 'They've been using you, Gino. Who gave you the names? Who told you where to go and when?'

He thought of Hanrahan, smiling in the darkness of San Lorenzo in Lucina. 'What does it matter?'

'Because they're just playing with you, Gino,' the cop insisted.

He laughed. 'You think I don't know that?'

Sara's face, compassionate, loving, stared at him. 'Then why do it?'

He waved the gun in front of her. 'Because this is what he deserves.'

'He's our father,' she said. 'He deserves our pity. Not our hate. If I can forgive you . . .'

The little cop seemed puzzled. Gino watched her face in the half-light. It could have been an image from a painting. She seemed so placid, so sure of herself. 'Please,' she said. 'We can belong to each other. We can heal ourselves if we want. Don't let them use your fury for their own ends. Don't give them that pleasure. Or they win.'

He listened hard in the dark space beyond them. They had to be there. The rats chattering away in the darkness, shredding what little was left of his soul. But all he could hear, deep inside his head, was the refrain of the music: Cannonball Adderley's alto chanting 'Mercy, Mercy, Mercy, Mercy' with an insistent lilting sadness, like a gospel singer praying for absolution.

'If you talk to people I know, Gino,' the little cop said, 'there can be justice for them all. Your father. For these people who led you to do these things.' The cop hesitated. He was hardly holding the gun now. 'Isn't that what you want?'

Fosse thought again of the Irishman, his hot breath in his ear, saying those hated words in San Lorenzo in Lucina. How it would be so easy to make things right if only Michael Denney could be persuaded to flee from behind the high walls of the Vatican. He would like to see Hanrahan face justice, he thought. There was, when he considered it, so much he could tell them.

The cop's hand went up and grasped the gun. Fosse let go, let him take it.

Nic Costa's eyes flashed at Sara. 'Try to find your father. He must be hiding somewhere while the lights are out. Keep him safe until I say so. I don't know if the right people are here or not.'

In another situation, Costa knew, she would have kissed him quickly on the cheek. But Gino Fosse was still on a knife edge. Neither of them wanted to push their luck. Her hand reached out and squeezed his, then she was gone, a fleeting figure vanishing into the black maw of the church.

Fosse stared after her, a wild animal look in his eyes, part fear, part rage. Nic Costa felt, for a moment, afraid. 'Where is she?' Fosse asked. 'Will she come back?'

'Sure, she'll come back,' he said, trying to sound confident.

'I didn't know,' Fosse said. 'I did it to the others because they were whores. That's what they were for. I didn't know . . .'

Fosse's black eyes stared into his. 'It haunts me. I don't want it in my head any longer.'

A part of Gino Fosse wasn't mad at all, Costa thought, and then he let his mind go blank, unable to countenance the possibilities that lay within what he'd just heard. There was no time. People were moving through the shadows, big, dark bodies, men in jackets, men with a purpose. Costa wondered who would get there first, who might be in the church already. He'd tried to cover as many options as possible.

Someone brushed past him. An arm reached down towards the altar rail, some coins fell in the box there and, in a sudden, aching flash, the lights of the canvas burst into life.

Costa blinked at the image on the wall. It looked alive. If he tried, he thought, he would hear the assassin's breathing, feel the strength of the light pouring out from the canvas, trying to shed its redeeming grace on them all.

Then a familiar face, half lit by the yellow electric lamps, pushed between them.

'Where the hell is he?' Falcone demanded, snatching

the gun away from him. 'Denney? What have you done with the bastard?'

The people he called should have been here now. He could hear someone else moving through the darkness. They needed more light than this single wan pool of yellow in one corner of the nave.

'I never saw him,' he replied honestly.

'One way in, one way out,' Falcone hissed. 'For Christ's sake. He knew this place like the back of his hand. He's gone. He must be gone.'

He said nothing, trying to think. One minute, she said. Just a little time to talk and to keep him safe. Though they must, he now realized, have spoken already that day. Was there really anything else left to say?

'And you . . .' Falcone's finger jabbed into his shoulder. 'You just can't stay away, can you?'

'I think, sir,' he replied, 'you should consider your position.' He looked into Falcone's cold, bleak face. 'You can't carry on with this now. It's bound to come out.'

Falcone shook his head. 'What do I care about my position? To hell with it!'

Without warning he snatched a pair of handcuffs from his pocket, slammed one end on Gino Fosse's wrist and locked the other to the iron railing. Costa looked into Fosse's eyes. He was scared.

Falcone took Costa by the arm, peered closely into his face. 'This bastard killed your partner. We're walking away, kid. We're done with this mess.'

The painting shone at him from the wall. He was unable to take his eyes off the figure in the background: Caravaggio himself, watching the murder which came from his own imagination, pitying the victim bleeding on the ground, pitying too the assassin led by fate to be the instrument of his death.

Falcone was dragging him now, by the arm, away from the scene. He struggled.

'Jesus!' Falcone threw Costa against a pillar, and snarled into his face, 'I want you out of harm's way, Nic. I don't want any more dead men sitting around in my head.'

'No,' Nic Costa said softly. 'I can't let this happen.'

There were more bodies moving. Maybe they were the people Falcone expected. Maybe someone else. He thought he heard Teresa Lupo's voice rising in the clamour. From somewhere a camera flashed. People were beginning to shout. On the far side of the church a set of lights suddenly came on. Banks of bulbs followed them, marching around the ceiling as someone found the switches.

Costa looked at Falcone. The inspector's bright eyes were darting around the church, trying to make sense of it all.

'This has got to stop,' Costa said, pushing himself out of Falcone's grip. He fought free with a sudden jab, then raced the few yards to Gino Fosse. They were there. Two men. He pushed in front as they closed in on Fosse, raising their hands, two barrels beginning to gleam in the wan light. He fought to take his eyes off the figures on the wall: the stricken man, his white tunic red with blood, the furious, naked attacker.

There was a noise that could have been the angry, leaden sky outside, a burning flash of bright light so intense it seared a raw, sharp pain somewhere behind his eyes. Nic Costa stared at the image on the wall: a young bearded man, watching in agony and amazement the bloody, vivid scene he had created. Then the face faded and with it the bright, life-giving light.

Sixty-six

Leo Falcone had two appointments in his diary that chill October day. One was mandatory. For the second he would be an uninvited, unwelcome guest.

Disciplinary proceedings always left him cold. This was his third appearance before the tribunal in twenty-five years with the force. He knew what was required: an admission of some limited form of guilt, a display of penitence, the silent acceptance of a formal token of reproof. Perhaps they would dock his pay or make him attend some course of 'retraining'. It was possible that he would be demoted, though he believed that unlikely. The Questura was scarcely overflowing with experienced officers to take his place.

Falcone's position was plain. Whatever else had gone wrong, Gino Fosse was dead and the city was rid of a vicious, psychotic killer. He had lost officers to this man. His team had worked day and night trying to bring him to justice. Denney may have escaped, along with his daughter. There was more bloodshed than anyone wanted, even, he privately believed, those who initiated Fosse's game and made its existence known to official quarters when it suited them.

But none of this could be easily laid at his door. The investigation they had ordered found no evidence of collusion between himself, the Vatican and the criminal parties who had gathered at San Luigi dei Francesi to kill the fleeing cardinal and his wayward son. There was talk in the wilder parts of the papers about a cover-up. The last, snatched pictures of the shooting in the church, taken by the woman journalist Nic Costa had sent there, continued to do the rounds. The gunmen had escaped. They would, he knew, never be found. So be it. This wasn't the first time the authorities had acquiesced in order to forestall a greater furore. Given the nature of Roman politics, he doubted it would be the last. And the media had short memories. Soon there would be another scandal to occupy them, another face to sell more papers.

The hearing lasted ninety minutes. He walked out with a reprimand. They had been persuaded by his argument that a conspiracy, if it existed, and he felt sure this was impossible, could only have begun over his head. They were moved by his genuine grief for his lost men. They were willing to give him the benefit of the doubt. This time, anyway.

At the end, after announcing a verdict which had clearly been decided before he entered the room, the commissioner led him to the door, taking his arm. 'None of us is untouchable these days, Leo,' he said. 'We live in changed times. Take care. I can't save you again.'

Falcone didn't want to look into his eyes. Maybe the man would see the bitter amusement lurking there. Had Falcone fallen, the commissioner would have followed not long after, and they both knew it.

'I understand, sir,' he replied and walked down the corridor, thinking of what lay ahead.

For the sake of form – to let them know he was still in harness, his power undiminished – he then spent an hour in his office, taking reports concerning the stabbing of a tourist who made the mistake of hustling for dope at the station. At midday Falcone put on his coat and left the station. He could not, in all conscience, avoid what came next.

The crematorium was off the Via Appia Nuova, not more than two kilometres from the Costa family home. He watched from his car. There were perhaps twenty mourners, mainly men, in dark suits. A tall woman in over-elegant mourning clothes was pushing the figure in the wheelchair. Falcone sat listening to the radio for thirty minutes, thinking about the ceremony inside. It was a myth, a ritual. As a young cop he'd been called to a fatal accident at a crematorium once and come to understand the way they worked. This was a mechanical process. Messy, imperfect. It could be anyone's ashes you walked away with. No one would know. No one, if they were honest enough to admit it, really cared about detail. This was a dumb show to ease the grief of those still alive. Details hardly mattered.

The distant doors opened and they came out again, leaving in a slow procession of black cars. He followed them back to the farmhouse, parking opposite the drive, just out of sight. It was three hours before the last had left. Falcone got out of his car and looked down the drive. There was just the woman now. And the figure in the wheelchair.

He swallowed hard and wished he didn't have to go through with this. Then he walked up the drive, where he was met halfway by the woman.

'He doesn't want to see you.' She was attractive in an

old-fashioned way. Her eyes were bright and intelligent. She'd been crying.

'He doesn't have a choice,' Falcone said and kept on walking.

There was a table by the wheelchair. On it sat a bottle of old Barolo, almost empty, and a couple of glasses. And a white alabaster urn, a small thing, so bright and shiny it could have been plastic.

Falcone poured himself some wine, looked at the man in the wheelchair and said, 'You're cultivating expensive tastes for an invalid, Nic. That meagre pension we're giving you won't buy many cases of this stuff.'

Costa looked terrible. He'd put on weight while confined to the wheelchair. His face had puffed out. There was a distinct red tinge to his cheeks. Falcone knew what men looked like when they sat on the edge of a pool of booze, wondering whether to dive in. It had happened to so many cops. It was part of the job for some. He'd never expected Nic Costa to be among them.

'Why are you here?' Costa asked. His eyes were bleary, his voice cracked.

Falcone pulled the envelope out of his pocket. 'I brought your mail. They've been intercepting it, in case you hadn't guessed. Nothing to do with me. I've been lying low in Sardinia for the last couple of weeks. Enforced vacation. You probably heard.'

Costa gazed at the long white airmail envelope. It had the farm's address on the front, written in a long, sloping, feminine hand. The letter had been scissored open at the top.

'You know where they are?'

Falcone glanced at the postmark. 'Says here this was posted in the Florida Keys. Guess they're long gone from there now. Somewhere in the States, I imagine. Not a clue in the letter. The way Denney and the woman got out of here in the first place is still beyond me. He'd plenty of money with him but that doesn't explain everything. Maybe he had more friends than we knew. The Americans say they're looking for him, on our behalf you understand. Lying bastards. They're holed up somewhere with new names, a new house, new lives, promising to keep their mouths shut. We won't see them again. That's my take on things anyway. I could be wrong. It happens.'

Costa looked at the letter. It couldn't contain anything important. They would never have passed it on if it did.

'Take it,' Falcone said, pushing the envelope across the table. 'It's for you. Personal. Like I said, this wasn't my decision. They had to do it, though.'

It contained a single page. On it, in the same elegant hand, just five words: 'I thought you were dead.'

Falcone watched him, trying to assess his reaction. 'Can't blame her,' he said. 'We all thought that at the time. We forgot you were such a stubborn little bastard.'

'Sorry to disappoint you.'

'Hey,' Falcone snapped. 'A word of advice. A man in a wheelchair should avoid self-pity. It's not becoming.'

Costa reached for the Barolo and refilled his glass.

Falcone calmed down a touch and took a seat at the table. 'A lot of people were pleased to see you pull through, Nic. And then . . . this. It's like you're dead again somehow.'

'Is this you talking? Or your friends? Or Hanrahan? Tell me that.'

'Just me,' Falcone said. 'No one knows I'm here. Hanrahan's skulking somewhere back in Ireland, keeping his head down. Won't last for ever, of course. He's too damn useful to them. Just for the record, he's not my friend. Never was. Never will be.'

Costa's eyes were fixed on the neatly tended garden with its rows and rows of tidy plants. Falcone wondered if he was still listening. 'I heard it on the radio,' he said. 'You got off with a reprimand. So no one pays for this. No one except Gino Fosse.'

'You could look at it that way, I guess.'

'There's some other way to see things?'

Falcone shrugged. He was getting tired of this.

'Why are you here?' Costa asked again.

'I don't want any more victims. I've got enough on my conscience as it is. Nic . . .' He was back staring into the wine glass as if all the answers lay beneath its thick meniscus. 'I'm sorry your father's dead. I never knew him. People who did, say he was a good and honest man. We could use more like that. But don't think you can take his place. You don't belong in that wheelchair. You haven't earned that yet.'

Costa said nothing and gulped at the wine.

Falcone pulled up his chair and got close to him. 'I talked to the doctors. They said this isn't a permanent disability. You could be out of that chair in three months, maybe less. You could be back to your old self in six. If you turned up for the physio sessions. If you wanted to.'

'Get out of here,' Costa snarled.

The woman had returned. She'd been eavesdropping. She was carrying a bottle of mineral water and a couple of glasses. She put them on the table and removed the wine. Costa avoided her eyes.

'Listen to him, Nic,' she said. 'Please.'

'Bea, you don't know who this man is.'

She gave Falcone a cold stare. 'I know. I read the papers. I still think you should listen to him.'

He scowled and took the glass of water all the same. Falcone looked at the woman. He was grateful. Then he nodded and she retreated once more.

'Here.' He reached into his jacket, took out something and placed it next to Costa's hand. It was his old ID card, the one he'd thrown into Falcone's face a lifetime before.

'I'm back at work on Monday. I've got a desk with your name on it. I've got work for you.'

'Work?'

'Yes! Work! Let's face it. What else are you going to do? Drink yourself stupid day in and day out and call on the housemaid every time you want to take a piss?'

'I'm a damned cripple,' Costa yelled at him.

'Then learn to walk!' Falcone bawled back. 'Jesus . . .' The older man stood up. 'Look. I'll say this once. I need you, Nic. You're a smart cop. We can't afford to lose you. There's something else too.' Falcone eyed the horizon sourly. 'You remind me of what happened. How I screwed up. Maybe it'll make me think twice in the future.'

Costa's interest was stirring, Falcone could feel it.

'Don't think for one moment this is sympathy. I'll ride you as hard as I always did. All the more so once you climb out of that damn chair.'

'Go to hell,' Costa spat.

Falcone smiled. He recognized the moment. 'Thank you. By the way, I went back to work a few weeks ago. They said I showed up too early. Sent me back to do a little more time.'

There was something different in Falcone's eyes. Self-doubt maybe. An empty, dead loneliness. Or just the mask of a clever actor.

'Monday,' Falcone repeated. 'I'm not asking you to like me. Just to keep me company. Stay off the drink this weekend. You need to sweat some of that shit out of your system. And if you've got any questions . . .' he nodded at the urn on the table, 'ask him, not me.'

Then he set off down the drive, a tall man, beautifully dressed in a dark suit, but stiff, uncomfortable with himself in some way Costa hadn't noticed before.

A light breeze was coming in from the north. The wind was gently tearing the last few leaves from the old almond tree in the drive. They scuttered around the departing Falcone's feet. Through the bare branches Costa could now see the distant roof of the austere old church on the Appian Way. 'Domine, Quo Vadis?' Lord, where are you going? His father's reason for rebuilding the old farmhouse, for making this place the Costa family's home.

He shivered in his thin jacket. The wine wasn't enough to keep him warm. He looked around for Bea. She had moved into the house before his father died, caring for them both. He took her for granted, he knew. There seemed no other way.

'Bea!' he yelled. '*Bea!*'

She didn't come. Maybe she was watching him from the house, thinking about what Falcone had said. Maybe she was wondering why a woman in her mid-fifties should be looking after a man almost thirty years younger, a cripple who refused his own chance of redemption. Maybe she was thinking Falcone was right.

'Bea,' he cried, one last time. There was no reply.

It was cold now. The light was fading. If he had one more drink he knew what would happen, where his mind would go. To the bedroom upstairs and the night, the single night, he spent with Sara Farnese.

This was important. Nic hoped Bea was watching.

He grasped the alabaster urn with his right hand then, with his left, took hold of the gnarled grape vine that wormed its way up the patio pillar. Struggling, short of breath, feeling a distant sensation run down his injured spine and press a little movement into his half-dead legs, he dragged himself upright and looked at the field.

It was immaculate. Bea had called in men to help her. The green heads of *cavolo nero* were rising in spite of the season, forcing themselves upright, working towards the sky.

His fingers shook as he fumbled at the lid. Then, with a single determined movement, he tipped the urn upside down. Grey ash and dust spilled out onto the rising wind, gathered in a fleeting grey cloud then vanished, scattering across the land a lifetime of memories, an abundance of love and shared grief, gone in the blink of a disbelieving eye.

He clung tightly to the vine, watching this mortal smoke disperse. It was nothing. It was everything. It was gone. It would never leave him.

Then the breeze stiffened. The page on the table, with its five words written in a firm, elegant hand, fluttered in the wind, rose and began to tumble through the air, flitting across the arid ground, turning and turning before it disappeared into the scrub by the road.

He watched it vanish, wishing he could run again.

Nic Costa felt no wiser. Just a little stronger, perhaps, and that, in the circumstances, was as much as he could bear.